PRAISE FOR *Alara's Call*

"Breathe deep. Relax. Sink into a world similar yet strikingly different than our own. A lavish world where mantle clocks, crinolines and epaulettes coexist with sword fighting and martial arts, visions and supernatural gifts. Follow the journey of a young woman called to serve her God yet struggling with the scope of that service. Gaze at this new world with soft eyes. It will surprise you. It surprised me. It touched my mind and heart. It was my first taste as an adult of the potential of speculative fiction. I am forever grateful for that."
  —Robynn Tolbert, Author of *Daughter of Anasca*

"*Alara's Call* weaves a layered adventure in an intricate setting, full of rich detail and complex characters who battle immense odds. Readers seeking a story with depth and heart won't be disappointed by this inaugural work by Kristen Stieffel."
  —Rebecca P. Minor, Author, Artist, and Founder of the Faith and Fantasy Alliance

"Kristen is a talented, thoughtful writer with fantastic storytelling instincts. *Alara's Call* is sure to please lovers of great fantasy stories."
  —Ben Wolf, Award-Winning Author of *Blood for Blood*

"*Alara's Call* was beautifully drawn in every aspect, from the worldbuilding down to the characters and their motivations. I became so attached to Alara and Dorrel that I couldn't put the book down—I absolutely adored their relationship and how they fought for each other!"
  —H.A. Titus, Author of *Forged Steel*

"Alara's conflict in this story is very real world and compelling in spite of the fantasy backdrop. The novel is well written with a combination of lovely, flowing prose and interesting personal conflict. It is a wonderful mix of women's fiction and fantasy that would serve as an excellent introduction to the first-time seeker, while holding the attention of the seasoned reader."

—T. J. Akers, Author of *The Final Paladin*

"Stieffel's exquisite writing style and detailed setting drew me into her fantasy world from the very first page. In Alara, she has created a heroine unlike any I've ever read—a rare balance of faith and audacity, humility and fierce combat skills. *Alara's Call* will make you laugh, cry, smile, and ponder some of life's deepest questions."

—Laurie Lucking, Author of *Common*

"*Alara's Call* is a fantastic beginning to The Prophets Chronicle series! Creative and exciting, it's full of action, political intrigue, and a beautiful romance. These characters will capture your heart!"

—J. M. Hackman, Author of *Spark*

"An intriguing story with a clever heroine that is not to be missed. *Alara's Call* is a fresh tale, breathing new life into the genre, while still giving us the familiar struggles and triumphs we crave."

—Amy Brock McNew, Award-Winning Author of *Rebirth*

"As a prophet myself, I've always loved fantasy because it's the lone genre where prophetic words are still honored, or even treated as 'normal.' Yet in most such stories, these words are long-past delivered, only left to be fulfilled. *Alara's Call* is a refreshing and compelling addition to the genre precisely because in this story, the prophecies happen in real time. And the prophet herself is wrestling with a call very few of her countrymen share. Kristen has written a concise, compelling adventure that absolutely will keep all readers riveted. But for those of us who intimately resonate with Alara's gift—and the daily challenges it brings with it—the story hits home on a much deeper level. This is a very special book with a destiny of its own. Prepare yourself to be moved."

—Lisa England, Writer, Maker, & Coach,
www.thatfierydance.com

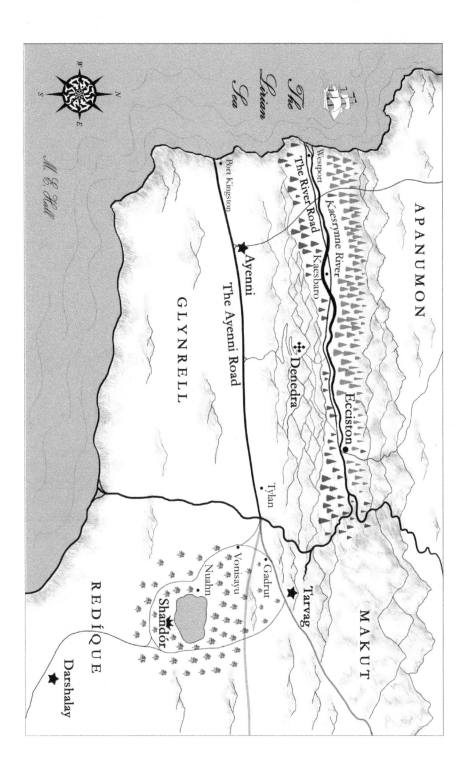

# Alara's Call

To Valarie —
Diligently Pursue
Your Call!!
1 Peter 4:10
Kristen S.
FPEA 2021

**Coming Soon:**

*Lena's Privilege*
The Prophet's Chronicle, Two

*Dorrel's Commission*
The Prophet's Chronicle, Three

*Gered's Ascension*
The Prophet's Chronicle, Four

# Alara's Call

## KRISTEN STIEFFEL

Love2ReadLove2Write Publishing, LLC
Indianapolis, Indiana

Copyright © 2017 Kristen Stieffel

Published by Love2ReadLove2Write Publishing, LLC
Indianapolis, Indiana
www.love2readlove2writepublishing.com

Map © 2013 Mary Elizabeth Hall www.maryelizabethhall.com. Used by permission.

Library of Congress Cataloging-in-Publication Data is on file at the Library of Congress, Washington, DC.

ISBN: 1-943788-19-7
ISBN-13: 978-1-943788-19-4
Library of Congress Control Number: 2017953973

This is a work of fiction. Names, characters, incidents, and dialogues are products of the author's imagination and are not to be construed as real. Any resemblance to actual events or persons, living or dead, is entirely coincidental.

Cover Design by Sara Helwe (www.sara-helwe.com)

*To Phyllis Kirkpatrick*
*1920-2009*

*She took me to church until I rebelled*
*and took me to the library, always.*
*She exemplified Proverbs 22:6,*
*"Train children in the right way, and when old, they will not stray."*
*Thanks, Grandma.*

# Chapter 1

## A CERTAIN CURATE

"Alara," the general said, "you must decide whom you trust more—me, or your father."

The breath shuddered out of her. "You, sir."

"Then do as I say."

Alara shivered and pinched her lips between her teeth. They rode in the general's curricle, drawn by a pair of black horses. He drove the cart himself, presumably to avoid having a driver present to overhear. The clopping of hooves on paving stones echoed down a dark, empty street shrouded in morning mist.

Defying her father was bad enough. Defying the prime minister could be seen as treason. Unfortunately for her, they were the same man.

She clenched her hands to stop their trembling. It didn't work.

General Rariden grasped her fingers in one of his brawny, weathered hands. "Listen. If I can convince the foreign minister to suspend your father's treaty for review, we can prevent Ambassador Pavud from taking you to Makut. But if I can't, we'll do what we must to get you to safety."

"Thank you, sir." Alara drew a deep breath. "But our Redeemer has said, 'If you're pressed into service, do what is asked, and more besides.'" She sighed. "That rather implies I should go to Makut as the treaty requires."

He let go of her hands. "Not while I'm living." His baritone voice dropped to a gentle rumble. "The prophet Digalo wrote, 'A leader whose directives contradict Scripture forfeits the support of believers.'"

Father's action surely contradicted Scripture. "You mean you would—"

"If I hadn't been out of the country when he pushed the treaty through Parliament, I'd have stopped it then." Though retired and more than seventy years old, Rariden was as robust as a man half that. Only thinning gray hair and a deeply lined face revealed his age. In his dark-gray suit and plain black cravat, he epitomized the distinguished statesman. "I am sorry about that."

"Why should you be? I suppose he waited until you were away for just that reason."

"Huh. You know your father well."

She scarcely knew him at all. But she was familiar enough with his politics.

The carriage turned the corner, and the spires of the meetinghouse emerged from the mist ahead. "I may have left government," Rariden said, "but I still carry some influence."

"That's a gross understatement."

He smirked. "Your father has forfeited my support. So I'll do what I can." His eyes narrowed. "You will not go to Makut on my watch."

Alara and General Rariden crossed the dew-damp side courtyard of the meetinghouse. Captain Palon Madrew approached from the other direction, impeccable in her dark-blue full-dress uniform, a peaked cap shading her slate-blue eyes. They met in the center of the yard.

Palon tipped her hat to the general. "Sir."

"What did you find?"

"Ambassador Pavud is to arrive at Ravendyn at nine o'clock. Perhaps we should we leave now."

"I can't." Alara turned toward the side entrance of the meetinghouse. "I'm officiating."

"Your sister will understand." Palon blocked her. She stood six inches taller than Alara, though they were equally muscular. "Your safety is at stake."

"You two are the only ones who understand my safety is at stake."

"No, your brother is with us." Rariden pulled his mouth into his characteristic half-smirk and turned to Palon. "But she's right about the rest of the family."

"I suppose so. But we can't wait about when a whole crew of Makutians is coming."

"A crew?" Alara's heart beat faster. She had expected only Pavud and a few attachés.

"An ambassador always comes with an entourage and a military escort. And there's a full battalion of soldiers stationed at the embassy."

Father hadn't said anything about a military escort. Of course he hadn't. "You're being alarmist."

"You could do with more alarm." Palon jabbed a finger at her. "You shouldn't even be here. You should've stayed abroad, where they couldn't reach you."

"My sister asked me to officiate at her son's naming. I couldn't refuse."

"Mm-hmm." Palon flicked invisible lint from her sleeve. "And you hoped to visit Dorrel during your leave."

Alara shrugged. Oh, she longed for his gentle strength just then. But it was impossible.

"Before I send the two of you off, let me at least try to find a diplomatic solution. I'm still hoping we won't have to resort to . . ."

Rariden hesitated.

Alara used a mock-sweet voice. "Running away?"

"Retreat."

Palon snorted. "Treason."

The sunrise shone through the tall latticed windows of the meetinghouse. Alara sat on the rostrum with the rector, but for once she would rather have been in the pew with the rest of the family.

Mum's auburn hair was coiled and pinned up in a pouf around her head, much like Alara's. But her mother's bejeweled coiffure and glistening turquoise gown, like the other ladies' gowns and the gentlemen's dark suits and satin cravats, looked more suitable for an evening ball than a morning prayer meeting. Probably because the service included the naming of the prime minister's grandson.

The rector moved to the lectern and read off the list of congregational concerns—the usual matters of illnesses and deaths and, because so many politicians were in attendance, vaguely worded requests for Telshi's will in various situations.

Father, tall and broad-shouldered, stared ahead with a blank expression. Perhaps he was distracted, too.

The rector shuffled to the last note in his stack. "Lastly, Shenevra Wyndur begs our prayers that those traveling today will have a safe and successful journey."

Alara glared at her mother, who appeared unconcerned, with her gentle smile and the sparkle in her pale green eyes. But then Father was good at convincing people there was nothing to worry about, especially when there was. How could Mum ask for safe travels, when she knew where Father wanted to send her?

After offering supplications, the rector read the next Scripture and called for a time of silent confessions. Alara ran through her usual list: impatience, selfishness, incompetence . . .

*Kenna, forgive me for not discerning Your will. For getting Palon and the others mixed up in my problems. Forgive me for the wicked thoughts I've had about my father. But how can I serve You if he sends me to a land where they worship other gods? There must be another solution than rebellion. Please show me what to do.*

Praying for a vision never worked. Visions came only when Kenna chose to send them, not when Alara thought she needed them.

All she knew of Kenna's will for her was a vision she'd had more than a year ago of mission work. There was no reason to believe Kenna's will had changed.

But could Her plan require defying Father and putting the others at risk?

Alara offered a verse her superior at the mission had insisted she memorize. *Make my heart penitent, make my manner humble, and make my will match Your own.*

The rector gave the assurance of pardon, and the congregants replied, "Ocha." He took out the songbook and read the page number. A sound like autumn leaves in the wind filled the room as people paged to the proper place.

The song's lilting melody underpinned pastoral lyrics depicting the people of Telshi as sheep tended by Kenna, their loving Redeemer.

*Kenna, You've blessed me with the gift of foresight, and I thank You. You've showed me many things — Jaselle and Bayor's marriage, my mission work . . .*

Her voice wavered. She gave up trying to sing.

*But You never showed me that I'm meant to be a curate. I've never seen myself on a rostrum, leading worship. Please show me Your will.*

The songbook wobbled. She pulled her arms closer to her body to steady her hands.

After the song, the rector said, "Now, Jaselle Kordelyon and Bayor Lorengen will bring their son to receive his name. Jaselle's sister, Curate Alara Kordelyon, will officiate."

Jaselle and Bayor rose, and he shifted their two-year-old daughter from his lap to that of Alara's younger brother, Camrun.

She and Camrun had little in common but their parentage and the high forehead and pointed chin of Father's side of the family. His utter faithfulness—when everyone else in the family thought her paranoid—demonstrated a concern he had never before shown. And it proved he, too, trusted Rariden more than Father.

Alara took a deep breath and stepped forward, smoothing her long, pale-blue curate's vest. Its straight lines couldn't accommodate the petticoats fluffing up her skirt. She should have worn something simpler, but Mum had already proclaimed her underdressed.

Jaselle had Mum's willowy build and oval face, but she and Alara shared the Kordelyon black hair. Bayor looked taller than usual, a wide smile crossing his round face. Jaselle carried the baby and stood on Alara's right. Bayor took his place on the left.

"Kindred," Alara said, "the Kordelyons have gathered in this meetinghouse for centuries."

*Meetinghouse* seemed an inappropriate term. A thousand people could sit in that building, and it was overfull that morning. Frescoes of Scripture scenes decorated the vaulted ceiling. Sunlight glinted off brass chandeliers. More like a palace than a house of worship.

At the mission where Alara served, the villagers met in a wooden shack with no glass in the windows.

"We are privileged to bring a new member to the family of Telshi." Alara glanced at her father, who grinned broadly. It was the first time in a long time she had said anything that pleased him.

"Mairah, our creator, we give thanks for this, Your greatest gift. In Your goodness You have wrought, from Bayor and Jaselle's love for one another, a new life." Ah, good. Her voice hadn't caught in her throat as it usually did at that point in a naming.

Of course, that was because she was distracted.

Focus!

"Ahbay, our counselor, thank You for this joyous day. Guide Bayor and Jaselle as they raise their child to be strong in body, mind, and faith."

Jaselle handed Alara the baby, a stocky three-month-old. Few people delayed naming a baby, but Jaselle had waited until Alara could be there.

Alara swallowed the lump in her throat. "Kenna, our redeemer, abide with this community and strengthen us as we offer ourselves as examples of faith to our newest member, Gejo Lorengen." Alara's voice quavered—she couldn't help it. The privilege of being the first to say a child's name publicly always drew tears. But this wasn't just any child —he was her nephew.

Maybe the rector would forgive a little quaver.

She passed Gejo to her brother-in-law, took a deep breath, and cleared her throat. Tears clung to the corners of her eyes. "Holy Telshi, great Three-in-One, we thank You for new life, for Your word, and for Your spirit dwelling in us. Ocha."

Apart from the quaver, it wasn't bad. Perhaps no one would notice the tears.

Still, her superior back at the mission, if he were present, would say she hadn't been paying attention.

And he would be right.

Bayor and Jaselle returned to their seats, and Alara took the lectern. She opened the songbook and announced the page number. Sheets ruffled. The piano played. The people sang. After only a few bars of music, Alara neither heard nor saw them.

*Camrun sits in a carrel at the National Archives with three books open before him. He makes notes on loose sheets of paper with a pencil.*

*The librarian approaches—a thin man with a bald head and pale, wrinkled skin. He carries a folio-size antique book several inches thick, its dark-brown calfskin binding broken at the spine.*

*"Thank you." Camrun makes room for the book.*

*The librarian places the book on the desktop. "May I ask what you're studying? Perhaps I can help."*

*Camrun takes off his spectacles and rubs his eyes. "I'm researching the constitutional basis for the abolition of the monarchy."*

*"Ah. You'll want some of the chamberlain's chronicles, then. I'll pull the relevant ones for you." The librarian takes two steps away, but turns back. "You'll want a larger table."*

Alara blinked, her sight returning to the present, though the vision of Camrun's future hung in her mind's eye like an interrupted dream.

The piano and singers had fallen silent. The songbook lay on her left foot. She picked it up and bumped her head on the underside of the lectern as she stood. She laid the songbook on the lectern.

The rector came alongside her. "All right?"

She nodded, though her knees wobbled. She sat in her chair.

He gave the final reading and the sermon. "Before we depart," the rector said, "let us thank Telshi for the blessings we have received."

For a moment, no one moved.

Father stood. "I am thankful that, after long delay, we shall finally end the trade embargo with Makut." He sat.

A few people applauded.

The rector raised his hand. The clapping died down. He chose not to criticize that breach of decorum.

A long silence followed. No one chose to follow the prime minister.

The rector turned to her. "Curate Kordelyon, will you dismiss us?"

Alara stepped to the front of the rostrum and raised her hands. "Holy Telshi, ruler of all, we thank You for Your many blessings, not least that of living in a country where we are free to worship You. Bless this day, bless our nation, and bless Your children as we go forward in the assurance of Your good will. May the blessings of Mairah, Kenna, and Ahbay be with us now and throughout all our days. Ocha."

The others repeated the word of affirmation, then rose, stirring a rustle of coattails and crinolines. Alara leaned her elbow on the lectern. Trembling, she hung her head, covering her eyes with one hand. *Kenna, help me understand what You showed me.*

The rector leaned closer. "Curate, are you sure you're all right?"

She nodded.

Mum climbed the rostrum steps and rubbed Alara's back. "You had a vision."

The rector patted Alara's hand and withdrew.

Alara raised her head to look at Mum. "You could tell?"

"I know that look. What did you see?"

"Camrun, working in the archives." Alara searched the room. He was halfway to the door. Alara descended the rostrum steps to follow him, but in the crowd, movement was slow.

Outside, the worshipers gathered in the courtyard between the meetinghouse and the rector's manse. Alara couldn't see Camrun.

Palon joined her. She smoothed her short brown hair with one hand before putting on her cap with the other. "Is this meetinghouse always so packed?"

"Not usually. Not at sunrise." Alara pressed through.

"You suppose they turned out because the Kordelyons were bringing a new member?"

Dozens swarmed around Jaselle and her baby.

Alara kept her voice low. "It seems likely."

Palon waved at the wide lawn, full of buffet tables laden with silver platters of fruit, soufflés, and pastries. "We don't get this sort of spread at the barracks chapel."

"We don't usually get it here, either. This must be Father's doing."

"Alara!" Bayor's grandfather broke through the crowd and shook Alara's hand with both of his. "After watching you grow up all these years, it's a pleasure to see you serve so faithfully. Well done."

"Thank you, sir. It's kind of you to say so."

"Indeed," Alara's father said from behind. "She's made us all proud." He put his arm around her shoulders.

She flinched, then stiffened, in that unfamiliar embrace.

Mr. Lorengen smiled and released Alara's hand. "Indeed she has."

"Do help yourself to breakfast."

Mr. Lorengen thanked him and went to the buffet.

A young man in a dark suit approached. "Prime Minister, how soon do you think the embargo will end?"

"Ah." Father nodded, showing his best concerned frown. He removed his arm from her shoulders. "Yes, the free trade agreement has been held up by a certain curate we all know." With a hand on the other man's back, her father guided him aside. "But let me assure you . . ." They moved away.

Her cheeks burned.

Mum sidled through the crowd, coffee in one hand and a small plate of food in the other. "What did Mr. Lorengen have to say?"

Alara shrugged. "Oh, 'well done,' that sort of thing."

"It was done well."

"But I choked up."

"So?"

"I could have done better."

Palon folded her arms. "Room for improvement is different from not good."

Alara shot her a grimace sidelong.

Palon looked the other way, as if pretending not to notice.

"You're too critical of yourself." Mum took a sip of coffee.

Alara opened her mouth to answer, but Palon elbowed her. With a bob of her head, she indicated where Alara should look.

Across the courtyard, Rariden talked with three politicians. The men spoke, faces broadly animated, gesticulating in turns. The foreign minister shook his head, spun around, and walked away. The others went in different directions, leaving Rariden alone.

He met Alara's eyes. He pointed to her and then, with a flick of his wrist, to the gate.

Palon grabbed Alara's hand and tugged her toward the street.

Mum called after them, "Don't skip breakfast."

Alara pulled her hand loose. "In a minute, Palon. I have to find Cam."

"In a minute?" Palon squawked.

Alara stood on her toes, craning her neck. Being shoulder-high to nearly everyone didn't help. Finally, she spotted Camrun in the line at the coffee urn. She worked her way toward him, Palon close behind.

Alara tugged Camrun's arm. "I need to speak with you." The three of them withdrew to a corner near the stone wall of the manse. "I had a vision."

"What, just now?"

"In the meeting. I saw you in the National Archives—"

He rolled his eyes. "I'm a historian. Where else would I be?"

"Will you listen?" She related everything she'd seen, even the broken binding and the spectacles.

"I don't wear spectacles."

"Not yet. You'll be researching the constitutionality of Reyshara Kordelyon's abdication."

"Why would I do that?"

"I don't know, I'm just telling you what I saw. If it's in a vision from Kenna, it's Her will, and it's important."

He snorted. "Thus spake the prophet Alara."

"Important enough to jeopardize your freedom?" Palon grabbed Alara around the upper arm and yanked. "Let's go!"

Camrun's eyebrows pushed together, creasing the skin between them. "You got the signal from the general?"

"Yes, but I had to deliver the vision first."

Camrun grimaced. "Let's go."

Alara's heart squirmed inside her. Palon pulled her toward the gate. Camrun followed.

Near the street, Father intercepted them. "Captain Madrew, whatever sport you girls have planned will have to wait. Alara is needed at home." He smiled. "We're expecting guests."

Palon's long, smooth face betrayed nothing. "Yes, Prime Minister."

Father took Alara's arm. "Shall we go?" He escorted her to the carriage, where Mum stood waiting.

Alara's limbs stiffened. She climbed into the carriage.

Camrun and their parents followed. Father closed the door, and the carriage rolled away, leaving Palon behind.

# Chapter 2

## FOR THE GOOD OF THE COUNTRY

Flags flew from the peaks of the twin guardhouses, fluttering and snapping in the wind. The Glynrellan national flag, dark blue and red separated by a diagonal band of gold, flew from the left tower.

From the right tower flew the Kordelyon family flag: a raven, its wings spread, on a field of royal blue. It held in its right claw a scroll of Scripture, and in its left a sword. Above its head hovered a crown—an anachronism that had been expunged from the family crest until Alara's father put it back.

Four precisely matched chestnut horses drew the carriage up the long, curving drive, climbing to the crest of the hill topped by the family's ancestral home, Ravendyn.

The manor's wide marble steps led to a portico and ornately carved oak doors blackened with age. Cream-colored marble walls stretched up sixty feet, capped by a blue slate roof through which grew a forest of chimneys.

A year doing missions work abroad had given Alara a new appreciation for Ravendyn's beauty. Furthermore, she finally comprehended what great fortune Telshi had granted her family. She had always known they were better off than most. Mission work had revealed the magnitude of the difference.

Inside, the crystal chandelier held no candles but scattered the foyer with sunlight from the high windows. The marble-tiled floor led to a curving staircase covered in thick red carpet. Alara walked up, Camrun and Mum close behind.

Father, as usual, headed straight for his office.

Camrun followed Alara into the sitting room of her suite, which brought their mother in as well. "What is going on? Both of you are behaving very oddly, and so is Palon Madrew."

Alara sat sideways on her desk chair and rubbed her neck, which had turned stiff and cold.

Camrun stood beside her, arms folded. "Ambassador Pavud is coming this morning."

Mum sighed. "Is that what this is about?" She sat on the end of the settee near Alara. "Do you really think your father would put you in danger?"

"I think he's too blinded by ambition to realize what he's done."

"Alara! That was a disrespectful thing to say."

"He hasn't shown any respect for my work."

"We all admire what you do, baby. There will be plenty of time for mission work after you return from Makut."

"If she returns," Camrun grumbled.

Mum glared at him. "Your father has promised me she will."

The look Alara exchanged with Camrun confirmed that he, like she, could recall too many broken promises.

Alara changed into tan riding trousers and a green shirt. While waiting for Palon, she sat at her desk and pulled her journal close. She stroked the knotwork triquetra tooled into the leather cover.

Now nearly full, the journal had seen her through two years and hundreds of miles.

The night before, when she'd studied the Scriptures seeking a solution, she'd filled page after page with notes and questions and prayers. Yet she'd come no closer to resolving the problem. General Rariden's way seemed the only one.

She turned to a fresh page and recorded the morning's conversation with Rariden and her vision of Camrun's future.

Shortly after the mantel clock chimed half-past eight, Palon burst in. "Where are your bags?"

"A private came for them half an hour ago."

Palon frowned. "Which private?"

"I don't know. Which one did you send?"

"None!"

Alara winced.

"All right, we'll find your bags. Are you ready?"

"Nearly." She went to her dressing room, where she shouldered her saddlebag and took a wide-brimmed leather hat from the shelf.

"And this." Palon grabbed the scabbard from its hook near the door. Her strong alto voice was subdued for once. "I just got word that the home secretary sent new orders to the northern border patrol. If Curate Kordelyon turns up at the border, she's to be sent back to Ayenni."

Alara belted on the scabbard. "I'm not to leave the country?"

Palon's mouth twisted into something half smirk and half grimace. "Those orders weren't sent to the Makutian border."

Alara closed her eyes. "Kenna, help us."

"Ocha. Let's go." Palon walked to the door.

Alara returned to her desk. "How can we go if—"

"Hasn't Rariden trained us both since we were five? We can evade the border patrol."

Alara stowed her journal, clerical register, and Scriptures in the saddlebag.

She and Palon matched strides down the hall to the back stairs. There, a couple of privates in dark-blue fatigues stopped them.

Palon waved her hand to one side. "Out of the way, fellows."

The private on the left saluted. "Begging your pardon, Captain, but the prime minister told us to bring the curate to his office."

Palon's stiff posture grew even more rigid. "All right, let's go."

The two privates escorted them to the main hall, a wide, wood-paneled corridor, then around a corner, down a narrower hall to a pair of white doors.

Palon extended her hands.

Alara handed over her hat and saddlebag. Then she opened the doors and stepped through. Arched windows with white casings framed the desk on two sides. Paintings the Kordelyons had collected over the centuries decorated the walls. An intricately patterned knotted silk rug covered the floor.

Father stood behind his expansive mahogany desk, sorting papers. "Please sit down." His once jet-black hair had grayed at the temples during his years in office. The heavy lines on his face made him look many years older than Mum, though they were both in their mid-fifties.

Alara sat rigidly in an upholstered armchair in front of the desk. Her innards fluttered like a bird in a too-small cage. The Scriptures she'd studied the night before jumbled together in her brain.

He sat. "Alara, you're aware the Makutians are anxious to implement the free trade agreement—"

"As are you."

"Yes, but you've been holding things up. It's bad form."

"Bad form?" Alara wailed. "You put my name into a treaty without consulting me, and I'm the one accused of bad form?" That awful whine revealed too much. She pushed her voice lower. "If I were any other citizen, you would never have done that."

"You are not any other citizen. You are the prime minister's daughter."

She leaned forward. "I am a cleric with a ministry to tend. But you expect me to abandon my work and do a diplomat's job instead."

"Such visits are common between ruling families."

"I couldn't go now if I wanted to." She shifted back in her chair. "I was only given leave for Gejo's naming and Camrun's commencement." She had hoped to make it to Denedra for Dorrel's doctoral commencement as well. "I'm due back at the mission in two weeks for the solstice festival."

"Don't worry. I already wrote to tell the prelate you have more pressing duties—"

"More pressing than serving the church? I hope you didn't put it to her that way."

"It's taken care of, Alara!"

"Do you care that once I cross the border, I cease to have any rights? Women are chattel in Makut. Thanks to this treaty, I would be considered Prince Velek's property."

Her father rubbed his forehead. "Where do you get these ideas? It only says 'Prime Minister Kordelyon shall present his daughter Alara to His Royal Highness the Crown Prince Velek.' That's all. Just be presented to him."

"General Rariden said that, in Makutian, for a woman to be presented to a man means she's given to him *as a present*. At best, a forced marriage. At worst? Slavery. How could you do this to me?"

"You're overreacting."

"Am I? The way that document is written, Velek could do anything he wanted with me. Anything."

"That's Rariden's interpretation."

"And what is Prince Velek's interpretation? If he just wants to meet me, why doesn't he come here? Or we could meet on neutral ground, in Redíque."

"I can't speculate about the prince's thinking. And you can't delay diplomatic proceedings just because Rariden has made you paranoid." Father stepped out from behind his desk and sat in the chair next to hers. His voice softened a little. "Has he so filled your head with war stories that you can't imagine things in Makut might have changed in fifty years?"

"They haven't changed enough to grant women any degree of

liberty. And the persecution of believers there is even worse than in Apanumon."

"Alara, please. Prince Velek is your cousin Bóhjetien's friend." He chuckled. "Even if you don't trust my judgment, don't you trust Boh's? Do you really think any friend of his would hurt you?"

She hadn't thought of that. Her cousin Boh and Velek were lifelong friends. That had to count for something. Or did it?

"Alara, I would not put you in danger."

"Then come with me. I'll feel safe if you're there."

He stood and returned to his desk. "I can't." He flipped through some papers. "Parliament will vote this week on my proposed budget."

"You're implying that your political maneuvering is more important than my ministry."

"Maneuvering?" He stabbed her with his steel-gray eyes. "My job is to do what's best for all Glynrell—not just you, and not just the church. You come from a long line of leaders who often sacrificed their personal desires for the good of the country. This once, you can do the same." He erased his ferocity with a broad smile. "I know you dislike playing the courtier, but it really is no different from one of your trips to Redíque."

"It is different. No one ever forced me to go there against my will."

He cocked his head. "True. But as Digalo wrote, you must 'submit yourself to those whom Ahbay has given authority.'"

"Digalo also wrote, 'Only misery derives from abandoning the path of Telshi.' You know my path led to the mission, not Makut."

"You spent a year at the mission. Maybe Telshi has another path for you now."

If that were so, Kenna presumably would have revealed it to her directly.

"Besides, the Scriptures instruct you to obey your parents."

"Scripture says 'parents must protect the dignity and purity of their children.' You know both will be endangered in Makut."

He straightened, rigid. "Young lady, are you accusing me of violating Scripture?"

"I am saying no person's dictates may supersede the will of Telshi." That statement surprised her, because she hadn't thought of it.

"And what book does that come from?"

She quavered. "None." It came from Kenna, surely. But she couldn't say that. "It's . . . a conclusion . . . based on study."

"Is it."

Alara took a deep breath. "Kenna said, 'Ahbay has a plan for every believer's life, and Mairah gives each one a gift with which to serve others. One must fulfill that plan through the diligent employment of one's gift.' How can I use my gift to fulfill my calling if I wind up in a Makutian gynaeceum?"

His laugh was stiff. "At least there would be plenty of unbelievers to preach to."

She glared at him. How could he make light of such a thing? Telshan missionaries were often beaten and tortured by Makutians. Sometimes murdered.

"Alara. As a Kordelyon, and as the daughter of the prime minister, you are required to perform this official function. I am sorry it interferes with your work. I am sorry it is contrary to your wishes. But it is for the good of your country, and you will do it."

Her shoulder muscles drew taut as a bowstring. *Kenna, help me.* She stood and stalked toward the door.

He followed and grabbed her arm. "Sit down."

"I need to speak with Palon."

"No. Sit down."

"Then will you please send for General Rariden?"

He shoved her toward the chair. "Sit. Down. And be quiet."

Alara sat there a long time, praying silently, while Father worked silently. Behind him, in a bookcase between the two windows, the clock chimed nine.

Father dropped his pen into its brass holder. "Let's go meet our guests, shall we?"

She followed him out, alternately rubbing the palm of one hand with the thumb of the other. *There's no way out now, is there, Kenna? My only comfort comes from knowing You are with me. Frankly, that's not much help.*

In the foyer, Mum stood at the foot of the stairs, chatting with some of the assembled dignitaries. Camrun and Rariden talked together near the front doors. Camrun had changed into riding clothes and put on his sword. As they spoke, he ran his fingers through his caramel-colored hair, a sure sign he was agitated.

As Alara approached, Rariden met her eyes.

She left Father's side to join them.

"You young people look out of place in your riding clothes," Mum said. "You could have waited until after tea to change."

"Why?" Camrun put one hand on his sword hilt. "Just to placate the people who want to enslave my sister?"

Rariden clapped Camrun's shoulder. One of the cabinet ministers excused himself.

Mum sighed, glancing toward the ceiling. "Heavens, Camrun."

A bugle sounded from the guardhouse. The butler, a thin, gray-haired man in the blue-and-black livery of the household staff, opened one of the double doors just far enough to slip outside, then shut the door behind him.

Alara craned her neck to see out one of the narrow windows flanking the doors. An empty carriage stopped in the drive.

Ambassador Pavud and the soldiers with him all rode horseback. After they dismounted, the ambassador and an officer wearing gold-braid epaulets climbed the steps.

The butler opened both doors wide. "Ambassador Pavud and Commander Sturg."

Father and Mum walked forward and shook hands with the ambassador, a broad-shouldered man with a bit of a paunch. Streaks of gray ran through his pale-brown hair.

The commander removed his peaked cap, tucking it in the crook of his left arm.

Father shook his hand. "Commander. This is my wife, Shenevra Wyndur."

Mum put out her hand. Sturg ignored it.

"Commander," Father said, "I understand our ways differ from yours, but please honor our customs. To refuse a handshake is an insult."

"Beg pardon." Sturg made a slight bow as he shook Mum's hand.

Father extended his arm. "Alara, you remember Ambassador Pavud."

She stepped forward and extended her hand. "Sir."

He wore a wine-colored suit with a cutaway coat and a black waistcoat. He shook her hand as if it were raw sausage. "Ma'am. It's a pleasure to see you again."

She couldn't return that pleasantry.

Father introduced Commander Sturg. Alara put out her hand. "Sir."

The commander stood stiffly, his eyes not focused on anything. The high collar of his black dress uniform touched his jaw. He was taller than the ambassador and stocky, with short blond hair, darkly tanned skin, and features that seemed carved by a hatchet. His bow was slight and his handshake lighter and more fleeting than the ambassador's. "Your Highness."

She dropped her hand. "I'm not a highness, I'm a curate."

A momentary frown creased his brow.

After Father had introduced some of the dignitaries, Mum smiled and gestured toward the parlor. "Please come in to tea."

Father took Alara's arm and guided her into the room. The vaulted ceiling stretched over a collection of richly upholstered settees and ornately carved tables. Windows looked southward over the drive and the gardens that ran down the hill. Father led her to a sofa near the window. She glanced about for Rariden and Camrun.

At the innermost end of the room, near a life-size portrait of Alara's ancestor Reyshara Kordelyon, servers drew coffee and tea from chubby silver urns. Others moved through the room, offering dainty pastries from vast platters. Camrun waved to Alara from the coffee urn. Palon stood by the kitchen door as if on guard duty.

"I'm glad this matter is finally coming to a conclusion, Prime Minister." Pavud took the chair on Father's right. "His Royal Majesty King Domat is most eager to end the trade embargo."

"As are we, Ambassador." Father accepted a cup of tea from a server. "But we didn't expect a military escort."

Pavud made a politician's smile. "The king wants to ensure nothing stops your daughter from arriving in Tarvag on time."

Alara declined the server's offer. "On time for what?"

"The fifteenth," Father said. "The deadline for implementation of the treaty. You have cut it close, Alara." He grinned a little too broadly. "Still, you have a week and a half to get there—plenty of time."

"Indeed," Pavud said. "The carriage can also accommodate a maid, if your daughter wishes to bring one."

"Alara?"

She rubbed her hands down the legs of her tan riding trousers and gripped her knees. Palon couldn't pass for a housekeeper, especially not in full-dress uniform. And Alara wouldn't risk taking any other woman into Makut. "That won't be necessary."

They continued talking politics. Alara still couldn't see Rariden, and now Palon had vanished also. Camrun leaned against the archway leading to the foyer.

The fruit and pastries might as well have been dirt. The dryness of her mouth and the sourness of her stomach made eating impossible.

After what seemed an age, Father stood. "We shan't keep you any longer, Ambassador."

Pavud stood also. "Thank you, Prime Minister. We can leave as soon as she has changed."

"These are my traveling clothes."

Pavud barely glanced at her. He looked at her father, who smiled as if he were campaigning.

"You will humor my daughter, won't you, Ambassador?" Father held out his hand to Alara.

Reluctantly, she took it and stood.

Everyone returned to the foyer, where Camrun handed Alara her hat and saddlebag.

Alara shouldered the bag and whispered, "Where's Palon?"

"Tell you later."

"She can't travel with us armed like a man," Pavud said.

"Of course. Alara?" Father held out his hand.

She frowned.

He scowled.

Sighing, she removed the sword belt. As she handed over her weapon, she whispered, "This is insulting."

Father passed the sword to the butler and took Alara's arm. They walked toward the doors. Camrun fell in step alongside her.

"Kind of you to see your sister off," Father said as they walked onto the front steps, "but why are you in riding clothes?"

"I'm going with her."

"Nonsense, Camrun." Father stopped and turned to face him. "You have commencement in just a couple of days."

"Exams are over. I can skip commencement."

"Thanks, Cam," Alara murmured.

"You're not going," Father said.

"I already sent for my horse."

Father leaned close to Camrun's face. "Your sister's obstinacy is bad enough. I won't be defied by my only remaining son."

Camrun's eyes narrowed. He drew himself up a little taller. "If Kyvern were here, he'd do the same."

Father turned away, dropping Alara's arm.

Mum took his place, putting her arm around Alara's shoulders. They walked silently down the steps.

Sturg jogged past them, tugging his cap on. He headed for his horse.

The ambassador gestured to the man standing near the carriage. "Prime Minister, this is Lieutenant Hanik."

The lieutenant was almost as tall as Sturg, but slender. He had a narrow face, and his hair was the color of new bronze.

Alara's trunk and suitcase were tied to the rack on the back of the carriage. Hanik opened the door and stood aside.

She put on her hat. "I prefer to ride. Where's my horse?" The strong wind blowing from the west threatened to take her hat away. She tightened the chinstrap.

Hanik showed no expression, but the ambassador frowned. "That won't do, Prime Minister."

"Alara, please cooperate," Father said. "I told the grooms not to prepare your horse."

Mum squeezed her shoulders. "I realize this is off-putting, but you must trust your father. Besides, with Cam along, nothing's going to happen to you."

"Cam can't go along," Father said.

Mum stared, wide-eyed. "Why not? He wants to. And it will ensure Alara's safety."

Father leaned closer to Mum. "There is no threat to Alara's safety."

Mum's voice was soft but tense. "Quite a few ladies who survived the war would disagree. Since you refuse to go with her, Camrun must." She hugged Alara. "Take care, baby. We'll see you soon. Telshi go with you."

Alara clung to Mum's shoulders. "And with you." Her voice cracked. She blinked back tears and searched the crowd gathered on the stairs. Where were Rariden and Palon? After a moment, she let go.

Mum hugged Camrun. "Stay close to your sister."

He tugged his wide-brimmed hat firmly onto his head. "Count on it."

Pavud and Sturg mounted their horses first, and Camrun and the soldiers followed suit. Father handed Alara into the carriage.

Mum waved. "Have a safe trip!"

Alara waved back as the carriage pulled away.

The Ayenni road ran from the seacoast in the west to the farmlands in the east. Paved with hexagonal stone blocks, the road carried traders and businesspeople of every sort. They hauled loads of granite from the mountain quarries, cases of wine from the Kaesrynne Valley, and bushels of grain from the lowlands. Shepherds on foot in tattered dungarees shared that wide road with students on horseback and bankers in polished ebony carriages. Rich and poor alike gaped at the Makutian procession. The road, like a river, swept Alara away.

*Kenna, is this really my path? Preaching in the gynaeceum? I realize the church has made inroads in Makut, but—*

She didn't want to preach there. She wanted to return to the mission in Apanumon, where she had friends.

Better still would be a meetinghouse in Glynrell. A curacy of her own. Except the rector who ran the mission had made it plain she was unqualified for such a post. Although she knew of an available one, she tried not to think about it.

*Kenna, show me what to do.*

She closed her eyes, but no vision came. She took out her book of Scriptures, a thick volume bound in tan sheepskin. The gold lettering on the spine and cover had mostly worn away. Many of the creamy pages' wide margins were filled with her notes.

She opened to the chronicle of Digalo. He had spent much of his career preaching the news of Kenna in Glynrell when it was a backward, heathen country. It seemed fitting to read his story, since she was being taken to a backward, heathen country.

Camrun rode close to her right-hand window. From time to time he caught her eye and smiled. Heavy gray clouds hung above him.

*Kenna, thank you for Camrun. I've never said that, have I? Forgive me for all the times I compared him unfavorably to Kyvern. Since Ky died, Cam's been terrific.*

Soon the clouds released their rain. Another road ran down the mountain and through the hills to meet the Ayenni road. At the crossroads, a little village of stone houses with slate roofs offered travelers respite. Alara expected the troops to stop there to break out rain gear. She wanted a chance to stretch her legs.

But they pulled overcoats from their packs and passed through the village without stopping. Camrun scowled and, with some difficulty, likewise unpacked his coat.

Alara looked out the left-hand window, past Lieutenant Hanik, to the mountains in the north.

Through the veil of rain, she could barely make out the granite buildings of the cloister halfway up the side of Mount Denedra. She wished she could fly—across the foothills, up the side of the mountain, into the tallest tower of the abbey, where the prelate kept her office. She'd be safe there.

But if she were back at Denedra, she probably wouldn't be up in the abbey with the prelate. Instead, she'd be down in the stables with Dorrel.

# Chapter 3

## At a Distance

Near sundown, Commander Sturg halted his troop where the Ayenni road cut between two low hills. The northern one was broad and mostly flat. Sturg dismounted, then walked through waist-high rye.

The hill offered a good view of the rolling land all around. There were no large trees nearby. That long grass wouldn't offer cover for cavalry, but infantry easily could hide in it.

The rain had eased to a fine drizzle. The strong wind that had brought the storm in from the sea continued to blow, tossing the grass like waves on a lake.

Sturg turned to Sergeant Korig. "Clear this ground and build a fire."

Korig organized some privates to do the work. They used their sabers as scythes to cut the grass, which was taken to the horses.

The carriage would have to stay on the road. Just as well. That way, the girl would be kept at a distance.

The carriage door opened. The girl stepped out. What was she thinking?

She met her brother, and they sat on the wet pavers and did stretching exercises.

"Hanik!"

The lieutenant, arms folded, was just watching the Glynrellans. He looked up at the sound of his name. "Sir?"

"Get her back in the carriage."

Hanik saluted and walked over to the girl. Sturg couldn't hear what was said, till she raised her voice.

"I beg your pardon!"

Hanik said something more, gesturing toward the carriage. She stood, brushed off her trousers, and walked straight toward Sturg.

The worst thing about being assigned to the embassy in Ayenni was dealing with headstrong Glynrellan women. And every Glynrellan woman he had ever met was headstrong.

She strode forward, dressed like a man, her pants, shirt, and hat not much different from her brother's. Sturg wondered if Prince Velek knew what he was getting.

"Commander," she said, "I've been shut in that carriage all day. You must allow me some exercise."

She spoke in Sturg's language, not her own. Her Makutian was better than his Glynnish.

He glared at her. She glared right back.

Her eyes were green.

His stomach heaved, unsettled by the brazenness of her stare.

He gazed above her head. "Please return to the carriage, Your Highness."

"I told you once, I'm not a highness."

He flung the back of his gloved right hand across her cheek. Her head lashed to one side.

Instantly, Camrun Kordelyon's sword lay beside Sturg's throat. "Don't touch my sister."

Ambassador Pavud approached at a quick pace.

The girl glared at Sturg through narrowed eyes and drew off, arms folded.

Camrun took a step forward, forcing Sturg back. "This is why I joined my sister. I knew she'd be treated poorly."

"Begging your pardon, Mr. Kordelyon," Pavud said. "We are unused to such brazenness."

"That's no excuse for violence."

"If you'll put away your sword, sir," Pavud said, "we can discuss this rationally."

Camrun took a step back and sheathed his sword, but his arms remained poised to draw.

"Commander," Pavud said, "you must admit that such treatment is inappropriate for the prince's bride."

Sturg would admit no such thing.

"And you," Pavud said to Camrun, "must admit your sister's demeanor was disrespectful."

"My sister withholds respect only when she doesn't receive the respect due her."

"May we agree," Pavud said, "she will be treated with due respect if she will do likewise?"

"Of course. But remember her title is curate. A rank earned—not inherited."

Pavud made a small bow. "Understood, sir."

Camrun eyed Sturg. "Commander?"

He nodded, slightly.

Camrun stepped back, keeping his eyes on Sturg for several moments more. Then he coaxed his sister back into the carriage, where she belonged.

Alara dropped onto the carriage seat and threw her hat on the floor. "I would rather be out in the rain than cooped up in here. You know that."

"Yes, but give these fellows a wide margin. There's no point antagonizing them."

She sighed. He was right. Not that she would say so.

Camrun looked over his shoulder, then climbed in and sat across from her. He switched to Redíquan and lowered his voice almost to a whisper. "Listen." He leaned forward. "The general and Palon are following us."

"What? Cam—"

"This is the general's plan, so do not argue. They shall come at midnight and disable the guards. Then we go to Denedra." He winked.

If he started teasing her about Dorrel the way Palon did, she'd kick him.

"Perhaps it is better if we do not. With you along, I daresay they shall not be too awful." She rubbed her cheek. "As long as I keep my mouth shut."

"Really? When have you ever done so?"

She wasn't going to admit to his being right about that, either. "This is ridiculous. Father says go to Makut. Rariden says go to Denedra. I do not wish to do their will. I wish to do Kenna's will."

"Ah. And what word do you have from Her upon that matter, O wise prophet?"

She kicked his shin.

He kicked hers.

She huffed, folded her arms, and looked out the window.

"You heard Pavud refer to you as 'the prince's bride.'"

"Yes." She closed her eyes. Granite bricks dropped into her stomach. "Do you think Father knows their intent, or did Pavud trick him?"

Camrun shrugged. "Does it matter? Either way, we must get you away from these pigs."

"Thank you, Cam." She put out her hand to him. "You have been a good brother to me, and I have never thanked you for it."

He held her hand. "Do not lie, Alara. I have been beastly to you for many years."

That was true.

But she'd been beastly as well, and there was no telling who'd been

beastly first, because it had been going on for as long as they could
remember.

Lieutenant Hanik brought blankets, a canteen of water, and a
supper of cold ham and carrots. Alara and Camrun stayed in the
carriage, while the others sat in their tents in the increasingly heavy
rain. The ambassador had a large wall tent, but the others, even the
officers, had only pup tents.

Three men patrolled the perimeter of the camp. If Palon took one
and Rariden the other, the third might raise an alarm before they
reached him.

Alara glanced out the window to see whether anyone was looking.
She drew a piece of oilcloth from her saddlebag, wrapped her books,
and put them away. "My raincoat is packed." She jerked her thumb
toward the baggage rack. They continued to use Redíquan. It seemed
prudent, though they had no assurance the Makutians were ignorant
of that language.

"Palon shall bring another for you. And your horse, also."

Soon it was fully dark. Clouds hid the moon, making it impossible
to tell the time. Raindrops rattled against the roof.

No night had ever seemed so long.

There was no sleeping. Even if she hadn't been waiting, quaking,
for Palon's signal, the lightning and thunder would have kept Alara
awake. And what if the Makutians couldn't sleep, either?

A flash of lightning. A double-rap on the carriage door. A roar of
thunder. Alara's tremulous limbs snapped to attention. The rapping
had come from her right. The door facing away from the Makutians'
tents.

"Go," Camrun whispered.

Alara sloughed off the coarse wool blanket Hanik had given her,
leaving it on the seat. She stepped onto the road and slung her
saddlebag over her shoulder. Camrun followed and drew his sword.

Lightning flashed. She saw the tents, but nothing else beyond the carriage.

When the thunder rumbled, she ran westward.

Only the feel of pavers under her boots and the occasional flash of lightning told her she was keeping to the road.

One flash revealed a horse ahead. She slowed to a walk, while her heart ran on. Rain dripped off the brim of her hat. "Willow." In response came a familiar nicker.

Another lightning bolt. Alara edged forward, one hand outstretched, until she touched warm, wet horsehide. She threw her saddlebag over Willow's withers and glanced back up the road, waiting for lightning to show whether anyone followed.

Soon enough, she got a glimpse of a horse and rider. Palon.

"Well done, Alara."

"I didn't do anything but run away."

"Which was exactly what was needed, so well done."

Alara rummaged in the pack on Willow's rump until she found her buckskin duster.

"There's a saber on your pommel," Palon said.

Alara pulled on the coat, then found the sword belt and strapped it on. Hoofbeats approached. Camrun, with Rariden close behind. Alara mounted her horse, and they all galloped toward Denedra.

"Commander!"

Sturg sat up. "What?"

Outside the tent, Sergeant Korig said, "The princess is gone."

Sturg swore, then pulled his boots on. He stepped out into the dim predawn light. Half the tents had been knocked down in the storm.

"Where are the guards who were on duty?"

Korig pointed to the edge of camp, where Hanik was checking a private's eyes, as if looking for signs of concussion. Two others sat nearby, bruised but not bloodied.

Sturg strode over. "What happened?"

Hanik looked up. "They were all knocked out by blows to the head, Commander."

"Not severe enough to break skin? Not enough to kill them?"

"No, sir."

Fists on hips, Sturg frowned at them a moment, then turned his back. Punishing them would have to wait. He called Ult, who served as his aide.

The boy was fourteen, all gangly arms and legs. His little brown spaniel followed at his heels.

"That dog of yours is meant to be a retriever," Sturg said. "See if it can get the girl's scent from the carriage."

Ult ran down to the road. The spaniel scampered behind, ears flapping.

The ambassador emerged from his tent. Sturg gave a brief report.

"We passed the religious cloister yesterday," Hanik said. "The one on the mountain."

Pavud, arms folded, looked that way. "Denedra."

Sturg nodded. "That's where they'll likely go. Korig! Take two men and Ult and the dog and overtake them."

The ambassador watched Korig leave. "I'll go on to Tarvag with my people and alert the king there may be a delay." He turned to Sturg. "But every noble family will be there, Commander, expecting a wedding on the fifteenth. You must get her there on time." Pavud walked toward his tent.

"By any means necessary, Ambassador?"

"Of course."

# Chapter 4

## DENEDRA

The storm continued until nearly dawn. Alara shrugged out of her waterlogged coat and draped it over Willow's haunches to dry.

Mid-morning, they crested a hill. Before them rose the southern slope of Mount Denedra. The cloister's towers grew from its flank, an outgrowth of pale gray granite quarried from within the mountain.

"If we're lucky," Alara said, "we'll get there in time for dinner."

"We've already been lucky." Rariden twisted in his saddle to look behind them. The hilltop offered a view for miles around. "They haven't caught up to us."

On the other side of the hill, the horses splashed across a stream and onto the road that zigzagged up the face of the mountain.

They reached Denedra's south gatehouse just before noon. By then, the sunshine had mostly dried them out. The gatekeepers greeted them cheerfully as they opened the gates.

Alara led the others through the grounds. Terraced gardens rimmed with sand-colored brick flanked the courtyard. The campus contained cloister and university, a jumble of levels and towers added on at different times as the occupancy grew. Denedra felt as familiar as Ravendyn. Returning was like going home.

On the north side of the campus, three long stables ran perpendicular to the cloister. A plateau stretched northward to a sheer granite face that still showed marks where stonemasons had cut away blocks for the buildings. The eastern end of the face ran into the crevice that formed the north side of Denedra Pass.

Alara rode up to the large wooden doors of the first stable. She dismounted and stepped inside. "Hello? Professor Sheeno?"

A familiar bellow came from the end of the corridor. "Who's there?"

"Alara Kordelyon."

A portly, balding man in dungarees and a linen shirt approached from the far end of the building.

"Hello, Professor. Good to see you."

"And you. What brings you back?"

"That's a long story." She introduced the others.

Sheeno led them down the broad corridor, opening gates to empty boxes. Wide, short window slits under the eaves brought in a clean, post-storm breeze that lightened the musk-and-manure odor of the stables.

Willow whinnied giddily at a bay stallion in a neighboring box. The stallion, Toban, whickered back. Willow pulled her reins out of Alara's hand to stand alongside the gate of Toban's stall. They rubbed their necks together, strands of her chestnut mane mingling with his black one.

"Oh, you missed your sire, didn't you?" Alara rubbed Willow's neck. She gave Toban a pat on the shoulder before separating the horses and leading Willow into the roomy box across from Toban's.

While she was loosening the girth on her saddle, she heard, from the other end of the building, the voice she'd been anticipating. Or dreading.

"Who was it, Professor?"

Sheeno looked from the speaker to her and back again with that familiar cold glare.

Alara pulled off her gloves and stepped out of the stall to shake Dorrel's hand. "It's so good to see you again."

"And you, Alara." Sinewy and a foot taller than she, Dorrel had deep-set eyes almost as dark as the shock of coffee-colored hair that spilled into them. He took her hand between both of his. "Your hands are like ice." He snatched his hands back and looked away, first to Sheeno, then Willow, then the window. "You weren't out in that storm, I hope."

Alara blushed. "Afraid so."

The professor frowned. He couldn't start in on them again. It was just a handshake.

Camrun stepped in. "Dorrel. Good to see you." They shook hands.

"And you. How've you been?"

Camrun looked at Alara with a wry grin. "I've been better."

Dorrel looked up, his brow creased. "General Rariden?"

Rariden also shook Dorrel's hand and introduced Palon.

"Pleasure to finally meet you, Mr. Chevallon," Palon said. "I've heard a lot about you."

Dorrel's eyebrows went up. He looked at Alara, who could do nothing but scowl at Palon.

"Or is it Dr. Chevallon now?" Camrun asked.

Dorrel made a small snort, almost a laugh. "Not yet. Commencement isn't until next week."

Sheeno addressed a girl who had come in behind Dorrel. "Help get the tack off these horses, then get them some water. Dorrel, why don't you fetch a few more first-year students to help?"

The girl started toward Willow's stall.

Dorrel stopped her with a hand on her shoulder. He turned to the professor. "I'll look after Willow myself."

"She can do it—"

"You'll excuse me if I feel a bit proprietary toward Willow."

Sheeno glared at Dorrel but nodded.

Dorrel sent the girl to fetch the others, then smiled weakly at Alara before heading into Willow's stall.

She'd never heard him talk back to a professor.

Alara lifted the saddle from Willow's back. The side wall of the box came almost to Alara's shoulder; she set the saddle on the edge of the wall.

Dorrel draped Willow with a blanket.

"Alara," Rariden said, "we need to speak with the prelate."

"Let me take care of Willow—"

"Go on," Dorrel said. "I'll look after Willow like she was my own."

"Sometimes you behave as if she is your own."

"No, but Toban expects me to look after his get"—he raised his voice—"don't you, boy?"

Toban whickered.

General Rariden stepped into the gate of the box. "Alara."

She looked from him to Dorrel.

Dorrel pulled off the rest of Willow's tack, and Alara was in his way when he went to hang it up. He grinned at her. "You're keeping the general waiting."

"Yes. Right." Oh, she missed working with him. "All right, then." She patted Willow's withers in parting. Her gaze lingered on Dorrel's face as she turned toward the general. Her eyes caught up with the rest of her head. "Sorry, sir."

She took him and the others to the main building, up the spiraling stone steps toward the central hall. Behind her, Palon whispered something to Camrun, who snickered.

Alara didn't care to know what had been said.

Through the cavernous great hall, past the library, down a narrow stone corridor, they reached the antechamber of the abbey. There, a seminarian at the desk sent word to the prelate's office.

The abbey was the oldest part of Denedra. Its windows were glazed with bull's-eye panes. Ancient tapestries hung on plastered walls yellowed with age.

In a few minutes, they were shown up another set of spiraling stone stairs to the prelate's office, a small room in the central tower.

Bookcases lined the walls, leaving barely enough space in the room for the desk.

Prelate Dalys was heavyset and just a little taller than Alara. Her hair, once brown, had turned mostly gray. She was nearly the age Alara's maternal grandmother would be, if Grandmammá were still living, and possessed the same sort of regal serenity.

After Alara made introductions, the prelate gestured Alara and Palon into wooden chairs facing the desk. The letter atop a pile on the corner of the desk bore the Kordelyon crest at the top and, at the bottom, her father's outsized signature.

General Rariden explained why they had come.

"I understood from the papers there was some confusion about the treaty's wording," the prelate said. "You believe the Makutians interpret it differently than we do."

Rariden nodded.

"We heard the ambassador call her 'the prince's bride,'" Camrun said.

The prelate's eyebrows lifted slightly. "I see." Her eyes went to the letter. "This letter from the prime minister informs me your services are needed elsewhere." She tilted her head.

Alara couldn't respond. There were no words.

"Rather presumptuous of him, I think, to reassign one of my clerics without consulting me first."

"Ma'am, I have every intention of returning to the mission."

"I should think so." Prelate Dalys folded her hands on the desk. "The treaty has been a matter of some debate here. Some say, and I am inclined to agree, the prime minister not only impinged upon your free will and my authority as your superior. By exceeding the bounds of his authority, he also violated the will of Telshi."

Alara tried to laugh, but it came out like a choked-off cough. "I don't know whether I appreciate being the subject of doctrinal debate."

Prelate Dalys pursed her lips in a little smile. "I understand." She looked to Rariden. "General, Alara's obligation to the church requires that she return to her post in Apanumon. That means defying the prime minister"—she waved a hand toward the letter—"which I am prepared to do. But can you, as a statesman, assure me that her returning to Apanumon is the best solution?"

"It's not a solution," he said. "The only solution will be for Parliament to rescind the treaty. But in Apanumon, she will be protected in the meantime."

"How so?"

"Apanumon has no diplomatic relations with Makut. Their troops won't be able to reach her there."

The prelate nodded. "Very well." She lowered her eyes for a moment, then looked up at him. "How can we help?"

"Alara and Palon will need provisions for the trip to Apanumon."

"I'm going as well," Camrun said.

"You're coming back to Ayenni with me."

Camrun gaped at Rariden. "I'm seeing my sister to safety."

"Palon can do that. I need you to find historical precedents for overturning international trade agreements."

Camrun sighed. "And the arranged marriages of the pre-Telshan period, I suppose?"

"Probably a good idea." Rariden faced the prelate. "Also, if the Makutians deduce this is where she came, your militia will need to hold them off."

"I doubt it will come to that," she said. "Our walls are formidable."

Rariden nodded. "They served us well in the war, and I daresay they will again."

Leaning against the wall of Willow's box, Dorrel absentmindedly cleaned her bridle. The first-years were still buzzing about General Rariden.

They didn't understand his presence meant trouble.

Dorrel had toyed with the idea of riding to the capital to visit Alara, but Sheeno would disapprove. And he had long ago heard enough of the professor's opinion.

Besides, her family probably wouldn't appreciate his showing up uninvited.

On first seeing her in the stable, he'd flattered himself to think she was stopping on her way back to Apanumon to visit him. But then he'd seen the general and realized something was wrong. Probably to do with the treaty.

The sound of her voice startled him.

"Dorrel—imagine finding you here." Her tone was wry. She stepped into the box.

"As if you wouldn't know where to find me."

She chuckled. "I'm afraid I have to ask you—" She frowned at the chamois in his hand. "Were you cleaning my tack?"

His cheeks flushed. "Hope you don't mind."

"Of course not." One of her sweet, honest smiles brightened her face and his heart. "You probably did a better job than I would."

Behind her, Rariden and Camrun saddled their horses.

"You're not leaving already?"

"Cam and the general are going back to Ayenni. But . . . I need you to do me a favor."

"Anything."

"Show Palon and me the fastest way to Apanumon."

After seeing the general and Camrun off, Dorrel and Alara hurried to the dining hall. There, Palon had staked out a corner table and spread out a map.

So Palon had heard a lot about him. Well, he'd heard a lot about her, too. Alara's fondness for Palon sometimes bordered on hero worship.

After everyone was seated, one of the seminarians blessed the meal. Then the first-years came around with platters of roast beef and bowls of vegetables.

Palon sat on one side of the table with Dorrel and Alara opposite.

"The closest border crossing is north of Ecciston." Palon pointed to it. "But there's a large fort near there. Thanks to the home secretary, they'll be looking for you."

"Besides," Alara said, "that's east of here. The mission is to the west."

Palon nodded, chewing. She swallowed, then took a sip of water. "Ryol Pass is in the direction you need to go, but that'll also be guarded by the border patrol." She looked at Dorrel. "Could we head due north over the mountains?"

He shook his head. "The going is too hard." He tapped the map with the handle of his fork. "There's a pass north of Kaesbaro, but the terrain is so rough, hardly anyone goes that way." That trail wasn't even marked on the map.

"Is it guarded?" Palon asked.

"Not really," he said. "The border patrol delegated it to the militia, but the closest militia members live several miles south of the pass."

Palon nodded. "Just the thing, then."

He shook his head. "Willow isn't sturdy enough for that climb."

Alara scrunched her eyebrows. "She's Toban's get, isn't she?"

"Yes, but she has her dam's spindly racehorse legs."

That was the wrong way to put it. Her face scrunched up as if she might cry.

Palon looked at the ceiling. "You had to bring that up . . ."

"I'm sorry, but it's true."

As if it were happening again, Dorrel pictured Alara on her mare, Vinnaq, chasing a stag through the forest, over a line of gorse bushes, onto a rough slope of granite scree. Vinnaq's legs had crumpled like paper.

Alara's voice was hushed. "I should never have taken her over that jump."

"Any of us might've done the same," he said. "You were in the lead because you had the fastest horse."

"She wasn't bred for the hunt." Alara bit her lip.

Dorrel looked at Palon. "Your horse looks like a Chevallon charger."

She cocked her head. "So he is. You've a good eye."

He shrugged. "The army's been using our horses for generations."

"Centuries, you mean." Alara stared at her plate, pushing carrots around with her fork.

"If we can't take Willow this way"—Palon tapped the map where the trail should be—"what are we going to do?"

"We'll stop in Kaesbaro first." Dorrel speared a carrot. "My father has horses that can make the climb."

Alara looked at him. "Can Willow make it to Kaesbaro?"

"She made it here, didn't she? The trail down Mount Denedra isn't as rough as that one."

Palon took a sip of water. "How long will it take us to get there?"

"Toban makes the trip fast, but I doubt the others can keep up. Until we get to the river road." Dorrel eyed the road on the map. It ran alongside the river most of the length of the valley. He leaned closer to Alara. "Then Willow could outrun us all."

That coaxed a little smile out of her.

Dorrel continued. "If we leave now and ride through the night, we could be there by morning."

Alara blinked rapidly. "Ride through the night. Again."

"You rode all last night?"

She nodded, her face careworn.

He propped his elbow on the table, leaning his cheek on his hand. He looked over at Palon. "Maybe we should wait until morning."

"Can't risk it," she said, her mouth full. She swallowed and looked at Alara. "You'll just have to slog on."

Alara still picked at her food.

"You can't slog on with an empty stomach," Dorrel said. "Will you eat already?"

She grimaced, but she ate.

Shortly after midday, Sturg and his troop caught up to Korig outside the gates of Denedra.

"They won't open the gate, Commander," Korig said. "They won't even say whether she's here."

"Guard!" Sturg bellowed. "We demand entry!"

The gateman leaned out the window of the tower. "Beg pardon?"

"Diplomacy, Commander," Hanik muttered.

Sturg glared at him. "Fine. You talk to him."

Hanik called up to the tower. "We wish to see Alara Kordelyon."

"Sorry. Can't help you."

"May I speak to your . . ." Hanik hesitated. "Prelate?"

"I'll send word," the gateman said, "but I can't promise she'll come." He disappeared.

"She?" Sturg asked.

Hanik shrugged.

Whether *she* came was irrelevant. The prelate was unlikely to open the gates willingly. Sturg had already decided what to do. While they waited, he spoke with Ult. He wasn't strong, but he was nimble.

With the guard tower empty, there was no one to see Ult toss the grappling hook over the gate and climb. He was halfway to the top when another gateman appeared in the turret.

The tower jutted outward from the wall, so the man had a clear view of the gate. He bellowed in Makutian, "Get down!"

Ult continued to climb. The gateman nocked an arrow and drew the string of his longbow. "Get down!"

Korig raised his crossbow.

The arrow flew between Sturg and Ult.

Korig shot. The gateman fell back, struck in the neck.

Ult reached the top.

Another gateman stood in the window of the gatehouse. He—no, she—aimed an arrow at Ult. "Down!"

Ult looked back at Sturg.

"Come down, Ult," Sturg said. "It's too late."

Ult slid down the rope. He walked to Sturg's horse, pulling off his abraded gloves, eyes on his hands. "Sorry I wasn't quick enough, sir."

"It wasn't your lack of speed. They had more than one guard in the tower."

An alarm bell pealed.

Dorrel and Palon had finished eating, but Alara's meal was only half-gone.

"Can the kitchen supply us—" The alarm bell cut Palon off.

For half a moment, the air was heavy with silent hesitation. Then the dining hall erupted. Students jumped from chairs and ran from the room.

Palon jumped up as well, Dorrel and Alara following.

"Chevallon." Palon pointed to Alara. "Get her out of here."

"We can't leave now," Alara wailed.

"You are their objective." Palon strode toward the door. "No Makutian reaches his objective on Glynrellan soil while I'm breathing."

"Ocha," Dorrel said. "Still, I should muster—"

"You should follow orders, Sergeant."

How did she know his rank? Not that it mattered. "I need my sword."

"Where is it?" Palon asked.

"In the weapons locker"—he pointed in the direction the other students were going—"at the mustering area."

"Leave it."

The three jogged down the stairs to the stables and saddled their horses. Many students had come to do the same.

When she'd finished with her horse, Palon took off her sword and handed it to Dorrel. "I suppose that professor of yours can get me another."

"Any of the faculty can."

She nodded. They led the horses outside. "Get her to Kaesbaro, Sergeant."

"Yes, ma'am." He gave Palon a salute.

"Palon . . ." Alara cleared her throat. "Come with us."

Palon put on her cap. "I'm of more use here. And you're wasting time."

Alara hugged her. "Please be careful. You're my dearest friend."

"You're a liar." Palon pushed Alara back, but she smiled. "Dearest but one. I know that." She winked at Dorrel.

His stomach clenched. Alara blushed brightly, ducking her head.

Palon mounted and pointed her horse away from them. "I'll meet you in Kaesbaro." She followed the students to the mustering area.

Alara and Dorrel galloped across the pasture, while everyone else went the other way. "I can't believe we're leaving the fight," she said.

He couldn't either, but he wasn't going to disobey a captain. Especially not when she was so right.

At the gate, a girl climbed down the ladder from the gatehouse. "The alarm was on the south side."

"I know." Dorrel jumped down, opened the gate, and ushered Alara and Toban through. He paused before closing it. "Hold this gate at all costs."

Her eyes showed too much white, like those of a spooked horse. "Yes, Sergeant."

# Chapter 5

## THE BARRICADE

Sturg drew his men off, out of bowshot of the guard tower. "We need to reconnoiter. Look for a place to scale the walls after dark."

"Sir," Hanik said, "This place has hundreds of students, plus faculty and clergy. We're outnumbered fifty to one, at least."

"I know. But going back without the girl is impossible."

"Of course. But it wouldn't be rational for her to remain here, under siege."

Sturg narrowed his eyes. "You think she went out the back."

"She would likely feel safer in Apanumon, since their border patrol turned back the prince's last attempt to retrieve her."

Sturg dismounted and pulled the map from his saddlebag.

Hanik joined him.

The road from Denedra to the valley joined a larger road that ran along the river. Another road to the east crossed the Kovarn Mountains, which formed the border.

"If she has gone," Hanik continued, "we'll have to overtake her before she reaches the border. Otherwise we'll come up against the border patrol."

"We can handle the border patrol." Sturg compared the map with what he saw before him. The terrain around the cloister was rough but not impassable. The eastern side looked less craggy. "We'll go round the back and see whether we pick up her trail. If there's no sign of her leaving, I'll consider whether we should attack."

He didn't care for this last option. They were outnumbered. And he wasn't going to leave his men's bones at the gates of Denedra, as his predecessors had in the war.

Sturg crested a ridge and looked toward Denedra. They must be watching. He didn't know whether they'd attack when the troop reached the road on the north side of the cloister.

Crossing the mountainside meant going on foot and leading the horses, most of which had never crossed such terrain. Private Helk's horse slipped into a ravine, nearly taking him with it. He let go of the reins and kept his footing, but then he had to climb into the ravine to finish off the screaming beast.

Helk, a lanky young man with stringy, shoulder-length hair the color of straw, hiked back up with his horse's pack on his own shoulders. Pathetic.

When they finally reached the road, it showed many horses and riders had recently been there. So she was traveling under heavy guard.

Ult's dog picked up her scent. It headed toward a bend in the road. Sturg gave a short whistle, and it returned.

"You," Sturg pointed to Private Feolt. "Scout ahead. Report back as soon as you spot them."

While Feolt scouted, the men sat at the roadside, eating jerky and hardtack till he returned. Blood dripped from his right leg. "They're about a quarter-mile down-mountain, sir. It's a thickly wooded place, just past a curve in the road. Boulders on either side of the road, the space between them barricaded with logs."

"How many people?"

"I saw only a few sir, but I didn't stay long. They shot me." Feolt was short and thickset with dark brown hair. His tanned skin had paled.

"I see that." A handspan of arrow stuck out of Feolt's thigh. The arrow had gone through the leg and into his horse. "You were shot from the side, not the front."

"Yes, sir."

Sturg eyed Hanik. "They lined the road with archers."

Hanik nodded. "Glynrellan longbows are said to be formidable."

"True. Patch him up."

Hanik cut through the piece of shaft between Feolt and the horse, then pulled the shaft from Feolt's leg. The private got a bandage but no stitches. "I know it hurts like Shaedeis," Hanik said, "but it'll have to do for now. I'll make a proper job of it later."

Feolt nodded, then took a long drink from the flask of liquor Korig handed him.

Hanik left the arrowhead in the horse, covering it with a bandage.

Sturg spread out his map. Feolt fingered the location of the Glynrellan barricade.

"Where were you when you were shot?"

Feolt moved his finger south. "Just past that bend."

"All right." Sturg chose Feolt and another private to stay with himself and Ult and split the rest of the squad between Korig and Hanik.

"Each unit will take one side of the road on foot. Kill the archers quietly so as not to alert the others. After you've finished the archers, outflank the barricade. Then blow a signal horn. We'll attack on horseback from the front while you attack from the rear."

They loaded crossbows. Two units disappeared into the woods. Feolt led the rest down the trail to just before the bend where he'd been shot. There they waited.

Sturg heard nothing for a long time. That was good. "Ult, you hang back. Collect spent crossbow bolts and return them to the soldiers."

"Yes, sir."

A girl's shout of "Captain!" was followed at once by Hanik's horn.

Sturg drew his saber. "Charge!"

They galloped down the trail.

On the other side of the barricade, his men fought the Glynrellans. Swords clashed, but Sturg heard only the horses' hoofbeats. He roared like a bear as he neared the barricade, a chest-high stack of timbers.

His black charger easily leapt over. He came down amidst the brawl. One of the Glynrellans fell underneath the steel-shod hooves.

Sturg galloped on, making room for the privates to come behind.

A boy, sword raised over his shoulder, came at him. Sturg met him, his saber cutting into the boy's neck.

Sturg wheeled around.

The privates on horseback had likewise felled a couple of students. One of them was a girl.

Only Glynrellans would send girls to do such work.

Six students lay on the ground. Four more dueled his men.

Hanik fought a woman. She was getting the better of him.

Ult pulled a bolt from a body on the ground.

Where was Korig?

Up against one of the boulders, Helk was trying to get the pants off a blonde-haired girl. Her right arm hung limp and bloody at her side. She punched him with her other fist.

One of the students vaulted over the barricade. He sprinted up the trail toward Denedra.

A crossbow bolt in his back stopped him.

Ah. There was Korig.

A tall, burly student dueled Radig. Sturg moved forward and slashed the student's neck. He fell.

Radig took a step back, his breathing ragged and short. His sword arm was swathed in blood.

A crossbow bolt flew past Sturg and into the ribs of the woman fighting Hanik.

She didn't make a sound.

Hanik ran her through. The tip of his sword came through the back of her dark-blue jacket.

She took another swipe at him on her way down. With his sword buried in her, he couldn't parry. But he ducked, stepping back.

She fell onto her back in the dirt.

Another bolt went into the shoulder of a student. Two privates finished him off.

Hanik retrieved his sword.

Aside from the blonde, only one Glynrellan remained, dueling one of the privates.

Two more privates charged in and knocked him down. The one he'd been fighting cut his throat.

Sturg dismounted. "Fall in!"

Korig scrambled down the hillside. The others fell in, except for Helk, still wrestling the blonde.

"Helk!" Sturg hollered. "We haven't time for that. Finish her."

She said something so rapidly, Sturg caught nothing of it but "Kenna." One of their goddesses.

Her prayer was cut off by Helk's knife.

Sturg tallied the casualties. Korig and the others made sure all the Glynrellans were dead. As they did, they collected the weapons of those they'd killed.

Hanik knelt next to Radig, opened his medical kit, and ordered one of the privates to build a fire.

Ult came to Sturg with a Glynrellan arrow in his hand. "May I keep this, sir?"

"Did you kill the archer?"

"No, sir."

"Then you mayn't."

Ult dropped the arrow.

Twenty-one altogether. Five archers on each side of the road, and ten students behind the barricade.

Plus one who wasn't a student.

Sturg frowned at the body of the woman Korig and Hanik had killed. She looked close to thirty. Her hair was brown, cut mannishly short. She wore the full-dress uniform of the Glynrellan army with epaulets bearing the insignia of a captain.

Korig picked up her sword. He removed her sword belt and the dagger sheath on her right leg.

"No sign of the prince's bride?" Sturg asked.

Korig shook his head and cleaned the sword. "None, sir."

Sturg swore. She was getting away, while he and his men were stuck here bandaging wounds. Which probably was what the Glynrellans had planned.

Hanik twisted a tourniquet around Radig's upper arm. Below the elbow, a large piece of flesh had been carved away, revealing bone.

Korig sheathed the sword and held it out to Hanik. "Lieutenant?"

"No thank you, Sergeant." He didn't look up from his work.

"You dealt the final blow, sir."

"I don't care."

Korig shrugged and kept both sword and dagger.

"It's got to come off . . . doesn't it, sir?" Radig asked, his voice thready.

"Yes." Hanik measured a dose of laudanum into a tin cup and gave it to him.

Radig downed it.

After the men had collected their trophies, Sturg sent those not wounded to fetch the horses left up the trail.

A slice ran diagonally across Hanik's left forearm. Ult wrapped it hastily. While waiting for Radig's painkiller to take effect, Hanik inspected the wounded. Six of them, besides him and Radig. He gave a couple of the privates their stitches while the cauter heated in the fire. Those that didn't need stitches bandaged one another.

Once Radig was mostly senseless, Sturg himself put the dowel in Radig's teeth and held his shoulders down while Hanik sawed the arm off at the elbow.

Sturg studied his map. The road to Apanumon ran through the town of Ecciston. They'd have to go that way.

Hanik soon bled through his bandage. He saw to all the others, even Feolt's horse, before turning to his own injury. Unfortunately, Radig was their only other medic. So Korig held the edges of the wound together while Hanik stitched it shut.

Korig bandaged the long line of sutures. Hanik, his face pale, walked to where Sturg sat on an outcrop of rock.

Hanik cleared his throat. "Radig won't be able to ride for several hours, sir." Just a slight tightness in his voice. He had more fortitude than Sturg had figured. "We'll have to lead his mount till he comes around."

Sturg nodded. "I thought as much. The others?"

"Feolt can't put his full weight on that leg. But no one else is as badly hurt."

"Good." Sturg showed Hanik the map. "There's a Glynrellan fort just north of this town. But I don't expect any trouble. We have diplomatic papers. And word of this"—he jerked his thumb at the bodies—"won't reach them before we do."

# Chapter 6

## KAESBARO

By the end of the day, Alara was trembling. They had left Denedra without provisions. Her bow and quiver were in her pack, but she couldn't trust her shivering limbs. So she handed the bow to Dorrel. He shot a grouse, while Alara gathered watercress and mushrooms. They roasted the bird on a makeshift spit.

Apart from Palon not having caught up to them, the only problem was, once they'd finished eating and buried the fire, Alara didn't wish to get up again.

"Can't we just wait here until Palon catches up?"

Dorrel crouched by the little stream and washed his hands. "She said meet her in Kaesbaro. We'll meet her in Kaesbaro." He stood and dried his hands on his shirt. "Maybe you know her well enough to disobey a direct order, but I don't."

Sitting on a flat rock by the stream, her forearms on her knees, Alara drooped her head.

"I know you're tired, Lar, but we need to keep moving."

Tired? She was beyond tired. She had ascribed the trembling to not having eaten. Only it hadn't stopped. So it must be exhaustion.

She looked up at him. "You think Commander Sturg might catch us."

Dorrel looked in the direction of Denedra, though it couldn't be seen. They were down-mountain and northeast of it by close to twenty miles. The sun, setting behind her, cast an amber glow on his face. "He'll never get through Denedra. But he might get around it."

"With horses?"

Dorrel shrugged. "We need to ride."

She hung her head again, squeezing back tears. She nodded, got up, and rode.

Falling.

Alara wailed, grabbing the nearest thing that would break her fall. She leaned against Willow's neck, her breath quick and short, fingers laced into the mane.

"Lar? What's wrong?"

Alara tried to catch her breath, tried to speak, but could do neither. She just wept, pressing her cheek against Willow's hide.

In a moment, Dorrel stood next to her. "What's wrong?"

She wrung the words out. "I dozed off." She took a short breath. "I almost fell."

"Oh, Lar." He ran his fingers through his hair, scratching his head. "I'm sorry."

"I need to stop." She dismounted.

He stepped closer. "We need to keep moving."

"Oh, Dor, please." Arms folded over her midsection, she almost doubled over. "Can't we rest just a bit?"

The moon was in its last quarter. By its thin light, his face looked dark and gray.

She staggered to him and leaned against his chest. "I'm sorry. I wish I weren't so feeble."

He put his arms around her and rested his chin on her head, just as he used to. "Two nights with no sleep would make anyone feeble."

Alara held him tightly. For a minute, they kept silent, except for her sniffling.

"I have two options," he said. "You can lay down here—only we don't have any blankets—and get some sleep while I keep watch. Or . . ."

"What?"

He cleared his throat. "I can lead Willow, and you ride on Toban with me. You sleep, and I'll make sure you don't fall."

Sleeping sitting up on horseback wouldn't be restful. But neither would sleeping on the forest floor. "You think we should keep moving."

"Yes."

"Then we'll keep moving." She gave him a little extra squeeze before letting go.

While she mounted Toban, Dorrel gathered Willow's reins.

"Willow," he said. "Willow."

Alara looked back. "She fell asleep, didn't she?"

"Yes. Willow!" He patted the mare's cheek. She shook her head and snorted. "Come on."

He led her forward, alongside Toban, then got into the saddle behind Alara. Holding the reins of both horses in his left hand, he put his right arm around Alara's waist.

She leaned against him, folding her arms over his and holding his hand. His warmth and strength supplied those she no longer had. "This is just like the day I lost Vinnaq."

"It is not. You cried all the way back to Denedra. Your horse was dead and your arm was broken."

"But you held me just like this, and Toban—stepping as if walking on eggshells. I think he knew I was hurt."

"Well, he's that kind of horse."

"Yes, and he has that kind of rider." She tipped her head back. His cheek rubbed her hair. "Did I ever thank you for taking such good care of me that day?"

"Yes. Several times."

"Good." A fullness welled up in her chest and came out as a sob. "Oh, Dor, I've missed you so much."

He squeezed her a little tighter. "I missed you, too."

She was supposed to be sleeping. If she said more, she'd cry more and not sleep. So she shut up and slept.

Just before dawn, Dorrel and Alara crested a hill. Below, the silver-blue ribbon of the Kaesrynne wound through its namesake valley. Beyond the rolling green hills on the other side of the river rose the Kovarn Mountains.

Orchards and vineyards climbed the hills around them. At the base of a foothill, the trail they followed brought them to a road along the riverbank. The water churned with a gentle roar over boulders.

They stopped to water the horses and take a drink themselves.

"How far away is Kaesbaro?" Alara asked.

"Not far. We should get there in time for breakfast."

The road was wide enough for them to ride side-by-side. At times, the Kaesrynne bent away from the road, into the trees. Even when the bank was hidden from view, Alara could still hear the river, like the murmur of voices in another room.

As the sun rose behind them, Alara spied a mill on the opposite riverbank, not far from an arched bridge. The riverbed was less rocky here, and the water settled into a quiet rush, complemented by the splashing of the mill's waterwheel.

The horses' hooves made pounding echoes as they crossed the wooden bridge.

Dorrel smiled. "I love that sound. It means I'm home."

She looked up the road behind them. "How long do you think it will take Palon to catch up?"

"No telling."

"You're not going to insist we keep moving, are you?"

"No, she said she'd meet us here, so we'll wait for her here. Besides, you need a proper rest."

Alara relaxed a little. She had long wanted to visit Kaesbaro. Now that she saw what a cozy little village it was, she relished the idea.

The road ran straight through town, passing a handful of shops. At the butcher's, hams and legs of mutton hung in the window. A grocer had bushel baskets of fruit lined up on the porch.

They met a wagon coming the other way. The driver exclaimed loudly when he saw Dorrel. "Well, hello there! What brings you home early?"

Dorrel waved. "Long story."

Someone else called a hello, and again he answered but did not stop.

"Dor, if you see Tyana Nucol, stop and introduce me."

"How do you know of Tyana?"

"She's the one who organizes the donations Kaesbaro sends to the mission."

"Ah. Right. They live"—he pointed to a side street ahead and to the right—"up that way." Along the lane, cottages sported wide porches and brightly colored flower gardens. "We could stop in later."

Soon they approached a second bridge, but before they reached it, Dorrel stopped in front of a long, one-story building of gray and white stones. The slate roof had a shallow pitch. The blue-and-gold sign hanging from the eaves read *Chevallon's Livery*.

Inside, he picked out two open boxes near the tack room. Once they had groomed and fed the horses, Dorrel picked up Alara's pack and saddlebags and escorted her across the street to the West Bridge Inn, a two-story building of tan brick with dark green shutters and woodwork.

Dorrel pulled open the big green door, then followed Alara into the public room. It had a high ceiling, a small bar on the left side, and a fireplace on the right. Dorrel set her bags down and helped her out of her coat. He hung their hats and coats on pegs by the door.

Two elderly men sat in big upholstered chairs by the front window, talking and drinking coffee. At the far side of the room, a few people were seated at a pair of dining tables running parallel to the back wall. Unless Alara was mistaken, the back of one person belonged to Dorrel's father.

Dorrel flipped a flat hand up in front of his mouth and nose, a signal that meant *silence*. His grin signaled mischief.

He quietly crossed the room. "Excuse me, are these seats taken?"

Mr. Chevallon dropped his fork. He was out of his chair in a moment, grinning widely, enveloping Dorrel in powerful arms. "What are you doing here?" Though they had the same dark eyes and hair, Kester Chevallon stood several inches shorter than his son and had a much greater girth.

"Long story, Dad."

Kester stared at Alara for a moment as if he couldn't believe what he was seeing. "Alara!" He quickly embraced her. "Sorry, hope that wasn't too presumptuous." He stepped back, his hands on her shoulders. "It's just so good to see you."

"Not at all, Mr. Chevallon. It's good to see you, too."

Kester beamed at her. "What brings you here?"

She gave him half a smile. "That's the long story."

"Ah. After breakfast, then?" Kester pulled out a chair for her.

"If you don't mind."

"Of course not." Kester sat on one side of her and Dorrel on the other.

Soon, a thin, tall white-haired woman came from the back room, carrying a coffee pot. When she saw Dorrel, she nearly dropped it.

Dorrel rose, and she met him with a maternal embrace. She was taller than Dorrel, by an inch or two, and seemed all bones. "What in heaven's name are you doing here?"

He didn't answer. Instead, he gestured to Alara. "Marita, this is Curate Alara Kordelyon. Alara, this is Marita Graylin, chairwoman of the town council."

Marita shook Alara's hand vigorously. "A pleasure, Curate." Her hearty contralto voice contrasted her seemingly frail build.

"And for me, Chairwoman Graylin."

"Pfft. Call me Marita, please."

"And you must call me Alara," she said. "You're the innkeeper?"

"That I am."

"I need a room, if you have one."

Marita nodded. "I always have room for clergy." She picked up a mug and poured the coffee. "But have your breakfast first."

Before their breakfast was served, a stocky man a little older than Kester joined them. "Dorrel! How've you been?"

Dorrel introduced her to Kergam Risdun. The man's bushy gray eyebrows leapt into his shaggy hair. "Well, Curate, it's good to meet you after all this time. How are things at the mission?"

"Quite well, thank you. I'm on my way back there now."

"I hope you'll stop with us a little while."

"Yes, I'm waiting for a friend who's coming with me."

"Excellent! Then would you be willing to lead a prayer meeting this evening?"

"Oh. I suppose I could, if you like."

"Like? We'd like nothing better, eh?" He clapped Kester's back on his way around the table.

Kester nodded. "Surely."

Mr. Risdun sat opposite her. "Not that Marita doesn't do a fine job leading prayers. But it'll be nice to have it done by a professional."

Alara's heartbeat quickened a little. "Kaesbaro still doesn't have a curate?"

Mr. Risdun shook his head. "He died in the epidemic."

"Yes, I heard. But that was more than a year ago. I can't believe no one has taken the post." If the prelate hadn't sent her to Apanumon, Alara would have applied for it.

Dorrel shrugged. "I suppose no one wanted to come here."

*Telshi, I want to come here. I want to serve these people.* She had to confess this prayer was only half of the truth. What she really wanted was to be near Dorrel.

The doorway by the bar opened onto a stairwell. Alara followed Marita upstairs to an airy upper landing, then down the corridor that bisected the building. Marita opened the next-to-last door on the left.

Alara stepped inside. A thick quilt lay on the bed, and a woven rug covered the floor. She put her pack on a low chest under the window and pulled the curtain aside. The Kovarn Mountains rose above the tree-clad foothills that ranged around the town. "What a grand view." She turned back to Marita. "It's a lovely room. How much?"

Marita waved a hand. "I don't charge clergy."

"But I can't—"

Marita walked to the hall. "If Kergam Risdun has his way, you'll earn your keep." She smirked and closed the door.

Alara drew the curtains and pulled off her boots. Napping on Marita's down mattress under a fluffy quilt was much more comfortable than doing so on Toban's back. But she didn't have a strong arm around her or a gentle voice in her ear.

# Chapter 7

## CALLED UP

"What's this long story, then?" Dad asked.

Dorrel finished his coffee. "I need to explain it to Etton as well. Why don't you come with me so I don't have to tell it twice?"

They walked to the middle of town, where a road wound down from the foothills and crossed the main street. On one corner stood a long brick building. The sign read *Temir Glassworks*. Wide doors were propped open to catch the breeze. At the far end, two furnaces blazed. Glass blowers worked in front of the smaller one, while the larger supplied the people filling molds.

Dorrel led the way through the bustle, shaking hands and clapping shoulders.

In the middle of the building, Etton Temir inspected a rack of wine bottles. He held one up to the light, frowned, and tossed it aside. It landed with a crash in a wheeled bin to be fed back into the furnace.

Etton looked up, met Dorrel's eyes, and quickly moved to meet him.

Dorrel put out his hand. Etton shook it, pulling Dorrel closer to embrace him. A few years older than Dorrel, Etton was nearly as tall, but with a wiry build and sandy brown hair. "Welcome back! Early, aren't you?"

"Yes. Something came up. I need to talk with you. Privately."

Etton's grin faded.

He showed them into his office at the front of the building, where its window looked out on the main street. Etton's knotty-pine desk took up the middle of the room. A large green slate chalked up with orders hung on one wall. Etton closed the door, shutting out most of the roar and clatter.

Two ladder-back chairs sat in front of the desk. Dorrel stood behind one, bracing his hands on it. Dad pulled the other chair out and sat down. Etton moved behind the desk and pushed the wooden swivel chair aside.

Dorrel explained why he and Alara had come to Kaesbaro.

"You say you're under orders from Captain Madrew." Etton leaned on the edge of the desk. "But if she's disobeying the prime minister, should you be?"

"This plan isn't hers. It's General Rariden's."

Etton straightened, and his eyebrows rose. "Oh. Well . . . all right then. How far behind you are the Makutians?"

"They were at the front gates of Denedra when we went out the back."

Etton frowned. "No telling how long it would take them to get around." He rubbed his jaw. "A day, maybe?"

"Possibly less," Dorrel said, "depending on how sure-footed their horses are."

"Perhaps you two should leave for Apanumon now," Etton said.

"Captain Madrew told us to meet her here." And Alara needed to rest.

"Right." Etton opened a drawer and took out the paperboard folder that held the town militia's roster. "We'll just have to call up everyone." He pulled his squeaky chair close, sat down, and picked up a pencil. "Except you're not on my roster."

"I was called up when the alarm rang at Denedra."

"I never thought Druyun Kordelyon would make such a mistake where his daughter was concerned," Dad said as he and Dorrel walked home.

"Neither did I."

"Did you ever meet him?"

"No. Only her mother and siblings visited her at school."

"Not even when she was ordained. I remember that." Dad shoved his hands into the pockets of his dungarees. "Made me think less of him."

Dorrel nodded, eyes downcast.

"Now I think less of him still," Dad grumbled. "But it's good to see you and Alara together again. I never understood why you two broke it off."

"There wasn't anything to break off."

"Wasn't there?"

For a few minutes, they walked in silence.

"Even if there weren't," Dad said, "which I don't believe for a minute, there could be now."

Dorrel shook his head. "She has to go back to Apanumon."

Dad walked on a few paces. "Well, she won't stay there forever, will she?"

"I don't know . . ."

"And we have an opening for a curate, don't we?"

"Yes . . ."

"You could at least discuss the matter."

Dorrel sighed. He hadn't ever intended to admit this. "We discussed it, Dad. Her last year at Denedra."

"What's the problem, then?"

"She can't come here —"

"Why not?"

"Because her post is in Apanumon!" He waved toward the northwest.

"Well, if you're going to be obstructive—"

"I am not being obstructive. Everyone else is. The prelate, her father, Professor Sheeno . . ."

"What does Sheeno have to do with it?"

"He said since Alara was going to Apanumon and I still had to finish my doctorate . . . it was not a good time to start a courtship."

"Ah-ha. So your mother and I weren't the only ones who noticed."

"No." Dorrel wasn't going to admit exactly how much Sheeno had observed.

"Well, did he ever mention Galardi?"

"Not that I remember. Why?"

"He was the one who wrote, 'In due time, Telshi levels the rough ground for those who follow the Way.'"

Dorrel stopped and faced his father. "What is that supposed to mean?"

"It means a path may be blocked at one time, but at another Telshi can open it." Dad put his hands on Dorrel's shoulders. "The trail may have been rough then, but perhaps now it is due time."

"How can it possibly be due time? Her father signed a treaty that forfeits her freedom, the prelate and Rariden both told her to go back to Apanumon, and we have a squad of Makutians on our tail."

"You could still talk to her." He leaned a little closer, and suddenly Dorrel felt ten years old. "Promise me you will talk to her."

Dorrel hung his head. Of course Dad was right. But knowing that didn't make it easier to reopen a subject that had already caused so much heartache.

Sturg's squad never reached Ecciston. The dog led them westward and down-mountain along a narrow track where they had to go single file. Shortly before noon, they stopped in a little clearing to eat.

Sturg re-examined the map. The spaniel whined at him. He broke off a piece of his dried beef, and the dog ate it from his hand.

Sturg spread the map on the ground between himself and Hanik.

"The next nearest pass into Apanumon is this one." Sturg pointed to Ryol Pass to the west. "She must be going that way."

Hanik nodded. "She works at a mission in western Apanumon. A westerly route makes sense."

How did Hanik know where she worked? Sturg pretended it was common knowledge. "True."

The spaniel stepped on the map, sniffing Sturg's finger. He gently brushed the dog away. "Sit!" It sat, wagging its tail.

Except for Ecciston, the map showed no towns in the valley.

"There's no place for her to take refuge," Sturg said. "It shouldn't take long to overtake her, especially if the dog keeps on her scent." He scratched the spaniel's ears.

"It's not a bad tracker for its size." Hanik smiled.

Sturg took it for condescension. "No, not bad." He pulled his hand back. "But a war dog would be better suited to the job." Makutian Army war dogs stood as high as a man's waist and had teeth like those of wolves. The spaniel was barely knee-high to Ult.

"Perhaps," Hanik said, "but we must bring her to Tarvag unharmed. With a war dog, that would be unlikely."

Sturg grunted and stood. "While we're talking about it, she's getting farther away." He sent Ult to fetch the blanket the girl had used so he could get his dog back on the trail.

Dorrel slept until shortly after midday, when Dad woke him for dinner. They crossed the street to the inn and waited by the bar while Marita got Alara. She arrived still looking haggard. Wisps of hair had pulled loose from her braid and curled around her face, which was charming, but her cheeks were pale.

When she saw him, a little smile lightened her dark expression. "I hope you got some sleep, too."

"A bit."

Dad slapped Dorrel's shoulder and headed for the tables. Dorrel took a deep breath and held out the sword he had brought. "I know you prefer a rapier." He extended his arms, presenting the sword in his open palms.

She accepted the sword and drew it. "Wonderful balance." The blade, etched with a pattern of twining grapevines, glimmered in the light. "It's beautiful." She tilted her head. "Will it be all right if I wait until I get mine back before returning this?"

"It's yours. I—Dad and I want you to have it."

She narrowed her eyes. "Your mother's?"

Dorrel nodded.

She shook her head, sheathing the sword. She held it back out to him. "I can't."

He pushed it back to her with both hands. "You will." He kept his voice quiet, but firm. "It's a better sword than that army saber. We want you . . ." If only he could pour his feelings out through his eyes and into hers. "I want you to have this one."

She looked down at the scabbard. Her mouth opened and closed. She whispered, "Thank you."

His voice, too, was hushed. "You're welcome."

They stood like that for a moment. Then they joined his father at the table. Before she sat, Alara took off the army-issue sword belt and put on the one that had been Mum's.

After their prayer of thanks, Marita served a hearty meal of roasted fowl, steamed vegetables, mashed potatoes, and baked beans.

As at breakfast, Dorrel sat on Alara's left, while his father sat on her right.

"Kester, thank you for the sword."

He picked up a piece of bread. "You're welcome to it, Alara. Nya would be pleased for you to have it."

Alara sniffled and dabbed at the corner of her eye with a knuckle.

Perhaps she was remembering, as he was, the evening they had sat, hand in hand, in the chapel at Denedra during the memorial service for victims of the epidemic. Dorrel's mother. Alara's brother Kyvern. And too many others. The reading of the necrology had lasted half an hour.

"Besides," Dad said, a little too loudly, "Nya rather hoped that someday . . ."

Dorrel scowled at his father, willing him to shut up.

He snorted and looked away.

Alara smiled weakly. As usual, she pushed the bits of broccoli to the rim of her plate. Dorrel reached over with his fork, speared one of the florets, and ate it.

Across the table, Mr. Risdun raised his eyebrows.

Dorrel flushed. His mother would have scolded those poor table manners, but no one at Denedra ever complained.

Then Mr. Risdun smiled, which just made Dorrel flush more. Throughout the meal, Mr. Risdun peppered Alara with questions. First about the mission, then about her calling and her time at Denedra.

She didn't seem to mind, but when the questioning continued long after the dishes had been cleared, Dorrel considered putting a stop to it. Could Mr. Risdun not see how tired she was?

A tall, blond man stepped up to the table. "Excuse me."

Although they'd never been introduced, Dorrel had seen him before. He was an Apanumoni immigrant with a square face and tanned skin. His pale blue eyes were wide with alarm. Dorrel couldn't recall his name.

"You are the—" he hesitated, as if searching for words. "The doctor of animals?"

Given the man's agitation, Dorrel opted against quibbling over the fact that he had yet to receive his doctorate. He put out his hand. "Dorrel Chevallon. You're Sharine's husband, aren't you? I don't think we've—"

He smiled widely, and some of the tension left his posture. He shook Dorrel's hand vigorously. "Makedeliz Chasumapanim. You may call me Mak."

"What brings you?"

"This ram of mine has the swollen belly. I think it's the bloat."

Dorrel got up. "You'll excuse me?"

"Surely." Alara smiled.

Dorrel and Mak walked across the street to the livery. "What has he eaten?"

Mak rolled his eyes. "Alfalfa. A lot of it, I think."

"When?"

"Before sunup. This one . . ." He shook his head. "The others are content with grass. But the ram likes the alfalfa and will jump the fence to get it."

Inside the stable, Dorrel took his father's veterinary kit down from the top shelf of the tack room. The trocar was in the bag, but the stomach tube wasn't. He looked through the boxes on the shelf. "What have you tried?"

"When I first found him, I fed him cooking oil. When that didn't help, I fed him soap, as Papa used to."

Dorrel found the tube and tucked it into the bag. "Have you kept him moving?"

"As best as I could."

They returned to the street, where Mak's wagon and horses waited. Dorrel dropped the bag in the back before climbing onto the wagon's seat. Mak slapped the reins, and they headed east across the bridge, then northward up a winding foothill road. Mak's flock was scattered across the hill behind his small farmhouse.

He led Dorrel to a sheepfold next to the barn.

The ram lay on his right side. "Oh, no." Dorrel ran his hand down the animal's left side and felt the characteristic distension behind the last rib. "We have to get him on his feet."

"I must check on Sharine." Mak's voice sounded panicky. "She was supposed to stay with him to keep him moving."

Mak ran to the house, while Dorrel lifted the protesting animal to its feet. When Dorrel looked up, Mak was halfway across the yard, and Sharine stood in the doorway of the farmhouse. Heavily pregnant, she braced her back with her hands. Her blonde hair was tied up under a kerchief.

They spoke for a minute, then Mak kissed her cheek and gestured toward the house. She gave Mak a parting squeeze of the hand and went inside.

Dorrel took out the stomach tube.

Mak returned to the sheepfold. "She couldn't get him up again after he lay down."

"No surprise. He's a big one."

"You're not going to stick him in the side, are you? Papa once lost a ram that way."

"I'm hoping to avoid that."

Mak eyed the tube. "What's that for?"

"I'm going to put it down his throat, into the rumen, to relieve the pressure."

"You're joking."

"No, and you're going to hold him while I do it."

Mak frowned.

"It's better than the trocar."

Dorrel had brought it, but he didn't want to use it. As Mak feared, puncturing the ram's side could cause an infection.

The procedure was not pleasant, and the ram fought them. But it being two against one, they beat him. Once the pressure had been relieved, Dorrel gently removed the tube from the ram's gullet. He wiped the froth from the tube with a linen towel.

Once Dorrel was sure the ram was out of danger, he packed his bag. "Would Sharine mind if I washed up in her kitchen?"

"Of course not. Especially not after you saved this only ram of ours." Mak rubbed its head as if it were a dog. He stayed in the fold with the ram, while Dorrel walked to the house.

He rapped lightly on the door. When he heard Sharine's "come in," he poked his head inside. She was chopping vegetables at her kitchen table.

"Just came in to wash up."

"Thought you might. There's a kettle for you on the stove."

Dorrel poured some of the water from the kettle into the dishpan in her sink. A bar of soap and a towel sat nearby.

"What do we owe you?" She wiped her hands on her apron.

"I didn't have to use the trocar, so I'd call it a five-stater job."

Sharine bit her lip. "We don't have that much right now."

"You can pay me later." He waved one half-dried hand. "After the shearing."

She smiled, and her shoulders relaxed. "Thanks, Dor."

"Don't mention it." He went to collect his bag.

Mak offered to drive him home, but Dorrel insisted he stay. "You don't want to leave Sharine alone again."

"This is true." Mak walked Dorrel to the road. "I can't thank you enough for coming." He shook Dorrel's hand. "It's pleasant to speak the language of my people."

Dorrel headed toward town.

He hadn't realized Mak was speaking Apanumoni. Dorrel had sometimes helped Alara study when she'd taken it during her final year at Denedra. He must have picked up more than he realized.

# Chapter 8

## NEWS AND DEBATE

Alara answered so many questions—from Mr. Risdun and others who arrived—that she believed if they weren't interviewing her for the curacy, they were preparing to write her biography.

Near teatime, the door swung open, and a woman stepped in. "Curate Kordelyon?" She was a little younger than Alara and wore her brown hair in a braided bun, flyaway tendrils framing her round face and hazel eyes.

Alara had turned her dining chair to face the center of the room. "Yes?"

She squealed and ran across the room, leaving the door open behind her. She stopped at Alara's chair, bouncing on the balls of her feet. "I'm Tyana Nucol. I'm so excited to meet you!"

Alara stood and hugged her. "I am so grateful for all you've done for the mission and your letters to the children. It means so much for them to know they have Telshan kindred who care about them."

"Oh, it's my pleasure, Curate. I enjoy doing it."

One of the men pulled up a chair for Tyana, and another closed the door she'd left open.

While Alara and Tyana got acquainted, Marita served tea. Kester and Mr. Risdun got their cups and took them to the armchairs by the window. Others came in and took tables near the bar.

"Honestly, Kaesbaro is one of our chief supporters," Alara said. "You've all been exceedingly generous."

Ms. Amati, a stout, silver-haired woman almost as old as Marita, knitted a white cotton stocking without even looking at her hands. "Kenna said, 'Those who have much must give much.'"

One of the teenage girls asked, "Why are they all so poor there?" She sat cross-legged on the floor, wearing brown trousers and a lemon-yellow shirt. Her blonde hair was tied in a ponytail.

"Because in Apanumon, only the nobility own land," Alara said. "The landowner controls the distribution of goods and keeps all the profits. He's supposed to provide for his tenants in return, but most people only receive the barest necessities."

"I suppose that's why Mak emigrated," Mr. Risdun said.

"Partly," said a man on Alara's left. "But also because of the religious persecution." He leaned against the wall by the fireplace. He wore a loose white shirt and dungarees. Alara guessed he was close to her own age.

"Has the persecution eased up at all in your village, Curate?" Tyana asked.

"Not appreciably."

"Last time you wrote," Ms. Amati said, "you told us some young noblemen were trying to stop construction of the schoolhouse. Were you able to finish it?"

"Very nearly. It should be done soon. That bunch did turn up again, but I was in the militia at Denedra, and Rector Orizozabil served in the Apanumoni army before seminary. They weren't prepared for that sort of opposition."

Kester harrumphed. "You might mention you trained with General Rariden."

A murmur ran through the room.

Alara looked upward. "Thank you, Kester, for dropping names so I don't have to."

"Oh!" The girl in the yellow shirt yelped. "Could you train our unit?"

Alara looked at her. "Are you in the militia?" She looked too young.

"Only just," she said. "We haven't done much training lately—only calisthenics and sword drills."

"Those are good," Alara said. "I'm sorry. What's your name?"

"Shelon Balmon."

"Shelon, I'm going back to Apanumon as soon as my friend Palon gets here, but I could write to General Rariden and see if he has another student he can send to help with your training."

The fellow leaning against the wall snorted. "Talk to Etton Temir before you do, Curate. He commands the company, not Shelon."

He had the same high cheekbones as Shelon and the same slate-blue eyes, though his hair was a darker shade of blond.

Shelon looked over her shoulder and glowered at him, then stuck out her tongue. He just smirked.

Alara leaned toward Shelon and spoke quietly. "That must be your brother."

"How did you know?"

"I have a brother, too." She winked, and Shelon giggled.

As Dorrel approached the inn, through the front window he could see a larger crowd than usual gathered for tea.

He knew why.

Inside, more than a dozen people sat around Alara, teacups and saucers in hand. She was telling them how she and Palon had met as children, taking martial arts lessons from General Rariden.

Marita's son Regger stood behind the bar. He was as old as Dorrel's father and almost as short as Alara. His stout build and craggy, oblong face gave him a rougher look than his temperament warranted.

While Dorrel and Regger caught up, Alara's story shaded off into tales about the summers she used to spend in Redíque.

"Kenna said there is no peerage among Telshans." Mr. Risdun's eye took on the wicked glint he always got when he thought he was about to incite debate. "So how do the Redíquans justify keeping a royal family?"

Alara instantly, almost gleefully, entered into a discourse Dorrel had heard before. Her pet cause.

Dorrel couldn't begrudge his neighbors the chance to get acquainted with Alara when they'd supported her mission work for so long. But although her hands still gestured eloquently as she spoke, Alara's green eyes were dull with fatigue.

He wanted to chase everyone away so she could get some sleep. He wished he could take her into his own bed —

Dorrel turned around and leaned on the bar, arms folded. He hung his head. *Ahbay, help me.* Everyone else was eager for news from abroad or theological debate. All he could think about was bedding the cleric.

He lifted his head and looked from the teapot nearby to Regger. "Do you have any coffee?"

"Yep. Want me to bring you a cup?"

"Bring two." Dorrel turned back around and found Tyana.

Grinning, shoulders hunched, she whispered. "It's so good to see you." She hugged him, then stepped back and looked over her shoulder at Alara. "I can't believe you brought her."

"Huh. Neither can I."

"Will she stay?"

"No. She's on her way back to the mission."

A frown erased Tyana's smile. "Oh. Well, at least I have some things to send with her. Don't let her leave without them."

"Yes, ma'am."

"Pfft. Don't ma'am me." She gave his shoulder a playful shove and returned to her seat.

Alara's discussion of Redíque's constitutional monarchy digressed into an account of the abdication of Reyshara Kordelyon, but she got back to the point before summing up. "So, Mr. Risdun, you are quite right that monarchy is an un-Telshan form of government." She screwed her expression into a consternated frown. "Unfortunately, I have been unable to persuade my Redíquan cousins on that point."

A few people chuckled. The others must not have realized who her Redíquan cousins were.

Dorrel rubbed his forehead. His father approached and leaned next to him. "You should be getting some rest."

"So should she."

Regger brought the coffee. Dorrel sidled through the crowd to Alara's chair and handed her a mug.

She took it and gave him a wide smile. "Bless you."

Marita, finally, had the nerve to do what Dorrel didn't. "All right, you lot. If you want this girl to lead a sunset prayer meeting, you can't let her spend the afternoon talking herself hoarse." Marita handed Alara a cup of tea. "You shush now and drink that. It'll soothe your throat." She gestured toward the mostly empty platter of teacakes. "Are you finished?"

"Yes, thank you," Alara said, but Dorrel grabbed one before Marita took them away.

"You should get some more sleep before the meeting." Dorrel devoured the tiny cake in a single bite.

"Yes, as soon as I finish my tea." She stood, so Dorrel did likewise.

Tyana hugged them both. Then she and the others dispersed, except for Gylun, who'd been standing next to the fireplace. He stepped closer to exchange a handshake combined with a back-slapping half-hug with Dorrel. Then he turned to Alara. "Curate, my wife and I had a baby recently. If we bring her to the prayer meeting, can you do the naming?"

"Of course. I'd be honored."

"Thank you. We'll see you then." He clapped Dorrel's shoulder in parting.

When he'd gone, Alara leaned toward Dorrel. "And that was . . ."

"Gylun Balmon."

She moved to the settee and looked back at him with half a smile.

He followed and sat next to her, wanting to hold her hand, but both of hers were occupied with the cup and saucer. Instead he extended his arm along the back of the sofa behind her.

Dad and Mr. Risdun were talking quietly in chairs by the window, and a few other people gathered at the bar with Regger.

If Dorrel moved his hand just a little, he could touch one of the locks escaping from her braid. He longed to run his fingers through her hair. But it was always braided or put up in a bun. Or both. Besides, that would be a dreadful liberty to take.

She looked at him, and he looked away.

How was he supposed to explain everything he was thinking? It had started to make sense while his father was talking, but now he couldn't collect his thoughts.

"Dor—"

He turned back to her, his heart quivering.

"Am I wrong to be worried that Palon's not here yet?"

"Not at all." He combed his fingers through his hair. "Perhaps she feels she can't leave while they're still holding off the Makutians." He shook his head. "There's no telling, really."

"How long should we wait?"

"I don't know. She said meet her here. How angry will she be if she arrives and we've gone on without her?"

"Not very, I don't think. Not given the circumstances."

Dorrel nodded. "All right, then. We'll leave in the morning."

Alara sighed. "I'm not looking forward to taking to the road again." She sipped her tea. "But it doesn't seem reasonable to stay. Given the circumstances."

That night, Sturg's men feasted on pheasant, something most of them had never before eaten.

The spaniel whined at him. He tore a piece of meat from the bone and held it out. The dog deserved it, having retrieved the fowl during the hunt.

Sturg picked up his map and tipped it toward the light, scratching the spaniel's ears with his free hand. He judged they were about a third of the way to Ryol Pass.

After the meal, they pressed on, while the sun neared the horizon in front of them.

Ult and Sturg rode at the front of the troop, just behind the dog, which kept its nose to the ground.

The shadows lengthened, and the light darkened to orange.

Behind him, the men grumbled in low tones. Korig rode up alongside Sturg. "Commander, the men want to know when we'll stop for the night."

"We'll stop just long enough to light torches. Then we'll keep going till we catch her."

# Chapter 9

## THE FUTURE OF A NATION

Instead of taking an afternoon nap, Alara sat at the timeworn secretary desk in her room, opened her journal, and put into words all that had happened. As she wrote, her certainty grew—returning to Apanumon was Telshi's will. That was where Alara had been sent. Where she belonged.

But that conclusion only muddled her thinking about Dorrel.

Hadn't they agreed there was no point in courting? They had. She had a ministry in Apanumon; he had a practice in Kaesbaro.

That hadn't stopped them from exchanging letters twice a week for the last year.

He had complicated things further by giving her his mother's sword—an heirloom! And the way he'd cared for her since they left Denedra . . .

She dropped her pen and put her head in her hands. *Kenna, help me! I'm still in love with him. What am I supposed to do?*

She glanced out the window. Sundown neared, and she still wore riding clothes, her braid a mess. From the wardrobe she took out her vest and the one dress Palon had packed for her: a plain, long-sleeved linen chemise in a pale shade of lavender.

Alara untied her braid and started brushing her hair.

*Her father paces like a caged animal around his office. He is surrounded by the political cronies who run his campaigns. A secretary dashes in with a ballot report.*

*Horym, an elderly cabinet minister, is totting up election results, working atop her father's desk from the wrong side. "It does not look good, sir."*

*Her father falls into his chair. "How many reports are in?"*

*"Eighteen," Horym says. "Even if you carry the remaining four provinces, there is no way to gain enough votes." He puts down his pen. "You have lost the election, Prime Minister."*

*Her father clenches his head in his hands. Then his fists pound the desk. The blow knocks over Horym's inkbottle.*

Bracing herself on the edge of the dresser with one hand, Alara bent to pick up her hairbrush from the floor with the other. She sat on the edge of the bed, trembling.

She had been taught to communicate a vision to the person concerned as soon as possible. But she couldn't go to Father now. And one didn't put such things in a letter.

*Kenna, why give me a vision when I can't deliver it?*

She took several deep breaths to compose herself, but the vision reverberated like a nightmare. Trembling, she moved to the desk and opened her journal.

As she recorded the vision, she shivered at its import. *This is the first time,* she wrote, *that I've been shown the future not only of a person, but of a nation.*

When Alara returned to the public room carrying Scriptures, register, pen, and inkbottle, she found Tyana and a man helping Marita and Regger arrange the dining chairs in rows. Dorrel and Kester pushed the sofa to one side.

Dorrel frowned at her. His boots beat double-time as he crossed the room, looking dashing in his high-collared jacket, his sword on his hip. His waist-length jacket was made of lightweight wool in the cobalt shade the Chevallon family favored. It had no lapels, and the collar reminded her of Palon's dress uniform. He narrowed his eyes. "What's wrong?"

"Nothing."

The lines on his forehead deepened.

She ducked her head and lowered her voice. "I had a vision. I don't think I should talk about it until I deliver it."

"Oh. To whom?"

"I shouldn't say." She looked up and gave him a weak smile. "No one here."

He put out his hand, hesitated, then patted her shoulder.

Alara put her things on the bar. She wanted to hug him, but she dawdled, fiddling with her writing implements.

"Where's your sword?"

She rolled her eyes. "I can't wear it with a vest."

"Yes, but shouldn't you at least have it at hand?"

"Curate?" Tyana said.

Alara sidestepped so she could see around Dorrel. "Yes?"

"This is my husband, Stohan."

Alara put out her hand. "Pleased to meet you. Thank you for helping Tyana with the offerings for the mission. We truly appreciate it."

"My pleasure, Curate." Stohan's height was midway between Alara's and Dorrel's. He looked to be about Camrun's age, with a similar slight build. A shaggy head of brown hair topped his round face. He grinned, looking from her to Dorrel. "So you two—"

"Don't," Dorrel groaned.

Alara couldn't speak. Tension like a fist gripped her innards.

The door opened, and a woman about Alara's age came in. She wore a yellow-and-white calico dress and cradled a baby against her maternal curves. Gylun followed, wearing a brown suit, his shirt collar open and no cravat. But then, none of the men wore cravats. They were, however, all wearing swords, as were some of the women, which suggested Dorrel had said something to someone—possibly everyone—about the Makutians.

Gylun stepped close. "Curate, this is my wife, Laneesa."

A smile brightened Laneesa's soft, heart-shaped face. Her golden hair was done up in a bouffant bun much like Alara's.

Alara bent to see the baby, wrapped in a white crocheted blanket. Pink fists waved aimlessly. "She's adorable. What is her name going to be?"

"Sarya Balmon," Laneesa said.

Alara smiled reflexively and nodded. "A good scriptural name." She hoped to name her own daughter Sarya. Someday. If, Mairah willing, she ever had one.

She blushed. Dorrel stood right behind her. Alara distracted herself by opening her register and dipping the pen. After recording the particulars, she took a blank sheet from the back of the book and drew up a copy for the Balmons.

Shelon and several others—presumably the rest of the family—entered in the meantime.

Gylun signed the book and paper where Alara indicated, then took the baby from Laneesa while she signed.

Laneesa gasped and pointed to Jaselle's name, written just above her own. "This is your sister. Jaselle."

"Yes."

She giggled, turning toward Gylun. "Our names are in the same register as a Kordelyon."

He smirked and nodded to Alara. "Two Kordelyons."

"Now, stop." Alara took the pen from Laneesa. "You'll give me a swelled head. Though some would say it's too late."

Laneesa covered her mouth to stifle the giggles.

Shelon made faces at the baby.

"Shelon," Alara said, "how old are you?"

"Eighteen."

"Would you like to be a witness?" Alara held out the pen.

Shelon broke into a wide smile. "Yes, ma'am!" She carefully signed her name, then handed the pen to Dorrel, who signed as the second witness.

Alara surveyed the room. Several dozen people had already taken seats. Marita placed a bell on the polished-oak mantel.

Gylun and Laneesa sat near the fireplace. Alara glanced out the window. The shadows were long and the light fading fast. The hearth served as her rostrum. She picked up the brass handbell and chimed it three times.

When the last chime died away, she set the bell down and faced the congregation. "Kindred, Ahbay makes plans for us we could never imagine. I had not planned to come here. But—" her throat threatened to close. *Kenna, don't let me choke up.* "I cannot think of any more fortuitous circumstance, or any place I would rather be." She avoided looking at Dorrel.

"Let us pray." She bowed her head, wishing her voice would stop wavering. It did, but only because she recited one of the day's end prayers she knew so well she could rattle it off without thinking. The worst way to pray.

Fortunately, there were better vocalists than she to lead the singing. She taught from Digalo because she'd read so much of him recently. Then, after a second song, she stepped down from the hearth and called Gylun and Laneesa forward. They took their places.

"Mairah, we praise You and give thanks for this, Your greatest gift. In Your goodness you have wrought, from Gylun and Laneesa's love for one another, a new life."

Her voice caught in her throat. Tears stung her eyes. She blinked them back.

"Ahbay, thank You for bringing me here to take part in this joyous event. Guide Gylun and Laneesa as they raise their child to be strong in body, mind, and faith."

Laneesa handed her the baby.

"Kenna, abide with this community and strengthen us as we offer ourselves in aid to this family and as examples of faith to our newest member, Sarya Balmon."

Why did she always cry at namings?

Alara handed Sarya to Gylun, then dashed a tear from her cheek, hoping no one noticed. "Holy Telshi, ruler of all, bless this day, bless our nation, and bless Your people as we go forward in the assurance of Your good will. We thank you, great Three-in-One, for new life, for Your word, and for Your spirit dwelling in us. Ocha."

The others echoed the affirmation.

Gylun and Laneesa returned to their seats.

Alara called for the sharing of concerns and thanksgivings, though her mind raced ahead to silent confessions, knowing she had as much confessing to do as anyone. If not more.

After the meeting, so many people dropped hints about the open curacy, Alara's false smile began to pain her. She continually said things like, "I'm sure Ahbay has a plan." Finally, she followed Marita into the kitchen and sank into a wooden chair by the cast-iron stove.

Marita rinsed the dregs from a teapot and spooned fresh tea into it. "I realize they've pestered you mercilessly. But they mean well."

"Oh, surely. But putting them off is wearying."

"Well, I won't tell anyone where you're hiding." She filled the pot from the kettle on the stove and headed to the door. She hesitated before she pushed it open. "Except Dorrel, if he asks." She winked, then went out.

Was it that obvious? Alara put her face in her hands.

*Kenna, help me. It's a week, at least, from here to the mission. How am I supposed to keep my composure with him all that time?*

She sat there a few minutes more, listening to the burble of the kettle, fretting more than praying.

Pointless. She got up and left by the back door.

Dorrel scanned the room. Again.

Marita smirked. "She's in the kitchen."

But when he leaned through the doorway, the kitchen was empty. He went back to confront Marita.

"Well, she was there." Marita looked upstairs, but Alara wasn't in her room, either. "This lot wore her out. Perhaps she went to get some air."

Dorrel nodded. If she'd gone out, he knew where she would likely be.

Alara had just started brushing Willow's off hindquarter when she heard the door of the livery open and close. *Kenna . . .* She wavered between hoping it wasn't Dorrel and hoping it was. *Tell me what to say.*

He stepped up to the stall and rested his forearms on the gate.

As soon as she looked into his bottomless brown eyes, a warm flush of comfort welled up, soothing the chill tremor in her nerves. But she could say nothing.

He held her gaze until she turned away. He knew her well enough to know she would only groom her horse at such a time if she was upset. She felt transparent.

"What's wrong?"

She let out her breath in a long, ragged sigh. "I was just awful."

"When?"

"In the meeting. I wasn't paying attention. I recited words without thinking. At least . . ." Her voice stuck. She swallowed. "My mind was not on my work. I was thinking about Father, and Palon, and . . . instead of the prayers or the songs or Sarya. My mind should've been on Telshi, not on . . ." She made the mistake of looking at him. Tears threatened to flow, but she sucked in a short breath, swallowed them, and turned back to Willow.

Dorrel swung open the gate. In a moment he was next to her, resting his gentle hand on her shoulder. "Lar, you've had two rough days, and Mr. Risdun and the rest ran you through a gantlet. Besides, you have good reason to be worried about Palon and the Makutians."

"That's no excuse for being distracted while serving. Then, when I did get my mind on the service, I choked."

"So? Laneesa's mother called it charming."

She snorted and pulled Willow's blanket back into place.

"If you apply for the job, they'll give it to you."

Her heart thudded against her breastbone. Her hands shook. "Dor, just because I'm a seer doesn't mean I'm qualified to be a curate."

He stared at her for several long moments. "I can't believe you said that."

"It's true."

"It's irrelevant. You have a doctoral degree in theology, and the prelate ordained you. That qualifies you to be a curate."

She shook her head. "You don't understand . . ." Neither Dorrel nor the prelate had heard the criticisms Rector Orizozabil at the mission had leveled at her.

"The prelate believes in you. All those people across the street believe in you." He waved his arm in their direction. "I believe in you. Why don't you believe in you?"

"Because I know what's in my head," she wailed, pointing to her temple. "I'm a self-centered, poor excuse for a cleric. Preoccupied with worldly matters when I'm supposed to be *serving*." She couldn't hold back the tears any longer. She buried her face in his shirtfront, her arms tight around him.

The grooming brush fell to the floor.

"Oh, no, Lar—shhh." He wrapped his arms around her, smoothing her hair with one hand. "Don't cry, please."

Telling her not to cry didn't stop the tears. It never did. But her weeping abated after a minute.

"I'm sorry." She sniffled. "I always seem to wind up crying on your shirt."

Her emotions did run high, but they were genuine, and that was one of the things he loved about her. "I don't mind, sweetest." He squeezed her a little tighter, brushing his cheek against her hair. "Except I don't like to see you cry."

"I can't help it. I . . ." Her breath was ragged. "When I got to 'abide with this community,' I almost couldn't finish. It's a lovely village. I honestly can't think of any place I'd rather be. I meant that."

"I know you wouldn't say something you didn't mean. Especially from the rostrum."

"I wish I could apply. I really do. I'd love it here. But I must go back to the mission."

"Yes, but the prelate's not going to leave you there forever, is she?"

"I don't know. Rector Orizozabil says I'm immature and high-strung. I suppose if he has any say in the matter, I'll never have a curacy."

"Well, it's not up to him. That's the prelate's decision."

She nodded. Then she pressed her cheek against his chest. "Oh, love . . ." She let out a sigh. "So much for being 'just friends.'"

"It was a rotten idea, anyway."

"True." She stared at him, her eyes wide and bright. Then she stood on her toes and kissed him.

It was such a terrible relief, he practically crushed her against him. They had denied their affection for so long, finally giving in to it was almost painful.

"What are we going to do?" She leaned against him again.

He rested his chin on top of her head. "In the morning, we'll head for the border. When we get to the mission, we'll ask Rector Orizozabil to marry us."

She gasped.

Well, he'd botched that. He stepped back. "You will marry me, won't you?"

The breath went out of her in a rush. Then she made an exclamation that was half laugh and half cheer. "Oh, yes!" She threw her arms around his neck and kissed him again.

He held her tightly, lifting her off her feet.

When he set her down again, she sighed. "What if he says no?"

"Then I suppose we'll have to wait until General Rariden gets the treaty revoked. Then you can come home."

"That would depend on whether the prelate approves my transfer."

"She will, Lar."

"I don't know . . ."

"What did Rector Orizozabil do to you? You used to be the most confident person I know."

"Overconfident, you mean." She pushed away, retrieved the brush, and tossed it into the box of grooming tools. "The rector gave me a more accurate view." She picked up the box and headed for the tack room.

He followed. "No, he didn't. He's got you seeing only faults and not your capabilities."

"Pfft." She stood on her toes to lift the box back onto the shelf over her head.

He stepped behind her and easily pushed the box into place. Then he turned her to face him. "A self-centered person who's exhausted and scared wouldn't lead a prayer meeting after an entire day of interrogation."

She sniffled.

"Lar, please." He handed her his handkerchief. "Try."

Nodding, she blew her nose. "Who heads the board of trustees?"

He kissed her forehead. "You must've guessed."

She chuckled weakly. "All right. I'll speak to Mr. Risdun. But if Rector Orizozabil refuses to marry us, we may be waiting quite a while for the treaty . . ." She stopped and looked at him, wide-eyed. "If the rector agrees, that would void the treaty. Velek can't marry me if I'm already married."

"Most Makutians belong to the Kivatan faith. They don't respect Telshan marriages."

"Yes, but Velek is the crown prince. He can't marry just anyone. His bride has to be both royal and virginal."

"But you're not roy—" Centuries ago, before Glynrell became a democracy, the Kordelyons had been the royal family. And Alara was related to the Redíquan royal family on her mother's side. "That's why he wants you."

"I'm afraid so. Father claims that clause in the treaty isn't really about marriage. But even if he knew it was, I think he'd be quite gratified. Sometimes I think he's too fond of 'the old way,' as he puts it. The peerage and all that."

Dorrel frowned. "Has he not read the Chronicle of Kenna?"

"I suspect my father may not be as devout a Telshan as he would like his constituents to believe."

"Huh. Well, if Orizozabil says no, we'll find someone else. His isn't the only mission in Apanumon, is it?"

"No, but the next nearest is days away."

"That's all right. We put this off so long . . . I'm not willing to wait any longer."

She grinned and kissed him. Several times. For a long time.

Then he started laughing.

"What's so funny?"

He hugged her, resting his chin atop her head. "We're kissing in the tack room again."

"At least Professor Sheeno isn't here to catch us."

"True." He spent a few more minutes kissing her and reacquainting himself with her curves.

She pressed her hand against his sternum. "We should go back, you know. People will talk."

"I suppose they will." Not that he cared whether they did.

"Perhaps we would have been better off with Sheeno chaperoning."

"No." He kissed her again. "I don't think so."

# Chapter 10

## CAPTURE

Late in the night, the troop topped a hill. While Hanik and the others continued to follow the spaniel, Sturg paused. Downriver, moonlight shone on rooftops. A small town — only a few lights burning.

She might've stopped there for the night. That would be fortunate. Much easier simply to pluck her from a room at an inn than to overtake her on the road.

He keenly anticipated the pleasure of binding that she-dog hand and foot. Maybe he'd allow the men to use her. Maybe he'd take a turn himself.

No. Hanik would report such a violation of protocol. His loyalty to the prince plainly was greater than his loyalty to Sturg.

Besides, the prince couldn't marry a used woman. Sturg wondered whether Velek would mind a bride with a broken leg.

He kicked his horse forward to rejoin the squad.

Ahead of them, a horn sounded. A hunting horn. One long, low note. Then a pause just long enough for the blower to draw a breath, followed by a longer, louder blare.

Sturg galloped forward to take the point. "Arm crossbows!" He drew alongside Korig. "Can you tell where it came from?"

Korig nodded toward the trees ahead and to the left. "That way, but I'm not sure how far." He fitted a bolt into place.

"Silence him if you can."

Another blare sounded from the horn. Korig aimed toward the sound.

A figure sprinted down the road ahead of them.

"Korig." Sturg pointed to the runner.

Korig swiveled his crossbow and shot.

The runner fell. Again the horn sounded.

As they rode on, Korig and some of the others shot in the direction of the horn, but it seemed to move.

Soon, they reached the runner. A girl. She pulled at the ground with her elbows, dragging herself toward the town, Korig's bolt in the middle of her back.

Korig jumped down and drew his knife. He grabbed the girl's ponytail, pulled her head back, and slit her throat.

In harmony with the first horn, a second sounded, farther away. Possibly within the town.

Sturg swore. He whistled for the spaniel, which had gone too far ahead. It returned, barked once, then scampered back toward the town, stopping only a moment to sniff the corpse from which Korig removed the sword and the long blonde tress.

Something jarred Dorrel from sleep, though when he lay awake, he couldn't identify what had roused him or why his pulse beat so loudly in his ears.

While he pulled on his trousers, he heard it again. A horn in the distance. He shoved bare feet into boots. Pulled a brown leather hunting jacket over bare shoulders. Strapped on knife and sword. Grabbed quiver and bow. Jogged down the stairs.

He ran across the yard to the stable. As he put on Toban's bridle, he heard another horn, closer. No time for a saddle. He led Toban to the street, mounted, and galloped toward the east bridge.

Because if there was trouble, it would come from that direction.

The single note of the hunting horn was followed by a bugle: "To Arms."

Riders with lanterns approached at a gallop.

Gylun reached him first. Dorrel halted. Toban pawed the ground and snorted.

"They're here." Gylun glanced over his shoulder. "Etton's got two squads holding the bridge. He sent the rest of us to form the second line."

Other members of the militia ran toward them on foot.

From the east end of the street came shouts and the clatter of hooves and swords.

"I need a bugler," Dorrel called.

"Here." It was Ebrun, though Dorrel could hardly make out his features.

"Blow 'To Arms.'"

Ebrun lifted his bugle and sounded the call, twice.

Five cavalry, counting himself. He picked three of them to hold the crossroads, along with a dozen foot soldiers.

With Gylun and the rest following, Dorrel galloped to the inn.

Inside, Regger pulled back the curtain, releasing a bit of light into the moonlit street. He looked surprised to see them there. Then he tapped his chest and pointed to the street. *I'll come to you.*

Dorrel held out a hand, palm forward. *Stay there.*

Regger tapped his forehead with two fingers. *I understand.* The curtain fell back into place.

The hoofbeats of a single horse came toward them. Gylun drew his sword.

The rider carried a lantern hanging from a crook. Mr. Risdun.

"Should have thought of fire pots." He dismounted. "Gonna have quite a time fighting in the dark."

He planted his crook near the wall of the livery.

Ebrun sounded the bugle call again.

"Where are they?" Dorrel asked.

"Still at the bridge, near as I can tell," Mr. Risdun walked toward the door of the inn and tugged on the handle. The door didn't budge. He nodded.

Tyana approached at a run. "Dor!" A group of people followed her, including Stohan.

"Take a team and cover the back door." Dorrel pointed that way. She chose Stohan and three others.

Stohan shook his head. "I'll take the front." He grabbed a younger fellow. "You go with them."

Tyana hugged Stohan, kissed him, then ran with the others to the back of the inn.

Dorrel watched them go, hoping Marita had sense enough to wake Alara. "Gy, Mr. Risdun—"

"Under the circumstances, you could call me Ker." He mounted his horse.

"We'll take the point. Stohan, since you volunteered, you can form up the infantry behind us."

"Yes, sir." Stohan tossed off a salute. Shortly, the militia had arrayed themselves in front of the inn.

They waited painful long minutes, listening to the clatter and clamor grow closer.

Soon the flash of torches and a blaze of broken lanterns erupted at the crossroads.

"We should go to them," Gylun said.

Dorrel nocked an arrow. "We should hold our position."

Gylun looked across Dorrel to Mr. Risdun.

He squinted down the street, toward the mass of horses and people and flickering lights at the crossroads. "Dorrel's right."

Alara woke, heart hammering, hoping the bugle call she heard was only a dream. It wasn't. It sounded again, clearly. "To Arms."

She dressed. By the time she'd pulled on her boots, the call sounded again, closer, as if the bugler was right outside.

She glanced out her window. Below, Tyana and four others clustered around the back door.

Longbow, quiver, and army saber were soon slung over her shoulders. She strapped on Nya's sword belt while she jogged down the stairs.

In the public room, Marita poured kerosene from a lamp over towels stuffed into a kitchen pot. Three other pots also sat on the table. "Take those out and light them."

Regger gestured to the window. "But Dor said —"

"Don't I outrank Dorrel? Take them."

Alara's thundering heart deafened her. Dorrel was out there facing the Makutians.

Regger carried the pots outside.

"Alara. Take your position in that corner." Marita pointed to the kitchen door. "That'll let you cover the whole room."

Alara pushed a dining table into the corner and climbed on top of it. It gave her a better angle of attack and acted as a barricade to the kitchen door, should they come that way. She nocked her arrow. The orange flicker of the fire pots could be seen around the edges of the curtain.

Regger returned and bolted the door. He and Marita pushed the sofa in front of it.

A couple of other guests jogged down the stairs and into the room. Only one of them wore a sword.

Marita glanced at them. "If you fellows aren't ready for a fight, go back upstairs."

The armed man joined Regger at the window.

The unarmed one said, "Is there a spare sword?"

Alara tossed him the army saber.

Hoofbeats, at a gallop, drew closer. The riders carried torches.

Dorrel loosed an arrow. He couldn't tell if he'd hit anything. He loosed another.

A spaniel ran past him to the door of the livery, sniffing the space between the door and the dirt. Then it ran across to the inn and barked.

Tracking Alara like prey. Dorrel's innards tightened into a knot.

He shot again at the oncoming riders.

Mr. Risdun drew his sword.

A Makutian soldier on a black charger came at him. An arrow stuck out of the horse's left shoulder. The rider pointed a sword at Dorrel's chest. He wore a commander's epaulets. Sturg.

Dorrel dropped the bow, drew his sword, and reared Toban.

The black charger dodged Toban's hooves. As the horses passed one another, the commander swung at Dorrel's neck. Dorrel parried with an upward swipe of his sword.

The charger plowed into the infantry.

Dorrel turned to follow Sturg, but a Makutian private intercepted him. A short, thickset man. He swept his sword around wildly.

Dorrel blocked the saber and countered with a blow to the private's side. His sword sliced through the black uniform. A thin line of blood showed through the gap.

The black charger trampled a couple of foot soldiers.

The private came at Dorrel again with a cut toward his right shoulder. Dorrel parried with a circular motion that sent the tip of his rapier over the saber's guard and into the private's forearm.

Around him, swords clashed. People howled in pain.

The private didn't cry out. He tried to jab Dorrel under the arm.

But Dorrel nudged Toban into a sideways turn that left the private poking at nothing. Dorrel cut into the private's wrist with a blow that shook his shoulder as if he were hammering an anvil.

The private grabbed his saber with both hands. He didn't drop it. But when the sword came back up, it was in his left hand.

Dorrel reined back. Gylun fought a big, bearded Makutian.

Behind him, the sound of swords clashing was joined by the cracking and shattering of wood.

Outside, people shouted and screamed. Horses issued challenging whinnies, and their hooves fell with sickening thuds on flesh, not earth.

The door shook, battered by a force that rattled the hardware.

Alara drew her bow.

Marita and the others ranged themselves in the middle of the room.

Splinters flew from the doorframe. The door fell into the room, landing like a ramp on the sofa.

Sturg and his black charger filled the doorway.

Alara loosed her arrow.

The charger, climbing over the door, took the arrow in its side, just behind Sturg's leg.

Another arrow was on her bowstring in a moment.

Marita crouched and sliced the tendon above the hock of the horse's off front leg. The horse went down. Sturg pitched forward in his saddle onto the horse's neck.

Alara's arrow skimmed across his back, leaving a shallow trench.

Sturg swung down from the saddle. The horse tried to stand but fell to its knees.

Sturg advanced. Regger stepped between him and Marita. He hacked at Regger, who blocked the swing.

Two Makutian privates clambered over the door and sofa.

Alara let one arrow fly. It struck the first private through the shoulder. Her second grazed the other, cutting open his cheek.

Where was Sturg?

Regger lay on the floor, facedown in a widening pool of blood.

*Kenna, I don't want to kill anyone.*

She nocked another arrow and kept her eye on the door. *But if I must, give me strength.*

Sturg crawled on his belly underneath the tables. Swords clashed overhead, and he heard the wet thud of an arrow hitting flesh.

Velek's bride clearly was more trouble than she was worth.

He worked his way into the corner she was shooting from and braced his back against the underside of the table.

It went over in a crash of pottery and limbs. Arrows from her quiver spilled onto the floor. The table landed on its side.

She rolled away, jumped to her feet, and drew her sword.

A corporal came in, pushing the shattered door and trampled sofa aside.

The thin old woman who'd cut down his horse fought Private Merud.

Another private, an arrow poking through his shoulder, fought a middle-aged man. A second, younger civilian intercepted the newcomer.

Sturg stepped around the table and faced the girl. He supposed he had to take her alive. Not much point, otherwise. "Surrender and no one else has to die."

She frowned, her sword poised. She met his eyes like a man, as if calculating her odds.

"Never!" The old woman bellowed. "These. Pigs." The blow of her sword against Merud's punctuated her words. "Will not. Have. Their way. With us. Again."

The girl lunged.

Sturg parried. Circling, they traded blows. No matter which direction he came at her, she blocked him easily. Her speed was unnatural.

He tried to press her into the wall, but she swept his sword away and dodged past him into the center of the room.

Sturg spun and hacked at her knee.

She blocked that blow, too.

Merud had both hands on his sword as if it were a broadsword. He cut the old woman's shoulder. Her sword fell.

The girl's riposte came for Sturg's neck. He brought up his sword just in time. The blades rang, sliding together to the hilts.

"This is stupid," he growled. "Surrender."

For a moment, she glowered at him. "Never." Her fist landed in his right eye. He recoiled, shaking off the pain.

She lunged. He parried, dodged, circled behind her. He kicked her in the back. She went down, her head inches from the stone hearth. He bounded forward to pin her. She rolled onto her back and met him with both feet in his stomach.

Winded, he fell to one side. She jumped up, scampering to the center of the room.

The old woman lay in a heap on the floor.

Merud, blood running from a cut in his cheek, approached the girl from behind.

As if she could see him coming, she spun, lashing out with her foot. Her roundhouse kick landed on the side of his head. He staggered back into a table.

Sturg closed in and grabbed her wrist. He bent it back till the sword clattered to the floor.

She plunged the elbow of her free arm into his stomach. She twisted, trying to pull out of his grip. Merud came at her again. Her side kick to his chest knocked him back a step.

Sturg tightened his grip. She bent over, pulling his arm. What was she doing?

He tumbled over her shoulder and onto the floor.

When she stooped to pick up her sword, Sturg kicked her in the face.

She staggered.

Merud reached for her wrist.

She brushed his arm away as if making a circular parry. She gave him a right cross to the face, then brought her left fist into his solar plexus.

He doubled over.

She raised her clasped hands as if to pound the back of Merud's neck.

Sturg tackled her, sending them both clattering into a table and its chairs.

On the floor, a broken chair all around her, she hit him in the face with her elbow. Then she scrambled toward her sword.

Sturg grabbed her ankle and hauled her back toward him.

She rolled over. Her ankle twisted out of his grip. Her other boot heel hit his jaw.

Merud ran toward her, but she rolled away, and he staggered into the sideways dining table. It scraped across the floor.

She jumped to her feet.

Sturg stood. They had her.

He and Merud closed in.

He'd heard of such a thing but had never seen it. She crouched then leapt upward, each foot lashing out in a different direction. Her right foot hit Merud's chest. Her left got Sturg's belly.

While they recovered, she picked up her sword.

Sturg swung at her sword arm. For a moment it seemed he'd gotten through her guard. But she blocked his swipe, putting both hands on the hilt of her sword to push his away. He'd cut her arm but not deeply. Not enough to make her drop the weapon.

Merud attacked, but she parried his hasty lunge with a seemingly effortless sweep of her sword.

Either of them alone should've been able to defeat her. Yet she held them off, spinning, kicking, slashing. How could she meet Sturg's sword on one side, then swing about to parry Merud on the other?

And where were the rest of his men?

Two privates dueled the civilians. The others still were in the street. Held back by militia—amateurs!

Outside, men bellowed, and horses and women shrieked. Inside, swords clashed, and feet scuffled. Then a loud thud as the corporal dueling the younger civilian by the bar felled his opponent.

Finally. The corporal joined Sturg and Merud.

Sturg drew off, catching his breath, while Merud and Corporal Tormod fought her. It was as if each parry gave her momentum to parry the other man's weapon.

But they'd wearied her. She no longer attacked. It was all parry and riposte, left and right.

Sturg sheathed his sword and approached from behind.

She shifted her weight as if to meet him. He moved with her, while the others kept her engaged.

He caught her in a chokehold, clamping her neck in the cleft of his elbow. He pulled on his wrist with the opposite hand.

She lifted her shoulders, trying to break free. Tried to wedge her fingers between his forearm and the artery.

She squirmed and kicked. Her sword fell. She reached behind her head to grab his.

Sturg held fast.

Her head bent forward, then snapped back, into his face. Blood from his nose ran into her braided hair.

He tightened his hold.

She tried once more to kick, then fell limp.

He let her drop to the floor.

"Merud. There's rope in my saddlebag. Tormod, find me a horse."

Sturg bound her hands and feet. She wouldn't be out for long.

Dorrel advanced, his rapier clashing with the private's saber.

The private reined back, grimacing. Then he plunged forward with another offense.

Dorrel batted away the saber with a sweep of his arm. He swung the rapier in an arc over his head.

Then he brought it down, across the side of the private's neck. A crimson river flowed down the front of the torn uniform.

The private fell across his horse's neck, then slipped off into the dirt.

Dorrel reined back. "Mairah, forgive me," he gasped, only half meaning it. He looked around.

More bodies lay on the ground than he had stomach to count. One might've been Stohan.

The door of the inn was gone, the doorframe shattered.

The Makutian lieutenant advanced on Mr. Risdun, their swords ringing.

Gylun traded blows with the bearded sergeant. He seemed to be holding his own, so Dorrel moved toward the lieutenant.

A Makutian corporal stopped in the doorway of the inn, then went for the dead man's horse.

As Dorrel approached, Mr. Risdun cried out. He collapsed over the neck of his horse, a horrible gash across the middle of his back.

Dorrel closed in on the lieutenant. Their swords clashed.

Commander Sturg came out of the inn. Alara hung limply over his shoulder.

Dorrel's breath stopped.

The corporal brought the dead man's horse to Sturg.

"Stand down." The lieutenant's sword arm, barely a foot from Dorrel, froze. "We got what we came for. We'll leave you in peace if you stand down."

The commander slung Alara across the horse like a sack of grain.

Dorrel glared at the lieutenant. His sinews felt brittle enough to snap. He grabbed the man's sword arm above the wrist. Toban stepped backward. They pulled the lieutenant off his horse.

Sturg bellowed, "To me!" He galloped past, Alara still limp in front of him.

Dorrel spun Toban about and sent him into a gallop. The lieutenant rolled out of their way, escaping Toban's hooves by inches.

They raced down the main street, past broken bodies and walking wounded. Dorrel quickly gained on Sturg.

The horses' hooves made pounding echoes as they crossed the wooden bridge.

Something hit him in the back. Then a rope circled his shoulders. He was yanked off Toban. He fell, the rope collapsing around him.

Dorrel landed on his back, his head cracking against the hard-packed dirt road.

Toban pulled up short and looked back for his rider.

Pain shot through him when he sat up. It got worse when he tried to untangle himself from the rope.

A soldier rode past, then another.

Dorrel tried to get the rope off. Strong hands stopped him.

"Easy, Dor. You're hit." Etton helped him to his feet. He draped one of Dorrel's arms over his shoulders and wrapped an arm around Dorrel's waist.

Dorrel staggered. His head swam. He couldn't control his limbs.

What was he supposed to be doing? It was important . . .

A group of soldiers on horseback thundered past.

Nothing made sense.

He was asleep.

This was a dream.

Or a nightmare.

# Chapter 11

## THAT DARK ROAD

The pounding of hoofbeats at the gallop. The odor of blood and horsehide and man sweat. Dimly, in the moonlight, hooves on dirt. Alara's hands were tied behind her back. Her ankles were bound.

For a few seconds, she had no idea whether it was all real, and if it was, how she had gotten there.

The whole fight came back to her at once. *Kenna, no! Not the Makutians.* She tried to pull herself up. An arm pressed into her neck.

"Don't move."

Sturg.

Each time the horse's hooves hit the ground, her head throbbed.

The woman remained still and silent for the rest of the ride. Sturg stopped near the little campfire at the mustering area on the other side of the hill from which he'd first spotted the town.

He dismounted, leaving her on the horse.

"Let's have some torches."

Ult picked up two torches in each hand, and Radig lit them with a stick from the fire.

Sturg took a torch and held it up. He heard hoofbeats. He drew his sword in case they weren't Makutian horses. In the torchlight, he could dimly make out horses and men churning down the hill.

He called out. "Hanik."

No answer.

"Korig."

"Here, sir." Torchlight flickered across the sergeant's craggy face. He stopped near Sturg, dismounted, and took a torch from Ult.

"Roll call."

While Korig called the roll, Sturg glanced back at the woman. She was watching him. "Don't move."

She looked away.

"We're missing five, sir," Korig said, "including Lieutenant Hanik."

Sturg swore. "Take two men and find them. We'll wait here."

Korig and the others rode into the dark.

Sturg handed the torch to Radig and pulled the woman down. "The prince expects to get you in one piece." He pulled a rope from the saddlebag. "But that won't stop me from breaking your leg if I must."

She glared at him. "I can't run, can I? I'm hobbled."

He picked her up, over his shoulder, and carried her to a spot away from the fire, but close enough that she was still in its light. He put her down with her back to a pine tree, then tied her in place.

"May I sit?"

"No."

The packs had been left here with Ult and Radig during the raid. Sturg found Hanik's and unpacked the medical kit.

"Ult."

"Sir?"

"I was grazed by an arrow. You'll have to bandage it till Hanik can stitch it up."

Dorrel sat on a stool, leaning on a wide bar top. Shelves behind the bar held rows of bottles.

The inn? He was in the public room of the inn?

He looked around.

The room was full of people, but none ate or drank. Few even spoke. Many wore bandages.

How had he gotten there, and why were so many people so badly hurt?

Gylun sat in an armchair by the window, his eyes glazed over. One leg of his trousers had been cut off. A stool propped up his foot, and a blood-soaked bandage covered him from knee to hip. Another bandage swathed his arm.

In the back of the room, on one of the dining tables, lay a man. Mr. Risdun? A thin old woman leaned over him, stitching up his wounds.

A couple of people stood with her, handing her things she needed. A woman with a bandage on her hand hung up more lanterns to light the table.

Dorrel felt pressure against his shoulder blade, which hurt almost as much as his head. Then the pressure eased.

Something red flew past him into a basket behind the bar. A beefy hand picked up a square of folded linen from the bar top. The pressure resumed.

He looked over his shoulder. "Dad?"

His father's voice was unusually subdued. "Yes?"

"Was I knocked out?"

"No, you've been awake the whole time. Why?"

"How'd I get here?"

"Etton walked you back."

"Back from where?" Why was he at the West Bridge Inn? Dorrel tried to remember something from earlier in the day . . . but failed.

"Segra?" Dad's voice revealed an uncharacteristic panic.

Alara had kissed him in the tack room. So his being here had something to do with her. "Where's Alara?"

"Etton went after her," Dad said.

A woman came over. Like his mother, she was trim with delicate hands. For a moment, he thought it was Mum. But this woman's hair was pale with bits of gray, and her face was round, not narrow like Mum's. Tyana. She was Tyana's mother. Her eyes were red and swollen.

Where was Tyana? Alara wanted to meet her.

The tray Segra carried held a bowl of water and a stack of cotton cloths. She set the tray on the bar.

"I think he hit his head," Dad told her. "He doesn't remember what happened."

She looked into each of Dorrel's eyes in turn. Then she put her hands around his head, carefully probing his skull.

He yelped. It felt as if she'd stabbed the back of his head.

She tsked. "He's got quite a bump, all right. Could be a mild concussion." Segra lifted Dad's hand to examine Dorrel's shoulder. "It's not letting up," she called out. "It'll take stitches."

"All right," the old woman said. "Dose him up, but he'll have to wait."

Segra patted his hand before going toward the kitchen.

Soldiers. Firelight glinting on gold epaulets.

Dad again swapped the compress on Dorrel's back for a clean one. He tossed the blood-soaked cloth into the overloaded basket.

"Was I unconscious?"

"No," Dad answered. "I told you, you've been awake the whole time."

"I feel as if I just woke up." If he'd been awake, why couldn't he remember? "Where's Alara?"

Dad sighed. "Etton's gone to get her."

"Oh." But where was she that Etton had to get her?

Segra returned with a mug.

"If he's concussed, should you put him out?" Dad asked.

"We have to so she can stitch him up." She handed Dorrel the mug.

The concoction smelled vile, but he gulped it down.

"I've done all I can." The old woman's voice was cold. "He's in Mairah's hands now."

Two men lifted Mr. Risdun on a stretcher and took him upstairs. Two more carried Gylun to the table.

Dorrel leaned on the bar and tried to reconstruct his fractured memory.

He'd hit his head. So he must've fallen.

"What happened to my shoulder?"

"You were shot." Dad cleared his throat. "A crossbow. Falling on it didn't help. It's a miracle you didn't break your shoulder blade."

He'd fallen—no, he remembered a rope—he'd been pulled off Toban and hit his head when he landed.

It was like trying to remember a dream. Fragments came into view, then slipped away as he tried to take hold of them.

She kissed him in the tack room.

She asked how long they should wait for Palon.

Why would Palon come here?

She slept in his arms on Toban's back.

She agreed to marry him.

The commander threw Alara's limp body over a horse.

He shuddered. The Makutians had her.

Dorrel tried to stand, but Dad's hand on his good shoulder stopped him.

"I have to go after Alara."

"You're in no shape to go anywhere. Etton went after her. Sit down."

Dorrel sat. His head felt like a boulder. He folded his arms on the bar and laid his head on them. His tenuous grip on consciousness began to slip away.

Suddenly the old woman was looming over him. He tried to sit up, but her strong hand on his heavy head stopped him. "Don't."

"I have to go after her, Mairah." His voice slurred. The old woman's name wasn't Mairah, but he couldn't remember what it was.

"Don't fight the anesthetic, Dorrel. Sleep." She smoothed his hair with her fingers, just like his mother did. "I've got a couple of others to take care of first, then I'll get to you. All right?"

He couldn't answer because he couldn't think. Her touch and gentle voice lulled him to sleep, completely against his will.

After what seemed an eternity, Korig and his privates returned with Lieutenant Hanik, Corporal Tormod, and two riderless horses.

Hanik dismounted. "Sir, some of the townsfolk came after us. We engaged them about halfway between here and the bridge. When Korig's party arrived, that drove the Glynrellans into retreat."

"Casualties?"

"Helk was killed at the bridge, and Feolt at the inn. Arteg was killed in the final skirmish."

"The enemy?"

"I lost count of the Glynrellan casualties."

Sturg nodded.

"The princess?"

Sturg pointed to her, and Hanik headed that way.

"She can wait," Sturg said. "See to the men first." All were wounded, even Korig.

"Yes, sir."

While Hanik did his stitching and bandaging, Radig kept watch atop the hill.

The rope constricted Alara's arms and chest. Her hands grew numb, pinned between her back and the rough pine bark.

She almost didn't care. She almost wished they had killed her. Because they would take her to Tarvag, and what waited there was worse than death.

*Oh, Telshi, what have I done? Hanik lost track of the casualties?* She'd seen Regger and Marita wounded, and the fellow using the spare saber. *How many more in the street? Dorrel? Please, Holy Mairah in heaven, protect him.*

*Kenna, forgive me. Forgive me for running away, for bringing my problems to Dorrel and his neighbors. Forgive me for hurting these men and*—this was the hardest thing to pray—*forgive them for what they've done. They take their orders from Prince Velek, or from the king. I suppose I should pray forgiveness for them, too, and for the ambassadors and my father . . . but I'm not ready for that. I'm too angry! Help me!*

Sturg had said no one else had to die. Which meant some already had. *Ahbay, comfort those who mourn.*

Oh, she was not going to cry in front of these . . . pigs.

*Mairah, Dorrel said Marita is a healer. If that's so, then pour Your healing power through her and onto the people in Kaesbaro. Preserve them in this trial and make them whole. Keep Your healing hands on these men and their medic. And me, I suppose, though perhaps I got what I deserve.*

Her whole face ached, especially the left eye, which she couldn't open. Her right cheek felt as if it would show Sturg's bootprint forever. Her sword belt was gone. Had they left it, and Nya's sword, in the inn, or had they taken the sword as a trophy? She didn't wish to ask and perhaps lead Sturg to believe it was more valuable than it really was. Because it was priceless.

Lieutenant Hanik prioritized the men for treatment. He took off his jacket and rolled up the sleeves of his black shirt. A bandage wrapped his right forearm from wrist to elbow.

If he was the medic, who had bandaged him? And when?

Some of the men made lewd remarks about her. Sturg told them, using Makutian words she suspected were vulgar, to shut up.

After Hanik finished Sturg's stitches, he slung his bag over his shoulder and approached her. "I'm going to untie you so I can treat your wounds. But if you try anything —"

"I'm hobbled."

"—the commander will make good on his threat. Understand?"

"Yes." Besides, they outnumbered her eleven to one. It had only taken three to beat her.

He untied her and looked her over.

She wasn't in bad shape, considering. Although she had lots of bruises, her arms had taken only a few glancing cuts, except for the gash Sturg had given her upper arm. It wasn't very deep, but it was several inches long.

He gently fingered the slit in her shirtsleeve. "You'll have to take this off for me to bandage you." His voice was low and soft.

"Of course. But they don't all have to watch me do it."

He nodded. "Ult!"

A slim, blond teenager ran over. He was instructed to unpack a tent and string it up as a screen between "the princess" and the squad.

His doing so resulted in a burst of hoots and taunts from the other side.

Hanik rolled his eyes, which might have made Alara laugh, had she not been quaking. She was shielded from the others, but could she trust him?

She had no choice.

Fingers trembling, she unbuttoned her shirt and removed it. Though she wore a sturdy underbodice, she felt naked.

The alcohol stung her wounds, but his touch was light. He did the job more dispassionately than a Glynrellan doctor would have. After bandaging the smaller cuts, he cleaned the long, deep one. "This will take stitches. I have laudanum, if you want it."

"No, thank you." It couldn't be wise to be senseless around this bunch.

Hanik called Ult and asked him to fetch something. A word she didn't know.

Ult returned a minute later with a tin flask. He shook it, producing a tiny sloshing sound. "It's nearly empty, sir."

Hanik handed it to her anyway.

"No, thank you."

He narrowed his eyes. "Are you sure?"

"Of course. I don't know where it's been."

Ult laughed, and Hanik gave a small start and a snort. Perhaps a stifled laugh of his own. "Ult, hold her hand, and keep the arm straight." He wrapped a linen cloth around a wooden dowel already chiseled with the imprints of teeth.

She clenched it in her jaw, weeping, praying, growling, while he stitched the wound. As if her arm were on fire, searing pain flared down the limb. She gripped poor Ult's hand so hard, she might have broken fingers. Each stab of the needle, each tug of a suture, she accepted as punishment for bringing her problems to Kaesbaro.

By the time Hanik finished, she lay limp, her limbs trembling, her face drenched with tears and sweat. He covered the stitches with salve and a bandage, then gave her a cloth to dry her face. He had the decency to look away while she buttoned her shirt.

Ult packed the tent.

Hanik put away his supplies. "You said you prefer to ride."

"Yes."

"You'll have to, now. The ambassador took the carriage to Tarvag."

"Fine."

He untied her ankles and helped her to her feet. He kept a firm grip on her arm until he'd brought her to a horse. "Remember what Commander Sturg said."

"I remember."

He nodded.

They all mounted, and with half the men carrying torches, Sturg led them at the quickest pace possible on that dark road.

# Chapter 12

## GOING AFTER HER

Half asleep, Dorrel rolled over. He wasn't in the dormitory at Denedra. He lay in his own bed at home. Segra sat in the chair by the window, bathed in bright sunlight. "Segra?" Why was he home, and why was she there?

"How do you feel?" She dropped her sewing into the basket at her feet and came to him.

"Fine." He sat up. "What time is it?"

"Settle down." She pressed his shoulder. "You can't be fine."

His confusion blew away. "Alara—did Etton find her?"

She sighed. "I'm afraid not. He was wounded, too."

Dorrel remembered mangled bodies in the road. He wasn't sure whether it was a memory of reality or a dream. "How many?"

"Wounded? Thirty-two, including yourself."

Himself? Oh. A bandage covered his right shoulder. "And . . . dead?"

Segra swallowed hard. "Oh, Dorrel . . ." She took a deep breath. "Seventeen."

Dorrel moaned, covering his face with his hands. *Mairah, help us.* He looked up. "Tyana?"

Her eyes wrinkled, and she bit her lip. "She's unharmed, but . . . Stohan died at the inn. Trampled. She's devastated." Segra sobbed.

He grabbed her hand. "I'm so sorry. I shouldn't have—"

"Don't, Dor." She shook her head. "You all did what you had to do."

"Did we?" He scrubbed his face with his hands. "It's all a blur." Gaps riddled his memory. He pushed back the covers.

"Dorrel, please . . ."

Still in the trousers he'd worn the night before, he got out of bed on the side opposite from her.

"You're in no condition—"

"I have to go after Alara." Dorrel opened the wardrobe. He tossed clean trousers and a shirt onto the bed.

"You're not . . ." She took a couple of steps backward. "Let me see that bandage." She reached into her sewing basket and drew out a pair of scissors.

Dorrel sat on the trunk at the foot of bed and turned his back to her. The scissors pressed cold against his skin as she cut the bandage off. "I was shot, wasn't I?"

"Yes. You should be in pain."

"I'm not."

"Sweet Mairah . . ." She pulled the bandage away, and her warm fingers prodded the skin. "It's healed."

He tried to look. "What, completely?"

"Yes." She dropped the scissors on the quilt and ran her fingers through the hair on the back of his head. "That lump on your head is gone, too."

He rubbed his head as if he didn't believe her.

Her voice quavered. "I haven't seen Marita work a healing so thoroughly in . . . ages."

"Just as well, since I have to go." He stood.

With a firm hand on his shoulder, she shoved him down. "The skin's healed, but the stiches are still in you. Let me pull them out." A seam ripper from her basket did the job. "You shouldn't try to go after them, you know. Those brutes would kill you without thinking twice."

He didn't doubt that. But what they'd do to Alara would be far worse. "I can't let them take her."

She sighed. "All right, that's the last of it." She tossed the shredded sutures into a wastebasket. Then she walked briskly out the door. "Kester," she hollered, closing the door behind her, "your son thinks he's leaving."

Dorrel dressed while downstairs, Dad and Segra spoke in faint murmurs.

He pulled aside the curtain. Though the sky overhead was clear, dark clouds loomed over the mountains in the south. He glanced at the clock on his dresser. Almost midday. The Makutians had come late at night. They had a huge lead on him.

His father's slow, heavy footsteps trod up the stairs.

Dorrel took a haversack out of his trunk.

Under the haversack lay an old mail shirt that had belonged to his grandfather. He snorted. Had he thought to wear it last night, he might not have been stopped by that bolt.

His armor—an old brigandine and a newish gambeson—were still in his trunk at Denedra with his militia uniform. The mail shirt would have to do. He put on a wool undershirt meant for winter, shrugged the mail over it, then pulled on a cotton shirt. Too much for summer. Not enough for a battle.

Dad opened the door.

"I'm going after her." Dorrel went to the wardrobe for his hunting jacket.

It wasn't there.

Of course not. It would be in the laundry, blood-stained, with a hole in it.

His drover coat would get in the way during a fight. He took out a close-fitting jacket of black leather and put that on. It fit snugly over the other layers.

Dad's hand still rested on the doorknob. "Shall I saddle Toban for you?"

Dorrel sighed. "Yes, please."

Dad turned to go.

"Thanks for not trying to stop me."

"I'd go with you, but I'd only slow you down." He went downstairs.

Dorrel packed quickly. As he pulled things from the top drawer, he saw the suede money pouch he kept there. It held about twelve staters.

There was no telling how long he'd be gone or what sort of supplies he might need along the way.

He tossed the pouch into the haversack.

Dorrel strapped on his sword and hunting knife and took down his hat. He jogged down the stairs.

In the kitchen, Segra muttered while stuffing provisions into a saddlebag. She gave him a glare. "I don't know what your father is thinking. Neither of you seems to realize how dangerous—"

"It's more dangerous for Alara than me."

She inhaled sharply and nodded. She took a couple of peaches from a bowl and tucked them into the bag before handing it to him.

"Thank you, Segra."

"You're welcome." She sighed. "Oh, for the love of Mairah—" Her voice cracked. "Be careful. We can't lose you, too."

He smiled weakly. He had no words.

As he walked across the yard to the stable, Dorrel considered taking Willow. But he'd make better time without her. Toban could carry them both home. He'd done it before.

Just before dawn, Sturg led them off the road and into the forest. Alara guessed they were still west of Ecciston. But their route took them south of the town and its fort. Her only hope was escape. Or the border patrol.

They rode all through the day and past sundown and never saw another person.

It rained gently, intermittently, throughout the day. She wouldn't complain—wouldn't give them cause to think her self-centered or demanding, though in truth she was often both. But after the sun went down, she shivered uncontrollably in her wet shirt.

By the time it became too dark to ride, the rain had stopped, though drops still fell from branches overhead. They found a clearing, and Sturg snapped orders at his men as if they didn't already know how to make camp.

When Alara dismounted, Hanik stood close by. She sat and began stretching her legs, first in front of her, then splitting them right and left, leaning along the length of each one in turn.

"Curate, you oughtn't . . ." Hanik began. But the enlisted men started their barrage, half of which she was pleased not to understand.

"I'll do as my teacher told me. I don't care what they think."

Hanik frowned.

He stood next to her, arms folded, while she stretched. She thought her chance of escape would come when she asked for privacy to relieve herself. But Hanik fashioned a latrine for her with an extra tent. She could tell by his footsteps that he stayed close.

They returned to camp, where Ult had already pitched her tent. She thanked him. He blushed and ducked his head.

Hanik gestured for her to sit, then took out a rope and tied her ankles. He looked away briefly, then took off his jacket and stepped behind her, holding it open.

"Here."

"No, thank you."

"You're shivering. And because your shirt is wet, your . . . undershirt . . . can be seen. Is your pride more important to you than your modesty?"

It was not. Especially not under the leers of those men.

She put on the black wool jacket, wrapping it tightly around her.

The sleeves reached her fingertips. The forearm of the right sleeve had been sliced open, the edges of the cut stained with blood.

A hunting party returned with the spaniel and some fowl. Once the men had eaten, Hanik brought her a plate of food and a cup. He dismissed Ult, who went to get his own dinner.

Alara balanced the plate on her lap and murmured a prayer of thanks before picking up a wing.

Hanik sat cross-legged nearby. "Why do Telshans always pray before eating?"

"Because food comes from our Creator. Not to thank Her would be rude."

"I've heard religious talk that made less sense. But explain something to me. I'm told Telshans claim there is only one god."

"Yes, we have the word of Telshi through the prophet Galardi, 'Your God Telshi is One. There is no other.'"

"But you pray to a mother, and a father, and your prophet Kenna." He flicked long, thin fingers out in turn. "That's three gods."

"Kenna isn't a prophet. She's God in flesh. She is Telshi."

He shook his head. "This is the religious talk that makes no sense."

*Thank you, Telshi, for putting my schooling to work here.* "Your father, what work does he do?"

Hanik wrinkled his forehead, raising his eyebrows. "He was a banker."

Was. What a blunder. Still . . . "He was a banker. He also was a son and a father. One man, three aspects. Telshi is the same. Mairah the Creator, Ahbay the Counselor, and Kenna the Redeemer. Not three deities, but three persons of the One deity."

"I never heard it said that way before."

She backtracked to her blunder. "May I ask what happened to your father?"

"He died in the epidemic."

"I'm sorry. My older brother did, too."

"I've heard it said everyone on the continent lost someone."

"I believe that's true," she said. "But here's my comfort. I know my brother Kyvern is in heaven with Telshi, where there's never any sickness. Of course, since he was a physician, I wonder what he'll do."

This attempt at humor failed to provoke a smile.

"I was told," she continued, "your people believe all the dead go to Shaedeis—the underworld."

He nodded.

"Does that give you comfort, to believe your father is there?"

"I don't believe in Shaedeis," he said, "or heaven, or any other thing for which there is no proof."

"Then I pity you."

He frowned at her.

She decided that was enough preaching for one day.

The soldiers took turns guarding her tent. Hanik had bound her ankles again and tied her hands behind her back. But once she was alone, she tucked her legs through the circle of her arms, bringing her hands to the front. She untied the rope with her teeth as Rariden had taught her. Then she removed the rope from her ankles.

She peeked out of the tent. One private patrolled the space between her and the campfire. She waited for him to give up and nap, or go off to relieve himself, or even just look the other way long enough for her to scramble toward the cover of the forest. He didn't. Neither did the guard who relieved him. So she went to the rear of the tent and lifted it.

A boot landed near her fingers. "Don't even try."

She snatched her hand back. Alara stopped watching the sleepless guards and curled up in her bedroll. Sturg had made sure she knew her horse, tent, and bedroll had been inherited from one of his men, a private named Feolt who'd been killed in the village.

She wrapped herself in Feolt's blanket and Hanik's coat and prayed for Dorrel and his neighbors and for Dorrel and for Feolt's family and for Dorrel—until she fell asleep.

Toban woke Dorrel shortly before dawn by snorting in his face. He groaned, pushing the horse's nose away, and sat up. The sun illuminated the eastern end of the Kaesrynne Valley.

How much time had he lost? He should've been up at first light. "Arrgh, Toban! How could you let me sleep so long?" He stood and feebly tried to brush the rain-dampened mulch off his trousers.

He found a stream and drank deeply, then washed his face and hands.

Toban stood still while Dorrel dug into his saddlebag. The food, wrapped in oilcloth, was mostly dry. He took out a large chunk of raisin bread.

"All right, boy. Let's go get Alara." Toban whickered as if in agreement. Dorrel mounted and headed eastward, munching his bread.

The Makutians' trail was easy to follow. Where Glynrellans would carefully pick their way through a forest in single file, the Makutians had plundered through several abreast. They might as well have cut themselves a boulevard.

# Chapter 13

## AN UNFORGIVABLE AFFRONT

In the morning, Alara struck her own tent, though Ult offered to do it for her. "You've your own to do," she said, "and there's no point my sitting idle."

While she rolled up the tent, Hanik did the same with his.

"Lieutenant . . ." She hesitated. "I mean no disrespect . . ."

He waited.

"I've nothing to keep the sun out of my eyes. But I found Private Feolt's cap in his pack. Will the others mind if I wear it?"

Hanik glanced over his shoulder at them, then stuffed the tent into his pack. "If they do, they can take it up with me."

They rode relentlessly that day, forgoing a noon meal. Near sunset, most of the troop went hunting. Alara was left with Hanik, Radig, and Ult to make camp.

Those with two hands pitched tents. Radig cleared the ground for a fire. Alara was afraid to ask where or when he'd lost his arm.

She looked for a chance to bolt, but Hanik stayed close, his eyes continually on her.

Once all the tents were up, they collected firewood. Alara found a fallen pine and snapped off a few pieces from the jagged edge of the broken trunk. Each chunk was about the size of two of her fingers.

Ult frowned at her. "What're you doing?"

"Smell that?" She held it out to him.

He sniffed, then wrinkled his nose. "What is it?"

"Turpentine." She gave him the Glynnish word, because she didn't know the Makutian one. "They're good fire starters."

"Oh."

She and Ult built the fire, and Hanik told Ult to light it.

The boy looked dumbstruck. "I can't, sir."

"What?"

"I don't know how."

Hanik huffed. "Very well." He headed for his pack.

Alara handed Ult a piece of pine. "We'll have to teach you."

Hanik returned with flint and steel, and Alara showed Ult how to light the fire starters and place them under the tinder.

It was nearly dark when Sturg and his hunting party returned to camp. The woman sat by her tent, Hanik less than an arm's length away. Ult prodded the fire with a long branch.

"Ult! What're you doing?" Sturg strode over to him.

"I'm tending the fire, sir. I lit it myself."

"Lieutenant, I didn't ask you to teach him to light a fire."

"He didn't, sir," Ult said. "The curate did."

Sturg glared at the woman. She smiled at him. That put his stomach in a knot.

She got up and came toward him. "He's too old to not know how to light a fire."

"That's for me to decide."

She gestured to the blaze. "He's obviously capable."

Audacity might be acceptable in her father's house, but in front of the men, it wouldn't do. He drew back his hand.

Hanik slid between them and caught Sturg's wrist. "I believe Prince Velek would agree his bride already has too many bruises."

Just like Hanik to use the prince's name to cover insubordination.

Before Sturg could say anything else, Korig dropped their catch at her feet. "Get to cooking, then."

She glanced at the animal, a mountain goat, and smiled. "Of course." She held out one hand. "I'll just need a knife to skin it."

Sturg ignored her. "Korig, cooking is Merud's job." He waved Merud forward and pointed to the goat. "Get to it." While Merud took the animal away, Sturg stepped closer to Korig. "Never mind arming her. Didn't it occur to you that letting a prisoner cook your food is unwise?"

The woman spoke up again. "If all you could find is an old mountain goat, you wouldn't want to entrust it to a poor cook like me, anyway."

Was she being obnoxious on purpose? Sturg spun on her. Before he could think of a response that didn't involve slapping her, Hanik turned on her, too.

"Sit down, and be quiet."

She gaped at him. "I—"

"Just. Be. Quiet." Hanik pointed to her tent.

Surprisingly enough, she sat and was quiet.

Alara drew her knees to her chest and wrapped her arms around her legs. In Sturg's absence, Hanik hadn't been so demeaning to her.

Once the men had eaten, he brought her a piece of meat and some dried fruit. "How do you expect me to keep him from hurting you if you provoke him?"

"I wasn't trying to provoke. I was just—talking." After a brief prayer, she picked up the meat. "You didn't seem to mind my talking." She took a bite. The meat was tough.

"No," Hanik said. "But he isn't used to conversing with women as equals."

She swallowed. "And you are?"

He shrugged. "I've spent more time with Telshans than he."

"Really? Where?"

"In Redíque. I went with Prince Velek on some of his visits." He smirked and switched to Redíquan. "Listen: I had the honor to serve in the company to guard the royal . . ." He frowned. "That's wrong."

"The company that guards."

"Yes, thank you. The company that guards the royal family. I accompany Prince Velek on state visit."

"Did you go with him to Shandór last winter?"

He raised his eyebrows. "Yes. How do you know he go there?"

"Mehrialéna wrote to me about it."

"Ah." Hanik nodded. "She is your—how do you say it?"

"Cousin."

"Cousin."

Alara ate a dried apricot. "I gather he went to buy horses from Bóhjetien." Her cousin was almost as renowned for his horses as the Chevallons were for theirs.

"There was talk of horses. But most it was to visit. They are friends."

She nodded.

"Do you think," Hanik said, "the friend of your cousin would be bad?"

She stared at her plate. "No, Boh would not befriend someone evil. But though Prince Velek might think the treaty is fair, I think—" she shook her head. "The prophet Galardi wrote that marriage must be founded on love, not politics."

Hanik frowned.

Ult grabbed a branch to put on the fire.

"Not that," Sturg said. "It's too big."

Ult stood, propped the branch diagonally on the ground, and put his foot on it as if to break it in half. When that didn't work, he drew his knife.

"Not your knife!" Alara called. "For the love of—" She leaned over, reaching for the pack in front of his tent, next to hers. She'd seen him use a hatchet while they built the fire. She pulled it out. "Use this."

Hanik grabbed her wrist.

"Shaedeis!" Sturg charged across the clearing.

She opened her hand. Hanik took the ax.

"I wasn't trying to arm myself." She couldn't disable them all with only a hatchet, not when they had sabers. "I was just trying to stop him from damaging his knife."

Sturg yanked the hatchet from Hanik's grasp, holding it near its head. Backhanded, he struck her across the face with the handle. She splayed onto her side.

She lay still. So much for not provoking him.

Hanik jumped to his feet.

Sturg stood over her.

Alara tensed.

Sturg kicked her in the ribs.

"Commander!" Hanik shouted.

Sturg kicked her again.

Hanik grabbed the commander's upper arm, pulling him away.

"Don't try such a thing again," Sturg told her, "or this lot'll get what they're after."

The enlisted men cheered and hooted.

Sturg shook off Hanik's grip, then spun and strode toward Ult. His big hand went around the boy's thin bicep. "Never leave a weapon within a prisoner's reach."

Ult's eyes grew wide. He, too, got a blow from the ax handle.

Alara crawled into her tent.

Hanik followed, which brought on a round of goading from outside.

"What're you doing in here?"

He knelt just inside the flap of the tent. "I'm sorry I wasn't able to stop him." He sighed. "How bad are you hurt?"

"I'm fine."

"Don't be absurd."

"If my ribs were broken, I'd know. Please leave, Lieutenant."

He turned but hesitated. "You'll tell me if you've sharp pains with your breathing."

"Of course."

He picked up the ropes he'd used to bind her hands and feet. He leaned forward, his voice low. "You're fortunate I didn't tell the commander you untied them last night."

She nodded. "Thank you."

"I won't bother tying you again if you'll not bother trying to run."

"You understand why I tried."

"Of course. But you understand that because you escaped from us once, we are doubly vigilant now."

This was surely true.

"I wish to give you some dignity, ma'am. But you must promise cooperation in return."

*Kenna, show me what You want. Am I to go to Tarvag, or Apanumon, or Kaesbaro?*

"Curate?"

Kenna said if one was pressed into service, one should do what was asked, and more besides.

"All right, Lieutenant. I promise."

Hanik put the ropes aside. "Thank you." He left. She pulled off her boots, wrapped herself in Feolt's blanket, and wept.

*Telshi, it is written that You can turn evil things to good purposes. Please work on these evil events and bring something good out of them. Even if the good is me preaching in a Makutian gynaeceum. Ocha.*

Dorrel stopped for the night at a place where a rocky outcrop provided shelter. He ate a cold supper—a boiled egg and bread. He didn't build a fire lest the Makutians see it.

His healed shoulder perplexed him, though he was unspeakably grateful for it. Why should he be so fortunate?

For years, people had claimed Marita had supernatural healing ability, but Dorrel hadn't believed it. If Marita could heal people, why had Mum and so many others died in the epidemic?

But if Marita couldn't heal, why was he sitting there as hale as the day he'd left Denedra? *Mairah, if it's true you've given Marita this gift, I thank you for it.* Otherwise, he might still be laid up in bed instead of pursuing Alara's kidnappers. *Please heal Mr. Risdun and Gylun and the others, also.*

Still sweltering in his multiple layers and mail, he lay atop his blanket. Toban was already asleep. "Glad you can sleep, boy." Dorrel stared at the stars. *Ahbay, help me find Alara and bring her safely home. Kenna, protect her.*

How he longed for Alara's body next to his. He could almost imagine her wrapped in the blanket with him, their arms and legs entwined.

On the fourth night, Alara was awakened by a heavy footfall near her head.

A man in her tent.

She sat up. "Get out!" She tried to scoot outside.

He straddled her. Grabbed her throat in one hand. Pushed her head to the ground. "Shut up, she-dog." Korig. He stank like rotting meat.

"Hanik!"

Korig's hard hand moved to cover her mouth. He pulled at her blanket, groping for the buttons of her trousers.

She looped one arm around his neck. The other she crossed in front of his chest. She pulled her knees up against his backside, tipping his putrid bulk forward. She grabbed his elbow and arched her back, shoving with arm and hip until he rolled over. They fell into the side of the tent, bringing the canvas down over them.

He hollered. Probably profanity.

She leaned down, sliding her arm from his chest to his neck. She grabbed her own sleeve with the other hand.

He bucked like a wild horse, but she tightened her grip, closing her forearms around his neck like a vise. He kicked futilely. Untrained boor.

When Sturg had choked her, she thought her head might burst open. Korig must feel the same.

He fell limp.

She jumped up, pawing at the canvas to clear it off her head. Her foot landed on part of him—an arm, perhaps—as she scrambled away.

This was her chance. She could make for the woods.

But Hanik blocked her way. "What happened?" The blade of his sword reflected the dim firelight.

"Korig attacked me."

He stiffened, shoulders back. He looked her up and down. "You don't seem the worse for it." His eyes darted to the crumpled tent. "And he's not moving."

"He should've known better."

"Huh. True." He raised his sword. "Don't move."

She clasped her trembling hands behind her back like a soldier at ease. Others had emerged from their tents. No chance of escape now.

Hanik nudged the pile of white canvas with a toe. "Korig!"

A groan.

"Sergeant! On your feet." Hanik stood back.

Sturg stepped in. "What the Shaedeis is going on here?"

Hanik kept his eyes on her. "Korig attacked the princess, and she bested him." Again he nudged the sergeant with his boot. "A double failure."

Sturg grumbled, "Never try to take a Glynrellan woman alone."

Alara's stomach turned. They had a procedure for that?

Korig stumbled out of the remains of the tent.

By now, every soldier in the camp was watching.

Hanik stood nose-to-nose with Korig. "That was an unforgivable affront, Sergeant."

"Why treat her as if she were the queen already?" Korig rubbed his head. "She's just a woman." Some of the listeners hooted similar sentiments.

But someone — Radig, perhaps — said, "Well it wouldn't do, would it, Korig, for Prince Velek to accept a used woman."

Someone said, "True," and others murmured agreement.

Korig snorted. "Only the priests care about a woman's purity. The prince isn't a proper Kivatan and neither am I, so what does it matter which of us uses her first?"

Hanik laid his sword alongside Korig's neck. "That was a treasonous remark, Korig. An assault on the prince's bride is likewise treason. And treason is punishable by death." Hanik took a step forward, forcing Korig back. "If you touch her again, I will kill you."

Korig lifted his spread hands and retreated again.

Sturg grabbed Hanik's arm and pulled him back. "You mayn't kill my top sergeant."

"He at least ought to lose his stripes."

Sturg said something Alara assumed was swearing. He turned his head, slightly, toward Korig. "Dismissed, Sergeant."

Korig walked away.

Sturg stepped closer to Hanik. His voice was so low she could hardly hear. "It's well known you were sent to Ayenni for no other reason than to escort that she-dog to Tarvag. Just do that, and leave the discipline of my men to me."

Hanik sheathed his sword. "Korig mayn't have guard duty over her again."

"Fine." Sturg returned to his tent.

Hanik hung his head, shoulders slumped. Then he straightened and returned to Alara.

Her heart still raced, and her limbs trembled.

He stopped a few feet away. "I'm sorry. I'll see that Korig is punished for this."

She folded her arms. "How can you?"

The waning crescent moon gave little light, but the fire shone enough on his face for her to see his smirk. "I have connections."

"Do you."

Hanik's expression turned stern. "This should never have happened. I'm sorry for it." He put his hand to his face, rubbing first one cheek, then the other. "I'll make sure it doesn't happen again." He glanced back at what was left of her tent. Then he pointed to his own. "You can spend the rest of the night in my tent."

Her stomach heaved again. "I beg your pardon?"

He made a little bow. "I'll stay out here."

"I see." She climbed into the tent and lay there, shivering, unable to sleep, while outside, Hanik paced, keeping guard.

From then on, Hanik stopped using his tent. Instead, each night he slept on the ground in front of hers.

As the squad made its way eastward, Alara and Hanik conversed at length in Redíquan. He said he appreciated the opportunity to practice. His vocabulary and syntax improved daily. Whenever Sturg was out of earshot, Ult joined in as well. He learned quickly.

"Prince Velek is the friend of your cousin Bóhjetien," Hanik said one day. "So he would not harm you."

"Oh. Because he would not wish to offend Boh?" Alara's tone was sarcastic.

"Certainly." Hanik could not have understood how insulting this was, even if she'd tried to explain. "Besides, as a royal bride, you would never be subjected to the sort of . . ." He thought for a moment, then switched to Makutian. "Degradation practiced during the war."

"You say that, but I might've been."

He didn't try to deny it.

Hanik told her many stories about the prince. About his diplomatic visits, his patronage of the arts, and his charitable work. He seemed determined to convince her that Velek was a good and noble man.

Alara was convinced only of Hanik's loyalty.

Dorrel's sleep was filled with nightmares spawned by Marita's war stories. During the day, the need to forage slowed his progress. His food had run out.

He'd hoped the border patrol would intercept Sturg's squad, but it seemed unlikely. The main roadways had border crossings, but elsewhere pairs of horsemen patrolled the border. And each pair had dozens of miles to cover. Sturg must know that, which was why he'd left the road.

Dorrel wasn't sure when he crossed the border, but he thought he'd already done so when the Makutians' trail turned south onto a road that ran up the mountainside to a narrow pass. That surely would've slowed them down.

Toban, accustomed to traversing the Denedra Range, took that unfamiliar ground with sure-footed ease, as if he traveled it every day.

The crest of the pass gave Dorrel a sweeping view of the country below. Pine-covered mountains descended to green hills that rolled away ahead of him.

He could just make out a group of horses galloping down the wide road that ran out of the hills. Although they were too distant for him to discern any details, Dorrel felt they must be Sturg and his troop with Alara.

Their long lead had been shortened to just a few hours. Although the Makutians traveled at a good speed, Dorrel was encouraged. He ruffled Toban's forelock. "Old man, you are magnificent."

Toban whickered.

Dorrel pointed him down the road.

*Ahbay, thank you for seeing us this far. Mairah, give us speed and strength to finish the task.*

He kept his eyes on the troop until a hill blocked his view. "Never mind," he said, as much to himself as to his horse. "We'll be upon them in no time."

Then, of course, Dorrel would have to fight the entire squad to free her. He didn't want to think about that.

# Chapter 14

## GADRUT

Alara's poor skewbald gelding had stitches in his side, but like her, he was healing reasonably well. Horses and riders alike were exhausted, but after they descended the last foothill and turned onto the main road, Sturg pushed them harder still, sending them into a gallop.

The gelding's gait faltered often. "He won't be able to keep this up much longer," Alara told Hanik after an hour of that grueling pace.

"None of them will," Hanik answered, "but we're not far from the fort at Gadrut. You can see the town there." He pointed to a thin line of gray stone wall a few miles straight ahead.

Alara's heart shrank. The site of some of the Makutians' worst war crimes.

Hanik didn't seem to remember or care. "We'll change horses there."

Shortly after noon, they reached the town's western gate. Only then did Sturg slow them to a trot. He led them eastward to the town square. There they turned south and rode to the fort at the town's southern gate. Sturg didn't give the order to dismount until the heavy wooden gates had been barred behind them.

Grooms, most younger than Ult, sprinted across the courtyard from the stables to take the horses. Sturg conferred with the fort's commander.

Alara stretched her arms over her head, then sat in the dirt to stretch her legs.

The fort's soldiers stared at her. Nevertheless, she continued. Hanik looked away. He ought to be used to her post-ride exercises.

"Hanik!" Sturg bellowed from across the yard. "Get that woman inside!"

Hanik bent over and gently grasped her arm. "You heard him."

She frowned but stood and walked with Hanik to a door on the left side of the courtyard. It opened into a kitchen. A portly, middle-aged woman with gray hair tied up in a dingy kerchief curtsied. Hanik asked her to bring them water and something to eat.

It was still two days till the wedding. They could reach the capital before nightfall.

The fort's commander agreed to supply Sturg with fresh horses and a wagon. He didn't even comment on the woman's outrageous behavior.

Sturg took leave of the commander and went to the kitchen. Hanik and the woman sat at a rough pine table eating sandwiches. Those two had become awfully cozy.

Hanik shot to his feet.

"You," Sturg said to the cook, "take this woman and get her proper clothes."

Eyes suitably downcast, the cook curtsied and showed Kordelyon's daughter out of the room.

Sturg turned to Hanik. "I'm having a wagon hitched up. We'll take her to Tarvag in that."

"Yes, sir."

"It'll be slower going, but I won't have her seen in the capital riding horseback—in pants." He glowered in the direction the women had gone. "Bad enough she had to be seen here like that."

The Makutian horses had torn up the packed earth of the main road. The prints showed they'd broken into a gallop, so Dorrel did likewise. A lesser horse would resist, but Toban needed no urging to sprint to the town ahead. He seemed to know what was at stake.

By now Dorrel saw the folly in attempting to wrest Alara from the troops. Even if he somehow armed her with his knife, the two of them couldn't take on a whole squad.

He could only track them to their destination. What he'd do when he got there, he didn't know.

Dorrel reached a crossroads marked by a tall signpost. One placard pointed behind him to Tylan, a Glynrellan town. His mother's family shipped wine to a wholesaler there.

To the south was the Redíquan town of Vonisayu. The sign that pointed east read Gadrut. His stomach twisted.

Marita, along with thousands of other women, had been held prisoner there.

On the outskirts of town, he passed a large field surrounded by a wrought-iron fence. Inside were row upon row of gray stones. He was puzzled at first. When he realized what it was, he shuddered.

A burial ground. He'd heard of them but had never seen one.

Somewhere near would be the mass graves where the Makutians had buried the victims of the prison camp.

A guard stopped him at the town gate, but when Dorrel said he was going to Tarvag, the guard waved him through with no further questions. Between the gate and the town square, he lost the trail. Bustling people and ox-drawn carts had obliterated the hoofprints.

He stopped at a tavern near the square and tied Toban up at the trough. Dorrel let him drink a bit, then strapped on his feedbag. It was almost empty—he'd have to buy supplies before he left town. He patted Toban's shoulder, then headed inside.

Slatted blinds covered the only window, making the room gloomy. At least it was cooler inside. Sweat pooled under the woolen shirt on Dorrel's back.

He pushed his hat off, letting it hang from his neck by the chinstrap. He stepped up to the bar, wondering how to inquire about the soldiers without arousing suspicion. He started by asking for food.

The bartender brought him a bowl of soup. "Six shillings."

"I'm sorry, I only have Glynrellan staters," Dorrel said. "Can you take them?"

"Glad to." He took Dorrel's gold stater and gave him back four large silver crowns and four dull-gray shillings.

Dorrel stared at them. It was more than he expected. "What's the exchange rate?"

"One-and-a-half staters to a sovereign, last I checked. What did you get when you went over?"

"Sorry?"

"When you changed your sovereigns for staters before going to Glynrell, what did you get?"

"But I—" Dorrel shook his head. "I didn't. I mean—I'm from Glynrell."

The bartender's eyebrows shot up. "Really? You don't sound like it."

"Thanks. Guess I had a good teacher." Dorrel pocketed the change and started on his soup.

The bartender poured a refill for a fat man at the other end of the bar.

"I heard a bunch of soldiers came to town." Dorrel hoped he sounded casual. "I thought they'd have filled your place by now."

The bartender snorted. "You'd think so. But they went straight to the fort without stopping." He shrugged. "Maybe they'll come in the evening."

"They won't." A skinny, elderly man sat at a table nearby, smoking a pipe. "They've gone."

"How can they have gone?" The bartender leaned his portly frame across the bar. "They just got here."

"I tell you, they've gone." The old man's beard wagged as he talked. "Left the fort almost as soon as they came. Only they left with a covered wagon."

"Was that woman with them?" the fat man asked.

The old man shrugged.

The bartender wrinkled his brow. "What woman?"

Half the fat man's drink disappeared in a gulp. "The one who rode in with them."

"I didn't see any woman."

The fat man laughed. "Then there're a couple things you didn't notice!"

"They were all riding." The bartender sounded testy. "In pants."

"Was probably that Glynrellan girl of the prince's." The last of the whiskey disappeared down the fat man's gullet. "They ride all the time."

"That's just an old tale," the bartender scoffed.

The elderly man shook his head. "Oh, their women ride. And fight. I've the scars to prove it."

The bartender stared at one patron, then the other, before turning to Dorrel. "Is that true?"

Dorrel nodded.

The bartender frowned. "You'd let your wife wear pants and ride a horse?"

"Well, I'm not married—yet—but in fact," he almost laughed, since the woman they were talking about and the one he was about to mention were the same person. "The woman I'm to marry is a better rider than most."

The fat man guffawed. "Better than you?"

"I wouldn't say that." Dorrel smirked. "But she's beaten me in a sparring match more than once."

"Every married man would have to admit to that," the bartender said.

They all laughed together, and Dorrel returned to his soup.

Alara was on her way to the capital, he was certain, in that covered wagon. They'd take her straight to King Domat's palace. Wherever that was.

"Do you think that was your princess?" The bartender refilled the fat man's glass.

At the risk of spoiling the fragile camaraderie, Dorrel had to put the man right. "Not 'princess.' We have no royalty."

"Sorry," the bartender muttered. "Meant no offense."

"None taken. When did the soldiers come through?"

A group of customers entered and seated themselves at a table.

The bartender shrugged. "A few hours ago." He stepped out from behind the bar to serve the newcomers.

Dorrel would have to infiltrate the palace and get her out by stealth, not by force. But he couldn't do that looking like a scruffy stable hand. And after six days of hard going, he looked scruffier than ever.

One of the people from the table approached. "Excuse me, sir. Is that your horse outside? The bay?"

"Yes."

"It's a fine horse."

"Yes, he is."

"How much?"

"I didn't buy him. He was a gift."

"Not how much did you pay for it. How much do you want for it?"

Dorrel shook his head. "He's not for sale."

"Come, now. How much?"

Dorrel speared the man with a glare. "That horse is priceless."

The man's eyes narrowed. "Really. Where's he from?"

Would answering this question cause more trouble than not answering? "The Chevallon Stables."

The man's eyebrows shot up, disappearing under the fringe of graying blond hair covering his forehead. "How'd you come by a Glynrellan horse?"

This ability to fool the locals was uncanny. "I am Glynrellan."

"Oh." The man's face went blank. Then he offered his hand, and Dorrel shook it. "I'm Trobed, a trainer at the Homuk Stables. I'm authorized to pay up to five thousand sovereigns for a good stallion."

Dorrel shook his head.

Trobed continued. "If you come speak to the owner, he might pay ten thousand."

"Not for twice that. Not for ten times that."

"Well . . . do you ever stud your horse? We pay fair fees."

"I'm sorry," Dorrel said, "but I haven't time."

"Well, if you pass by on your way home, please consider the offer."

Dorrel smiled in a way he hoped looked sincere. "I will." He considered his uncle would kill him if he let a Makutian breeder get hold of Chevallon stock.

Trobed rejoined his companions.

By the time the bartender returned, Dorrel knew what to do first. "Is there a barber nearby?"

While the bartender gave directions, Dorrel reached into his pocket and drew out six more staters. "Would you please change these for me?"

The bartender's eyebrows shot up. "Of course, sir. My pleasure." His voice dropped. "I can take them to Tylan to buy wine. Not that it's allowed, exactly." He winked. "But the customers like your wines much more than ours."

Dorrel shrugged. "Of course."

The bartender took the money and handed Dorrel nine gold sovereigns. "Well, if that woman really was your—what do you call her?"

Fiancée. Sweetest. "Curate."

"If that was her," the bartender said, "that trade agreement will finally go through. Then I won't have to make the trip. My regular suppliers can do it for me."

Unoccupied, the barber sat in one of his chairs reading a newspaper. When the door opened, he jumped, tucking the newspaper under the counter. "What can I do for you, sir?"

Dorrel hung his jacket and hat on the bentwood rack before sinking into the vacated chair. "A haircut, please, and a shave."

"Yes, sir." The barber draped a cloth around Dorrel's neck. Scissors clicked in his ears.

If he posed as a groom, he could say he'd taken a horse out for exercise. But the guards would know the palace grooms.

"Not too much off the top."

The barber chuckled. "Leave the ladies something to run their fingers through, eh, sir?"

Dorrel smirked. "Something like that." One lady, anyway.

Better than posing as a groom would be pretending to deliver a horse. Toban was fine enough for any royal stable. He still drew compliments after a week of hard going.

The barber stirred up foam in a mug. He slathered it on Dorrel's face, opened a straight razor, and began scraping off the six days' growth.

Fortunately, Dorrel could pass for a Makutian. He'd fooled two people already.

The barber didn't offer a choice of aftershave. He just splashed something on Dorrel's face that smelled sour.

"Do you have a washroom?" Dorrel rose from the chair.

"In the back, sir."

"Perfect," Dorrel said, though he doubted it would be.

The washroom was just a narrow closet, the basin a small pottery bowl. Still, the barber brought him a kettle of steaming water, and a sponge bath was better than none at all. Dorrel dried himself with a towel that smelled like dust.

He'd only brought one change of clothes—black leather hunting trousers and a white shirt. He put them on, then cleaned his jacket with a chamois. It was warm enough to go without a coat, but it provided another layer of protection over the mail.

He couldn't get a good look at himself in the tiny mirror over the washstand and wasn't at all satisfied with what he could see. He was just a student, a stable hand. Even if he could bluff his way into Domat's stable, how was he to get any farther?

*Ahbay, if this is the stupidest idea I ever had, please stop me.*

# Chapter 15

## THE GYNAECEUM

Wearing a faded, threadbare dress too small for her bust and flimsy suede slippers too big for her feet, Alara bounced along the road in the back of a covered wagon with Hanik, two privates, Ult, and the spaniel.

Canvas flaps covered the back of the wagon, so Alara had no view to inform her of their progress. Eventually they stopped, and Hanik handed her down.

Immense white marble walls surrounded a large courtyard. The central keep of the palace rose overhead. Its gleaming white towers might have been lovely, had they not held such dismal prospects for her. Wings spread from the sides of the keep, forming a courtyard between.

Sturg dismounted and said to Hanik, "Take her to the gynaeceum."

Hanik saluted, turned to Alara, and gestured to a door on the right.

Alara looked back over her shoulder. "Goodbye, Ult. Thank you for everything."

Ult waved. "Thank you, Curate."

Sturg grabbed Ult's arm above the elbow and walked away, pulling Ult after him.

Hanik took her through a hallway between the kitchen and the scullery, up a spiral staircase, past four floors. They stepped into a narrow passage. Halfway along, a wide corridor intersected it. They turned left. Sunlight spilled through tall windows at either end of the hall, forming a lattice pattern on the floor.

Hanik opened the first door on the right and leaned into a tiny office. "Alara Kordelyon is here."

A gray-haired woman sat behind a narrow desk. The corner of her mouth twitched slightly. Her eyes roamed over Alara's shabby attire, and she frowned. She took a key from a desk drawer and brought it to Hanik. "Last door on the left, sir." She curtsied. "I'll bring the maids shortly."

Hanik walked with Alara back the way they had come. A stocky blond soldier waited in the passage that led to the stairs. He saluted as they approached.

Hanik saluted in return. "Private."

"Welcome back, sir."

"Thank you. This way." Hanik led them down the hall. He opened the door and waved Alara into the room.

An upholstered couch flanked by ornately carved chairs faced a row of tall windows that poured in sunlight. The room was decorated in shades of peach.

She never had cared for peach.

Hanik stayed in the doorway. "Please make yourself at home."

She snorted. "Not likely."

In the hall, the private inhaled sharply.

Hanik met her gaze. "There's probably a bath through there." He pointed to a door. "No doubt you want to wash."

She nodded. It was hard to be friendly now, here, knowing what was coming.

He closed the door. The key clicked in the lock.

For a moment she stood there, staring at the golden doorknob. She turned to survey her prison.

Through the doorway she entered a dressing room. To the right, a bathing room decorated with the delicately painted tiles for which Redíquan artisans were renowned. A brass bathing tub sat at the far end. Straight ahead, a bedroom.

A high four-poster bed, draped in heavily embroidered curtains, dominated the room. The two mullioned windows in the outer wall could not be opened.

She hammered the diamond-shaped panes once with a huff. Then she drew a deep breath and returned to the dressing room. Its window was likewise fixed.

In the sitting room, she tried the paned doors that opened onto the balcony. The handles gave, and the doors swung inward. She loosed her tight breath and stepped onto the balcony. A subtle breeze stroked her filthy skin.

She leaned over the railing. Seventy feet to the ground, maybe more.

In the dressing room, she found no spare linens, only opulent, garishly colored clothing. She slammed a wardrobe door.

She could strip the bed sheets to make a rope, but would there be enough? And once she got down, how would she get past the guards?

If she started now, she might be done by nightfall.

Someone knocked on the door.

Striding into the outer room as if she were, indeed, at home, Alara met the woman from the office, two teenage girls, and a tall, thickset woman about Mum's age.

"Your Highness." The gray-haired woman curtsied. "I'm Maube, matron of the gynaeceum. If you need anything, the maids will get it for you."

The girls curtsied.

Maube held a hand out toward the other woman. "This is Rafal, our ladies' nurse."

Rafal curtsied. "Your Highness, I can change your bandages while the girls prepare your bath."

"Ladies." Alara raised her hands. "I'm not a highness, I'm a curate. If you won't use that title, please just use ma'am. And no more curtsying, please."

"We can comply with that in private, ma'am." Maube gave the girls a stern look, and they nodded. "But we must apply the queen's protocol in the presence of the royal family."

"Thank you." Alara went into the bedroom, followed by Rafal. "The cuts are healing nicely. They mightn't need new bandages."

Alara unbuttoned the borrowed dress and pulled it off, followed by her waist-long underbodice. "As for these"—she fingered the bruises across her abdomen—"nothing seems to be broken."

Rafal paled.

Alara was unaccountably pleased by that response.

"Begging your pardon, ma'am. I wasn't told about those." Rafal looked away, moving the basket that had been hanging from her elbow to a nearby table. "I only was told to see if you needed new bandages."

Maube's eyebrows twisted into a fretful expression. "The soldiers. Did they . . ."

"They beat me up," Alara said, "but from the looks of them, I gave them almost as good as I got."

"But did they . . ."

Alara wanted to make her say it.

"Did they offend your purity?"

Korig's stink and strength still gave her daymares, but Alara knew what Maube meant. "No."

Maube relaxed.

*Never try to take a Glynrellan woman alone.*

Alara shook off the memories. "Glynrellan women are trained to defend themselves."

Maube startled as if Alara had shouted.

Rafal removed the bandages. Her hands were cold and not as gentle as Hanik's. "Most of these don't need dressings any longer. Just this large one, I think."

The long welt ran horizontally across her upper arm a few inches below the shoulder. Puffy red skin swelled around the black stitches.

Rafal cleaned the area with an antiseptic that stung, but its coolness eased the wound's heat. "I'll put on a new bandage after your bath, ma'am."

Alara heard the attendants in the bathing room, stoking the fire in the stove and drawing water from the pump. Maube brought her a white linen robe.

She could dismiss them and start on the sheets. But Hanik was right. After six days on the road, she desperately wanted a bath.

The sheets would wait.

Alara tipped her head back over the rim of the tub. She had been praying continually since they left her. *Abbay, please help me escape.*

She needed to get rid of the attendants, who were chatting in the dressing room, and get to work on the sheets. She got out and wrapped herself in a towel. As soon as they heard her splashing, the girls returned.

She shooed them out. "I can take care of myself, thank you."

After drying off and putting on a robe, Alara combed and braided her hair. She stepped into the dressing room, gripping the end of her braid.

The attendants, who had been sitting on a bench, bounced to their feet.

"Is there something I can use to tie this?" Alara asked.

Farpar drew a thin white ribbon from a small basket on the dressing table. "Please, ma'am, let me." She tied the braid.

Rafal slathered the stitches with salve and bandaged her arm.

After she'd gone, the attendants took turns pulling dresses from the wardrobes. The fashion in Makut was immodestly deep necklines, garish prints, and color combinations that made her eyes hurt.

"Oh, no, please," she said, when they showed her the tenth such gown. "Ladies, may I have a plain dress? Like yours, Ebena." The blonde-haired attendant wore a plain yellow shift.

"Oh, ma'am, that isn't suitable for such as you."

"Where are my shirt and pants, then?"

The girls looked at one another as if silently negotiating who would answer. The task fell to Farpar. "Sorry, ma'am, but Maube said such things aren't suitable for a lady and sent them down to the furnace."

"Furnace? That was presumptuous." Alara plunked onto the cushioned bench and folded her arms. She took a deep breath and released it. "Please find me something plain."

Ebena and Farpar exchanged glances. "Princess Navka favors simple gowns," Farpar said. Ebena nodded, and they went out.

Alara sighed, glad to be rid of them. Once the door closed, she dashed to the bedroom and pulled the top sheet from the bed. Too bad she didn't have a knife or scissors; it would have made the job easier. She tore at the sheet with her teeth.

Some time later, the outer door opened. Alara shoved the torn strips under the cover.

She met the attendants in the dressing room. Farpar held a couple of dresses in her arms. Ebena held up one of them. "How's this, ma'am?"

It was a bilious shade of green, but at least it was all one color. Alara took the other dress from Farpar. Velvet the color of claret, trimmed with white lace at the neckline and sleeves. "This will do."

Ebena folded the other dress and put it into one of the cupboards.

They had another dispute when Alara learned the oddly-cut dress required a corset. Glynrellan women hadn't worn corsets since before the war. She gave in only because she wanted to get back to making her rope more than she wanted to avoid the corset. Nevertheless, the dress was still too small through the shoulders and sleeves. Princess Navka must be young, or slender, or both.

Ebena gestured to the brushes, glass jars, and clay pots on the dressing table. "If you'll have a seat, ma'am, we'll make you up."

"You mean paint my face? You won't."

"But —"

"No." Alara folded her arms.

Ebena opened her mouth to speak.

"That is final, Ebena."

Ebena ducked her head. "Yes, ma'am. Shall we do your hair, then?"

"My hair is done." The tight braid wasn't suitable for appearing at court, but it was perfectly suitable for shimmying down a makeshift rope after nightfall.

"But —"

"You must stop arguing with me, Ebena." Heavens! She sounded like Grandmammá Shardamayn.

"Yes, ma'am. Sorry." She looked to Farpar, and they withdrew.

The instant the door clicked shut, Alara returned to her work. But soon the door opened again.

Again, Alara hid the torn strips.

In the sitting room stood a gray-haired woman wearing a multicolored paisley dress. She was several inches shorter than Alara. An attempt had been made to contort her portly figure into an hourglass shape, using a corset that must have been even more painfully laced than Alara's. A thin gold circlet crossed her brow.

Alara refused to be cowed. "Yes?"

She raised her eyebrows. "Princess Alara?"

"No, Curate Kordelyon. And you are . . . ?"

She straightened her shoulders and drew herself up a bit. "I'm Queen Jorin."

Alara nodded, the closest she would come to a curtsy. "Ma'am."

The queen did not offer her hand. "I hope your rooms are suitable."

"Yes, thank you."

She moved to a chair. "You may redecorate to your liking. Inform Maube of your wishes, and she'll see they're met."

"What if I wish to go home?"

"My dear girl," the queen answered, "you are home."

Alara refused to sit and chat with her would-be mother-in-law. She folded her arms. "I disagree."

"Please sit down."

Alara stood beside, and slightly behind, the queen's chair. "No, thank you, ma'am."

"You'll address me as 'Your Majesty.' And you've yet to offer me a curtsy."

"Begging your pardon, Your Majesty, but as a Glynrellan, I'm not required to curtsy to anyone."

The queen turned in her chair to frown at Alara. "Do you treat your Redíquan relatives so poorly?"

"King Jentiérri understands that, since the abdication of Reyshara Kordelyon, Glynrellans need not defer that way."

"Really!" Queen Jorin turned away from Alara. "You'll need to learn some new manners, my dear, if you intend to succeed at court."

"I don't want to succeed at court. Not this court or any other. I only want to serve the people of Telshi."

Queen Jorin glowered at her.

*Kenna, she does not seem open to preaching. What am I supposed to do? Is this truly Your path for me? What about Dorrel?*

The queen stood. "I daresay my husband could've made a better match for his son."

Alara wanted to ask, then, why he hadn't, but she'd been impertinent enough for one day. She would get further with diplomacy than impudence. Besides, she was still praying. *Kenna, if this is the path You have chosen for me, tell me what to say.*

The queen straightened her massive, crinoline-supported skirt before turning toward the door. "Still, you're the one he chose, so we'll do our best to help you . . . adjust. Is there anything we can do for you to that end?"

"Yes. I wish to see Ambassador Divreenan."

Queen Jorin shook her head. "You mayn't entertain a man here."

"I don't want to entertain him here. I want to be taken to the embassy."

"That isn't possible."

"Why not?"

"You mayn't leave the palace." The queen said this as if it were obvious.

Alara almost asked whether that meant she was never to leave, but she didn't want to hear the answer. Another argument might be more convincing, from a Makutian perspective. "The ambassador has a duty to see me so he can tell my father I'm here."

"My son has already sent word to Ayenni of your safe arrival." The queen apparently saw no contradiction between *safe* and Alara's bruised face.

# Chapter 16

## DISCONCERTING

Commander Sturg sent Ult to the newsagent to fetch a week's worth of papers. After a quick bath, Sturg put on his dress uniform, as all soldiers did while on duty at the palace. The commander of the royal guard provided an office. Sturg had finished his third cup of coffee and started on his second newspaper when a private summoned him to General Kabed's office.

As he walked upstairs, Sturg planned what to say. He'd refrain from criticizing the woman. He'd just say it was an honor to have escorted the prince's bride. He considered apologizing for the delay, but since that was her fault, he decided not to.

He was surprised to find Prince Velek standing in the general's office. Sturg stood silently at attention in front of the general's broad pine desk.

Kabed was a short, thick man with a wide face and grizzled hair. His stoutness was solid muscle. Velek was nearly as tall as Sturg, but soft.

The general clasped his hands on the desktop and stared at Sturg for several long moments before speaking. "Commander Sturg, your orders were to bring the princess to Tarvag unharmed."

"Yes, sir."

"Explain why you failed to do so."

Had Hanik not taken the woman to the gynaeceum? "Sir?"

"My mother's nurse saw the princess," Velek said. "She has stitches in her arm, and she's covered in bruises."

"The ambassador's orders were to use any means necessary, Your Royal Highness."

"You found it necessary to beat her black and blue?"

"She put up quite a fight, sir. We had to defend ourselves."

General Kabed scowled. "From a woman?"

"She's well-trained, General. She held off two of us for several minutes."

Velek and Kabed exchanged a glance. "Perhaps you picked the wrong squad for this mission, Commander," Prince Velek said.

"Perhaps you picked the wrong bride, sir."

Velek's eyebrows shot up, but he said nothing.

General Kabed stood and stepped around the desk. He grabbed the front of Sturg's jacket, turning Sturg to face him. He slapped Sturg backhanded. "Insubordination won't do." The general returned to his seat.

Sturg made a small bow. "My apologies, Your Royal Highness."

"Commander, I could almost forgive the injuries done when you and your men were defending yourselves." Velek folded his arms. "But you kicked her when she was lying on the ground. How do you explain that?"

Hanik. He must've given the prince a report, making himself look good and Sturg look bad. "She needed to know further attempts to arm herself would be inadvisable."

Velek shook his head. "She was disarmed and beaten. Once that was done, further punishment was just vindictive."

Sturg remained silent.

Velek sighed. "General, I leave the discipline to you."

He walked out.

General Kabed sat at the desk for a minute, then stood. "Follow me."

The general headed for the door. Sturg turned and followed him downstairs and out to the courtyard.

Several of his men, and many of the palace contingent, were in the courtyard, going about their duties. So were some of the stable hands and other palace staff.

General Kabed led Sturg to the middle of the courtyard. "Commander," he said, in a voice loud enough to be heard in the kitchen, "you were to deliver your charge unharmed. You failed to do so. Put your hands behind your head."

Sturg did so. He braced himself.

Spinning, Kabed kicked him in the ribs.

Sturg staggered, then righted himself. He kept his hands clasped behind his head.

"How many times did you kick her when she was down?"

"Twice, sir."

This time, it was a side kick to his abdomen.

Kabed stared at Sturg for a few moments. "Dismissed." He walked away.

"Thank you, sir," Sturg muttered.

He hoped he wouldn't be ordered to serve with the palace guard on the day of Velek's wedding. Because if he ever saw the woman again, he would likely kill her.

The bed sheet was twice as long as her outstretched arms. Alara had torn it into twelve strips and had knotted most of the strips together. She hoped she hadn't miscalculated the distance to the ground. As she picked up another strip, the outer door of the apartment opened. She quickly hid her work.

Only Queen Jorin would presume to enter without knocking.

Why would she return so soon?

When Alara stepped into the sitting room, her nerves jangled at the sight of a man standing there. He had a soft, round face and pale brown hair graying at the temples.

"Curate Kordelyon." He stepped toward her.

She stepped back.

"I'm so pleased to meet you."

Only one man would dare enter her room. "I'm afraid I can't say the same, Your Royal Highness."

He sighed, retreating a step. "I understand."

She could guess what he'd come for. He wasn't muscular. She could beat him.

"Please, sit down." He gestured to the couch.

She did not move.

He sat down and watched her for a moment. "My father is anxious to get the formalities out of the way."

She clenched her jaw.

"We expected you several days ago. That would've given you more time to settle in, but now . . ." He faltered. "Guests are already arriving from the other districts. The wedding is set for the day after tomorrow, and my father sees no reason to delay. Not when so many of the nobility have traveled so far."

"The day after tomorrow. The fifteenth."

"Yes."

So that was what Ambassador Pavud had really meant when he told her father she needed to be in Tarvag *on time*.

"Will you please sit down?"

"No."

"Please. It's rather uncomfortable talking to someone who insists on standing on the other side of the room."

Her cousin Mehrialéna had called Velek dull but kind. And he was Bóhjetien's friend. She could at least give him credit for that.

She took the chair. "If you're uncomfortable, imagine how I feel."

He looked away. "I'm sorry. I never wanted any of this. It's all my father's doing."

"I see. So I'm not the only one who has to put up with a domineering father."

Velek grunted. "No."

"You said guests are arriving. Will Bóhjetien be one of them?"

"I'm afraid not. I was . . . dissuaded from inviting him."

"Is that because, if he were here, he would try to stop you?"

He shrugged.

"Have you spoken to Boh about this at all?"

"Ha! More like he spoke to me. When I last saw him, he gave me quite a lecture before I could explain the treaty wasn't my idea."

"Didn't it occur to you that his displeasure might give you reason to reconsider?"

"Curate, please understand, I fought this for months." He leaned forward, propping elbows on knees. "But I can't disobey the king."

"I see."

"I'm told there was a misunderstanding about the way his request was phrased."

"Yes. It was deceptive of Ambassador Pavud to slip that in."

"I suppose so. But now we're bound by the treaty."

"No, we're not. Accept the Glynnish interpretation." She switched to her language. "I've been presented to you. Done. Now let Ambassador Divreenan arrange an escort to take me home."

He clenched his hands, knuckles whitening. "I can't. Disobey. The king."

She huffed, stood, and paced the floor. "Why not?"

"If I don't remarry, my father will disown me."

Alara kept quiet, though she wanted to scream, *Be disowned, then!*

She took a deep breath. *Remarry.* She had forgotten he was a widower. The matter called for more care than she had considered.

Alara pinched her eyes shut. "So in spite of the misunderstanding, in spite of my refusal, you're going to"—she choked, swallowed—"to force yourself on me anyway?"

"No, of course not." His voice was remarkably gentle.

She looked at him. "Then let me go."

"I can't."

"Then what's the point?"

He propped one elbow on the arm of the couch and covered his eyes. "The point is the crown prince has indulged his grief long enough. The family honor is at stake. It's for the good of the country." His sour tone told her the words weren't his own.

"Yes, I got a 'good of the country' speech as well." She walked to the window and looked out on the half-timbered houses surrounding the palace.

"I'm truly sorry. The king has forced me to this."

She turned, back to the wall, arms folded. "To keep from being disowned."

Velek dropped his hand. "Disowned. Disgraced. Yes."

"Then why not marry a Makutian girl? There must be dozens who'd leap at the chance."

"Maybe a few." He shook his head. "But no Kivatan father would let his daughter marry me. Not after . . ." He scrubbed his face with both hands. "Not after the way I chastised the priests after Leerda died."

Little about the matter had appeared in the press. All Alara knew of it had come from her cousin Mehrialéna. "Can you tell me what happened?"

He slapped the arm of the couch. "Leerda was a Makutian princess by marriage and the daughter of a Temhainite duke by birth. She and the baby should've received a state funeral."

"Mehrialéna said it was disappointing."

"Ha! Her gift for understatement . . ." Velek cleared his throat. "The priest said the gods had revealed Leerda's weakness and removed her so a stronger woman could take her place." He put his head in his hands. "I didn't want a stronger woman. Leerda was bright and sweet. I wanted her." His voice choked.

Tears pricked Alara's eyes. Much as she wanted to fill the silence, she held her tongue. His grief needed space, not words. How long had it been? Five years? Six? She couldn't remember.

Not that it mattered.

He breathed deeply, then looked up, blue eyes rimmed with red. "That was the day I lost faith in the Kivatan gods. I'd never thought much of them before. They're crazy, you know. Capricious. But when the priest said that . . . I lost my mind. I don't even remember what I said. I just poured out fury on that poor old man as if . . . as if it would bring my wife and daughter back." He slumped back, limp, as if exhausted anew by furious grief. "In front of all the nobility. Now I'm branded an infidel."

*Ahbay, teach me how to counsel him.* Her cousins had been there. "How did Bóhjetien advise you?"

"He was no help, though he usually is. His talk of the will of Telshi —"

"Boh said *that* was the will of Telshi?"

"He said Telshi is sovereign and nothing happens without Telshi's approval."

"Pfft." Alara returned to the chair and sat. "Bóhjetien isn't the one who went to seminary. Listen to me." She stared at him until he looked her in the eyes. "A wife and daughter dying in childbirth is *not* the will of Telshi. That is the work of the Adversary."

"Is your god not omnipotent, then?"

"Yes, Telshi *can* do anything. That doesn't mean Telshi *will* do anything."

"You make Telshi out to be as capricious as the Kivatan gods."

She stiffened her spine as if Grandmammá Shardamayn were watching. "I beg your pardon. Telshi is not capricious. Telshi is kind — kind enough not to shuffle people around like pawns on a chessboard."

"So we are left to our own devices, then?"

"Not at all. Mairah gives us life. Ahbay will guide if we listen. Kenna will save us if we let her. But Telshi will not impinge upon our free will."

"You mean Leerda's death was a matter of her free will?"

"Not *hers*. But did she have a physician attending her?"

"Of course not. Only—"

He cut himself off.

Alara could guess his point. "Only men are physicians, and a man mayn't attend a woman in childbirth. Correct?"

His countenance fell. He nodded.

"I put it to you, Your Royal Highness, that Leerda and your daughter were not the victims of Telshi, but of Kivatan . . ." It took her a moment to recall the Makutian word. "Misogyny."

He covered his face with his hands, and a sound emerged—a sob, maybe. He scrubbed his face with his hands. "You said 'the work of the Adversary.'"

"Yes. The unjust death of innocents? Without a doubt."

He grunted and scrubbed his face again. "You've done more for my grief than your cousin did."

"Well, Boh can hardly be blamed. He's an equestrian, not a theologian."

Velek's shoulders jerked, almost as if he were laughing. "Yet you see the problem, Curate. My father guessed that since the Kivatan fathers wouldn't have me, a Telshan father might."

"The problem is he oughtn't ask the fathers, but the daughters."

"That gets me nowhere. I may not be a Kivatan any longer, but I'm no Telshan, either. Undesirable in every quarter." He looked her in the eye. "Including you."

"Sir, it's not that you're undesirable. It's that the entire situation is unconscionable."

"No doubt it is. But what can I do? If I disobey the king, he'll remove me from the line of succession."

"So? You have brothers. Aren't they just as capable of continuing the line as yourself?"

"Ha! Better, as the presence of my nephews proves." He stood and walked to the window.

"But if the king already has heirs through your brothers, why do you need—"

"If I'm disowned, I'm not the only one who'd be disgraced. My mother wouldn't be queen anymore. I can't let that happen to her."

"Why wouldn't she be queen?"

"My father will divorce her to give precedence to my half-brother Uked's mother. A divorced woman has no standing in Makutian society."

She closed her eyes, pinching back tears. So many casualties, Hanik lost count. For this? "You'd put me, my family, my friends, through all this—to protect your mother's social standing?"

He spun, glaring at her. "How much would you do to protect your mother?"

She closed the distance between them. "My mother derives her worth from her relationship with Kenna, not from her social position."

His voice turned sharp. "Your society is very different from mine."

"Yes, but you expect me to leave my society, where I'm valued for my gifts, and trade it for yours, where I'm not valued at all."

He took a step closer. "That's not true, Curate—may I call you Alara?"

She folded her arms and took a step back. "No, you mayn't."

He sighed. "You're valued by me."

"Oh, yes," she said, "because not only am I related to the Shardamayns, I'm also descended from the royal house of Kordelyon."

"Those are my father's reasons. You're everything he could ask for —"

"Everything except willing."

"You're also my friend's cousin, and Boh thinks highly of you. Which means I do too." Velek sighed. "I had hoped we could at least be . . . friends."

"Friends? After so much violence? You expect me to play along with this hoax just because Pavud deceived my father?"

"Your father understands how beneficial this alliance could be—"

"But he didn't understand that you intended to hold me to the Makutian meaning of 'presented.'" At least, she hoped he didn't. "He was only thinking about what he wants—increased trade. A boost to our economy before the election."

"That's good for your country, isn't it?"

"It should be possible to lift the embargo without treating me like chattel."

"I have no intention of mistreating you, Alara—"

"I told you not to—"

"Will you stop interrupting me?" Velek yelled. "It's extremely rude and disconcerting."

"Well, get used to it. Because I'm going to be much more rude and disconcerting than this before it's over. As for mistreatment"—she gestured to her black eye—"your people have already seen to that."

He sighed. "I'm sorry. Commander Sturg has been disciplined for injuring you."

"Oh." The words *Sturg* and *disciplined* didn't fit together.

"He was instructed to bring you safely. He didn't, in spite of Lieutenant Hanik's efforts to protect you." Velek's tone turned gentle. "He did try, you know."

She looked away, disarmed by the kindness in his eyes. "I know."

"He tells me the two of you got along rather well."

"Considering the circumstances, yes."

"I'm glad. He has always been a respectable soldier. That's why I sent him to be your escort. Unfortunately, my father thought you needed a higher-ranking officer to . . ." He faltered, raising open hands.

"To intimidate me into coming?"

His arms dropped. "I'm afraid so."

"He could've sent a general. I still would've run."

Velek nodded. "Since you're here now, I hoped you'd reconsider."

She shook her head.

"I know you've been hurt. Please let me try to make it up to you."

"Hurt? Hurt doesn't begin to describe it. Fighting broke out. How can you make it up to the wounded? Or the families of the dead? And you can't possibly make it up to me, when the abuse will only increase."

"I have no intention of abusing you."

"Then what is your intention?"

He spread his hands. "Am I so terrible? I know Mehrialéna thinks I'm dull but—" He grasped her hand. "Give me a chance to win you over."

She pulled away. "You're Boh's friend, and I respect that, but I can't . . ." For some reason, Alara felt she shouldn't mention Dorrel. "You can't win me over. Too many people were done too much harm."

"Fine." He walked toward the door. "The marriage is just a sham anyway. Keep a lover, I don't care." He turned back. "If someone else gets you with child, it will all be part of the pretense."

Her stomach churned. "Doesn't that defeat the purpose of producing heirs?"

"My purpose is only to protect myself and my mother from ruin. Choose anyone you want."

She shook her head.

"A Telshan, if you like."

Dorrel was no more likely to agree to such a travesty than she.

Alara looked him in the eye. "That's apostasy, what you're suggesting." She walked away. "Forced to marry a stranger because of a translation error?" She didn't like the rising anguish in her voice, but she couldn't stop it. "And then handed off to another . . . like a whore —" Her voice broke. She stood at the balcony windows, staring blankly out. "I'd die first."

"You wouldn't." He folded his arms. "I know that much about Telshans."

Suicide was anathema. But less so than what he proposed.

She turned to face him. Her voice turned cold and dry. "Don't try me."

# Chapter 17

## THROUGH THE CIRCLE

Dorrel approached the high stone walls of Tarvag. The city marched up a gentle rise of land, a cap of gleaming white spires at its center. The palace.

What bothered him most, even more than the intimidating walls, was the lack of trees. Kaesbaro and Ecciston were filled with them. But from the gate, he could see only a few sorry, straggly-looking specimens along the streets of Tarvag.

The gates stood open. A guard stepped forward and tipped his cap. "Here for the wedding, sir?"

As good a bluff as any. "Of course."

"Have a good stay, then, sir." The guard bowed.

"What's the quickest way to the palace?"

"Straight ahead, sir, then left at the Circle."

"Thank you." Dorrel rode through the gate.

"Thank you, sir." The guard bowed again.

Dorrel had never wished to visit the big cities he heard people speak of. Even though Alara spoke fondly of Ayenni and Darshalay, he had no desire to see them. He enjoyed the countryside, and he imagined cities to be crowded and noisy. Tarvag was both of these, and filthy as well.

Buildings three and four stories high loomed on either side. Most were plain brick boxes with few windows, all squeezed together with no space between. The narrow streets were lined with rubbish.

Most people walked. A few drove wagons pulled by oxen. Dorrel wove through the bustle.

The road opened onto a round plaza filled with people. Streets radiated from it at each compass point. A massive statue of a man on a horse towered over the hub.

King Domat's palace stood at the other end of a long, wide street that sloped upward from the Circle. Dorrel pointed Toban that way and quickened to a trot.

The palace walls loomed overhead. Twenty feet of smooth white marble. He'd need a grappling hook to make that climb. The palace beyond was made of the same stone. The central keep stood eight stories high—the spires taller still.

They had imprisoned Alara in there, somewhere. How to get in? How to find her? Where to start?

He crossed the street. Getting some distance from the imposing wall let him see more of the palace's windows.

Tall, carved wooden gates, flanked by turreted guardhouses, faced the Circle. Perhaps he could slip in through a service entrance at the rear.

It took a long time to pass the east side of the palace. Almost as long as from Kaesbaro's east bridge to the west bridge. On the north side, the gates were identical to those on the south and as heavily guarded.

His heart sank. But he continued his survey.

On the west side of the palace, a group of people stood in the street, looking up at the windows.

"Who is it?" an old woman asked.

"One of the king's wives," answered a younger woman.

"No," a man said, "that dress is too plain."

Dorrel had forgotten the Makutians' faith permitted polygamy. Alara being forced into marriage was revolting. For her to wind up as one among several would be an atrocity.

"Not thin enough to be Princess Navka," the young woman said. Those around her concurred.

"Could it be that Glynrellan princess?" the old woman asked.

"No telling. Nobody's seen her." The man still stared. "Unless that's her."

Dorrel followed the man's line of sight to a balcony on the fifth floor of the west wing. It required an effort of will to keep the prayer of thanks that welled in his heart from pouring out of his mouth.

It was her.

Velek had gone. Before returning to her rope, Alara went onto the balcony to pray. A warm breeze met her. The balcony faced west. Sunset glowed warmly over the city that ranged down the hillside.

She still knew nothing of Ahbay's plans. She didn't know if she was supposed to serve in Apanumon, or Kaesbaro, or Tarvag, or not at all. She didn't know whom—or whether—she was to marry.

But then, no one else knew such things, either. Why should she be different?

She recited aloud a prayer for day's end. She was in the midst of praying for deliverance when she noticed the people in the street below waving at her.

Though it was rude not to wave back, interrupting her prayers would be irreverent. She braced her hands on the marble rail, bowing her head. She prayed to Mairah for a speedy recovery for Regger and Marita and all those casualties Hanik had lost count of.

*Kenna, I'll preach in the gynaeceum if that's Your will. But it's not going well so far. Show me the path You want me to follow. In the clergy or out of it, I will be Your servant. Ocha.*

She lifted her head. Below, amid the milling people, stood a large bay stallion.

Toban. She'd recognize him at any distance. And Dorrel.

She almost called to him, but that would be futile. He was too far away.

The people around him waved hats and scarves, trying to get her attention. She waved, but her eyes were only on him.

Toban stood still as a statue. Dorrel kept his eyes on Alara. It had to be her. That posture was one of prayer. Who else in Domat's palace would be praying?

The setting sun bathed the walls of the palace in an amber glow. But Alara's face seemed dark. Bruised? He hoped he was wrong. But with the sun full in her face, it couldn't be a shadow.

The people around him waved. Dorrel raised his arm also, but with a different purpose.

He held his palm outward to her. *Stay there*. Then he raised his index finger and swung it in a circle. *Will come around the other side.*

With two fingertips, she tapped her temple. *I understand.*

"What was that?" one of the women asked.

"Some kind of Glynrellan salute," a man answered.

The first old woman squinted. "Is it the princess or not?"

"I suppose so."

"She's not a princess," Dorrel snapped. "She's Glynrellan."

The man next to him looked up. "Yes, that's true, technically. At least for the time being, eh, my lord?"

Dorrel stared at him. "My lord?"

"Oh. I mean . . . that is . . . begging your pardon, Your . . . Your Grace, but not knowing your proper title, I —"

"It's all right." Dorrel didn't wish to waste time sorting out the mutual confusion. "Forget it."

"Thank you, um . . . sir. No offense meant."

"None taken. Good day."

"And a good day to you, sir."

Dorrel glanced back at Alara's balcony. She was gone, the doors closed.

As Dorrel rode away, several others tossed "good day, sir" or "good day, Your Grace" at him.

He studied the people for the first time. All of them were dressed shabbily. Not in rags, but in ill-fitting, worn-out clothing of poor construction.

Dorrel had never given his clothing much thought. But his mother had always insisted he dress well, and Segra was an excellent tailor. Dorrel's riding trousers, his wrinkled shirt, even his jacket—a hand-me-down from an uncle—were all better made than anything these people wore.

And he had seen no one else on horseback.

Maube locked the doors to the balcony. She had come in with Farpar, who brought the dinner tray.

"It's five stories up," Alara said. "Do you think I'm going to fly away?"

"I was told to lock them so you don't do yourself an injury."

So Velek not only took her threat seriously, he'd passed news of it along.

Maube left her with Farpar and the dinner. Alara didn't feel like eating; her stomach was in a knot. How did Dorrel mean to get inside? But if they were going to escape, she'd need sustenance.

So she ate.

After she finished, she sat on the edge of the couch, arms wrapped around her middle, praying silently.

*Makutian noblemen and women sit in the high-ceilinged throne room. Their new king paces serenely up the red-carpeted aisle between banks of gilded chairs.*

*Sunlight glows on tall marble columns. The heir steps up the dais to the throne, his mother on one side, his first wife on the other. He turns to face his people.*

*A page, a small blond boy, bears a red velvet pillow. On top of the pillow is an imperial crown, trimmed in ermine.*

*A thin old man, bent with age, mounts the dais: a Kivatan priest, engulfed by heavy, ornately embroidered robes. He takes the crown in both hands and places it on the head of the new king.*

*"May the gods of our ancestors grant you long life, Sovereign King." He turns to face the assemblage. "King Domat is dead. Long live King Uked."*

Farpar's voice seemed to come from a long way off. "Ma'am? Are you all right?"

It took a moment for Alara's eyes to focus. "Yes. I'm fine." She trembled all over. "Please take away the tray and leave me alone."

Farpar took the tray and knocked at the door for the guard to let her out.

When the door clicked shut, Alara jumped from her seat and paced the room, clenching her fists and loosening them.

Uked would succeed Domat. That meant Velek would be removed from the line of succession. The king's plan would fail.

She dropped to her knees, bracing her arms on the coffee table.

*Kenna, until that vision about the election, You only showed me minor things. Who would marry whom. Which job a person would get. Whether someone would run for local office. Now, these are matters of national—international—import. Why are You showing me these things?*

**I am making your will match my own.**

For nearly twenty years, Kenna had been sending her messages. But never had Alara heard Her voice so clearly.

*Oh, Kenna! That's what I have prayed for, but everything is such a muddle. I can't deliver a vision to Prince Uked now. It's impossible! Besides, Dorrel's coming.*

**What happened to "in the clergy or out of it, I will be Your servant?"**

*Yes. What shall I do? Should I try to see Uked now? Or go with Dorrel?*

**Get up and go. You will know when it is time to share the message.**

The people in the street might mistake Dorrel for a nobleman, but the palace guards surely had a list of invited guests. Better to stick with the "delivering a horse" ruse than try to impersonate nobility.

A commotion started on the south side of the Circle. A large party of horsemen and two carriages came around the hub and up the street toward the palace.

He circled around a block of houses to come up on the group from behind. One of the horsemen at the rear looked Dorrel in the eye.

"Come up from Jabok, have you?" Dorrel guessed such a group must've come from the nearest large city.

The Makutian smiled. "Yes, and you?"

"I've come from Gadrut."

"Really? I didn't think there were any noble houses near there."

"No. I'm just bringing this horse from the Homuk Stables."

As if offended by this lie, Toban whickered and wagged his head.

"It's a fine horse," the man said.

"Yes, he is, isn't he?" By now the party had passed through the gate. "If you don't mind," Dorrel said, "I'd better go on ahead. Someone's expecting me."

"Of course. Will I see you at dinner?"

"Save me a seat!" Dorrel galloped around the side of the palace and found the stable. He refused assistance from the groom.

"He's an unruly brute. Quite dangerous." Dorrel led Toban into the narrow stall. It didn't give Toban room to turn around, and it hadn't been mucked out in days. But the manger was half-filled with oats, so Toban didn't seem to mind. "I wouldn't want any of you to get hurt."

"Very kind of you, my lord." The groom bowed. "I'll just bring water and leave the rest to you."

"Thank you. I'll be back shortly."

Dorrel headed across the courtyard toward the western wing. He brushed past servants as if he belonged there. No one said a word.

A stair near the kitchen spiraled up into the palace. He jogged up five floors, hoping he hadn't miscounted the levels from the outside.

He stepped into a narrow corridor. Halfway down its length, it was crossed by another, wider hall. He walked cautiously to this intersection. In the hallway on the right, a private stood outside a door. That must be Alara's room. Who else would have a guard?

The private put a hand on his sword.

"Pardon me, but I'm lost." Dorrel walked down the hall. "Can you direct me to Prince Velek's suite?"

The private's eyes narrowed. "Why do you need to know?"

"Well, you see . . ." Dorrel unleashed a side kick to the guard's stomach, knocking the wind out of him. He gripped the guard's shoulders and cracked his head against the wall. The private dropped unconscious. Dorrel found a key in the guard's coat pocket.

He slipped into the apartment, quickly closing the door behind him. Alara was kneeling in front of a table, leaning on her arms. She lifted her head. Her face was covered in bruises, and her eyes were red.

She ran to him, burying her face in his chest. Her arms tightly encircled his ribs.

He held her, brushing his cheek across her hair. Then he held her at arm's length so he could see what they'd done to her.

Gently, he cradled her chin, eyeing the purple and green blotches on her sweet face. His stomach clenched. "Tell me what happened."

"When they broke into the inn, I got beat up. That's all."

"Really?

She cocked her head to one side. "I would not lie to you."

"You've been crying."

She closed her eyes and swallowed. "I had a vision."

He'd never seen her so upset by a vision. But there was no time to talk about it. He reached for the doorknob.

Alara stopped him. "Do you have a change of clothes?"

"Not with me. Why?"

"I'll never get out of here dressed like this." She grabbed the voluminous skirt in her fists. "Makutian women don't ride."

He rolled his eyes. "We'll take a carriage. The grooms think I'm a Makutian nobleman. They'll probably give me one if I ask." He took her hand and led her out of the room.

"Why do they think that?" Alara stepped over the fallen guard. She stopped, pulling her hand out of his.

He looked back at her. "What?"

Alara gestured to the guard. "Bring me his trousers and coat. And the cap." She slipped back into the room.

Brilliant.

Dorrel quickly stripped the guard of his outer garments and took them to her.

In the dressing room, she had her arms twisted behind her back. She blew out an exclamation of disgust. "Undo these laces, love." She turned her back to him.

He dropped the guard's uniform on the bench. "You want me to help you undress."

"The thing is so stupidly designed, I can't do it myself."

He shook his head and unthreaded the laces. Too often he'd fantasized about taking her clothes off, but such a circumstance was beyond imagining.

She pulled the dress off, discarding it along with the bulky crinoline.

He should have looked away but couldn't. The corset cinched her waist into an unnatural shape, pushing her breasts up so they looked as if they would explode. The bloomers hid everything else.

A chuckle burbled up, but he choked it into a snort.

Her cheeks flushed red. "It doesn't feel as comical as it looks." She reached for the guard's jacket. "I'd take off this torture device, but I haven't any other sort of underbodice." A bandage surrounded her upper arm.

"What's that?"

She pulled the coat on. "Just a cut. It happened in the fighting."

He was healed, and the cleric was wounded. *Mairah, why?* He glanced at the lace in his hand. "Are there more of these?"

Alara started buttoning the coat.

"In the wardrobe, perhaps. Why?"

"To tie up the guard."

She grinned slyly, then went through a door to a bedroom. She returned with several strips of torn sheeting.

"Ha! Well, you weren't waiting idly, were you?"

Alara finished buttoning the black wool coat—just like Hanik's—then picked up the guard's trousers and pulled them on. She could barely get them over the bloomers. When she did, four extra inches of pant leg flapped at the ends of her feet. She rolled up the hems, tucking them to the inside. Her face still flushed hotly. She had imagined a lot of things with Dorrel, but never changing her clothes in his presence *before* they were married.

She coiled her braid atop her head and pulled the cap over it before stepping into the outer room.

Dorrel had dragged the guard inside and tied his hands behind his back with the lace from her dress. A strip of sheeting bound the guard's ankles. Dorrel tied another strip around the guard's mouth as a gag.

"Well, do you think I can pass for a man?"

He frowned. "Only if no one looks closely."

They jogged down the spiraling steps to the ground floor and walked past the kitchen. The staff was busy preparing supper. No one looked twice at them.

Side by side, they strode across the yard. The sun had sunk below the outer wall, shrouding the courtyard in shadow. In the stable, only a pair of lanterns shed any light.

Two stable hands stood chatting at the far end of the stable. When one of them stepped forward, Dorrel waved him off. "No, thank you.

We can handle it."

Alara saddled the mare in the stall next to Toban's. The groom craned his neck, looking past Dorrel to Alara. She moved around the horse, turning her back. Alara led the mare out. Dorrel followed.

They mounted and rode across the courtyard. As they approached the gate, Alara hung back, staying out of the torchlight. She adjusted the cuffs of the trousers so her feet were covered. Those satin slippers would surely give her away.

While Dorrel spoke to the guards, her heartbeat pounded in her ears. The grooms did keep calling him "my lord." Yet he was speaking plain Glynnish. Maybe they thought he was on Ambassador Divreenan's staff. If so, they were using the wrong form of address.

One of the guards glanced at her, but despite the poor fit of the uniform, he didn't give her a second look. Dorrel thanked the guards. Then they rode through the gates.

Alara took several slow, deep breaths to calm herself.

Dorrel turned westward. "Where's the nearest meetinghouse?"

She was glad they were both thinking along the same lines. There was just one problem. "I don't know. The church operates clandestinely here. The persecution is even worse than in Apanumon."

"Hmm." Dorrel grimaced. "We might be able to make Tylan by daybreak."

"Perhaps. But the Makutians will have fresh horses."

"Yes, but we have a head start." Dorrel prodded Toban to a quicker pace. "Let's at least head out of town. We'll stay off the road to make it harder for them to track us."

Alara had no faith in this plan. Staying off the road wouldn't help if Sturg used Ult's dog to track her again. "I think we should go to the embassy. There's a curate on staff there."

"All right. Which way?"

"I'm not sure, exactly."

He snorted. "Then how are we supposed to get there?"

"It's close by, Dor." She looked up and down the adjacent streets. "Divreenan once said it's near a place called the Circle. I take it that's some sort of—where are you going?"

Dorrel had turned Toban southward. "To the Circle. We passed through it on the way in. Didn't we, old man?"

Alara followed, her borrowed mare cantering to catch up. "How did Toban get to be an 'old man?'"

"By rendering distinguished service." Dorrel patted the stallion's chestnut neck. They soon reached the Circle. "Now what?"

She gazed up the streets that radiated, like spokes, in every direction. "It's on the east side, I think." What remained of the sunset was fading fast. She put it to her back and headed down the eastward street.

Dorrel pulled Toban alongside her mare. "Lar, what if the ambassador just turns you back over to them?" The question hung in the air for a moment. "Isn't he one of the ones who wrote the treaty in the first place?"

"He is. But I don't know where else to go."

# Chapter 18

## War Dogs

Sturg lay atop his bed, still dressed. It was too early for sleep, but he had nothing to do. So he lay there, concentrating on the pain in his ribs.

He almost wished Korig hadn't shot that woman at Denedra. The one who had nearly beaten Hanik. It might've been better to let her live and Hanik die.

Someone rapped on his door. "Sir? General Kabed wants you in his office immediately."

Sturg rolled out of bed. He pulled on his boots, then jogged upstairs to the general's office.

"Commander Sturg," Kabed said, "the princess seems to have escaped."

Sturg's blood rushed in his ears. "She was in the charge of Commander Evment's men, sir."

"They can't find her. I want you to help them."

Sturg took a deep breath, then let it out slowly. He couldn't lose his temper in front of the general.

But he wanted nothing more to do with the prince's bride.

"Princess Navka went to visit her," Kabed said. "She found the door unguarded and unlocked. The guard was inside, bound hand and foot, wearing only his shirt and undergarments. The princess released the guard. He told Evment a man attacked him in the corridor."

"Did he describe this man?"

"Tall, slim, dark-haired, wearing black leather riding clothes."

Sturg frowned. That description fit the militiaman who'd unhorsed Hanik. But Korig had shot him.

General Kabed continued. "She hasn't been found in the palace or the grounds, but she wasn't seen leaving. Evment's men will soon begin searching the streets around the palace. I've ordered the city gates closed. Since you and your men know her on sight, you'll lead the search."

Sturg was almost glad she'd escaped. Bringing her back, where Evment so far had failed, would help redeem him. "Sir, we should use the dogs to track her."

"Is that necessary? They'll head westward, obviously."

Sturg didn't admit he was excited by the prospect of watching a pack of war dogs tear the two Glynrellans, horses and all, to pieces. "Maybe not. This fellow most likely is Glynrellan, but he might be Redíquan. He might even be Makutian, from one of those Telshan groups one reads about in the papers."

Kabed frowned.

"If they hide nearby, the dogs will make a house-to-house search faster."

Kabed nodded. "All right, then."

Wandering the neighborhood searching for the embassy put Dorrel's nerves on edge. "I wish you had better directions."

"Sorry." Alara's tone was more petulant than apologetic. "Since I never intended to be in Tarvag, I didn't memorize the address. But the only place we're sure to find a curate is the embassy."

"Which is you-don't-know-where."

"Oh, stop!" She glared at him. "I am doing my best!"

He winced. Why were they bickering now of all times? "I'm sorry. But I do not want to get caught roving these streets."

"Neither do I!" Alara wailed.

"Lar. I'm sorry." He took a deep breath. "Divreenan said it's on the east side of the Circle. And?"

"I can't remember." Alara closed her eyes as if thinking, or praying. Perhaps both.

Dorrel glanced left and right, front and back. *Ahbay, You didn't bring us this far to fail now, did You? Help us.*

Alara paused at an intersection, looking up and down the cross street. "Of course," she breathed. "Thank you, Ahbay." She turned her horse. "This way!"

She galloped northward, toward a crenellated tower of white stone. Atop it flew a tricolor flag: horizontal bands of green, white, and yellow. Redíque.

Brilliant girl. He spurred Toban to catch up with her. Redíque had no part in the treaty.

In a nearby street, dogs barked.

Marita sometimes told war stories about the Makutian army's wolf-like dogs. About how a pack of them could take down a horse and rider, killing both and leaving nothing to burn but the bones.

Without needing to be told, Toban sprinted ahead, reaching the embassy gate half a minute before Alara's mare.

A gray stone wall surrounded the embassy. Dorrel spotted a guard in the stone turret near the arched wooden gate. "Guards!"

Behind Alara, a dozen dogs swarmed up the street, howling like a fierce winter storm. Gooseflesh rose on the back of Dorrel's neck.

The guard leaned out of the turret. "Who is there?"

Alara reached the gate. The dogs raced toward them, followed by horsemen.

Dorrel drew his sword and wheeled about, putting himself and

Toban between Alara and the oncoming troop.

She pulled the cap off. "I am Curate Alara Kordelyon. We need asylum!"

The guard disappeared from view, but they heard him inside, calling for reinforcements.

The dogs swarmed around them. Dorrel sent Toban into a capriole. He leapt, his hind legs lashing out, catching one of the dogs and hurling it across the street, where it fell, limp.

A crossbow bolt struck Alara's mare in the hindquarter. One dog had the mare's off hind leg in its teeth.

A tiny door in the gate opened. "In here!" a soldier called.

Alara jumped down. She kicked one of the dogs in the head. It fell back, dazed. She ran through the door.

"Open the gate!" Dorrel yelled. Toban reared and trampled a dog beneath his hooves.

"They are too close," the soldier called. "Come inside!"

A bolt struck Toban's shoulder, inches from Dorrel's knee. Two dogs leapt in unison, tearing into Toban's flank. He went down screaming.

Dorrel rolled away and sprang to his feet. He lashed out at the nearest dog, cutting its throat. The other he sliced open. Its entrails spilled into the street.

More dogs attacked. Several tore into the mare. Others came for Toban. Dorrel lifted his sword to meet them.

A bolt hit his right arm, just above the elbow.

"Get in here now!" The soldier hollered.

Sturg's enormous black stallion bore down on him.

"Dor!" Alara screamed.

He glanced toward her. Framed by the doorway, she strained forward. The soldier gripped her arms, holding her back.

A dog jumped at Dorrel, latching onto his left arm. He hacked his sword into its neck.

Sturg drew his sword.

Dorrel shook off the dead dog. He staggered back toward the gate.

A watery film covered his vision as he glanced once more at Toban's bloody hide.

A firm hand gripped his elbow, pulling him sharply back.

He stumbled into Alara's arms. They collapsed together onto the ground. The soldier kicked back a dog and slammed the door.

Sturg bellowed incoherently.

Outside, the horses screamed as the dogs tore into them.

"For the love of Mairah," the soldier, a captain, called to the man in the turret. "Put them down!"

Dorrel shook, sobbing. Alara sat behind him. He leaned against her. She wrapped her arms tightly around him, clasping her hands in front of him. Tears dripped off his chin, landing on her thin, strong hands.

The private in the tower loosed a shot from his longbow, then quickly nocked another arrow and shot again.

The screaming stopped.

The prayer was in Dorrel's head, though his constricted throat wouldn't make the words. Alara spoke for him.

"Mairah, thank you for Toban. He served us so well. Now it is time for him to return to you."

It was not time for Toban to return. He was young and strong and healthy. And he'd been so magnificent, done so much for them —

Alara rocked gently back and forth. "I'm sorry," she sobbed. "I am so sorry."

Sturg howled furiously as the door closed behind his quarry.

Five of the general's dogs lay dead in the street. The others were taking their fill of the horses.

In the gatehouse, a Redíquan private lifted his bow.

Sturg reined back, but the soldier wasn't aiming at him.

The Redíquan soldier shot the bay in the head, then the mare. Why? The animals were already done for.

"You can't harbor that woman!" Sturg called. "She's Prince Velek's."

"She's a member of the Redíquan royal family." The private spoke Makutian with a light Redíquan accent. "If Prince Velek wants to talk to her, he can take it up with the ambassador."

Sturg glanced at Korig, who had his crossbow trained on the gatehouse turret.

"Release her this instant!" Sturg said.

"We won't."

In a low voice, Sturg spoke to Korig. "Shoot."

Korig released his bolt, but the private dodged behind a merlon. He didn't reappear.

Sturg turned in his saddle to face Evment's corporal. "Take your squad and cover the rear gate. Send scouts to make sure there are no other exits."

The corporal saluted and left to carry out his orders.

Sturg turned back to Korig. "Sergeant, that man —"

Korig nodded, not taking his eyes from the turret as he fitted another bolt in place. "The one who killed Feolt."

"You said you shot him."

"I did."

"Maybe you missed." In truth, Sturg believed Korig's shot had struck. But obviously it hadn't been fatal.

Korig didn't argue. "It's not that strong a gate. A battering ram would make short work of it."

Sturg would need orders from the general before mounting a direct assault on an embassy, even to get the prince's woman. "Stay here. I'm going to brief the general. If he agrees, I'll return with two more squads and a battering ram."

Chain mail glinted through a rent in Dorrel's sleeve where the dog bit him. Alara thanked Telshi for Dorrel's foresight. That might mean the quarrel hadn't done much harm either.

Dorrel covered Alara's clasped hands with one of his own. With his free hand, he rubbed the tears from his cheeks. "Let me up, Lar."

Reluctantly, she let go. Maybe he didn't need her to hold him anymore, but she needed to hold him.

He stood. He pulled the quarrel from his arm and threw it onto the packed earth of the driveway. Then he picked up his bloody sword. He unbuttoned his jacket, reached inside, and drew out a handkerchief. He held it out to her.

She buried her face in it. She wasn't ready to stop weeping. But there was business to do, so she composed herself as best she could.

When she looked up, he'd taken out a chamois and was solemnly cleaning his rapier.

"Dor, I'm so sorry."

He slid his sword into its scabbard. He crouched in front of her and cradled her bruised cheek in his hand. "You have nothing to be sorry about." He stood and held out his hands.

Gratefully, she took them and let him pull her off the ground. She fell against him, wrapping her arms tightly around him.

"You're safe now." His voice sounded like gravel. "That's all that matters."

They leaned against each other, unmoving, until the officer behind her spoke. "Sir? Shall we bandage your arm?"

"What?" Dorrel looked at the torn sleeve. "It's not too bad."

Alara examined it. His arm bled, though not badly. "Let them wrap it before we see the ambassador."

He nodded and followed the captain into the guardhouse. Once the bandaging was done, the captain led them up the long arc of the driveway to a flight of broad stone steps. The white, crenellated tower loomed over them.

He showed them through a wide, marble-floored foyer. Ahead, a staircase curved upward. On the left, a pair of doors opened into a sitting room. "Please make yourselves comfortable. The ambassador shall join you presently."

The doors clicked shut behind him.

The room was paneled in dark wood and carpeted with a floral-patterned rug. The settee and chairs were covered in brick-red leather.

Dorrel walked to the fireplace. He leaned heavily against the mantel, which came up to his shoulder, and stared into the empty grate.

Alara took a step toward him. "Dor . . ." He didn't look up. She stepped closer still, reluctant to intrude on his grief but unable to bear hers alone. Quaking, she wept again. "Dor, I need you to hold me."

In two long strides, he closed the space between them and wrapped his arms around her. He stroked her hair with one hand. "I'm sorry, sweetest. I didn't mean to ignore you."

She sniffled. "I know."

"You're shaking."

"I can't make it stop."

"Well, don't try. It's been that sort of a day."

"Week, you mean."

"Yes. Cry some more if you need to."

"Not now. I'm trying to keep a clear head."

"Well, my shirt is ready when you are."

She chuckled feebly. "Thanks, love." She tipped her head up to kiss him.

His embrace was so fierce, it drove the breath out of her.

The door opened behind them.

Sheepishly, Alara turned to meet the ambassador, but she scarcely noticed him. She ran to the man who came in behind him. "Boh!"

He held her tightly. "Alara, thank Ahbay you are safe." Then he gently pushed her to arm's length. He was tall and lean with the same oval face and auburn hair as Mum. And his eyes were a light gray-green, just like Kyvern's. "Safe is not the best word, perhaps? But at least you are here."

"Yes," she said. "Oh, it is so good to see you."

"And you." Bóhjetien wore a cream-colored suit with no cravat and an open shirt collar. "This must be Dorrel Chevallon." He put out his hand.

Dorrel's eyebrows rose. He shook Bóhjetien's hand.

Alara giggled. "Yes. Dor, this is my cousin Bóhjetien Shardamayn."

They exchanged pleasantries. The ambassador hung back. He was a middle-aged man wearing a brown suit with a crisp, white silk cravat. His light-brown hair receded a bit at the temples. He stood in the doorway with a folder of papers tucked under his arm.

Finally, Bóhjetien introduced them. "This is Ambassador Rabicanoh."

The ambassador shook their hands. "A pleasure to meet you both. We are pleased to have you here, though I understand from the captain your freedom did not come without loss. I am very sorry."

Dorrel nodded.

Alara sank onto the couch. She put her hand in Dorrel's and drew him to sit next to her. The ambassador and Bóhjetien took the chairs facing them. Dorrel and Alara explained how they came to be there.

"You told the guard you need asylum," the ambassador said. "Of course, you have it. But King Domat shall certainly protest—"

"He may protest as much as he likes," Bóhjetien said. "I shall give him the same response he gave me."

Alara inclined her head a little toward him. "Which was?"

"Nothing."

She smirked. "I thank you for trying, anyway."

Bóhjetien shrugged. "The important thing now is to get you home." He turned to Rabicanoh. "Can you make arrangements with the Glynrellan ambassador?"

"Certainly, Your Royal Highness."

"Very good." Bóhjetien sighed. "I am glad neither of you was badly hurt in the battle."

"I would not call it a battle," Alara said.

"Not this." Bóhjetien gestured toward the street. "The one in which you were captured. I read of it in the papers."

"I have not seen the papers, and I did not see much of the fighting." She hesitated. "How bad was it?'

"Bad," Dorrel said.

She winced.

Rabicanoh passed her his folder. "I thought you might wish to see these." The folder contained clippings from the *Ayenni Daily Journal*. The headlines were horrid.

*Makutians at Denedra, Militia Unable to Hold Pass*

*Curate Kordelyon Captured*

*Seventeen Dead in Kaesbaro Battle*

*Prime Minister Denies Wrongdoing*

Palon had died before they even reached Kaesbaro. As Alara read each story, her tears and quaking increased, until finally she fell on Dorrel's shoulder, sobbing. He wrapped his arms around her. The folder and clippings slid to the floor.

Rabicanoh collected the papers and slipped out of the room.

Bóhjetien remained while Alara cried herself out. "The ambassador is seeing to your accommodations."

She turned Dorrel's handkerchief over in her hands, unable to find a dry corner. "Would you send for the chaplain, please?" She tucked the handkerchief into her pocket.

"Certainly." He got up and tugged the braided-cord bell pull hanging next to the fireplace.

Alara leaned forward, elbows on knees, her hands clasped. It seemed impossible to imagine the world without Palon in it. Her death left a void in Alara's heart almost as great as the one left by Kyvern's passing.

Dorrel slipped one hand around her wrist, poking his long fingers between her palms, prying one hand away. He held it tightly.

A servant came in answer to the bell. Bóhjetien asked for the chaplain, and the man bowed out of the room.

Ambassador Rabicanoh returned with a gray-haired man in the dark green dress uniform of the Redíquan army, the bars of a captain on his epaulets. Above the row of medals on the left side of his chest was embroidered the triquetra of their faith.

"Good evening. I am Chaplain Ivepafras." They stood to meet him, and he shook their hands. "I understand you have had quite a week.

What may I do for you?"

"Marry us," Dorrel said.

The chaplain stared, jaw slack, eyebrow lifted. Alara couldn't blame him. She'd be stunned, too.

Ivepafras took one armchair. Bóhjetien took the other, and the ambassador pulled up a wooden side chair from against the wall. Alara and Dorrel resumed their seats.

Ivepafras gazed at them a moment, then drew a deep breath. "You must know it is not that simple."

"I do," Alara said. "But I also know I cannot leave this building an unmarried woman."

Ivepafras nodded. "Neither can you rush into this —"

"It may seem abrupt to you, but I assure you it is not," Bóhjetien said. "My cousin has known this man for years."

"I see." The chaplain turned to Dorrel. "How long have you been courting?"

"Honestly?" Dorrel turned to Alara with a weary smile. "Two years?"

She smirked. "Hard to say."

Bóhjetien snorted. "It was at least four summers ago that letters to Alara began arriving at Shandór twice weekly from Kaesbaro."

Dorrel coughed and scrubbed the lower half of his face with one hand. "I didn't think anyone would notice your mail," he muttered.

"You have no idea," she groaned.

"Begging Your Royal Highness's pardon." Rabicanoh moved to the edge of his seat. "Regardless of the duration of the courtship, to marry off the crown prince's intended in his own capital . . . sir, that would be enough to start a war."

Dorrel stiffened.

Bóhjetien sank back, braced his elbow on the arm of the chair, and propped his forehead on his fingers. "You are right, of course, Ambassador." He looked at Alara. "I am sorry."

Had there been any tears left in her, she would have started crying again. "I understand."

There was a long silence.

"She's not his 'intended,'" Dorrel muttered.

"Well, of course not." She kissed his cheek. "I'm yours. Only he doesn't know that, does he?"

Dorrel fell against the back of the settee. "What do we do, then?"

"For now," Rabicanoh said, "rest. We shall have dinner shortly. I sent word to Ambassador Divreenan you are here. We can meet with him in the morning."

"Yes," Bóhjetien said. "Him and, I daresay, Velek."

Sturg brought the dogs back to the kennel master. As the handlers drove them into their cages, he recalled blustering about their being better suited to tracking the woman than a little spaniel. Still, Ult's dog had done well. And none of those wolfish monsters had ever given Sturg the sort of friendly companionship that spaniel did. Then again, neither had anyone else. Except, maybe, his late wife.

He cursed himself for getting sentimental in his old age—he wasn't that old, was he? No. Barely over forty.

As Sturg walked briskly across the courtyard to the palace, he slapped his gloves against his thigh absentmindedly.

He headed for the general's office, but Kabed's lieutenant directed him to the council room instead. There, a long ebony table surrounded by twenty chairs filled the room. Prince Velek sat at the head of the table, General Kabed on his right and Commander Evment on his left. Evment, too short and flabby for such a prestigious command, looked pale.

"Commander Sturg." The general gestured to the seat next to him. "Did you find her?"

Sturg paced the length of the table. "She reached the Redíquan embassy just ahead of us, sir. The dogs took their horses, but the two of them got inside before we caught up." He stopped at the chair Kabed had indicated but didn't sit.

General Kabed looked puzzled. "The Redíquans?"

Sturg shrugged.

"Of course the Redíquans," Prince Velek said. "They'll protect her as a member of their royal family."

"The embassy isn't heavily fortified." Sturg said. "With your permission, General, I'll return with more troops and a battering ram."

"You'll not." The prince raised his voice. "Thanks to your actions, we may already be on the brink of war with Glynrell. I won't risk a war with Redíque as well. The last time we tried such a thing, we were beaten."

Kabed stared at his hands on the table. The general hadn't fought in the war—he wasn't quite that old, though nearly so. "Your Royal Highness, we still should keep a guard at the embassy, in case she tries to leave the country in the night."

Prince Velek turned his head away for a moment. When he turned back, he nodded, his expression sad and rather pathetic.

Sturg expected to be dismissed, but he wasn't.

"Commander Evment," the general said, "what did you learn about the man who helped her escape?"

"A nobleman fitting the description the guard gave was seen leaving with a soldier about that time," Evment said, "but no one saw the princess."

Sturg tensed. "What 'nobleman' was this?"

"The grooms said he came with the party from Jabok," Evment answered.

"And what do the people from Jabok say?"

"Only one member of the party knew him. He said the nobleman is from Gadrut and was meeting someone in the palace. He must have a friend stationed here, and the two of them went for a drink." Evment sounded confident.

Sturg would crush him. "Do your soldiers often socialize with noblemen?"

"Well, I don't know—"

"Does anyone know this nobleman's name?" Sturg leaned across the table, braced on his outstretched arms.

"No . . ." Evment looked positively watery.

"What noble family is from Gadrut? Have your men found him or their comrade at any of the nearby taverns? Are any of your men unaccounted for?"

"N-not that I'm aware of," Evment stammered.

"Fool." Sturg straightened. "The guard's uniform was stolen. The 'soldier' seen leaving with the 'nobleman' was the princess."

"On horseback?"

"She's Glynrellan, you idiot." Sturg threw his gloves on the table. "She probably wears pants more often than a dress. She rode with us from Glynrell to Gadrut." He snorted. "She's probably a better rider than you."

Evment spluttered.

Kabed turned to Sturg. "Do you know who this man is?"

"Yes, sir. He's a Glynrellan militiaman. We fought him in the town where we found the princess. He killed Private Feolt and unhorsed Lieutenant Hanik."

Prince Velek looked up. "Didn't Sergeant Korig shoot that man?"

"Yes, sir."

"Yet he survived to commit this intrusion."

"It was dark, and they both were at a gallop."

Velek nodded.

"Commander Sturg." Kabed stood. "Return to the embassy with reinforcements and keep it guarded."

Sturg saluted, collected his gloves, and turned to go.

"Commander," Velek said.

Sturg turned back.

"Tell the Redíquans I wish to meet with the ambassador in the morning."

# Chapter 19

## WHAT MUST BE SETTLED

Dorrel woke up disoriented in a huge bedroom with sunlight angling sharply through the windows. He'd slept past sunup. Again.

The previous day came back at him in a rush.

Those hideous bruises on Alara's face.

That fierce race up the street, Sturg close behind.

The terrible cries of the horses. Toban going down in a pack of war dogs.

The newspaper clipping listing Regger and Stohan and his other dead friends and neighbors.

He caught his breath, choking back a sob.

Lying there feeling sorry for himself would do no good, so he got up, bathed, and put on a suit of clothes borrowed from one of the staff.

Someone knocked at the door. He trudged to the sitting room, still barefoot.

Captain Barláhtiay, the officer who'd met them at the gate, stood in the hall. He was a little shorter than Dorrel and solidly built, his pale-brown hair cut short. He held his peaked cap under his arm. "I am sorry to bother you, sir. Ambassador Rabicanoh says Prince Velek and Ambassador Divreenan are expected shortly after breakfast. Come to the foyer when you are ready, and a servant shall show you to the dining room."

Well, at least he hadn't missed the meal. "Thank you."

"You are quite welcome. Also, my men recovered the horses last night. We are preparing pyres in the front courtyard."

Unable to speak, Dorrel just nodded.

"The laundress has the things that were in your bags. And the saddler has your tack. What he cannot repair, he shall replace."

"That's not necessary."

"Perhaps not, sir, but it is being done anyway."

Dorrel's voice creaked. "Thank you."

The captain made a slight bow before departing. Dorrel eased the door shut. He moved across the room and lowered himself onto the thickly stuffed sofa facing the fireplace. He hadn't thought about having to light the pyre.

He sank deep into the seat, stretching his legs out in front of him.

Another knock.

He didn't want to talk to anyone. "Who's there?" he yelled.

"Your intended."

Anyone except her. He jumped up and opened the door.

He grabbed her and buried his face in the soft skin where her neck met her shoulder and kissed her there. She giggled.

He rested his chin on her shoulder.

"I overheard Barláhtiay talking about the pyres." She pressed her hands against his back.

He sighed and straightened.

She wore a lemon-yellow gown with white lace trim. The neckline was wide and rather deeper than he was used to seeing her wear. A tan line showed where the collar of her shirt had been. Her hair was pinned up in a puffy bun.

"Thanks for saying the prayer yesterday for Toban." He still held her waist.

"You didn't seem up to it."

"My voice wouldn't have worked if I'd tried." He shook his head. "I'm not sure I'm up to lighting the pyre, either."

"If you ask Captain Barláhtiay, I'm sure he'll see to it."

Dorrel gaped at her. "No! I'll do it myself. It wouldn't be right not to."

She patted his shoulder. "Well, I suppose you're up to it then, aren't you?"

He kissed her. "You know me better than I know myself." He kissed her again, and hugged her, and kissed her again.

Alara nudged him away. "Go put your shoes on before this gets out of hand."

After breakfast, while they sat in the dining room finishing their coffee, a server stepped in to announce Prince Velek's arrival.

Rabicanoh took them to a large room down the hall. Double doors stood open, revealing a long, wood-paneled room where high-backed chairs upholstered in dark green velvet surrounded an oval table. A man in a blue-green brocade suit stood to the left of the table. Dorrel knew who that must be.

Dorrel's borrowed suit was dark-blue wool with a cutaway coat and a black waistcoat. When Ivepafras had brought it to him, he thought it too formal. Now it seemed he was underdressed. The ambassador's charcoal-gray suit and Bóhjetien's tan one, while more conservative than the prince's, were of finer fabrics than Dorrel's. And their lace cravats, though not as elaborate as Velek's, were more formal than Dorrel's linen one.

Sturg and his lieutenant, both in dress uniform, stood near the wall behind Prince Velek. Every muscle in Dorrel's limbs drew taut. He was pleased to see the green smear of a half-healed bruise around Sturg's right eye. A bruise the size of Alara's fist.

Bóhjetien shook Velek's hand. "It is good to see you, my friend. I do not think I have ever before been in Tarvag without being welcome in your home."

"Not my doing, I assure you."

Bóhjetien turned to Dorrel and Alara. "Velek, I believe you have met my cousin Alara."

Velek made a little bow, and Alara nodded.

Sturg bristled and glared at her.

Only because he didn't wish to disgrace their host did Dorrel refrain from crossing the room to give Sturg a few more bruises.

"And this"—Bóhjetien gestured toward Dorrel—"is her fiancé, Dorrel Chevallon."

Velek's gaze returned to Alara. "You did not mention an engagement."

"It did not seem prudent to do so."

"Indeed," Velek said.

Alara turned to the server. "I believe the laundress sent up a package."

"Yes, Curate." He went into the hall, returning with a bundle wrapped in brown paper and twine.

"You may give it to Lieutenant Hanik."

Hanik stared first at the package, then at Alara with a quizzical look.

"The clothes I wore yesterday," she said. "The guard's uniform is cleaned and pressed. It is in better shape than when I got it."

"You have spent too much time in Makutian uniforms, Curate."

"Yes, I have, Lieutenant."

Dorrel frowned at her. How could she banter with one of the men who kidnapped her?

Rabicanoh smiled, gesturing to the chairs on either side of the table. "Please, let us sit." He took the seat at the head of the table.

Bóhjetien pulled out a chair for Alara, then sat between her and the ambassador. The Makutians sat on the opposite side of the table. Once Dorrel had settled into his chair next to Alara, Rabicanoh asked the server to pour the tea.

While the server distributed teacups, Alara asked, "Are we expecting Ambassador Divreenan?"

"Yes," Rabicanoh answered. "Any moment."

After a minute with no sound but the clinking of china, Velek gestured toward the courtyard. "May I ask . . . what are the structures outside?"

"Funeral pyres." Rabicanoh stirred his tea. "For the horses that were killed yesterday."

"You perform funerals for animals?"

"We cremate the dead because decay breeds disease."

"Full funeral honors are reserved for animals that render admirable service." Alara put her hand on Dorrel's knee.

He covered her hand with his.

Sturg leaned toward Velek and murmured something, but Velek interrupted. "Speak up, Commander."

Sturg glared at Dorrel. "One of those horses was stolen from the palace."

Alara used her sweet-sarcastic voice. "Do you want it back?"

Sturg broke his gaze from Dorrel to glower at Alara. "No. It was an old mare, no good for eating. Only for the dogs."

Dorrel's stomach turned. Sturg must know Glynrellans didn't eat horseflesh.

"We appreciate your disposing of the remains," Velek said. "But the owner must be compensated."

Alara leaned toward him. "And Dorrel must be compensated for the loss of his horse, which was no old mare."

Ambassador Rabicanoh and Prince Velek both looked about to reply when a server stepped into the open doorway. "Ambassador Divreenan."

Divreenan walked in, wearing a glaring purple and yellow paisley. He was a rotund, middle-aged man, older than Rabicanoh, nearly bald, with only a thin gray fringe of hair. Behind him were two men, younger than Dorrel, in plain gray suits.

Divreenan crossed the room to Alara. He clasped her hand in both of his. "Curate Kordelyon, I'm so glad to see you."

"Ambassador." She pulled her hand back. "Dorrel, this is Ambassador Divreenan. You've heard me mention him."

She said this so lightly, as if they were meeting him at a party, that Dorrel nearly laughed. Almost everything she'd ever said about Divreenan had been invective.

Dorrel shook hands with Divreenan, who then introduced his attachés. They sat, and the server served them tea and topped off everyone else's.

Ambassador Rabicanoh placed his hands flat on the table. "Your Royal Highness, I can surmise why you are here. But of course we must hear you say it."

Velek nodded. "The matter is rather complicated by this news of Curate Kordelyon's engagement. My instructions from the king are to bring her back to the palace immediately."

"Out of the question," Bóhjetien said. "You know I have objected to this from the start."

Velek leaned across the table. "And you know I am bound by the king's wishes."

Bóhjetien smiled gently. "I have told you many times, my friend, how your bonds may be loosed."

"Your counsel has caused me more trouble than I care to discuss."

Bóhjetien shrugged. "I said what I must."

"That is not what we must settle today," Velek said, "even if we could."

"What must be settled today is the matter of my cousin's freedom, which is not negotiable."

"Gentlemen." Divreenan straightened his papers. "If one reads the treaty in Glynnish, understanding that when one person is 'presented to' another it simply means an introduction has been made, then the clause in question has, in fact, been fulfilled, since Curate Kordelyon came to Tarvag and met the crown prince."

"But if one reads the document in Makutian," Velek said, "the clause has not been fulfilled, because she should have remained under my protection."

"Protection?" Dorrel tensed. "Take a look at her, and explain how you define 'protection.'"

Velek clasped his hands on the table. "I have apologized to the curate for the injuries done to her before she arrived at my home."

"He did," Alara whispered.

Dorrel glowered at her. She pleaded with him through her eyes.

"Ambassador Divreenan, is Prime Minister Kordelyon aware of Sergeant Chevallon's actions?" Velek asked.

"Not at all," Divreenan said. "Nor am I. To what actions do you refer?"

"Sergeant Chevallon crossed the border without documentation, infiltrated a royal palace, and removed a member of my household—"

"Liberated a prisoner," Dorrel said.

The prince ignored him. "All while in civilian clothing."

"I'm not regular army."

Alara squeezed her eyes shut.

"Begging your pardon, sir." Velek opened a folder of newspaper clippings. "According to your own newspapers, the militia unit at Denedra, of which you are a member, was called up more than a week ago. Which means you, sir, are on active duty. And out of uniform."

Dorrel's mind raced, along with his heart.

Velek was right.

He hadn't even thought about his uniform. There hadn't been time at Denedra. And Etton didn't tell anyone to get in uniform. Even if he had, Dorrel couldn't have worn his. It was in his dormitory room.

Besides, he couldn't have gotten past Gadrut, let alone into the palace, in uniform.

Which was, of course, the whole point.

Velek droned on about international law and clandestine operations, and Alara tightened her facial muscles, which meant she was trying not to cry.

Rabicanoh held out a flat hand as if signaling a halt. "Your Royal Highness, Mr. Chevallon has been granted asylum. I shall not extradite him without orders from King Jentiérri."

Was that a bluff? Dorrel found it hard to breathe.

"Such orders shall not be forthcoming, I assure you." Bóhjetien jabbed a finger at Velek. "Dorrel is under my protection. We shall not give him over. You must yield on that point."

Velek's eyes narrowed. "You wish me to yield on every point, but I cannot."

"Then we are at an impasse."

"It seems so." Velek stared at his clasped hands. He let out a long, deep breath. "I had hoped we could settle this as friends, Boh, and avert an all-out war."

Dorrel's furious trembling deadened, as if a weight held his nerves in place.

"We can renegotiate the treaty, Your Royal Highness." Divreenan fidgeted with his papers. "We wish to halt the aggression as much as you do."

Velek looked up. "Prime Minister Kordelyon had best do his own negotiating this time, Ambassador, to avoid any further misunderstandings."

"Ah." Divreenan stared at the sheaf in his hands. "I am not certain when—or, indeed, whether—such a thing shall be possible."

The tension in the room grew stiffer, along with Velek's posture. Velek speared Divreenan with a glare. "I urge you to persuade him to come. Because, in addition to the trade agreement, we must sort out the matter we were discussing before you arrived."

Divreenan looked from the prince to Rabicanoh. "And that was?"

"Reparations," Alara said. "But with no clear victor, and no declaration of war, how do we proceed? How do we compare that mare to Dorrel's stallion? Can you put a price on the wound in Dorrel's arm, or Hanik's?"

What did she know about Hanik's wounds? Dorrel hadn't seen him wounded.

Velek dismissed this with a wave of his hand. "Casualties must be counted as combat losses. Soldiers cannot be penalized for the results of open combat."

"But this was not a state of war," Alara said.

Dorrel put a hand on her arm. If she pressed that point, she'd have Dorrel guilty of murder. He did regret the private's death, but he didn't wish to go to prison for it.

"We can't be held liable for defending ourselves," Sturg said.

Dorrel glared at him. "Defending? Let's not get into the question of who was defending whom."

"No." Sturg met Dorrel's eyes. "That wouldn't serve any of us."

Dorrel hadn't expected to agree with Sturg on anything. "Exactly."

Alara patted Dorrel's hand. Ah, she understood. He drew his hand back.

Rabicanoh's brow furrowed. "Deciding upon appropriate reparations is complicated by the fact that we have only the newspaper accounts of what happened at Denedra and Kaesbaro."

"You were at Kaesbaro," Sturg said to Dorrel. "Can't you give an account?"

"I was shot, unhorsed, and knocked senseless. I left the next day."

"We shall have to write to get a full report," Divreenan said. "Who chairs the Kaesbaro town council?"

The second attaché's pen hovered over a piece of fresh paper.

Dorrel answered, "Marita Graylin."

"As the crown prince has suggested"—Rabicanoh nodded toward Velek—"it would be better to negotiate face-to-face with all concerned in attendance. Not only Prime Minister Kordelyon, but also Chairwoman Graylin and Prelate Dalys."

"A summit?" Velek's eyebrows rose.

Rabicanoh nodded. "Precisely. Rather than sending letters back and forth with demands and counteroffers, let us assemble all parties in an open forum. There is historic precedent." He turned to Bóhjetien. "Is there not?"

Bóhjetien smiled. "Certainly. Since the treaty that ended the last war was written at Shandór, it would be fitting if a meeting there could avert another war."

"An excellent idea." Divreenan laid his hands on the table. "When shall we convene?"

"That shall depend upon how long it takes everyone to get there." Rabicanoh looked at Alara. "Which is farther from Shandór: Ayenni or Kaesbaro?"

"Kaesbaro."

"It was six days from there to Gadrut." Hanik's comment earned him a sharp glare from Sturg.

After a few minutes' discussion, they concluded that four weeks would be more than enough time to get news to everyone and for delegates to travel to Shandór.

With Divreenan's second attaché acting as amanuensis, they composed a missive to the concerned parties. When he'd read it back and everyone approved it, the attachés removed to an office to make copies to be dispatched by military courier.

"If I may, ambassador," Alara said, "I would like to write some letters to include in the diplomatic pouches."

"Certainly. Mr. Chevallon, you may do the same, if you wish."

"Thank you, ambassador." Dorrel was almost as eager to send news home as he was to get news from home.

"Velek," Bóhjetien said, "I need your assurance that Alara and Dorrel shall have safe passage from Makut to Redíque."

"That is beyond my ability to promise." Velek closed his folder. "But I shall take your request to the king."

Bóhjetien nodded.

Rabicanoh stood. "Then we shall adjourn and reconvene at Shandór in four weeks."

They rose. Except Alara, who folded her hands atop the table.

Divreenan turned to her. "I am glad we shall be able to work things out satisfactorily, Curate."

She didn't look at him. "Ambassador Divreenan, dozens of people are dead. Things are far from satisfactory." She looked up at Velek. "Your Royal Highness, may I have a word with you privately?"

Velek's eyebrows shot up. "Certainly, Curate." He sat back down.

Dorrel leaned close to Alara, whispering. "The vision?" He couldn't imagine anything else it could be.

She nodded.

He straightened, patted her shoulder, and left the room.

A server closed the doors, leaving Alara and Velek inside.

Dorrel didn't know whether to wait for her, within earshot, or get on with what he had to do. The others stood around talking, and he couldn't bear Divreenan's simpering.

"Come," Bóhjetien said. "You have an unhappy task to prepare for, yes?"

Yes. But Dorrel still eyed the conference room doors.

"Velek is my friend. He can be trusted. Besides . . ." Bóhjetien looked at the door, then back to Dorrel. "She could beat him."

Dorrel turned his head aside, snorting out something like a laugh. Bóhjetien clapped his shoulder and accompanied him out the front door.

From the topmost step, Dorrel got an appalling view of the chest-high pyres. Black cloths had been draped over the corpses.

Captain Barláhtiay waited between the pyres. When he saw Dorrel, he took a few steps forward.

Dorrel trod down the steps and across the drive to meet him.

"The one on the left is yours, sir."

Dorrel had cremated horses before, but never one so much in his prime. Never one lost in combat.

The wind shifted, stirring the sharp smell of kerosene.

He reached for the shroud.

Barláhtiay's hand lashed out, grabbing Dorrel's wrist. "You do not wish to see."

"Yes I do."

The captain shook his head. "Do not, sir. Remember him as he was."

He stopped resisting, and Barláhtiay released him.

Dorrel took a step back.

A private arrived, carrying a pair of unlit torches.

*Mairah, forgive me. Toban is dead, and Prince Velek is threatening war. I never thought freeing Alara would lead to this. I just wanted her to be safe.*

She was safe. But her safety had come at such a great price—could that be part of Ahbay's plan?

*Ahbay, help me. I just did what I thought was right, the best way I knew how. I didn't mean to start a war.*

But it hadn't started with him. It had started with the Makutians sneaking that "presented" clause past Divreenan. And Dorrel had done the right thing. He'd done the only thing he could do.

*Kenna, save us. This mess not being entirely my fault doesn't stop it being awful and unjust. Not just what happened outside the gate. Everything. Stohan and the others—I killed a man! Dozens of people are dead, Alara was horribly beaten, and we may soon be at war.*

Kenna said Telshi could rescue the faithful from their enemies, and Telshi would guard those who believe and give them peace.

*Telshi, rescue us, guard us, and give us peace. Ocha.*

After the doors closed, Alara took a deep breath and released it slowly. From her jaw to her hands, every muscle had drawn taut. "I gather Bóhjetien has told you something about our beliefs."

"A great deal."

"Has he told you some believers receive supernatural gifts from Telshi? The ability to heal, or speak foreign languages, or see the future?"

"I've heard something of the kind. But surely that's just superstition or trickery."

"I beg your pardon, but it's neither. I'm a seer. I sometimes receive visions from Kenna showing me the future."

"Really. But you didn't foresee any of the recent events?" He almost sounded sarcastic.

"Kenna only shows me what She thinks I need to know. And She only reveals things that are Her will. But that's beside the point. The point is, when I receive such a vision, I must inform the people it concerns."

"Why are you telling me this?"

"Because I had a vision, and it concerns you."

Velek's eyebrows lifted. He waited.

"When your father dies, you won't succeed him. Prince Uked will."

He narrowed his eyes. "When will this happen?"

"I don't know. In the vision, Uked didn't look very old. In his late thirties, I suppose. Maybe forty."

"He's thirty-seven now."

A heavy silence hung between them.

"As odd as this sounds, Your Royal Highness, I must request an audience with your brother so I can tell him."

Velek frowned. "You'd return to the palace? After all that's happened?"

"It'd be far easier if he'd come here, but I doubt he would."

"I doubt he'd grant you an audience at all."

She doubted it, too. But she had to—

"I'll tell him." The moment Velek spoke, peace flooded through Alara, washing away her tension. The vision wasn't for Uked—it was for Velek.

"That will do, sir. Thank you."

"But I don't expect him to take it seriously."

"Do you take it seriously?"

"I . . . I'll have to give it some thought." His eyes drifted as if he were thinking of a place far away. "It gives me much to consider. More than you know." Velek frowned, his expression as grave as if he'd been told his father were already dead.

When Alara and Velek stepped into the hall, Hanik and Sturg snapped to attention.

With a silent nod, she took her leave of the prince and headed for the doors. Men pushed both doors wide open and fixed them in place with large lead doorstops.

Alara paused at the top of the steps. Dorrel, head bowed, stood in front of the pyre.

There was a funeral to conduct, and she was totally unprepared. Would Chaplain Ivepafras expect to do it? She turned to find him and nearly crashed into the ambassador's wife. "Oh! I beg your pardon, madáme."

Mrs. Rabicanoh, a pudgy, middle-aged woman with an elaborately piled and curled blonde coiffure, stopped in the doorway, the chaplain beside her. She smiled. "No harm done, Curate." She stepped aside and continued down the steps.

Chaplain Ivepafras carried a handbell and a book of Scripture. "Did you wish me to assist, or would you prefer to do it yourself?"

"If you would read the Scriptures, that would be ideal. I have barely given it a moment's thought."

He nodded. "Quite understandable. I was going to suggest the fourteenth chapter of Rychiana and selections from the fifth Canon."

Her eyes went heavenward in thanks. "Lovely. Thank you for thinking of it."

"Well, I had all morning. You had other things to attend to."

Many soldiers and some of the staff had begun to file out, moving around those on the porch and making their way to the courtyard. They gathered in a loose group on the drive, between the steps and the pyres.

Alara accepted the handbell from Ivepafras.

Velek stood on the top step, near Bóhjetien. He opened his mouth, hesitated, then blurted, "May I stay?"

"Of course," she said.

Hanik did not betray any surprise at his prince's request. He'd been stone-faced all morning. But Sturg had, more than once, allowed his feelings to show. Now his eyes darted to the prince, and his jaw clenched.

Ambassadors Divreenan and Rabicanoh emerged, and everyone moved down the steps. The others joined the congregation, but Alara and Ivepafras stood with Dorrel and Barláhtiay.

"Are you ready?" Alara asked.

Dorrel nodded.

She turned to face the assembly, then chimed the bell three times. "Kindred, we gather to commit to eternity these two beasts of burden, who have rendered exemplary service not only to their masters, but to me." Her voice cracked, and tears sprang to her eyes. For once, she let them. "Let us pray."

Heads bowed.

"Telshi, you put us over the animals so we might use them to our advantage. Yet you also gave us the responsibility of caring for them. We have done so to the best of our ability. Yet through circumstances beyond our control, we lost these."

Her voice creaked again. A tear escaped, rolling down the side of her nose.

If Rector Orizozabil were there, she would omit the next part, replacing it with something less likely to stir her volatile emotions. But he wasn't, so she said aloud what she'd been praying silently since the previous evening. If anyone didn't like it, well . . . she could take the criticism.

"Ahbay, Dorrel lost not only a magnificent steed, but the companion of half a lifetime, one he raised from a foal and trained himself." She pushed the prayer out despite the constriction in her throat that threatened to strangle her. "Comfort him in his grief. There will never be another to equal Toban, but guide Dorrel as he searches for one that might fill his purpose."

Dorrel sniffed. She didn't dare look at him.

"Ocha," she said, and the congregation echoed.

While Ivepafras read the Scriptures, Alara drew out the handkerchief she'd hidden in her sleeve.

When the chaplain finished, she and Dorrel each took a torch, which a private lighted. A drummer and a bugler played a dirge.

Dorrel moved to one pyre and Alara to the other. She went around it, poking the torch between the logs to light the kindling in many places, so the flames would do their job as quickly as possible. Dorrel did the same.

Sturg paced next to his horse in the driveway, near Velek's carriage. He glanced their way with a scowl.

The blistering heat soon made it uncomfortable to stand near the pyres. Alara had to raise her voice for the second prayer to be heard over the roar and crackle of the twin infernos.

"Mairah, yesterday we committed to you the spirits of Toban and this nameless mare. Today, we give you their substance. You create all things from the dust of the earth. To such dust, when life departs, all things must revert. Take the remains of these lifeless bodies and use them to foster new life."

"Ocha."

After a minute's silence, those in attendance solemnly drifted away. First Divreenan's carriage then Velek's rolled along the curved driveway, around the edge of the broad green where the pyres burned, and out the gates.

Alara drew close alongside Dorrel and twined her fingers with his. He squeezed her hand, tightly, and stared into the flames.

"We still have Willow," she said. "That was my consolation when I lost Vinnaq. Willow can carry on the bloodline."

He nodded.

"Not that the Ecciston Chevallons don't have others in his line, but —"

"I know what you meant, Lar." His grip on her hand eased a bit. "Thank you for that prayer. About finding another to fill the purpose. I needed that. I—" He cleared his throat. Then he let go of her hand and put his arm around her shoulders, pulling her close. "I hadn't known what to pray for."

# Chapter 20

## BEING IN THE SERVICE

Dorrel kept vigil over Toban's pyre, prodding the timber when necessary to keep the flames hot. Alara lingered awhile at the mare's pyre, but Dorrel could read impatience in her fidgeting. Barláhtiay's men repeatedly offered to do the work for them. Dorrel declined, but eventually Alara accepted the offer. She patted Dorrel's arm and walked inside.

The sun was high when Mrs. Rabicanoh came after him. "I know you feel this is your duty, Mr. Chevallon, but please allow others the privilege while you come in to luncheon."

Dorrel watched the plume of smoke rise to heaven. Flakes of ash drifted about the courtyard. It wasn't only duty. He owed Toban that much. And more. But he also didn't wish to be a rude guest.

A mock pout pinched her face. "If you do not come, I shall be very cross, and the others shall have to bear the brunt of my fury."

She'd shown herself to be such a kind hostess, he couldn't imagine her having any sort of fury at all. His lips squirmed as if trying to remember how to smile. "Well, I can't have that, ma'am."

One of the privates who had stayed close all day was the fellow who had put the horses out of their misery. Dorrel handed him the poker he'd been using. Then he went to his room to wash up. He combed ash from his hair.

When he returned to the foyer, Mrs. Rabicanoh paced, wringing her hands. "Oh, Mr. Chevallon. The curate is in the library." She pointed to a room just off the foyer, opposite the sitting room. "Please speak with her while I find Chaplain Ivepafras."

Dorrel crossed the foyer and stopped in the archway that opened into the library. At a writing table covered by books and papers and a tea tray, Alara sat sobbing into a tea towel.

He crouched next to her chair. She put her arms around him and leaned on him, sobbing and shuddering for another minute.

Finally she sniffled, and drew a few deep breaths. "Oh, Dor, it's so awful. And it's all my fault . . ."

"What? No, Lar."

"If I'd just done what Father told me to—"

"They'd have forced you to marry Velek, and you'd have been treated like . . . like a prisoner of war."

"And Palon and the others wouldn't be dead."

She wouldn't like his reply to that. So he remained silent and held her while she wept.

Chaplain Ivepafras leaned into the room a few minutes later. "Shall I join you?"

"Please." Dorrel gripped her shoulders. "Lar. Come here." He drew her to a little chaise longue upholstered in wine-colored velvet.

Alara leaned against its one arm, and Dorrel sat next to her. Ivepafras drew up the chair from the writing table.

She took a deep breath. "When all this began, I did not know what to do. Father sent me one way, Rariden another . . . when we stopped in Kaesbaro, and I had time to think about it, I realized my place—" She sniffled again and took another deep breath. "I am a seer, Chaplain. Last year I had a vision that I would do mission work in Apanumon. That is my post. That is where I belong. It seemed returning to the mission was Telshi's will."

Dorrel wrapped his arm around her shoulders. "Surely. The violence is the prime minister's fault for trying to take you away from that."

"But had I not run away, forty-one people would not be dead."

The chaplain let this statement hang in the air for a few moments. "But does that make their deaths your fault? Are they not the fault of those who wielded the weapons?"

She slapped her chest. "I wielded weapons!"

"So did I." Dorrel drew away. "I killed one of those men myself. I'd have killed them all to stop them from taking you."

"Oh, Dor . . ." She stroked his cheek.

"You were doing Telshi's will, and I like to think I was, too."

"Certainly," Ivepafras said. "The Scriptures tell us a marriage such as the Makutians would impose upon you is contrary to Telshi's will. As I understand it, your father was deceived by the Makutian ambassador's phrasing of the request."

Alara nodded.

"And who is the father of deception?"

She winced. "The Adversary."

Dorrel got a chill.

Ivepafras leaned toward them. "You chose not to follow your father's plan, and people were killed. But that plan was the product of deception—of the Adversary. Kenna showed you a plan that was the product of Her truth. As Her servant, you were bound to submit to Her will."

"But so many casualties . . ."

"As servants of Telshi, we continually battle the Adversary. And the prophet Galardi says that in such conflicts, Telshi's servants often suffer. You are one of the casualties. Would you rather obey Kenna's will and be kidnapped and wounded, or abandon Her and be safe?"

"I could never abandon Kenna. But—"

"Those who gave their lives were members of your army—your militia, yes?" Ivepafras looked at Dorrel, who nodded. "They all knew being in the service might cost their lives." He smiled gently. "They chose to defend you with their lives, because it was the right thing to do. Not only for you, but for their country, their church, and their Telshi."

"Ocha." Dorrel let go of Alara's hand and put both arms around her, because she was weeping again.

The Rabicanohs' private dining room was a windowless chamber set far back in the embassy, near the kitchen. White-painted wainscoting trimmed the walls below pale green and white paper. An oil-lamp chandelier lit the room. The round table, covered in white damask, was set for five with white china rimmed in gold.

Bóhjetien and the Rabicanohs were waiting for them. Once Alara and Dorrel sat, Ambassador Rabicanoh led them in prayer. A pair of men in white coats served them.

There was little conversation.

After the meal, once the servers had cleared the dishes, Bóhjetien pushed his chair back and slapped his thighs. "I know just the thing." He looked at Dorrel. "I must put you both to work."

"How so?" Dorrel asked.

Bóhjetien smirked. "You are an equestrian, are you not? Captain Barláhtiay has a troublesome pupil. Just the thing, I think, for a Chevallon to put his hand to. And we must keep Alara from introspection for a little while."

Dorrel stared into the space in front of him. He looked to Alara, her bloodshot eyes like a mirror of sorrow.

Her voice was tight. "I could do with some air." She put her hand on his knee. "And it's not like you to sit idle."

He squeezed her hand. "Right." He stood. "Let's have a look at this pupil, then."

The three of them changed into riding clothes and met Barláhtiay in the rear courtyard. He took them across the gravel yard, around a carriage house, and across a broad lawn to a pair of stables.

While Bóhjetien and Alara went into the first stable, Barláhtiay brought Dorrel to a small, wiry man near the doors of the second stable.

Barláhtiay introduced Dorrel. "This is Thente Lémoroh, our head trainer." They shook hands. "I would like Mr. Chevallon to see Bastion."

Lémoroh's skin was wrinkled and darkly tanned, his head covered with bushy salt-and-pepper hair. He sent a groom to fetch the horse. "Darshalay is supposed to send us finished three-year-olds, but Bastion came to us lacking discipline."

Dorrel wondered why Lémoroh hadn't finished the horse himself.

Every equestrian knew of the all-white horses Redíquans used for ceremonial functions. But Dorrel had never seen one before. The groom returned with a huge white stallion a hand taller than Toban. Nothing Dorrel had heard or read adequately described the refinement of the parade horse's conformation. If Bastion's chest were broader and his legs thicker, he could be taken for a charger.

Barláhtiay took the reins from the groom. "He knows his maneuvers, but his piaffe and passage lack finesse. And he refuses to stand still."

"He is fractious," Lémoroh said, "and has thrown several men."

"I suppose you can handle him." Barláhtiay smiled. "You are one of the Ecciston Chevallons, are you not?"

"Nearly. My father's from there."

Barláhtiay handed Dorrel the reins.

Dorrel checked the cinch and stirrups, then mounted. Bastion shuffled his feet, sidling.

Dorrel signaled a halt, but Bastion kept at it. Dorrel tightened the reins and deepened his seat, but the movement continued.

"You see why we cannot use him," Barláhtiay said.

"He wants to move. We'll let him." Dorrel put the horse through a few paces around the grassy yard. Bastion occasionally tossed his head and snorted. When Dorrel asked for a capriole, Bastion did it almost gleefully. Then, without permission, he reared.

Dorrel pulled the reins tight, winding them around his hands.

Bastion whinnied, then bucked. The force rattled Dorrel back and forth, and every muscle in his body fought it. He pulled back hard on the reins, drawing the horse's head up and back. "None of that."

Bastion whinnied in protest and stamped his foot.

"That one does not like his paces," Lémoroh said, fists on his hips. "Only the gallop. And he likes his airs above ground too much."

"Does he? Well, he can have them, then." Dorrel ran Bastion through all of the airs a few times before returning to the paces.

Alara and Bóhjetien, meanwhile, raced in circles around the embassy grounds on a pair of slender chestnut horses with spindly legs.

By the time a servant announced dinner, Bastion was willing to do what was asked, even the piaffe and the halt.

"Well done!" Dorrel jumped down and patted the horse's head. He turned to Lémoroh. "Do you have something I can give him?"

Lémoroh grabbed an apple from a basket inside the stable door and tossed it to him.

Dorrel caught it and fed it to the horse. "Well done, Bastion."

"You have bested most of these fellows, sir," Lémoroh said. "Few can keep a seat on Bastion once he starts to buck."

"I haven't been thrown since I was a kid." Dorrel rubbed Bastion's nose and neck.

"You may think he has learned his lesson, but he has not. He shall try it again."

"Of course he will." It would take time and trust to break a habit that bad. "But he won't get away with it next time, either."

Alara and Bóhjetien had already taken their horses back to the first stable. Dorrel took Bastion into the other.

"The grooms shall take care of him, sir," Lémoroh said. "You ought not keep the Rabicanohs waiting."

"I ought not walk away from this horse after I've been punishing him."

A stable hand showed Dorrel to Bastion's box and brought him grooming tools.

When he was nearly done grooming Bastion, Alara arrived. She leaned on the box's gate. "Boh didn't rush you, did he?"

"Not at all." Dorrel brushed Bastion's right front quarter and patted his neck. "It was just the thing. After this week, I needed something . . . normal."

She nodded, her eyes drifting away.

"I mean . . . I don't know anything about diplomacy or espionage or . . . war. But I know horses."

"Yes, you know horses better than anyone. Even Boh. You realize he only suggested this because it's what he would do in a similar situation."

"Well, he is a true equestrian, then."

She smiled, just a little. "He said the same thing about you."

The afternoon's diversion did keep Alara's mind off the bloodshed. Mostly.

Later that evening, as sunset approached, Bóhjetien led her and Dorrel down a wide, wood-paneled corridor, past sitting rooms and offices.

At the end of the corridor, above an open set of double doors, hung a gleaming triquetra. Through the doorway, the chapel's beamed ceiling rose two stories high.

Tapestries of scenes from Scripture covered the left wall. The right wall contained three arched, diamond-paned windows. Kerosene lamps in sconces and tall candelabra flanking the rostrum filled the chapel with a glow like the sunset outside.

They took seats near the front. The Rabicanohs came and sat with them.

Before the service began, a couple of privates brought in a washstand.

"Oh . . ." Alara moaned. Just what she needed. And Dorrel, too.

Dorrel leaned closer. "What?"

"It's surely appropriate, but I'll need a handkerchief."

Mrs. Rabicanoh handed her one.

The meeting followed the usual order of worship. By the time for silent confessions, the light outside was dim.

Chaplain Ivepafras stood next to the washstand. "Kindred, in recent days a peace of fifty years was shattered. The violence came to our very gates. Those who feel they have blood on their hands may come forward to receive absolution."

Trembling, Alara stood and walked to the rostrum. Dorrel followed. Behind him, the private who had put down the horses.

The chaplain poured water on their hands and dabbed some on their heads. "Kenna, Your sacrifice alone atones for the sins of the world. Remind these warriors, who drew blood in Your service, that by Your grace Your children are forgiven. Mairah, we pray for Your healing hand upon the wounded. Ahbay, we pray for Your comfort upon the families of the fallen."

*Kenna, forgive me. Had I known the cost, I wouldn't have fled. I would've—*

She felt her prayer interrupted, as if Kenna laid an invisible finger on Alara's lips. She unfurled the handkerchief. Dorrel put his arm around her and ushered her back to her seat. She leaned on his shoulder, weeping, while the chaplain read from the newspaper clippings the names of the Glynrellan dead.

"Captain Palon Madrew . . ."

# Chapter 21

## Departure

On the day that should've been Prince Velek's wedding, the incensed nobility raised a tumult. Some called for the expulsion of the Redíquan ambassador. Others said Chevallon and the woman should be hanged in the Circle. Sturg agreed.

Velek promised everything would be settled at the summit, but his words had little effect.

The nobles started leaving after lunch. Kabed called up Sturg and his men to help Evment's people direct traffic in the courtyard and the streets around the palace.

But Hanik was spared this miserable duty. He had been transferred back to his former post as Velek's bodyguard.

Once the trains of horsemen and carriages had gone, Sturg was called to Kabed's office. The general told him to sit. It was an order, not an invitation, so he sat.

Kabed handed back Sturg's recommendation that Korig be promoted to sergeant major. It was marked "denied" in large, red letters.

"Commander, how could you recommend such a man for promotion?"

"Sergeant Korig is an exemplary soldier, sir."

"Exemplary soldiers don't attempt to cuckold the crown prince."

Only Hanik would've reported that incident.

"His behavior was unworthy of a sergeant major's stripes."

Once denied a promotion on such grounds, a soldier was unlikely ever to get a chance at another. At least Korig didn't know the application had been made. Sturg never need speak to him of it.

Kabed handed over another paper—a written reprimand to be added to Korig's service record. He pushed pen and inkbottle across the desk. "As the officer in command, you should've written this, not me. Sign it."

Sturg signed.

"My lieutenant will fetch Korig. When he gets here, you'll give him his new assignment." Kabed handed over a sheaf of papers. "And you'll cut him to corporal."

Sturg roiled, fighting to contain the heat in his veins. He stared at the papers.

Korig was being transferred to Nidug, a small town far from anywhere. There was nothing for a soldier to do there but put down the occasional peasant uprising. Another blow from which Korig's career would never recover.

Sturg then understood how Corporal Radig must've felt when Hanik said his arm had to come off. Before Sturg could grasp what the loss of Korig would mean to his command, the general continued.

"Korig proved himself unfit for foreign service. And so did you, Commander."

The pages rattled in Sturg's hand. He put them in his lap. Every muscle quivered.

"I haven't decided what to do with you yet, but you'll not return to Ayenni. You'll remain here, on inactive duty, till the summit."

Sturg rose, dropping Korig's orders on the desk. "Whatever you wish to do, General, do it now. The summit is of no concern to me."

"But you're of concern to the prince. He demands you attend."

Sturg sat. "Yes, sir."

A silent minute later, the lieutenant showed Korig in. Sturg gave him the requisite dressing down, removed the sergeant's insignia from his sleeve, and gave him his new orders.

"Commander," the general said, "I'm told you took a sword from the princess."

"Yes, sir."

"I'll have it."

How many injustices must he endure because of Hanik's duplicity? "Yes, sir."

Kabed sat down. "Dismissed."

Sturg and Korig walked down the corridor side by side. Korig had, to his credit, displayed no emotion through the whole absurd scene. Once they were out of earshot, Sturg muttered, "That all was against my will."

"Thank you, sir." They descended the stairs. "What could he want with that sword?"

"Who knows? He's my commanding officer. He has a right to ask." But few officers ever exercised that right anymore. "Maybe the prince wants it."

They left the palace and headed toward the barracks.

"The prince should've fetched his own woman, then. If he had, we mightn't have three men dead."

Sturg agreed, but it wasn't something that should be said aloud. "Don't let anyone else hear you say that."

Korig entered the barracks, while Sturg went to the gymnasium nearby to feed his tension to a punching bag.

The meeting at the embassy had been bad enough. Sitting through days of such politicking at the summit would be torturous. And the woman. Her very presence would mock both him and the prince.

And how dare Hanik feed reports to the general behind his back?

Each blow of his fists against the bag sent a jolt up his arm that burnt off his anger. Or maybe stoked it.

Alara thought training Bastion was just the thing Dorrel needed to occupy his mind and hands. Not only during that first day of mourning, but through the week that followed, while they were essentially under siege. They couldn't leave the embassy, because the Makutians would presumably arrest Dorrel—or execute him—on sight.

He insisted on giving the horse's name in Glynnish, instead of the Redíquan *Vestan*. The others didn't seem to care, so Alara didn't correct him.

Alara had no such occupation of her own, although when the solstice arrived, she and Chaplain Ivepafras led the observance of the Resurrection of the Redeemer. What was meant to be a joyous celebration was instead subdued.

Once that had passed, Alara was left ruminating about Ivepafras's implication that the Adversary had played a part in the treaty negotiations. She spent her days in the library, filling sheaves of paper with study notes and speculations.

King Domat wanted to ensure Velek's line of succession, and her father wanted re-election. *Yet neither of these will happen,* she wrote. *Kenna has shown me this. That must mean—mustn't it?—that Her plans for Velek and for Father are related somehow.*

If only Kenna would speak to Alara again and tell her what to do. Little in her training had prepared her to cope with the Adversary interfering with her ministry, let alone with the politics of two countries. But Kenna said nothing.

One day at teatime, Bóhjetien entered the sitting room with a hefty, cream-colored envelope and a broad grin. He handed the envelope to Dorrel.

Alara recognized King Jentiérri's seal.

Dorrel broke it carefully. He withdrew the papers and read the first one, frowning.

"What is it?" Alara asked.

"Papers of diplomatic immunity." Bóhjetien filled his teacup. "For safe passage to Darshalay."

Dorrel unfolded the second sheet, which was vellum. He elbowed Alara. "Help me with this. I can't make out these letterforms."

It was no wonder. The page was so ostentatiously illuminated as to be nearly illegible. The Redíquan words "Majesty" and "King" were written in large script. The illuminated picture in the upper left hand corner was the capital in "His," but one could tell that only by deduction.

She sighed and leaned against him, reading aloud. "His Majesty the King requests the presence of Dorrel Chevallon—Oh, Boh," she looked up at him. "You did not ask—"

"I only told him Dorrel needed safe passage." Bóhjetien shrugged. "Anything further is his own idea."

Alara sighed again.

"Go on," Dorrel said.

"Can I sum up? Because it is just a verbose pile of—"

"Not again . . ." Bóhjetien rolled his eyes.

"—florid rubbish." Alara talked right over him. "Jentiérri is calling you to an audience."

"Me? Why?"

Bóhjetien took a seat. "Because you are engaged to his cousin, obviously."

"But the summit is in Shandór."

"We shall have plenty of time to go to Shandór after you meet Pappá," Bóhjetien said. "Besides, the rest of the family are in Darshalay, and they wish to meet you."

"Oh." Dorrel stared at the page.

"Do not worry, Dor," Alara said. "You shall get along fine. Besides, it is only fair. I have met your family."

"Only Mum and Dad and a few of the Arkens. Not any of the Ecciston branch."

Bóhjetien's teacup halted halfway to his lips. "You are related to the Arkens? Of the Arken Vineyard?"

"Yes. My mother was an Arken."

"Well, I hope you shall get us a bargain on claret." He sipped his tea.

Dorrel chuckled. "I'll see what I can do."

The following morning, after a sunrise prayer meeting and a lavish breakfast, the retinue assembled in the front courtyard.

A color guard headed the column. The soldier on the left carried the Glynrellan flag. On the right flew the Redíquan tricolor. In between rode a private carrying the Shardamayn banner, a field of green divided by a vertical band of white, the family crest in the center.

The escort included ten cavalry and two bowmen. Although a copy of Dorrel's diplomatic papers had been delivered to King Domat, there was no telling what the Makutians might try.

Except for Bóhjetien, who'd brought his own horse, each person had a white parade horse. Bastion had been saddled with Dorrel's tack, so expertly repaired one couldn't tell it had been damaged.

Alara put on her new hat, dark-blue straw with a black silk ribbon circling the crown. The ribbon ends threaded through the brim, and she tied them under her chin. She wore black trousers and a forest-green gambeson with diamond-patterned quilting.

In addition to the gambeson, Barláhtiay's armorer had equipped her with a sword and a brigandine. Like the one she'd worn when she served in Denedra's militia, its black leather shell was polished to a gleaming finish. She'd buckled it tightly so it skimmed her torso. Even if Makutians were, like the bartender in Gadrut, unaccustomed to seeing a woman on horseback, none would now mistake her for a man.

Dorrel wore a similar gambeson and brigandine.

Ambassador Rabicanoh shook their hands, and Mrs. Rabicanoh fell on each of them in turn, smothering them with maternal hugs as they took their leave. "Do have a safe trip. We shall see you soon."

Dorrel put on his hat. The laundress had worked wonders. The dark-brown felt was crisp, almost like new. Bastion obediently stood still after Dorrel mounted.

Bóhjetien drew his brown stallion into position on Alara's left. Dorrel was on her right. Barláhtiay took his place with the bowmen behind the color guard, then signaled to a soldier. The guards opened the double gates wide.

The procession rode through, flags waving gently. They used the passage pace, which Dorrel didn't enjoy any more than Bastion. But it was only until they left the city. He could stand the strutting for that long. It was meant, he supposed, to impress the Makutians.

The company rode toward the Circle. Curious citizens poked heads out of windows or stood in doorways to watch, doing plenty of gaping and pointing.

Alara remained poised, her eyes fixed straight ahead. He had never seen her look more regal.

Dorrel repeatedly had to restrain Bastion to keep him at the walk. The straight road and open countryside beckoned to them both. Dorrel wanted to give the stallion his head and let him enjoy a good run, but they couldn't risk breaking away from the others.

They reached their first stop early—well before sundown. A squad of soldiers sent in advance had secured rooms for them. The company put the horses up in a rather shoddy stable behind the inn. About halfway through their grooming, a stocky, middle-aged man glanced into the narrow stall where Alara was working on her mare, Spring.

"Oi!" he shouted. "What is she doing here?"

"*She* is grooming her horse," Alara replied, her voice cold.

Dorrel stepped out of Bastion's stall and headed for Spring's. The man grabbed Alara by her upper arm.

"I won't have a woman in my stable." He pulled her forward.

Alara pulled back. The grooming brush dropped from her hand. She made a fist.

Dorrel clamped his hand around the stableman's wrist. "Take your hand off my fiancée."

He looked from Dorrel to Alara and back again. But he let go. "You let your woman go around looking like that?"

Dorrel smiled at her. "I think she looks wonderful." This coaxed a smile out of Alara. Her hand loosened.

"Suit yourself," the man said. "But get her out of my stable."

Dorrel tightened his grip. "She will see to her horse, and none of you will put a hand on her."

"Why should I suffer a woman in my stable? My boys can do a better job."

"From the looks of the place, I doubt that." Dorrel let him go. The man walked away, muttering, and Dorrel returned to Bastion.

Once they'd finished, Alara said she needed a walk. So while most of the company remained at the inn, Dorrel and Bóhjetien and a trio of privates walked up the street with her.

It was the most like something from home Dorrel had seen in Makut. Posh shops with colorful window displays lined the street. It reminded him of the high street in Ecciston, despite the absence of trees.

For someone with short legs, Alara could walk uncommonly fast when she wished to. She was in full stride now, working off her anger.

A little girl, only about five years old, stood on a street corner on the other side of the road. A basket of flowers hung from her arm. The brightly colored clusters made a distressing contrast to her clothing's shabbiness.

Dorrel walked across the street. One of the privates followed.

The barefoot girl's dark-blonde hair hung greasy and stringy to her shoulders. One bruise smudged her right cheek and another showed where her thin, dirty arm poked out of a ragged sleeve.

"How much do your flowers cost?" Dorrel asked.

She didn't look at him. "Six pence a bunch, sir."

"How many pence in a shilling?" Dorrel asked the private.

"Twelve, sir."

Dorrel fished a coin from his pocket. "Why can't they use decimal coinage like everyone else?"

The private snickered.

"I'll take two."

She handed him two small sprays of flowers, each tied with a satin ribbon. Still she didn't look him in the eye.

He took the flowers and dropped the coin into her hand. "Thank you." He returned to Alara. He gave her the flowers and a kiss on the cheek.

"Thank you, love. That is very sweet." She leaned sideways and looked around him. "Yes?"

Dorrel turned. The little girl stood behind him. "Begging your pardon, my lord." She held up the coin in the palm of her hand. "You gave me a crown, not a shilling."

"Did I?" Dorrel crouched to her level, but she still wouldn't look him in the eye. "Well then —" He dropped a second coin into her hand. "There's another for being honest about it."

She gaped at it, then forgot herself long enough to stare at him, wide-eyed. "Oh, thank you, my lord! Thank you!"

"You're welcome." He stood, and she ran back to her place. "But I'm not a lord," he muttered.

Alara looped her arm around his waist and stood on her toes to kiss his cheek. "You are much more gallant than any Makutian lord."

"Indeed." Bóhjetien smiled after the little girl. "But you see, only nobility and soldiers wear swords. Since you are not in uniform, she naturally assumed you are a nobleman. And only a nobleman could dispense money that way." His brow furrowed. "It is odd, though, that she would understand Redíquan."

Alara tucked her arm through Dorrel's and walked, slowly, back toward the inn. "Glynnish, you mean."

"Who was speaking Glynnish?" Bóhjetien asked.

"Well, Dorrel, of course, he—" she stopped and stared at him.

"What?"

"The stablemen at the palace thought you were a Makutian nobleman."

"Yes." Dorrel smirked. "I realize my grades weren't spectacular, but I did pass Makutian."

"That is not the point. They thought you were a native."

"So?"

She turned to Bóhjetien. "And you are hearing him speak Redíquan right now?"

Bóhjetien looked as perplexed as Dorrel felt. "I have never heard him speak anything else."

"And you?" Alara asked the soldiers.

Like Bóhjetien, they had heard only Redíquan.

"I am hearing Glynnish." Alara laughed. "Dor, you are a speaker."

Bóhjetien's jaw hung open, and his eyes went from Alara to Dorrel. One of the privates whispered, "By all that is holy."

Dorrel shook his head. "Why would I be a speaker?"

Alara laughed again and threw her arms around his neck. "So you could infiltrate the palace and rescue me, obviously." She kissed him.

"I don't know, Lar."

"Dor, there is no other explanation." She hugged him, then stepped back, her hands on his shoulders. "A speaker!" She laughed and hugged him again.

Dorrel remembered Mak saying how good it was to hear his native language, but he decided against mentioning it.

# Chapter 22

## BORDER CROSSING

In the morning, Dorrel picked up his bags and stepped into the corridor. A Redíquan soldier stood there. "You weren't here all night?"

"No, sir."

"Oh, good."

"We changed the guard four hours ago."

"Ah." He couldn't fault them for caution.

Alara met him in the hallway, and they walked downstairs. In the public room, Barláhtiay's men kept a careful eye on the Makutians. A guard led them out into the street, where the horses were waiting. Soon they were on their way.

A few hours later, Barláhtiay sent a trio of archers to the front of the company.

Bóhjetien shifted his hat to raise the brim. "We must be near the border crossing."

Sure enough, after a bend and dip in the road, the flag of Makut appeared before them, a red field divided by a black X. It flapped from the turret of a guardhouse to their left.

A larger guardhouse, almost the size of the West Bridge Inn, stood to their right a bit farther away, flying the Redíquan flag. A wooden three-bar fence and gate marked the border.

Barláhtiay spurred his horse ahead to take the point.

Along the roofline of the Makutian guardhouse stood five men armed with crossbows. All aimed at them.

Alara spoke softly. "Dor, do you see . . ."

He didn't take his eyes from them. "I see them. Get back." He moved Bastion so the two of them were between the archers and Alara.

"That won't help," she muttered. "Not with their angle of attack."

She was right, of course, but what could he do? Bows creaked as the Redíquan archers nocked arrows and drew, guiding their horses with legs alone.

Bóhjetien sped up to join Barláhtiay.

The company halted at the gate while Bóhjetien and the captain talked to the border guards.

A thunk and a hiss. A bolt flew toward them.

"Down!" Dorrel yelled. Bastion reared.

Alara ducked, lying alongside her horse's neck. The bolt missed her.

The Redíquan archers loosed a volley from their longbows. Makutians fell back from the rooftop. Retreating? Wounded? No telling.

"Into the guardhouse!" Barláhtiay hollered.

Dorrel drew his sword. "Go!"

Alara spurred Spring and leapt the gate as if on a steeplechase.

Dorrel followed. Redíquan soldiers poured from their guardhouse and opened the gate. Bóhjetien and the rest of the Redíquan troops flowed through, then Barláhtiay. The archers came last.

There was much shouting on the Makutian side, but no more shooting.

Alara raced around the back of the guardhouse to a stable. There she dismounted. "Are you all right?"

"Fine. You?" Dorrel sheathed his sword.

She nodded and patted Spring's neck. "So much for diplomatic immunity."

"They shall answer for that." Bóhjetien jumped down from his horse.

A Redíquan captain joined them. "Your Royal Highness. What happened?"

Bóhjetien briefly described the attack.

The captain shook his head. "I shall have words with my counterpart."

"Be careful," Alara said.

He made a little bow. "I shall, Your Highness. Thank you for your concern." He turned to go.

Dorrel put out a hand to halt him. "I didn't hear an order to shoot. Just so you know."

"Very good, sir. Thank you." He bowed again and walked toward the gate.

A lieutenant approached. "Will you be staying long, Your Royal Highness?"

Bóhjetien shook his head. "No. We had best get away from Makut rapidly. But if you would, please see that the horses get water. We shall stop long enough to greet your troops."

The officer tipped his cap. "Very kind of you, sir." He sent a few enlisted people to tend the horses. The others formed up as if for inspection, and Bóhjetien led Alara and Dorrel down the line, shaking hands.

Finally the horses were refreshed and the canteens refilled, and Bóhjetien, Alara, and Dorrel had shaken every soldier's hand.

The border station captain returned. "My counterpart insists no order to shoot was given. The crossbowman on the roof shot of his own accord. He is among the wounded, but he will face disciplinary action."

"Thank you, Captain." Bóhjetien shook his hand. "Your troops have been most accommodating. We are grateful for your hospitality."

"It is our pleasure to serve, Your Royal Highness. Thank you for your time." He looked over his troops. "Common soldiers do not often receive visits from royalty."

Bóhjetien clapped him on the shoulder. "It is our privilege."

The company mounted, resumed formation, and headed south. Before long, Bastion was back to his antics, tossing his head or trying to sidle or switch to a canter.

The sun was high before Dorrel spoke up. "Captain, do you think it's safe to break formation?"

Barláhtiay glanced over his shoulder. "Yes, I suppose it is."

Dorrel grinned at Alara. "Race you."

Bastion tore down the road. Spring soon pulled ahead. Bastion caught up to her. Briefly, they were neck and neck. Then Spring dropped back, and Bastion galloped on.

Dorrel gave him his head, letting him run until he'd had enough. Then they walked until they found water—a little river bubbling over a ford. Dorrel dismounted and gave Bastion an apple from his saddlebag.

He removed every piece of tack: saddle, bags, even the bridle. Bastion tossed his head, whinnying, then rolled in the grass by the side of the road before getting up to graze and drink. Dorrel took out an apple for himself and sat with his back to a tree, waiting for Alara and the others to catch up.

Alara and Spring arrived at a canter. Alara turned Spring loose. "Printa could beat him in a sprint, but Vestan has more endurance." She sat beside Dorrel, kissing him briefly in greeting.

"What?" *Printa* was the Redíquan word for *spring*. "You mean Spring and Bastion."

She smirked. "You hear their names in Glynnish, don't you?"

"Yes." He watched the grazing horses for a few moments. "Until just now."

"Perhaps because Redíquan's not my native language."

"Oh. But I heard you in Glynnish at the embassy. At least, I think I did. Were you speaking Redíquan then?"

She used the Redíquan word for *certainly*.

"See, just then, I heard you in Redíquan, but at the embassy—well, I don't know what I heard."

"What you heard is irrelevant. You understood. That's the gift."

"Well, why didn't I have it before? It would've come in handy at school. My grades in Makutian and Redíquan might have been better."

"Your grades in Redíquan weren't bad." She leaned over and kissed him. "You had a good tutor."

He smiled. "True."

"Besides, the gift of speech and understanding comes from Ahbay. He'll put it on you when you need it and remove it when you don't. It's not as if I have visions every day, thanks be to Kenna. And does Marita heal every illness, every time?"

"No, obviously."

"I must say, it was disappointing to hear you speak Glynnish to everyone, when your Redíquan is fine. But since no one complained, I said nothing." She paused. "That Boh understood you should have been a sign. His Glynnish isn't that good."

They were silent for a minute or two.

"What does *vinnaq* mean, then?"

"*Beech*," she said. "That's why I named Willow after a tree, too."

He opened his mouth to speak, hesitated, then took a deep breath and told her about his conversation with Mak, down to that parting remark. "So I guess that was the first time."

"Perhaps. There might have been others you weren't aware of."

He frowned. "Did you feel this confused when you first learned you had a gift? I just wonder—why me and not someone else?"

"Oh, Dor," she moaned, "when you found me at the palace, that's exactly what I was thinking about. Praying about. Kenna, why me? I don't—" She choked.

"Can you tell me what you saw? In that vision about Prince Velek."

She took a deep breath. "He won't be king. His brother will."

He waited for her to say more, but she didn't. "Why does that trouble you?"

242

"Because it's not just about him! That vision is about a whole country—its future will be shaped by whoever is king. And the reason for Velek's removal—whether he abdicates or is deposed, I wasn't shown which—will have cultural ramifications as well. And . . ." She took a deep breath. "Perhaps I shouldn't say this, because I haven't delivered the vision yet—"

"I thought you told Velek at the embassy."

"Not that. I had one back home, too. About my father. Although I —oh, you're a member of the electorate, you have a right to know— only don't tell anyone else until I talk to him."

"All right."

"He'll lose the election."

"I should hope so. I surely won't vote for him again."

"Nor I. But these aren't the sort of visions I usually have. These concern the leadership of nations."

As if one of the ancient, illuminated scrolls on which Redíquan scribes had written the history of the church had unrolled before him, Dorrel saw the implications. Alara had foreseen turning points historians would write about for centuries. "That's . . . Lar, that's . . . prophetic."

She shook her head. "No, Dor. Prophecy is different. This is just . . ." She covered her face with her hands. "Just an awfully large responsibility for such a poor curate."

"Oh, we're not going through this again."

She looked at him as if he'd insulted her.

"You've spent most of your life speaking for Kenna, and you've always done so faithfully. It makes sense that She would entrust you with further responsibility. 'One who is faithful in a small task will be faithful in a great one.'"

She frowned.

"Moreover"—why was he the one giving a sermon?—"if Kenna needs someone to deliver Her message to world leaders, it's only logical She would choose someone who already runs in those circles."

"Oh!" She looked away.

He scooted closer and whispered in her ear. "You know I'm right."

Her expression was half frown, half smirk. "Yes, but your excellent apologia won't make it any easier for me to tell my father about the election."

Darshalay was bigger and noisier than any town Dorrel had ever seen. They rode through, receiving the same cheering and hand-waving they had in the other Redíquan towns they'd passed through, multiplied tenfold.

Alara smiled and waved in return, encouraging Dorrel to do the same. "You're not a soldier, you're a celebrity."

Dorrel did as she said, though it seemed preposterous.

Some students at Denedra—and in his first year he'd been one of them—saw Alara's tales from Redíque as self-centered. But after they became friends, he realized she only told them when asked. In fact, as she grew older, she only told them when pressed.

Alara usually referred to the Shardamayns as her "cousins in Redíque," which is why Dorrel had all but forgotten that her mother's cousin was the king.

And though everyone knew Dorváir was the ancestral seat of the Shardamayns, Alara only spoke of it as the "house" she stayed in when visiting Darshalay.

Dorváir sat on a hill near the center of the city. A long, straight road ran up to its gates. Its face was a broad cliff of white marble with six rows of windows peering down.

Many people lined the street, waving.

Someone threw an egg. It shattered against Bóhjetien's cheekbone and ran into the collar of his white linen shirt. He didn't turn his head to see where it had come from. He just drew a handkerchief and cleaned his face.

Despite his rank and the dozens of grooms at his disposal, Bóhjetien took care of his own horse. A true equestrian indeed.

While they groomed the horses, everyone exchanging comradely banter, Dorrel was content. But when they left the stables, Barláhtiay and his men went one way, toward the barracks, while Bóhjetien, Alara, and Dorrel headed toward the palace.

As they crossed the courtyard, Dorrel held her hand. "Is Ravendyn like this?"

"Not much." She raised her voice. "After Reyshara's abdication, the Kordelyons divested themselves of such trappings."

Bóhjetien, a few steps ahead of them, ignored her.

Alara's voice returned to normal. "Ravendyn is big. But probably no bigger than the Arken winery. Which I'd like to visit someday. Could we drop in uninvited?"

He put his arm around her waist and pulled her close. "Anytime."

Before they reached the wide, glass-paned doors, Alara's mother, Shenevra, ran out.

Alara darted forward to meet her in an embrace.

Alara's brother Camrun stepped through the doorway and jogged toward them.

Shenevra put a knuckle under Alara's chin and examined the bruises, which had faded to a sickly green. She tsked. "I hope you gave them as good as you got."

"Very nearly. But they had me three to one."

"Oh, baby . . ." Shenevra hugged her again.

Camrun met Dorrel, shaking one hand and embracing with his other arm. "Good to see you." He stepped back. "Quite a rescue operation."

Dorrel shrugged.

"Lar will tell you such heroics are beyond me. I'm glad they're not beyond you."

A single cough was the only reply Dorrel could conjure.

Shenevra smiled at Dorrel over Alara's shoulder. She let go of Alara and hugged him. "Oh, Dorrel, I can't tell you how grateful I am that you—" she choked. She smiled at him, then at Alara, then at him again, and hugged him again.

"I was supposed to make sure nothing happened to you." Camrun put his arms around Alara. "I'm sorry I let you down."

"Nonsense. You're not the one who let me down."

Camrun let her go but kept an arm around her shoulders. "Well, I'm pleased to hear you two are engaged finally." He smirked. "We've been wondering for years when that would happen."

"For the love of . . ." Alara pushed away from him and turned toward the door.

Bóhjetien, meanwhile, had exchanged a long kiss and a lingering hug with a tall, stately woman. She wore a taffeta gown trimmed with more lace than Dorrel had ever seen on one dress. Her mahogany-colored hair was piled on her head, decorated with tiny pearls throughout. She had a narrow face and a small nose.

Alara greeted her with a hug and introduced Dorrel.

"This is Domínarey, Boh's wife."

They shook hands, then Domínarey gestured toward the doors. "Please come in. We are having tea in the king's study."

Dorrel's stomach quivered.

Inside, marble columns held up a two-story, coffered copper ceiling tooled with an acanthus-leaf pattern. Domínarey led them through wide, high-ceilinged corridors decorated with extravagant tapestries and tall bronze statues and giant paintings in gilded frames.

Bóhjetien pushed open the double doors of the study, which was twice the size of the public room at the West Bridge Inn. Books lined the walls on three sides. The fourth had tall, arched windows looking out over a flower garden.

As soon as Bóhjetien stepped into the doorway, a little girl with long, strawberry-blonde curls dashed across the room. "Pappá!"

He crouched to meet her and scooped her up, balancing her on his hip. He kissed her cheek, and she put her little arms around his neck. "Look, Belissina. Here is Cousin Alara."

She looked at Alara, wide-eyed, but said nothing. Dorrel guessed she was about four years old.

Alara smiled. "Hello, Belissina. You do not remember me, do you?"

The little girl shook her head.

"Well, of course you do not. You were very small when I was here last. Heavens, that was two years ago, was it not?" Alara looked to Domínarey.

"Nearly." Domínarey patted her daughter's back. "Now Belissina, we have spoken all week about Cousin Alara's coming. Do at least say hello."

"Hello," she said, then hid her face against Bóhjetien's neck.

A woman stepped up. "She must get her reticence from your side, Domínarey. It cannot come from the Shardamayns."

"How very true." Alara smirked at her. "Dorrel, this is my cousin Mehrialéna."

She was taller than Alara and almost as voluptuous. Auburn hair framed her narrow face. Her eyes were a dark gray-green.

The prime minister was not present. But General Rariden was.

Alara hugged him. Dorrel had never seen her do that.

"It's so good to see you," she said.

Rariden held his hands to either side. Then, gingerly, he returned the embrace.

"Well . . . thanks be to Telshi you're safe." He patted her back. Alara let him go. The general extended his hand to Dorrel. "Well done, Sergeant."

"Thank you, sir."

Rariden pumped Dorrel's hand. "A rescue operation was obviously in order, but with my age, and Camrun's inexperience . . ." He exchanged a glance with Camrun. "We weren't able to do it." He clapped Dorrel's shoulder with his free hand. "Still, we couldn't have picked a better man for the job."

Dorrel could not imagine how to answer such an effusion from such a personage.

Bóhjetien led them to the far corner of the room. In a large wingback chair next to a window sat a thin old man with the slightest fringe of white hair. His suit was gray and plain—not much different from General Rariden's. His face was wrinkled, but his green eyes were bright.

Smiling, the old man stood and gave Bóhjetien half an embrace—because Belissina precluded an entire one—then turned to Alara.

"I am so glad to see you are well," he said. "Or should I say, as well as can be expected, hmm?" He winked.

"It is good to see you, Jentiérri." She introduced Dorrel, and the king shook his hand.

His grip was soft. Frail. He covered Dorrel's hand with both of his. "You have done us an inestimable service, young man."

"Thank you, sir. I did have . . . rather selfish reasons for doing so."

Jentiérri's laugh had a depth at variance with his thin chest. "Indeed. When Bóhjetien wrote, he told me you wish to be married. I have arranged matters with the prelate. We need only advise him of the day."

Alara giggled and kissed Jentiérri's cheek. "You are a dear. Thank you."

He returned to his chair, waving off their thanks as if getting the nation's prelate to perform someone's wedding were nothing.

Having tea with Jentiérri was one thing. It didn't take long for the tension Alara read in Dorrel's face and frame to fade. Jentiérri was masterful at putting people at ease.

But the next day was spent in gatherings of vast numbers of nobility, politicians, and distantly removed relatives. By the time they finished dinner—served in a hall bigger than the dining room at Denedra, and with nearly as many people—and retired to Jentiérri's study, Dorrel looked as if he would snap. Or collapse.

Collapse he did, into a settee upholstered in tapestry. Alara patted his shoulder. "Tea or port?"

He rubbed his forehead. "Tea, please."

She drew two cups while Domínarey served port.

Mum tsked. "A bit underdressed for dinner with the prelate, baby."

Alara stifled a sigh. Back home, her gown of blue and gold satin, trimmed with white lace, would not have drawn such criticism. But her skirt lacked a crinoline, which set her apart from the other ladies. "Sorry, Mum." She picked up the tea and turned.

Prelate Pomiren, a tall man with graying brown hair and a long face, took a chair near Dorrel. The prelate had sat with Alara at luncheon and quizzed her thoroughly about their courtship. She presumed Dorrel had been interviewed equally thoroughly at dinner, because then he'd been sitting next to the prelate.

Alara sat beside Dorrel, holding both teacups. He'd tipped his head over the back of the settee and closed his eyes. "I'm sorry, love. I know it's all very tedious."

"Exhausting." He lifted his head and accepted the cup she handed him.

Pomiren leaned into the lull. "Mr. Chevallon, I only wish your family were here. I have met all of Curate Kordelyon's relatives."

Dorrel's mouth twitched—an attempt at a smile. "I wish they were here, too."

"Nevertheless, the king believes we must proceed to free Curate Kordelyon from the unscriptural conditions of the treaty."

"He said that?" Dorrel glanced in Jentiérri's direction. "Does he realize what trouble he might be getting into?"

"Certainly," Pomiren said. "Some people disagree, but most I have spoken with believe, as I do, that here we must choose the Way of Telshi—or the way of the Adversary."

"Who disagrees?" Dorrel asked.

Pomiren shrugged. "Some politicians. A handful of noblemen. People who wish to maintain things as they are and not incite disaster."

Camrun took the seat next to Pomiren. "Disaster has already

occurred, has it not?"

"It has indeed," Pomiren said. "I have spent much time in prayer upon this matter, since the king first spoke to me of it. I daresay you have, also."

"Surely," Dorrel said.

Alara's throat clenched. The Adversary meddling in politics could be understood. But for their marriage to be dragged into the matter seemed impossible.

"Very good. Are we agreed, then, to choose the Way of Telshi?"

"Ocha." Dorrel's voice was heartier than it had been in hours.

But Alara's was weak, even though the choice was obvious. "Ocha."

Dorrel looked at her. "Are you all right?"

She nodded and cleared her throat. "Just . . . overcome." She leaned against him, and he squeezed her shoulders.

Pomiren tipped his head, smiling gently. "Then I shall see you at the meetinghouse tomorrow for sunset service."

Alara sat straight. "Sunrise, please?"

Prelate Pomiren waggled a finger at her. "The king said you would ask. Sunset. He insists."

Just like him. But she couldn't quibble about the time of day, when, in sponsoring their marriage, Jentiérri was risking a war.

# Chapter 23

## There Will Be Trials

Dorrel woke to a silent house. Alara had said few at Dorváir were early risers. Only the staff rose with the sun. She had suggested he meet her at a patio on the east side of the palace. He made a wrong turn getting there, but a housekeeper set him right.

Alara sat at a white wrought-iron table. Finely trimmed hedges rimmed the flagstones. Beyond the hedge bloomed a trio of magnolia trees. A couple of birds, hidden in the mist-veiled treetops, sang a call and response.

The sun had not yet risen. A kerosene lamp cast a golden pool of light over Alara's Scriptures, a paperboard folder full of journal pages, and a coffee service. He greeted her with a kiss on the cheek, and she poured his coffee.

He sat, and they held hands across the table. He waited.

She didn't speak. She just sat there, her brow lined with tension.

"Mairah," Dorrel said, "thank you for this day and for our friends and family. Ahbay, thank you for guiding us to safety and for leading Jentiérri and Pomiren to support our marriage. Kenna, we ask your blessings on what is meant to be a joyful day, and I ask that you please comfort Alara and reassure her she can tell me whatever's troubling her."

After their "ocha," she frowned into her coffee cup for a moment. Then she sucked in a deep breath. "Surely you know why I'm worried."

"I could guess a lot of reasons. I'd rather you told me."

"The Makutians are likely to declare war on Redíque for this."

"That's it?"

"Dor, my freedom and virtue are not worth even one life . . . how many would be lost in a war?"

"This is not only about your freedom. As Pomiren said, it's about following the Way of Telshi." He sipped his coffee.

She nodded, but her frown didn't fade.

"Alara." Dorrel waited until she looked at him. "When we agreed to be 'just friends,' I gave up praying that you would ever marry me. When I prayed about it at all—and after you left for Apanumon, it was a lot harder to pray about—I just prayed for a wife who would be supportive of my career. And a curate for Kaesbaro."

She looked away.

"I never put your name in those prayers, but I never forgot you could fill both roles."

Why was there a table between them?

"Come here." He took her hand. They left the coffee behind to sit on a marble bench under one of the magnolias.

He held her hands. "This marriage is an answer to prayer. But if it has negative consequences . . . well, don't the Scriptures say there will be trials for those who follow the Way?"

She nodded.

"I firmly believe this is the will of Telshi. Don't you?"

Alara hesitated.

His heart plummeted. "Alara?"

She opened her mouth but closed it again without speaking.

No, no, no. They had not gone through all this so she could back out. He cleared his throat. "Well, while I've been praying for a wife and a curate, what have you been praying for?"

"That Kenna would make my heart penitent, my manner humble, and make my will match Her own."

"Oh, that." There were times Dorrel wanted to throttle that rector in Apanumon, and this was one of them.

"Yes, that." She pulled her hands away. "I'm a cleric. Her will is supposed to be more important to me than what I want."

"And what do you want?"

"Oh, Dor." She sagged against him, her arms around his waist. "I want to be your wife, and I want to be Kaesbaro's curate. But I don't know whether those things are Her will. She hasn't shown me. I've never had a vision of myself on a rostrum."

"That can't mean it opposes Her will."

"Yes, but . . ." She sat up straight again. "Please don't repeat this to anyone."

He waited.

"In Tarvag, at the palace . . . She spoke to me."

"Spoke?"

"I heard Her as plainly as I hear you."

"What did She say?"

"She said She was making my will match Her own."

"And? If She is, then . . ."

"You're taking this rather well."

"How am I supposed to take it? Kenna trusts you with visions. Why shouldn't She speak to you as well?"

She huffed. "She hasn't spoken to me at all since that day. I have prayed and pleaded, but She is silent."

"Maybe She said everything She needed to."

"But all She said was I'm Her servant, and . . ." She paused, then looked up, grinning, her tension gone. "And She told me to get up and go."

"Go where?"

"Out of the palace." She leaned close to him. "With you."

He kissed her. "Well, then, what more do you need?"

She pursed her lips. "I just wish I could be sure this is the right time. But even if it is, I'm still afraid our wedding this evening"—she squeezed him more tightly—"will lead to a trial for those who follow the Way."

Mehrialéna's attendant finished applying the curling tongs to Alara's hair. Alara wore one of the gowns she kept at Dorváir: blue satin trimmed in black lace. A crinoline supported the skirt, and the wide neckline was revealing. She examined herself in a long mirror. "Do you think this is suitable for a curate?"

"Surely," Mum said. "Your ordination need not change your wardrobe." Her copper-colored gown was no less revealing.

"You think not? The last time I wore a dress like this, Rector Mirva dragged me back to the dormitory and made me put a scarf into the front to fill the décolletage."

"That was Denedra, not Darshalay."

Mehrialéna entered without knocking. She wore a yellow brocade dress with a crinoline even bigger than Alara's. She carried three boxes, two blue and one green, and handed them to Alara.

She recognized the first two. But the green box, a cube, was unfamiliar. "What is this?"

"Father wishes you to wear it. It was our great-grandmother's."

"Oh, no." Alara held it out to her.

"Alara, please. It is a simple thing he asks of you."

"No." Alara held out the box, shaking it.

Mehrialéna folded her arms.

"Baby, please." Mum took the box. "Humor him."

Alara sighed and took the first two boxes to her dressing table.

The long one held her sash, royal blue with a stripe of black down the middle. A silver multipointed star with the Shardamayn family crest at its center was pinned where the ends of the sash crossed. She draped the sash from one shoulder to slant across her torso to the opposite side. The crest sat near her hip.

Her collar, just like the one her mother wore, rested in the velvet lining of the second box. A circle of silver medallions, each joined to the next by a tiny silver link. Every second medallion held a sapphire. Mehrialéna's collar was similar, except it was gold with emeralds.

Alara lifted the collar over her head and placed it on her shoulders. It hung equally far down in the front and in the back, the silver cold against her skin.

Alara opened the last box and took out the tiara, a delicate filigree of silver dotted with diamonds and pearls. "This is too much."

"Certainly not." Mehrialéna said. "Jaselle wore it when she married. Now it is your turn."

"Humph." Alara faced the mirror and put the tiara in place. Sickly yellow-green blotches covered her right temple and cheek. "Tiara and bruises. What a lovely bride."

They walked downstairs to the rear courtyard, where the men and carriages waited.

As they crossed the rear foyer, Alara could see Dorrel through the glass doors. He wore a charcoal-gray suit and a blue waistcoat embroidered with gold vines. Camrun said something, and Dorrel laughed.

Her heart trembled at all they had weathered to reach that point. She felt truly blessed to have earned the love of such a kind, noble, brilliant man. That they should have achieved such happiness, while their friends back home were grieving, seemed unjust.

And Jentiérri, moving slowly across the floor in front of her, was sponsoring them, even though the cost to his nation was likely to be high.

Carriages lined the rear courtyard. The setting sun had just touched the roof of the west wing of the palace on the opposite side of the courtyard from where Dorrel waited with Camrun and the rest of the men. The women hadn't shown themselves since luncheon.

Jentiérri emerged, walking slowly but not leaning heavily on his walking stick as he had the evening before. Dorrel had previously only seen him in ordinary suits. But now he wore forest-green velvet with a gold lamé waistcoat and a gold circlet on his brow. Around his neck sat a gold collar studded with diamonds.

Jentiérri's butler, a muscular, middle-aged man, walked next to him. Domínarey trailed close behind. The butler handed the king into a carriage and climbed in after him. Bóhjetien and Domínarey followed, and the carriage left.

A moment later, Alara came through the doors with her mother and Mehrialéna. Alara's gown had a wide, deep neckline and petal-like sleeves long enough to cover the bandage on her arm.

Her hair was piled up on her head, but black tendrils curled down the sides of her face and around her neck, brushing her skin as she moved. A glittering tiara shone against the black backdrop of her hair.

It scarcely seemed possible this same girl had mucked out stables at Denedra with him. This sweet, gorgeous, remarkable woman who had agreed to marry him. His heart twisted.

One corner of her mouth turned upward. "Say something, Dor, or close your mouth."

He started to speak, then cleared his throat. "You really are a princess."

"No, I am a curate." She took his hand and climbed onto the carriage step. She hesitated and leaned down to him. "And so help me, I am never again wearing any of this rubbish."

The carriage stopped in front of the meetinghouse. Camrun jumped out and handed his mother down. Dorrel followed, giving Alara his hand.

When Dorrel looked up—and up and up—at the looming bell

tower, he couldn't believe the Shardamayns called it a meetinghouse. More like a meeting palace.

A flight of stone steps led to a colorfully tiled vestibule. An arched doorway opened into the meeting room. Above the doorway hung a massive gold triquetra.

The meeting room was vast, its vaulted ceiling capping marble pillars. The outer walls contained rows of arched stained-glass windows—portraits of the prophets.

Chandeliers filled the room with light.

The place was nearly full. While Dorrel and Alara walked down the aisle with the rest of the family, many eyes seemed to follow them. By the time the service began, no seats were left. People stood along the walls.

Jentiérri sat on the rostrum, next to Pomiren.

After the prelate's opening prayer, Jentiérri stepped to the lectern and read a passage from the prophet Galardi about the trials Rheedeka's father put Galardi through before allowing him to marry her.

Jentiérri returned to his seat, and the prelate took the lectern. His sermon was about the trials Telshi's followers often face.

"We have with us this evening," he said, "a couple who have come through trials more fearful—more deadly—than those faced by Galardi." Goosebumps rose on Dorrel's neck. It hadn't occurred to him, until Pomiren said it, that their ordeal had been one of scriptural proportions.

Dorrel didn't hear the rest of the sermon, so awestruck was he by the idea that, like Galardi, he would have "endured ten times the trials to earn her hand."

After a canticle, Prelate Pomiren stepped to the side of the lectern. "Now, Alara Kordelyon and Dorrel Chevallon shall come forward to be married."

Dorrel held out his hand, and she put her hand in his. He smiled, and she smiled back, and he thought his heart would burst.

They met the prelate at the top of the rostrum steps.

A boy in a gold and emerald collar—Bóhjetien's older son, Raynar—stepped up, carrying two gold rings on a red velvet pillow.

"The wearing of a ring on the third finger of the left hand," Pomiren said, "is so rooted in antiquity, its origin is unknown. We do know that Redíquans, Glynrellans, Makutians, and many others of every nation and every faith on the continent share this custom."

He took the rings, one in each hand, and held them up, overlapping.

"The circle is without end, as is the love of Telshi," he said, quoting Kenna. Pomiren lowered his hands. "Let these, then, symbolize your devotion to one another. Are you prepared to take the vow that shall require the rest of your lives to fulfill?"

When they answered, "Yes," he handed each of them the other's ring.

Alara held the gold band in her palm, and the prelate covered it with his own. "Alara," he said, "do you now, before these witnesses, promise to stand with Dorrel through all trials, to share all your material possessions, and to devote yourself fully and solely to him, body and soul, remaining a faithful partner and advocate for the rest of your life?"

"I do," she answered, in the same voice she would use if she were the one on the rostrum.

"Then place this ring on Dorrel's hand as a token of your pledge."

She did so, blushing and grinning more than any bride Dorrel had ever seen. He was doing a fair bit of grinning himself and only hoped he wasn't blushing.

Pomiren repeated the vow for Dorrel, who gave his "I do" perhaps more forcefully than necessary. Nevertheless, it was a relief to say it, to mean it, to look into her brilliant green eyes and know it was true.

The prelate folded their hands together and covered them with his own. "As our Telshi is eternally one, so may you be, until the end of your days."

"Ocha," the congregation said.

The resonance of the affirmation stunned Dorrel. He'd never heard so many people speak with one voice.

Pomiren released their hands. As she turned to go, Dorrel pulled Alara close and kissed her. She giggled.

"Stay," Pomiren said, quietly.

Wide-eyed, Alara looked toward the back corner of the rostrum, where Jentiérri's butler was helping the king out of his chair.

The prelate returned to his seat while Jentiérri moved forward. A thin, bald-headed man in an old-fashioned tabard, followed by a servant in the green-and-gold livery of Dorváir, mounted the steps on Dorrel's right.

Alara shook her head. A tiny, furtive movement. "No. No," she whispered.

Jentiérri glowered at her, his bushy gray eyebrows seeming to bristle.

"Oh, Dor." Her voice was soft, so as not to carry. "I'm so sorry."

The man in the tabard—a herald, he must be—opened a long, thin box.

Jentiérri took from it a sash like Alara's, except the ribbon running down its center was gold. The king put it over Dorrel's head and lifted the medallion. "This is our family crest. You are one of us now, and we are happy to have you."

Dorrel swallowed hard, his cheeks warming.

The king raised his voice to a grand level as if he were pronouncing a verdict. "Since ancient times, when a man performs great service to the crown, he is rewarded. Dorrel Chevallon has rendered quite a service, indeed. So."

The herald brought the king a broadsword. Its leather scabbard was tooled with a twining knotwork design.

"I hereby present to you this sword in honor of your valiant deeds." Then, sotto voce, Jentiérri added, "Utterly useless. Just for show."

Alara ducked her head as if stifling a laugh. "Put it on."

While Dorrel buckled the sword belt, the herald lifted a parchment. Beside the herald, the servant held a shield.

The herald read aloud. "To all and singular, nobles and gentles and others to whom these pronouncements shall come, by the principal herald and master of arms of the Kingdom of Redíque: Whereas anciently the valiant and virtuous acts of worthy persons have been commended with sundry monuments . . ."

The herald went on like this for some time, speaking of "prowess and valor" and "virtue and nobleness" without getting to the point. Eventually, he said, "Therefore, the aforesaid master of arms, in pursuance of His Majesty's warrant and by virtue of his office, granted by His Majesty the King, does by this record assign unto the said Dorrel of the house of Chevallon, the arms following: azure, on a bend or, a horse rampant argent."

Dorrel understood the words, but could not parse their meaning.

"Very good, sir," the king said. "Now explain the thing plainly, if you please."

The herald gestured to the shield. "The background is blue, with a diagonal stripe of gold"—his hand traced the stripe—"because these colors were assigned to your family by royal warrant in the days of Glynrell's monarchy. The horse, in a rampant pose, is white"—he glanced at Jentiérri, who frowned—"for reasons that shall soon be apparent." Jentiérri smiled, and the herald handed him the parchment.

"Your patent of arms." Jentiérri presented the parchment to Dorrel.

It contained elaborate calligraphy and illuminations, bordered with Redíquan knotwork designs. At the bottom of the page, yellow ribbons dangled from a large seal of green wax.

The king turned as if to take the shield, then muttered, "Oh, you give it to him."

The servant brought Dorrel the shield. It wasn't as heavy as it looked.

"Just for show." Jentiérri winked at Dorrel, who smiled.

The herald and the servant, who had briefly retreated, returned. The herald held another parchment, and the servant carried a flat, square blue box.

The herald started reading again. His language this time was even more florid, as he recited all the king's titles—there were quite a few—and Alara's lineage. Eventually, after an account of Dorrel's "brave and loyal" service to the royal family, he got to the part in which the king "therefore elevated, promoted, created, and established the aforesaid Dorrel, of the house of Chevallon, to the higher state, rank, title, and honor of prince . . ." at which Dorrel choked back a cough.

Alara rolled her eyes.

The herald kept talking, while Dorrel frowned a question at Alara, but she just said again, "I'm truly sorry."

The herald finished, finally.

The servant brought Jentiérri the box, from which he removed a collar like the one Alara wore.

"I realize there is no peerage in your homeland," Jentiérri said quietly, "but you shall humor us, yes? You have married a descendent of kings, young man. Do not forget that."

"I won't, sir." How could he, after all this?

"Now then." The king spoke in sonorous tones. "Having been elevated, promoted, so on and so forth"—he lowered the collar onto Dorrel's shoulders—"accept now the symbol of your state, title, and whatnot. Now, I know"—the king lowered his voice again—"you Glynrellans do not think much of such things. Hmm?" He leaned toward Alara with raised eyebrows. She smiled a little. He straightened. His hands still lay on Dorrel's shoulders. "This may be the badge of a rank your countrymen—and your wife—do not acknowledge. Therefore do not accept it as a badge of rank. Accept it as an heirloom." Jentiérri patted the links on Dorrel's shoulders. Tears glistened in the old man's eyes. "The last person to wear this collar was my late cousin Kyvern."

Alara inhaled sharply. Dorrel glanced sidelong at her. Her face was tight.

"Thank you, sir." Dorrel's voice had gone weak.

The king nodded, his lips pursed. "Ever meet him?"

"Yes. I admired him a great deal."

"Very good." Jentiérri gave the collar another pat, then squeezed Alara's hand before returning to the herald. He took the parchment and presented it to Dorrel. He took a deep breath, and his voice returned to its official mode. "Your letters patent."

Like the patent of arms, the page was heavily illuminated.

"Now then, we have arrived at the last item. Are you not glad?" Jentiérri gestured to Bóhjetien, who came forward with a sheaf of papers folded in thirds and tied with a red ribbon.

Jentiérri took the papers and faced Dorrel. "I understand you lost your mount in the fighting."

"Yes, sir." The sorrow, which had become quiescent, twisted again in Dorrel's gut.

"We hope this makes amends." Jentiérri handed over the papers.

Dorrel handed the patents to Alara and propped the shield against his leg. Brow furrowed, he untied the papers. They were handwritten in Redíquan, so he had trouble making them out. He showed them to Alara.

She gasped. "Vestan's pedigree."

Dorrel looked up, gaping. Bóhjetien grinned.

The king nodded. "My son tells me you have become attached to him. The reverse is likely, also. I am told he is a troublemaker, probably not as valuable as the well-trained horse you lost. Nevertheless, he is yours."

True, Bastion was not as well trained as Toban. But he hadn't had a single owner, let alone a single-minded single owner, as Toban had. He was still a magnificent animal. He'd never been given such a valuable gift. "Thank you, sir." Dorrel huffed. "Thank you seems inadequate."

"Nonsense." The king clapped Dorrel's shoulder. "All in the family, eh?"

Dorrel nodded, swallowing hard. Jentiérri had, with those simple words, reminded Dorrel that he had received such a gift before: when his uncle gave him Toban. That was in the family as well.

# Chapter 24

## THE GLITTERING NOBILITY

After the closing prayer, most of the congregation filed out, while Dorrel and Alara were shown to the office. A register lay open on the desk. The prelate had already recorded the particulars. All that remained was for them to sign.

Dorrel took up the pen. He signed the register and the marriage certificate. Then he handed the pen to Alara.

She dipped the pen in the inkwell, started to put it to paper . . . hesitated.

For a moment, his heart clenched. It was too late for her to have second thoughts. Wasn't it?

Abruptly, she bent and signed her name with unusual vigor. First in the book, then on the parchment.

When Dorrel saw what she'd done, his heart beat faster.

In the register, on the lines above and on the page opposite, were recorded several marriages and two namings. In each case, the bride or mother had the same surname as her husband.

And there, halfway down the right-hand page, Alara had signed her name *Alara Chevallon*.

"You don't have to do that." He looked to Pomiren, jabbing his finger at the page. "She doesn't, does she?"

The prelate looked over Alara's shoulder. "Oh. No. That is not the custom in your country. You need not do it if you do not wish to."

Alara handed the pen to Domínarey. "I wish to."

"Why?" Dorrel had never known a Glynrellan woman who took her husband's name.

"Because I would rather have your name than his."

That was something with which Dorrel could not argue.

Many well-wishers waited outside. It took a long time to shake all their hands and get back into the carriage. Alara carried the documents. Dorrel squeezed the blue-and-gold shield between his knee and her skirt. He hadn't thought about that ancient royal warrant in years.

"I'm truly sorry, Dor. If I had known Jentiérri was planning all that, I'd have stopped him. I didn't think he would. He knows how I feel about the peerage."

"Oh, come on, Lar." Camrun pulled the door closed. "It's not that bad."

"Not bad at all," Dorrel said. "Though I did feel a bit silly when the herald got to the 'prince' bit. What was that about?"

"The Redíquans consider Alara a princess." The clopping of the horses' hooves accented Camrun's sentences. "You married her. That makes you a prince."

Dorrel stared at him for a moment. "You're joking."

"I'm afraid not," Alara said.

"Honestly, baby, you're making too much of it."

"I am not, Mum. The whole business is just . . . shameful."

"Alara!"

"It's un-Telshan. I am proud to be descended from Reyshara

Kordelyon. She was one of the greatest Telshans ever. And it is shameful none of the Shardamayns ever thought to abolish their monarchy as she did ours."

"Nothing in Scripture forbids a monarchy," Shenevra said.

"But Kenna said all people are equal in the eyes of Telshi, and many of the prophets explicate that. Monarchy is contrary to egalitarianism."

"Yes, but this isn't about monarchy," Camrun said. "It's just Dorrel's investiture. A pointless bit of ceremony." Camrun turned to Dorrel. "No offense."

"None taken."

"Anyway, never mind what she says. Wearing Kyvern's collar doesn't affect your standing as a Telshan or a democrat." Camrun wore an identical collar. "I'm glad you have it."

Dorrel choked out a "thanks."

There was a long silence. Alara and Shenevra both frowned.

Camrun extended his legs as far as the ladies' crinolines would allow. "Of course, in the old days, investiture wouldn't be an issue for you."

"Why not?" Dorrel asked.

"In pre-Telshan times, a wife received her husband's title, but not the other way around. After the Telshan faith became dominant here, church leaders said it was a sexist, and therefore un-Telshan, practice."

"Unfortunately," Alara said, "instead of doing away with the peerage, the king just changed the rules to give each spouse the title of the other."

"Yes, so you wind up with a lot of couples who are simultaneously duke and duchess of one place and count and contessa of some other place." Camrun smirked. "Introductions at court can be almost comical." Shenevra slapped him lightly on the shoulder. "They never seem to realize how foolish it is."

"I don't care how foolish this is." Dorrel took the letters patent from Alara and put them aside on the seat. "It was worth it." He kissed her hand. The one on which she wore her ring.

She smiled.

Camrun groaned. "They should've had a carriage to themselves."

Shenevra shushed him.

"Well, Vestan's pedigree," Camrun said, despite her. "That's not foolish."

"Oh!" Shenevra rolled her eyes, then turned to look out the window.

Dorrel laughed. "Subtle way to change the subject." He turned back to Alara. "I can't wait to see what happens when we cross him with Willow."

She kissed his cheek. "I was thinking the same thing."

"Let's see . . ." Camrun looked upward. "Willow's sire was a Chevallon charger, and her dam was from the same line as Boh's racehorses. With Vestan being an imperial parade horse . . . you'll wind up with something strong, fast, and arrogant." He paused. "Like my sister."

Alara kicked his shin. He tried to kick her back, but since her leg was hidden in crinoline, he missed.

Dorrel was eager to get alone with Alara, but as soon as they stepped out of the carriage at Dorváir, Domínarey directed them to the dining hall.

"Just let us put these away," Dorrel said, but a couple of servants took the shield and the rest to put away for him.

"Nice try," Alara muttered.

At least they were seated together. But after dinner, they were compelled to join the others in the ballroom.

Caryatids forty feet tall lined the walls in place of pilasters, each figure holding a candelabrum. Between the caryatids, the walls were dressed in pale yellow silk. A gilded bas-relief of stylized vines and flowers decorated the frieze above. Fanciful frescoes covered the vaulted ceiling. He'd never seen anything like it. Alara's stories about the place had been more understated than he imagined.

At the inner end of the room, farthest from the wide double doors, a chamber orchestra sat on a dais, playing a concerto. The expanse of parquet floor was dotted with groups of people sipping port, sherry, and tea. A long buffet table near the right-hand wall displayed a vast array of pastries and sweets. While filling his plate, Dorrel whispered, "How long do we have to stay?"

"Too long, I daresay."

They tried to eat but were interrupted by greetings from myriad people whose names Dorrel would never remember. The glittering nobility, in their satins and brocades, insisted upon addressing him as "Your Highness," despite his attempts to correct them.

In a moment's lull, he leaned toward Alara. "Are they only going to play chamber music?"

She smiled. "That depends upon what they are asked to play."

Camrun handed his plate to her. "You two prefer three-quarter time, as I recall."

Dorrel grinned. "Right you are."

Alara took all three plates to a server while Camrun walked double-time toward the musicians.

Dorrel put his arm around her waist, and they moved toward the empty floor near the dais. She trembled under his hand. "At least this time," he said, hoping to ease whatever was making her nervous, "Sheeno and Mirva won't be glowering at us."

"No," she said. "Here, we have only supporters."

The musicians abbreviated the concerto and began a quick-tempo waltz.

Dorrel led her into a spinning flurry of steps, her skirt swirling. Alara laughed out loud. She wasn't trembling now.

They danced five dances before her smile faded.

"What?"

"Mum is glowering."

"Don't look at her. Look at me." His smile hadn't faded. "Why would she glower?"

"Because I'm monopolizing the best dancer in the room."

He pulled her closer and spoke quietly in her ear. "Isn't monopoly one of the advantages of marriage?"

She giggled and pushed at his shoulder. Ah-ha. She was trembling again.

"You had better ask Mum to dance before she becomes well and truly offended."

After Shenevra, Dorrel danced with Domínarey and several other ladies. Then he feigned exhaustion and begged a glass of water from a server.

Now where was his wife? In the sea of heads, he couldn't see hers. He waited near the tea table, drinking his water and hoping she'd find him.

Camrun, whose dark-blue suit was, apart from Rariden's, the only one in the room as conservative as Dorrel's, stopped next to him. "Noblemen, members of parliament, civil servants . . . I'd almost rather go meet that fellow who egged Boh."

Dorrel laughed. "I'll join you."

Camrun slapped Dorrel's arm with the back of his hand. "Next best thing. Have you met Tibaud?"

"I don't think so."

Camrun grabbed his hand and pulled him through the crowd. "Tibaud!"

A fellow nearly as tall as Dorrel, wearing a conservative black suit, turned toward them. His red hair and green eyes marked him as a Shardamayn. "Camrun! How are you?"

"Very well. Have you met Dorrel?"

Tibaud extended his hand. "I haven't had that pleasure." He spoke Glynnish, but with an accent. "I pray you and Alara will be very happy together."

Dorrel wasn't used to noticing accents.

"Tibaud is the Duke of Nuahn. We'll be in his neighborhood when we go to Shandór for the summit." Camrun clapped Tibaud's shoulder. "Will you join us?"

"I wish I could, but parliamentary business will keep me in the city."

Dorrel's eyebrows shot up. "You're a member of parliament as well as a noble?"

Tibaud raised one slim finger. "I'm an MP *because* I'm the duke." He shrugged. "A seat in the Chamber of Nobles is part of my duty. Though I confess, I enjoy the work so much, I might seek office even if I were a commoner." He winked at Camrun. "Should I ever be fortunate enough to become so."

Camrun laughed. "Well, Alara would be pleased, anyway." He glanced all around. "But don't let Boh or Lena hear you talking that way."

Dorrel felt in over his head. "Sorry?"

Camrun shook his head. "Our little joke among the antimonarchist faction of the family." He turned to Tibaud. "Did you hear about Boh being egged?"

"What, again?"

"The other day. Dor, you were there."

"Yes, but there's not much —"

"Dorrel?" Domínarey approached, three people trailing her. "May I introduce the Duke and Duchess of Olsage, the Marquess and Marchioness of Moridána."

Camrun smiled stiffly, an expression Dorrel had learned to interpret as the stifling of laughter.

"And their daughter, Lady Jahnvive."

Dorrel shook hands with the duke. "Pleased to meet you, Your Grace."

"The pleasure is all mine, Your Highness, certainly."

Dorrel answered the usual round of questions about what part of Glynrell he was from and how he and Alara had met. Domínarey and Tibaud stepped aside, speaking quietly.

Lady Jahnvive, meanwhile, leaned on Camrun's arm, flirting shamelessly.

"My lady, your glass is empty." Camrun took it from her. "Let me fetch you another."

Brilliant. Dorrel's own glass had been empty for some time. "I need a refill as well," he said to the Olsages. "Would you excuse me, please?"

The duke made a little bow. "Of course, Your Highness."

He parted from Tibaud and Domínarey with a wave and followed Camrun behind the dessert table and through a door to the kitchen.

"I can't take much more of this." Dorrel sagged against one of the worktables.

"Yes, and I can't take much more of" — Camrun put on a falsetto — "'tell me, Your Highness, why are you still available?'"

Dorrel laughed.

Camrun handed the sherry glass to a server. "Please take Lady Jahnvive another sherry." He turned back to Dorrel. "When a girl starts with that, she's only interested in the title."

"Well, marry her and take her back to Glynrell, where you don't have one."

Alara came through the door.

Camrun grinned. "That would be cruel."

"Not as cruel as leaving me out there while you take refuge in the kitchen."

"I'm sorry, sweetest." Dorrel hugged her.

"My idea, entirely," Camrun said.

"Yes, I saw that. You're smarter than I give you credit for."

"Ha! Smart enough to take the back stairs to the library. And if you tell Mína where I've gone —"

"Your secret is safe with us," Dorrel said.

Camrun shot them a parting grin before crossing the kitchen to the back stairs.

Dorrel kissed the side of Alara's neck. "He is smart."

He took her hand and pulled her past the bustling kitchen staff toward the stairs.

"Are we going to hide in the library, as well?"

"Of course not." He said nothing more until they were out of earshot of the cooks. "I assume you can find your room from here."

Blushing feverishly, she smiled and squeezed his hand.

Alara could not stop trembling. It only got worse as they neared her room.

The sitting room held a tapestry-covered couch and wing chairs. The stone fireplace was as high as Alara's shoulder. An equally large fireplace in the bedroom was covered by an embroidered screen. A housekeeper had closed the heavy satin curtains and lit a single kerosene lamp by the window. A wine-colored brocade spread covered the wide four-poster bed. The summer bed curtains, flimsy gauze embroidered with tiny gold flowers, hung from the tester inlaid with ivory and gold.

Alara let go of Dorrel's hand, lit a candle from the lamp, and went through to the dressing room. She put the candleholder down, then sat on the padded bench in front of the dressing table. The tiara went back into its box, and she began pulling out hairpins. Her hands still shook.

How could she be nervous? She had longed for this, prayed for this, for years.

Her mirror reflected the bedroom through the doorway. She watched Dorrel sit on the velvet-covered bench at the foot of the bed and pull off his boots.

*Kenna, help me. He's taking his boots off!*

She combed her hair. She glanced up at his reflection. He stood in the doorway, watching her. "Why are you staring at me?"

"Because you're beautiful."

She turned back to the mirror and touched her bruised cheek. "I'm a wreck."

He moved to stand behind her. "You are beautiful, and I love you." He rested his hands gently on her shoulders, and a wicked grin spread across his face. "And you're my *wife*." He bent over and kissed her neck.

She turned and kissed him.

He ran his fingers up the back of her neck and through her hair. It sent goose bumps across her scalp and down her neck. He took her hands, pulling her away from the dressing table.

She giggled. "Let me braid my hair."

"No." He ran his fingers through her hair again. Again it sent a shiver across her skin. "Leave it."

"It'll be a mess in the morning."

"I don't care. Leave it." He kissed her again.

She left it.

# *Chapter 25*

## ALL TELSHI'S CHILDREN HAVE GIFTS

Alara woke before dawn, as usual. The heavy curtains shut out any hint of predawn light. She couldn't see Dorrel. Only by his warmth and the sound of his breathing did she know he was there.

*Telshi, thank you for this wonderful man. You've answered his prayers and mine. Now, please just reassure me we haven't made a horrible blunder by rushing into this before settling the diplomatic business.*

She reached toward him but froze. He might not wish to be awakened at that hour. Not everyone enjoyed predawn study and prayer.

Besides, she relished that time alone with Telshi.

Alara slipped out from under the brocade coverlet.

Soon, she'd read a handful of Scriptures about equality and governance. She prayed awhile and took out the loose pages of her journal.

Camrun's opinion, that the investiture was just for show, was comforting, but she suspected it was the sort of comfort that came from hearing what you wanted to hear, rather than the truth.

*If I didn't respect Jentiérri so much,* she wrote, *I'd have been more insistent about putting a stop to that travesty.*

But she did respect him, so she hadn't fought him. Now she was left to discern whether Dorrel's acceptance of the regalia violated Telshan principles. Kenna, so far, was still silent, not only on that matter, but also on the diplomatic business.

She stepped onto the sitting room's balcony. To her left, the sun peeked through the trees, casting long shadows across the gardens below.

Bowing her head, she leaned on the railing. *Kenna, I'm confused. You said "the children of Telshi have no peerage, only peers," and Rychiana said "respect your elders." Galardi said "no one holds dominion by birthright alone," but Digalo said "submit yourself to those whom Abbay has given authority." How am I supposed to make up my mind when the prophets themselves disagree?*

She waited. Birds sang. A fountain splashed.

Rector Mirva had taught her that if the Scriptures seemed to contradict themselves, then the reader, not the text, was at fault.

*I'm missing something. What am I missing?*

Kenna had said, *Telshi gives each a gift with which to serve.*

Still in her dressing gown, Alara took the Scriptures to the library. There, she took down a concordance and hunted up paper and pen to make notes.

The barest glimmer of sunlight shone around the edges of the curtains.

The space next to him was empty. Dorrel listened, but the suite was silent.

He sat up. "Lar?"

He hadn't imagined it all, surely. He got up and opened the curtain. No, this was her room, and those were her clothes all over the floor. But where was she?

In the sitting room, a stack of handwritten pages lay on the writing table. He read a few lines—her journal. He turned away.

Pacing the room, he considered whether to get dressed and look for her. Perhaps she was on that same eastern patio. Or maybe he would find where they kept a coffee pot at this hour and let her look for him.

Before he made up his mind, she returned.

A triumphant smile emblazoned her face. Her messy hair was tied up fetchingly with a narrow lace scarf, and her silk dressing gown clung to her curves.

She held several loose sheets and a book of Scripture. Ink stained the fingers of her right hand. "Oh, Dor, I've had such a wonderful study this morning." She kissed him. "Did you ring for coffee yet?"

"No. How long have you been up?"

"An hour or two, perhaps." She tugged the bell pull next to the door.

"Do you often go studying in your dressing gown at dawn?"

"No, I usually dress first." She put the book on the writing table but kept the pages in her hands. "You know I've struggled with this investiture—" Her smile fell. "You're angry."

He sighed. "I'm not angry, sweetest." Not much. He put one arm around her waist and pulled her close. Her pages rattled against his shoulder. "I just thought my days of waking up alone were over."

"Oh, love, I'm sorry. You were sleeping so soundly. I didn't want to wake you."

He spent a minute kissing her, then said, "Next time, wake me."

She grinned. "I will."

He moved toward the bedroom, but as he stepped that way, she went the other.

"While we wait for the coffee, listen to this." She glanced at her sheets.

When she was so enthusiastic, he couldn't say no.

"There's much in the Scriptures about gifts, the most popular verse being 'Telshi gives each a gift with which to serve.' You have a gift, I have a gift—all Telshi's children have gifts . . ."

Dorrel chuckled, because this was a song they all learned as children.

"To some Telshi gives the gift of healing, to others speech"—she waggled her finger at him—"to others foresight. Others may receive the ability to teach or to raise funds or to govern. Governing, Dor! The ability to govern is a gift."

"Yes . . ." He sat on the settee, stretching his arms along the back.

"Those who hold power do so because it is the will of Telshi. No one holds dominion by birthright alone." She paced as she spoke, as she used to when she practiced her sermons in the garden at Denedra while he sat on a bench.

"We're instructed to submit to just authority and to respect our elders. And we're told the one who gives is more blessed than the one who receives, because the degree to which one gives to others is the degree to which Telshi will give to you." She looked up from her notes. "I have Scripture references for all of these."

"Surely."

"So . . ." Her eyes darted, scanning the page. "Ah. If the giver is blessed, then to refuse the gift denies the giver his blessing. Therefore, and I hate to say this, Camrun is right."

"What?"

"The collar and the title are gifts from Jentiérri. Accepting lets him have his blessing and shows respect for his authority and age."

"What about no peerage, only peers?"

"Whether you consider yourself better than others has more to do with what's in your heart than what's on your neck. Heavens, I've been quoting 'no peerage, only peers' half my life. That hasn't prevented my arrogance."

"So you no longer think it's a travesty."

"When did I say—" Someone knocked on the door.

Oh, that was a mistake.

"Would you bring up our breakfast, please?" Alara asked the

servant at the door.

He could only hope Alara would let it go.

But once the servant was gone, she continued. "I don't remember saying 'travesty.'"

Dorrel pointed to the pages on the writing table.

"For the love of—you read my journal."

"You left it out. I didn't read much. Just the last bit."

Alara straightened the pages and closed the folder. "I wrote that before I did my studying." She left her notes with the journal and sat next to him. "Governing—not that a king really governs in Redíque anymore—is Jentiérri's gift. Giving you the regalia is one of the only functions remaining to him. By accepting his gifts, you did him a greater service than he did you. Because to you the collar is just a memento of Kyvern. You'll never think of yourself as 'Prince Dorrel,' only Dr. Chevallon. And he'll be left with his few remaining functions and the memory of what authority a king used to possess."

"Is that a sermon," Dorrel asked, "or a prophecy?"

"Oh!" She jumped up and started to walk away.

He caught her around the waist, pulled her into his lap, and kissed her. "Thanks for having breakfast brought up. I don't want to go downstairs yet."

She pressed one hand against his chest, nudging aside the lapel of his dressing gown. "Neither do I."

The newlyweds were left alone until teatime, when their tray arrived with a note from Camrun: *Enough! You must come to dinner, at least. You can't leave Rariden and me to fend for ourselves with this lot any longer.*

Alara called it "extraordinarily cheeky," but Dorrel just laughed.

They reveled in their solitude for a few more hours, then dressed for dinner.

Alara took out a pale green moiré silk gown, trimmed with white tulle ruffles. A crinoline supported the wide skirt, and the puffed sleeves were big enough to hide hams.

Facing the mirror over his dresser, Dorrel tied his cravat. He'd never worn suits on so many successive days before. "I suppose you're used to dressing like this."

"Father keeps things at Ravendyn rather formal." She buttoned the dress. "But not like this."

The dressing room was as big as his bedroom at home. On one side stood Alara's dressing table, flanked by two massive, ornately carved mahogany wardrobes. On the other side stood an equally large wardrobe and the dresser. The staff had moved his clothes into them during the reception.

He took a gray brocade waistcoat from his wardrobe. "You won't find any occasions in Kaesbaro this formal. Not even in Ecciston."

"Well, that'll save on the tailoring bill, won't it?" She sat in front of her mirror.

"It seems absurd for you to leave an elegant, affluent home to marry a rural vet."

Alara twisted her hair into a bun. "Oh, yes. I'll desperately miss that straw pallet at the mission in the room I shared with the Orizozabils' two daughters."

"Ha! I'll stop worrying about your reduced circumstances, then." He pulled on his black cutaway coat and went to the sitting room.

A small calendar sat on the writing table by the window. The pages were elaborately illustrated with knotwork designs and fantastical creatures. He brought it back to the dressing room.

"When's your cycle?" He leaned against the doorframe.

She wound the tendril that fell along her left cheek around her finger, twisting it into a spiral. "It was last week." She did the same to the right side. "Why?"

His pulse quickened. "When did it start?"

"A couple of days after we left the embassy."

He counted off the days. "Ha!"

"What?"

"Mum always said Telshi's timing is perfect."

"That was Galardi—" She caught his eye. He shot her a mischievous grin. "Oh, for the love of—" For a moment, she turned back to the mirror. Then she rounded on him. "I am not a mare, Dorrel Chevallon, and so help me, if you ever refer to my being 'in season,' I will smack you."

He moved to stand behind her. "All right, I won't." He kissed the side of her neck and whispered in her ear. "Except you are."

She slapped his arm, which only set him to laughing.

Alara opened a jewelry box and frowned at its brilliant contents.

Dorrel sat on a low stool near the doorway. "Dad wrote back. He said we could have the master bedroom."

"We can't kick your father out of his room."

"He insists. It's the one adjacent to the nursery." He winked at her reflection in the mirror.

She blushed—he wondered if they could skip dinner in spite of Camrun.

Alara took out a pearl necklace and put it on.

"Never mind," he said. "We can sort it out when we get home."

She closed the box. "If we get home."

Though her words were quiet, they had the effect of an alarm bell on his nerves. He stood. "You think we won't?"

"You read the Makutian papers. They call me an adulteress and you a spy. They want us both dead."

"Don't you think Boh will provide enough guards to stop them if they try?"

"Probably." Her voice squeaked. "But what if they do try?"

He grabbed her hand and pulled her from her seat. "Come pray with me."

They knelt, facing each other, in the center of the room. Alara's skirt billowed all around. Dorrel held both her hands in his, heads bowed, foreheads touching. "Telshi, You've brought us a long way from Denedra. You've brought us together, and we're inexpressibly grateful. Continue to watch over us, and bring us home safely." He hesitated, trying to compose his next thought.

"The hand of the Adversary is in this." Alara's voice quavered. "Protect us from his schemes, and keep us in the center of Your will."

That summed it up. "Ocha."

Over dinner, Alara shared the results of her morning study with the others. Camrun approved, but Mehrialéna frowned. "Thus spake the prophet Alara."

Alara's cheeks flushed. She ducked her head, eyes on her plate. "It is just an inductive study."

"If it stops you from arguing about peers and peerage," Bóhjetien said, "I do not care what you call it."

Jentiérri was absent, so Bóhjetien sat at the head of the table with Mum on his right and Alara on his left.

There was nothing simple about the family dining room but its name. Stonework walls twenty feet tall held up a coffered oak ceiling. Tapestries faded with age hung on every side. And though the company included only those who were staying at Dorváir, they half-filled the long mahogany table, which could have seated four dozen.

They ate in silence for a few minutes. Then Camrun, a few seats down from Alara on the opposite side, said, "Lar, remember that vision you had? About my researching Reyshara's abdication? Father asked me to do it."

Alara's eyes widened. "And did you?" He couldn't have. It was too soon.

"Of course not! He asked me to determine whether the constitution left any room for the restoration of the monarchy."

"Oh, no." She shook her head. "No. He cannot be thinking of such a thing."

"He might think about it," Camrun said, "but it is impossible. There were a few ambiguities, originally, that might have allowed for such a thing. But they were all later resolved by Parliament."

"So you did research the matter."

"I did not have to. That is elementary history. The foundations of our republican government are rock solid." Camrun tapped the table with his index finger. "To restore the monarchy, even in name only, the constitution would have to be amended, which would require ratification by three-quarters of the provinces. It shall never happen."

"Thanks be to Telshi." Alara toyed with the food on her plate.

"All of which is secondary."

She looked up at him. "And the primary point?"

Camrun wore a wicked grin. "Your vision was wrong."

"No, it just has not happened yet."

"It shall not."

"It shall." She speared a bite of asparagus. "But not until after you start wearing spectacles."

# Chapter 26

## No Peerage, Only Peers

In the corridor between the dining hall and sitting room, Shenevra looped her arm through Dorrel's, effectively preempting his intention to sequester himself with his wife.

Alara sidled up next to him while the server was passing port. She put her hand in his, and they sat together on a settee. He put his arm around her shoulders, kissed her cheek, and whispered in her ear. "How long do we have to stay?"

The rim of the teacup half-hid her slight smile. "Too long, I'm sure."

He chuckled and kissed her again.

"Gracious!" Mehrialéna said. "Perhaps we should excuse the newlyweds."

Dorrel started to rise, but Shenevra speared him with a glare that could've come from his own mother. "I do hope you shall stop denying us your company, when we have not seen you in ages."

Bóhjetien laughed. "There is only one company they wish to be in, yes?"

Alara blushed brightly.

"There shall be plenty of time for that later." Mehrialéna sat in an armchair near Shenevra. "It is not fair that we should have heard so much about you for so long, and then be denied the opportunity to become acquainted now that you have married Alara."

The Shardamáyns asked about the Arken Vineyard and the Chevallon Stables, and he answered their questions until he was nearly hoarse.

Alara asked a server to bring water.

Shortly after he'd brought it, Jentiérri joined them.

"Pappá!" Mehrialéna left her chair so he could have it. "I did not expect to see you down here after that confrontation this afternoon."

Alara stiffened under Dorrel's arm. "What confrontation?"

Jentiérri accepted the cup of tea Domínarey brought him. "The one that brings me here. I thought you should know. Mr. Gralok, the Makutian ambassador, called on me this afternoon." He sipped his tea. "Mightily offended, you know. Sending word to Tarvag by diplomatic courier."

Alara nodded.

"Threatened to call off the summit, also."

"Did he?" Dorrel was about fed up with Makutian demands. "And what did he say about the border guard who shot at Alara?"

"Denied everything, you know," Jentierri answered. "Not under orders . . . acting on his own initiative . . . reprimanded by his commanding officer . . . that sort of thing."

"Huh." Meanwhile, they were calling for Alara's execution. And his.

"What shall we do?" Alara asked.

Jentiérri shrugged. "Let the diplomats sort it out. You proceed to Shandór as planned."

"I wrote to Velek," Bóhjetien said. "If the ambassadors cannot settle things, perhaps he and I can."

Alara sighed. "I hope so."

Talk turned to plans for the trip. They would leave in two days.

"Mina shall stay here with the children," Bóhjetien said. "Mehrialéna, I would like you to come to Shandór as hostess."

"Me? Perhaps I should stay with the children, and . . ."

"Lena," Jentiérri said, "please cooperate."

"But Mina is ten times the hostess I am."

"And infinitely more a mother until something changes, eh?" Jentiérri grinned at Mehrialéna, who ducked her head, blushing.

Dorrel hadn't thought her capable of a blush.

"Besides," Jentiérri said, "You much prefer Shandór to Dorváir, especially in the summer. You need not come back until autumn, if you wish."

Mehrialéna sighed. "Very well. It shall, at least, allow me to become better acquainted with Dorrel, yes?"

"Certainly," Bóhjetien said. "We should have a day or two before the summit begins."

"Bóhjetien," Domínarey said softly, "if there is an extra day or two, Alara and Dorrel would rather spend that time at the lodge, certainly."

"I cannot possibly go to the lodge," Mehrialéna said. "There shall be too much to do at the house."

"I was not speaking of you, Mehrialéna."

Mehrialéna frowned for a moment. Then her eyebrows shot up. "Ah! You are encouraging them."

Domínarey lifted her teacup and smiled.

Bóhjetien's cup landed in the saucer with a clatter. He leaned toward Dorrel. "My wife is a genius. Indeed, you must go to the lodge while we make the preparations."

"It is a brilliant idea, Mina." Alara pressed closer to Dorrel's side. "The lodge is on the east shore of the lake." Her voice dropped. "Miles from anything. As long as we're there, we needn't see another soul."

Miles from anything and anyone was precisely where he wanted to be with her. "Can we leave now?"

Bóhjetien agreed to move their departure up by one day, but not two. So the next morning was as blissful and leisurely as the previous one. But, while they sat in bed, the breakfast tray between them, Alara picked at her food, clearly preoccupied. Dorrel supposed it had to do with the Makutians.

He finished his coffee and got up to move the tray. "If you're finished . . ."

She topped off her coffee. "Yes, thank you."

He took the tray to the sitting room and left it on the coffee table. When he returned, she was in the dressing room.

"Camrun hasn't ordered us downstairs again, has he?"

"No." She'd taken out a linen shift. He hadn't seen her wear anything that plain since home.

"Then why are you dressing?"

She sighed. "Love, you know I adore you . . ."

"That sounds as if there's a 'but' coming."

"I need time alone with Telshi, also."

"Can't you do that here?"

She smirked at him. "Can you keep your hands off me that long?"

He grabbed her around the waist and kissed her neck. "That depends on how long 'that long' is."

Alara moved from the writing desk to the balcony and back again, several times, sighing intermittently. Ordinarily, her time in the Scriptures was soothing. Now she found only confusion.

Dorrel put his book down. "Is your morning devotional always so beleaguered?"

"Hardly ever." She sat in the desk chair. "Ever since Boh said he hoped I would stop arguing about peers and peerage, I've had a nagging feeling . . ."

"That you ought to argue about it more?"

"Yes!" She sprang from the chair and went to the balcony again.

He followed. Standing behind her, he put his arms around her waist and his chin on her head.

"I don't wish to be belligerent." She leaned against his chest. "I just want to . . ."

"Abolish the monarchy."

Her head drooped.

He kissed the back of her neck, then let go of her and pulled up one of the little wrought-iron chairs for her. He took the other. "Lar, your ministry isn't here. That's not your work to do."

"I know. Only the king and Parliament could do it. But they won't."

"What about Tibaud? Camrun said he's an antimonarchist. Hasn't he tried?"

"Of course he has. There's plenty of support for such a thing in the Chamber of Burgesses. But not in the Chamber of Nobles. It never gets out of committee. They'll never pass such a piece of legislation, unless . . ."

He waited out her hesitation.

"Unless Kenna pushes them to it, somehow."

He leaned forward. "You think She wants you to do the pushing?"

"Perhaps. I'm not sure. I have no standing with parliament. And it would be disrespectful for me, a junior cleric and once-removed cousin, to tell Jentiérri what to do. Besides, I've been going on about 'no peerage, only peers' so long, I don't know whether he'll hear me."

Dorrel folded his arms. "Your conclusion about my accepting the regalia doesn't help you there, either."

"I know." She put her head in her hands.

Someone knocked at the door. Dorrel went to answer it.

*Kenna, help me understand what—if anything—You want me to tell Jentiérri.*

**Bóhjetien.**

A shiver passed through her.

*But how am I to explain that although Dorrel could accept a collar, Boh can't accept a crown?*

*Dorrel willingly laid aside the collar. Reyshara laid aside a crown. She was the first. She must not be the last.*

Tears stung her eyes. *But I have spent years telling my cousins democracy is the only truly Telshan form of government. Why should they listen now?*

**It would not be the first time people failed to listen to a prophet. The message must be given anyway.**

Her pulse pounded in her ears like hoofbeats at the gallop. A prophet.

*But why was Jentiérri allowed to reign and Boh not?*

**Jentiérri failed to lay aside the crown.**

The trembling and tears intensified.

"The kitchen staff wanted to know—" Dorrel crouched next to her. "Oh, Lar . . ."

"It's not for Jentiérri. It's for Boh." She took a deep breath and wiped the tears from her cheeks. "It makes sense, really. Boh dislikes politics. That's why he spends most of his time at Shandór instead of here."

"Then perhaps he'll be willing to listen."

Some of the tension left her posture. "I hope so." She returned the desk to add these thoughts and Kenna's words to her journal.

"I told the girl from the kitchen we'd take lunch here."

"Thank you, love."

He sat down and picked up his book.

She picked up the pen but turned to him. "Remember when you said my vision about Uked was prophetic?"

"You said seeing and prophecy were different."

"Yes. A seer's vision is of Telshi's plan for the future, exactly as it will happen."

"And a prophecy?"

"Prophecy is a message. Sometimes it's a prediction of the future. But sometimes"—a chill crept up her neck—"sometimes it's a choice."

"Like when Digalo told King Pelyun that to follow Telshi, he could have only one wife."

"Exactly." Could she admit to the rest?

If she couldn't tell Dorrel, there was no one she could tell.

"No monarch since Reyshara Kordelyon willingly gave up a crown. So to convince others to do the same, it seems Kenna chose someone from her line who is arrogant enough to speak to royalty of democracy. She gave me foresight. As you said, I do run in these circles anyway." She gave him a twisted smile. "You were right."

"About . . . prophetic?"

"Yes." She dropped the pen and stalked the room. "But I can't . . . Dor . . ." Her tears resumed. "I'm a prophet."

He jumped up and blocked her mad pacing, enfolding her against his chest. "I can't think of anyone better."

She drew strength from his words and his trust. *Kenna, make me worthy.*

Despite her self-proclaimed arrogance, Alara lacked courage and words. Her praying so distracted her from the after-dinner conversation, she excused herself to sit on a padded bench in the corridor to pray properly.

*Kenna, why was it easier to speak to Velek than to give this message to Boh?*

She didn't need an answer. Surely it was because she couldn't fall back on "I've had a vision," which her family was used to hearing. This was not a vision. It was a prophecy—one that could change the course of a nation's history.

Despite Bóhjetien's disdain for politics, she expected him to tease her, as Camrun or Mehrialéna would, *Thus spake the prophet Alara.*

Mehrialéna's crinoline rustled as she approached. "You newlyweds have not had a spat, have you?"

"No, Lena. I was praying."

"Oh. I am sorry to have interrupted, then." She turned away.

"Lena? Tell Boh I need to speak with him, please?"

Mehrialéna nodded and returned to the sitting room.

*Kenna, tell me what to say.*

Bóhjetien soon emerged. "What is it, Alara?"

She stood. As she did, a sensation came over her she hadn't felt since her ordination. As if a great wind had blown through the hall, into her soul, filling her with the power of Ahbay's spirit.

"Bóhjetien, you know what Kenna said about peers and peerage."

"We are not starting this again —"

"Galardi wrote that citizens must submit themselves to the rule of just authority, and Redíquans have rationalized the perpetuation of the monarchy by calling it a just authority. But Galardi said no one holds dominion by birthright alone. The Canon decrees that authority is justified first by obedience to the precepts, and second by the approval of the populace."

"Are you accusing my father of violating some precept? Or are you saying the people disapprove of him?"

"Jentiérri is a faithful Telshan. But the fellow who threw that egg at you is not alone. Many Redíquans are antimonarchists. Yet the matter has never been put to a referendum."

Hands on hips, he made a noise that was almost a laugh. "Are you saying we ought to hold a referendum on whether to depose my father?"

"No. Jentiérri may serve out his days as he is."

"Oh, that is very generous of you —"

"These words are not from me, Boh!" Tears trickled down her face. She made no move to brush them away. "I wish I did not have to say them, but I must. Mairah knows the number of Jentiérri's days, and they are few. He is not asked to change."

The color drained from Boh's face.

"You are." She took a deep breath. "Reyshara Kordelyon set an example no other monarch has dared to follow. Kenna is asking you to follow it."

Bóhjetien stared at her for a moment, then turned his back on her and stalked away.

# Chapter 27

## SHANDÓR

Dorrel was accustomed to Dorváir being silent in the mornings, but on the day of their departure, the halls buzzed with servants rushing about, fetching and carrying supplies to the courtyard. Alara showed him to the morning room, a sunny spot with windows on two sides. Servers poured coffee, and the family milled about, talking excitedly of the trip.

"We shall breakfast first," Bóhjetien said, "and then have a walkabout."

Dorrel leaned close to Alara. "What does he mean, 'walkabout'?"

"Greeting the citizens. The Shardamayns often do on such occasions."

"Isn't that dangerous, given the circumstances?"

She frowned at him. "We're far from Makut, Dor. They can't reach us here."

"Can't they?"

Dorrel would rather have seen to the horses, but he couldn't say no to Domínarey, who'd been such a gracious hostess. With Alara on one side and Shenevra on the other, he walked through the massive front doors of Dorváir, down a walkway, and through a wrought-iron gate. The entire family went out, even Bóhjetien's three children, with only two soldiers watching the gate. Half the family went one way and half the other. They walked along the sidewalks, where a throng of people waited. They shook hands all the way down the block.

An old woman took his hand in both of hers. "Telshi be with you, Your Highness."

He'd given up on correcting people. "And also with you."

Many of the ladies gave Alara flowers, and a few even gave him some.

At the end of the block, they crossed the street and made their way back, passing Bóhjetien and his lot along the way. Then they crossed the street again and returned to the gate. By the time they stepped back inside the house, Alara's arms were so overflowing that Shenevra and Mehrialéna had to help her carry all the flowers.

The soldiers came in last and closed the massive doors behind them.

Alara walked to a large basket at the end of the foyer and dropped her armload of flowers into it. The others did likewise, until the basket overflowed.

Dorrel dropped his as well. "We're just going to leave them here?"

"I shall put some of them to use decorating the house." Domínarey walked past him and added her load to the pile. "I'll send housekeepers to the hospital with the rest to give to patients. They shall not go to waste."

"Ah. That's good." It still seemed as if the citizens had gone to a lot of trouble for nothing.

In the courtyard, the horses waited, free of baggage this time, since it was all on a wagon. Dorrel patted Bastion's neck and checked the fit of his tack. He wasn't accustomed to having others outfit his horse.

He looked across the yard. Seven of them traveling to Shandór, yet with the same number of guards that had escorted the two of them and Bóhjetien from Makut. Somehow, this seemed unwise, but if Barláhtiay and Bóhjetien had agreed, who was he to argue?

Alara half expected more wisecracks from Bóhjetien about her call for his abdication, but throughout the day's ride, he behaved as if she'd said nothing about it. Just as well. She really didn't care to discuss it further, so she wouldn't. Unless Kenna insisted.

"It's a prophecy," Dorrel said that night, while they settled into their room at a hotel. "He can't ignore it entirely."

Alara snorted. "He surely can. And likely will." She sat on the edge of the bed and pulled off her boots. "That's between him and Kenna now."

The following morning, Alara dug through her bags. "Blast."

"What?" Dorrel buttoned his shirt.

"Our brigandines are on the wagon."

His hands froze. "You think we need them here?"

She sighed and closed the valise. "Probably not. But . . ." She couldn't explain the feeling that had come over her. "I just feel compelled to wear it."

"Then we'll go down to the wagon and find it."

She shook her head. "No, no. I'm probably being silly." Yet stepping out of the room without armor seemed unwise.

In the hallway, no guard stood outside their door. Alara wasn't sure whether to take comfort from that or not. She and Dorrel walked downstairs to the dining room. None of the soldiers stood on guard duty. They all sat at a table near the door, eating. Barláhtiay rose when they walked in. "Your table is there, madáme. Sir." He pointed across the room to a round table in the corner.

"Thank you." Alara walked that way. Rariden and Camrun were already there, drinking coffee.

While Dorrel pulled a chair for her next to Rariden, she scanned the room again. "Should I be worried no one's standing guard?"

"Huh." Rariden put down his cup. "Yes. I was thinking the same thing."

Camrun dropped his menu. "You don't really expect trouble here?"

"No." Rariden smirked. "That doesn't mean we shouldn't be prepared for it."

"Hmm. I suppose even if Makutian bounty hunters don't come looking for you two, there's always the risk of antimonarchists having a go at Bóhjetien." Camrun handed her a menu.

Alara read it—a hand-lettered card describing three choices for breakfast. Nothing looked appetizing. And she had to stifle the irrational desire to ask one of Barláhtiay's men to fetch her armor.

Alara picked at her omelet, but she forced most of it down, along with some fruit and too much coffee. Her nerves jittered, though she wasn't sure the coffee was entirely to blame.

Bóhjetien emptied his cup. "We shall have a walkabout before we leave."

"Must we?" Alara crossed her silverware on the plate. "It may not be wise."

He frowned at her. "We have plenty of time to reach Shandór. We must not forgo our obligations."

Greeting his supporters probably wasn't obligatory, but she didn't wish to start another fight with him. So she folded her napkin and rose when he did.

Barláhtiay and his soldiers had finished their meal and left the room earlier, presumably to prepare the horses.

She grabbed Dorrel's hand as they crossed the lobby.

"What's wrong?"

"I don't know. I just feel . . . danger."

He put his arm around her shoulders. "You expect this to be different than in Darshalay? I was worried then, but nothing happened."

"I don't know. I've never before felt this kind of . . ." It took her a moment to find the word. "Premonition."

He gave her a squeeze, and they followed Bóhjetien and the others out the doors, down the steps, and into the street.

The crowd cheered at the sight of Bóhjetien. This time, the family didn't split up but instead moved in a file along the ranks of well-wishers. Alara kept her ears alert but heard not a single antimonarchist jeer.

But then, it wasn't really antimonarchists she feared.

Just as in Darshalay, ladies handed her flowers and gentlemen shook her hand. They all called her and Dorrel highnesses and went uncorrected, because it wasn't worth the bother.

Alara's nerves jangled like sleigh bells. A man shook hands with Mehrialéna. His posture was stiff, a bouquet clenched under his left arm. Alara stared, as if Kenna whispered, **Look**.

He let go of Mehrialéna's hand and met Alara's eye. He grinned. A little too much. "Mrs. Chevallon." His right hand reached for the flowers.

Before she could thank him for not calling her *highness*, he jabbed at her with a knife.

She grabbed his wrist, swinging his arm up and away.

The flowers hit the pavement. He punched her in the gut.

The air blew out of her.

Screams. Scuffling feet. Shouts.

She twisted his arm farther, but he kicked her knee.

She almost buckled. Kicked at his shin. Failed to knock his legs from under him.

He wrapped his other arm around her neck, pulling her close to his stinking self.

For a moment, he was Korig.

She screamed and rammed her knee into his hip. Didn't break the hold. She couldn't get her forearm up to his neck. She grabbed his shirtsleeve instead and tried to pull his arm away.

A fist darted into view. Collided with the man's temple.

The man's head snapped sideways. He went limp.

She dropped him. He fell, and the knife clattered to the sidewalk.

Rariden released his fist. "Grappling was never your strong suit."

She bent, hands on knees, trying to catch her breath. Not Korig. This man was clean-shaven, blond, and younger than the sergeant. "No, sir." She jerked upright. "Dor?"

Rariden pointed behind her.

Dorrel stood over a similar assailant, his foot in the man's back, the man's arm pulled backward at a painful angle.

Rariden jerked a thumb. "He's pretty good at grappling."

Alara laughed, a hysterical sound. "Yes. Yes he is."

"Tie these two up," Rariden bellowed in passable Redíquan. Barláhtiay's men rushed in, finally, and bound the assailants hand and foot. "Take them to the constable." Rariden looked about. "Bóhjetien!"

"Yes, sir?"

Bóhjetien, who had been at the head of the line, ran back to Rariden, who had been bringing up the rear behind Dorrel and Camrun.

"I think we must delay departure long enough to tell the police of this."

"Yes, certainly."

"It will be easier to keep Dorrel and Alara safe if we take them back inside and ask the constable to come to them."

"Yes, yes. You go. I shall send Captain Barláhtiay to the constable."

The family returned to the hotel and waited in the dining room —

by then mostly empty—for the constable to come.

Two guards took stations at the door.

*Kenna, forgive me for neglecting your warning.* Alara rubbed her head, which now ached more than her bruised belly. *Although if you really wanted me to pay attention, you might have spoken more clearly.*

What an awful prayer.

*Forgive me.* She lifted her teacup. Empty. She put it back on the saucer and pushed it away.

The hotel manager had closed the dining room for them. Dealing with the constable took the better part of the morning.

The manager approached, wringing a tea towel. "I hate to trouble you, constable, but I must serve luncheon to my guests."

"Ah, certainly. I think we are finished here." He stood and put his notebook and pencil in the pocket of his blue coat. "Again, I am most sorry this trouble came upon you in our town, Curate."

"No apologies necessary, Constable." She stood and shook his hand. Dorrel did the same. They saw him to the door.

In the lobby, Bóhjetien, Rariden, and Barláhtiay stood talking. The constable departed, and Alara and Dorrel joined the others.

"We no longer have time to reach Shandór by nightfall," Bóhjetien said, "so we will stop instead in Vielshay."

"But Reynami remained in Darshalay, did she not?" Alara turned to Dorrel. "I don't know if you met Reynami. She's the Duchess of Vielshay, so like Tibaud, she's a member of parliament."

Dorrel shrugged. "I don't remember."

She couldn't blame him. Sometimes she, too, had trouble keeping track of all the cousins.

"I doubt Reynami's steward will deny us hospitality." Bóhjetien frowned. "Especially given the circumstances."

Barláhtiay carried his hat under his arm. "I have sent word ahead with two of my men. They shall ensure the manor is secure. We can leave when you are ready."

"Thank you, Captain." Alara exchanged a glance with Dorrel, who nodded. "First, let us go to the baggage wagon for our armor."

The last leg of their trip—from the manor house in Vielshay to Shandór—wound through a dense forest of larch, beech, and ash. The terrain rolled gently. Shortly after midday, they left the forest road and moved onto a wide avenue lined with flowering dogwoods.

Not long after that, they topped a rise, and Dorrel got his first sight of Shandór.

The palace sat on a wide meadow bordering the largest lake he'd ever seen. It stretched away so far, the trees on the opposite shore were just a dark blur.

Shandór's blue slate roof was a sea of gables and conical turret tops, surmounting brilliant white marble walls. The central part of the palace ran parallel to the shoreline. From each end of it, a wing reached back toward the lake.

Several outbuildings had the unmistakable look of stables. Grassy fields along the lakeshore were cross-fenced with white five-bar fences like the ones at his uncle's ranch in Ecciston.

The road took them into a depression, hiding the palace. When they next saw it, they were hastening down a curving track to its gates. Hawthorn trees lining the drive bloomed with clusters of tiny white flowers.

A pair of soldiers emerged from the gatehouse. One saluted and the other blew the "attention" call on a bugle as the company rode past.

A round tower stood at the center of the façade, flanked by smaller towers at the corners. Ornately carved windows stared over the drive.

Bóhjetien took the lead from the color guard, taking them from the main drive onto a fork that went around the east wing of the palace. The gravel driveway wound past a garden of tidy hedges, color-filled flowerbeds, and shade trees with widespread branches. Across a wide expanse of short grass and past a copse of trees lay the lake, its windswept water glittering.

The drive curved to their right, ending at a brick-paved courtyard bordered on three sides by the stables Dorrel had seen from the road.

After the horses had been taken care of, the military escort headed for the barracks, while the others walked to what Bóhjetien called "the house."

Dorrel looked across the lake to the low, rolling hills on the far shore. He hadn't seen a mountain since leaving Gadrut.

They walked slowly along a sinuous path of octagonal pavers that wound through the gardens, past a swan-shaped fountain with water spilling from the beak.

At Denedra, Dorrel had sometimes missed home, but at least he was in the mountains, in familiar territory. Now he'd spent weeks not only far from home, but far from anything remotely like home.

Shandór's dozens of windows peered down at him. He grabbed Alara's hand.

She moved closer so her arm brushed against his. It made him feel a little less homesick. But only a little.

Bóhjetien opened a plain white door at ground level and led them through a large mudroom and down a wide corridor past the scullery and workrooms. Small paintings and needlework hangings decorated the whitewashed walls. It was much like the back rooms at Denedra.

They stopped at an office so small only Bóhjetien and Mehrialéna could go in. The others waited in the hall.

A slender, middle-aged woman with a gray-blonde braid wound around her head leaned over a floor plan. "I have put the Kordelyons in their usual apartments in the east wing, second floor." The housekeeper leaned sideways to see around Bóhjetien and speak to Shenevra. "Mr. Kordelyon is there now."

Shenevra smiled, brushed past Rariden, and hurried down the hallway.

"The prime minister's staff is on the third floor," she continued. "I have put the other Glynrellans in the east wing, also. When Prince

Velek's party arrives, I shall put them in the west wing with Your Royal Highnesses."

"Very good. We shall take tea in the green parlor." Mehrialéna stayed in the housekeeper's office, discussing further plans.

Bóhjetien took the rest of them up a narrow stair that led to a white door. He opened it, they stepped through, and all resemblance to Denedra ended.

They walked along a corridor wide enough for six people to go abreast without touching shoulders. The tapestries and gilt-framed paintings were proportioned to fit under the twenty-foot-high coffered oak ceiling. They passed closed doors decorated with gold filigree.

"These are the meeting rooms." Bóhjetien pointed to the doors but did not stop. He continued to an open space where the corridor intersected a wider hall. "And here is the great hall."

On Dorrel's right, the oak-paneled hall extended to a wall of windows overlooking the lake. The vaulted ceiling must've been forty feet high. Cases held pottery and other ornaments. Portraits covered the walls on either side. The gold railing of a gallery overhead ran toward the front of the building.

They turned left through an archway flanked by fluted columns and into a rotunda decorated with trees in brass pots. A cream-colored circular sofa with a conical backrest stood at the rotunda's center, an intricate starburst of multicolored marble tile radiating from beneath it.

Bóhjetien climbed the right-hand branch of a dual staircase, the arms of which curved upward to a landing above the archway.

Alara's hand trailed lightly over the golden balustrade. Halfway up she halted, gasping. There hung a portrait of Kyvern. "Boh. Is this Lena's work?"

He took a few steps back down. "Yes." His eyes drifted over it. "One of her better efforts, I think. She did it right after we got the news."

"It is just like him." She turned to Camrun. "Is it not?"

"Certainly."

Kyvern strongly resembled Shenevra. Mehrialéna had captured in oil the way his eyes crinkled when he smiled.

"Only she painted Ky wearing his collar." Alara started up the stairs again. "Since we rarely wear them, it is not really an honest portrayal."

"But it is lifelike," Dorrel said.

"Certainly," Alara said. "Remind me to tell Mehrialéna she has missed her calling."

"Ah," Bóhjetien said. "Is that also a word from Kenna, O wise prophetess?"

Camrun snickered. Alara hung her head.

Had Dorrel been holding an egg, he'd have thrown it at Bóhjetien.

Servants had brought their luggage up from the wagon, so Dorrel pulled off his brigandine and the sweat-soaked gambeson beneath it and changed into a clean shirt. They seemed unlikely to need armor in the palace. At least, not until the Makutians showed up.

Alara put on a plain cotton chemise. "Tea isn't for a half an hour." She pulled on her clerical vest. "I'm going to talk to my father now and get it over with."

He held her hand. "You don't want me to come?"

"I should do this on my own."

"Do you trust yourself to go without someone to stop you from punching him?"

"Hmm. I don't trust you not to punch him."

He kissed her hand. "You are very wise."

Alara's heart trembled. She knocked on the door of her parents' suite. Her father opened it. He wore a royal-blue suit with a black satin waistcoat.

"Hello, Alara," he said, as if greeting a lobbyist. "Come in. Shen," he called, while Alara moved into the center of the sitting room, "it's Alara."

Mum came out of the bedroom, wearing her crinoline and an underbodice. "Well, you changed quickly—oh, baby, is that all you're wearing?"

"This is not Darshalay, Mum. I'm a curate and ought to dress in keeping with my office."

Mum sighed. "If you must." She headed back to her dressing room. "Will you come help me into this gown?"

Alara followed and lifted the heavy gown of peach-colored moiré silk over her mother's head. "It's a bit much for summer, isn't it?"

"Perhaps." Folds of fabric muffled Mum's voice. Her head popped through the neck opening. "But it's always been one of my favorites." She started fastening the tiny pearl buttons. "What brings you?"

"I need to talk to Father."

"Ah." Mum turned away and pulled a jewelry box from her trunk.

"You might want to listen. It's important."

Alara headed toward the sitting room. Her father, arms folded, blocked the doorway. "I'm right here. Go ahead."

She took a deep breath.

He stared at her, his expression blank.

"You will lose the election."

A frown flitted across his face before being replaced by the mask of his political smile. "Now, how do you know that?"

She described the vision, every detail of it, down to Horym knocking over the inkbottle.

Mum clutched her jewelry box against her waist. "Druyun, you had better start planning now what you'll do. You could teach at the university, or"—she turned to Alara—"who will win?"

"You're taking it as a foregone conclusion she's right." Father frowned.

"She always is. You know Alara's never had a vision that didn't happen. Isn't that right, baby?"

Before Alara could answer, her father said, "Why do you keep calling her baby? She's a grown woman, for heaven's sake."

He was the one person who hadn't treated her like a grown woman. "I wasn't shown who will win the election. I've told you all I was shown." She sidled past him and made for the door.

"Now wait just a minute, young lady." He pursued her. "You cannot come in here, make a threat like that, and—"

"That was not a threat, sir." Alara paused, hand on the doorknob. "I only told you what I saw." She left without another word. He was working himself up to a fine bluster, and she didn't care to witness it.

Dorrel met Camrun in the hall and followed him back downstairs to the green parlor, a large room two doors down from the rotunda.

A grouping of settees and armchairs upholstered in forest-green leather filled the center of the room. A gold chandelier glittered in the sunlight.

Rariden sat in a chair, talking with two people on a settee.

"Professor Sheeno." Dorrel half-expected a rebuke for running off during an alarm, but Sheeno got up and gave him a pumping handshake.

"So good to see you." He slapped Dorrel's shoulder and gestured to Prelate Dalys. Her greeting was more subdued, but her smile no less broad than the professor's. They spent a few minutes catching up.

Men in suits stood in a cluster by the windows. The prime minister's people, probably. Broad, tall windows looked over the front drive and a fountain. Three tiers of marble basins spilled water into a pool lined with blue and green tiles. The open windows let in the music of splashing water and singing birds.

Soon Alara joined them. The prelate rose to hug her. "I am so glad you're . . ." She eyed the green splotch on Alara's right temple. "Not too badly hurt."

But the prelate couldn't see the stitches or the boot-size bruises smeared across Alara's ribs.

Instead of taking a seat, Alara moved to the tea service covering a half-round table against the left wall. Camrun was already there, loading his plate. Dorrel joined them, picking from the assortment of tiny sandwiches and cookies while Alara poured two cups of tea.

Shenevra and the prime minister arrived shortly, then Bóhjetien and finally Mehrialéna, whose gown was as elaborate as Shenevra's.

The room murmured and buzzed for some time as those who'd been in the attack described it to those who hadn't.

"Has anyone considered," Prime Minister Kordelyon said, "whether these assassins were in the employ of King Domat?"

A murmur washed over the room like a wave.

Bójetien stepped closer to Mr. Kordelyon. "What makes you say that?"

"Who else has cause to attack Alara? The Makutian papers have been calling for her and Dorrel's execution since they escaped the palace."

"I do not believe Velek would do such a thing." Bóhjetien frowned.

"I did not say he did." Mr. Kordelyon smirked. "But the king?"

Bóhjetien shrugged.

The chatter turned to what the Makutian papers said about the wedding and speculation over whether the Makutians would boycott the summit.

"They cannot," Mr. Kordelyon said. "For them to back out now would be an affront to Bóhjetien as well as to the rest of us."

Bóhjetien shook a finger at him. "Do not underestimate King Domat. His plans have failed, and he shall do whatever he must to recover his honor."

The prime minister snorted. "Yes. Apparently that includes assassinating my daughter and son-in-law. It shall not happen."

"Certainly not."

Alara tapped Dorrel's arm. She gestured toward the door, where the prelate stood. "We'll be back shortly. I hope."

He kissed her cheek. "The curacy?"

"No. I want to talk to her about . . . the other thing." The two of them left.

Shenevra looked from Dorrel to her husband and back again, shrugging at Dorrel with an apologetic smile. She seemed to be trying to get the prime minister to stop talking politics so she could introduce them.

Dorrel rather wished he would go on talking politics.

But finally she pulled him over. "Druyun, this is Dorrel Chevallon."

The prime minister put out his hand. "Good to meet you."

Dorrel shook it. "Sir."

"My wife has told me a lot about you. You've won her over, I'd say, as well as Alara." He smiled, sort of—a stiff mask.

"I've always got on well with Lar's family." Until he'd said it, Dorrel hadn't realized this was a rather pointed way of mentioning that Mr. Kordelyon was the only one in the immediate family who hadn't visited Denedra.

Camrun chuckled. "Yes, you get on better with me than she does."

Mr. Kordelyon made a similar chuckle. "That could be said of almost anyone, Cam." He gestured to Dorrel to step aside with him. Dorrel followed. Even if he didn't wish to give his father-in-law any deference, he supposed some was owed to the prime minister—albeit only while he remained in office.

Which wouldn't be long.

"I understand you're related to the Ecciston Chevallons."

"Yes."

"Why did your family leave Ecciston?"

"When my uncle inherited the business, my father chose to go out on his own."

"I see. And what does he do?"

"He's a farrier and keeps a livery."

Mr. Kordelyon nodded, pursing his lips. "And you're in the same line of work, I gather?"

"I'm studying veterinary medicine." For the first time, Dorrel wished, if all these outlandish things had to happen, they'd happened after he'd gotten his degree, just so he could honestly say he was a doctor.

"I see." Mr. Kordelyon folded his arms. "Dorrel, my wife thinks highly of you, and obviously Alara does, too." He made an artificial smile. "And I trust their judgment. Of course, every father thinks no man is worthy of his daughter. Still, now that you have married Alara, I expect you to take good care of her."

Even if this speech was just a show of paternal intimidation, it was in horribly bad taste. "Begging your pardon, *sir*." Dorrel loaded that honorific with all the sarcasm he could muster. "But I think I've done a better job taking care of her lately than you have." He spun around and walked out.

# Chapter 28

## THE HEIGHT OF ARROGANCE

Alara opened the door to the drawing room, a smaller room next to the green parlor. In the center of the room, three leather-upholstered armchairs surrounded a low, round table. Alara walked past them and around the large writing desk to open the bright floral curtains. Sunlight washed across the blond-oak paneling.

Prelate Dalys took the chair facing the window. "Thank you for suggesting we excuse ourselves, Curate. I didn't wish to offend your cousins by doing so. But we do need to speak privately."

Alara sank into the chair next to her.

The prelate smiled. "I received a request from the trustees in Kaesbaro."

"Oh." Alara hadn't expected such a letter to reach her so quickly, if at all, because the newspapers had listed Mr. Risdun as disabled.

"The timing is perfect. I dispatched one of our newly ordained curates to take your place at the mission."

"Oh."

"I'm sorry. Did you not intend to accept the curacy?"

"Oh! Oh, I'm eager to. And not just because of Dorrel. But if I'm not ready—"

"My dear, if a year with Rector Orizozabil didn't ready you, nothing would." The prelate searched her with an intense gaze. "A year ago, a cocky young lady came into my office insisting she was ready to lead a congregation." Her thin, pale eyebrows went up. "Have we lost that cocky young lady?"

Alara ducked her head. "Yes, ma'am."

The prelate's voice was gentle. "That's why you were sent, you know."

"I know." The words barely squeaked out. Alara took a deep breath. "But he often implies I'm not suitable for the clergy. And I've never had a vision of myself on a rostrum."

"Alara." The prelate leaned forward, her hands clasped in front of her. "You can't make decisions based on what you have *not* seen."

"I know. But my preaching is . . . awful."

"Nonsense." She stiffened. "Did Orizozabil say that?"

"Not in so many words."

"I have heard you preach many times. If you were awful, you would not have passed Rector Mirva's courses."

"But Rector Orizozabil says I choke up too much. But the only way to avoid choking up is to think about something else. But then he says I'm too distracted."

The prelate glanced heavenward. "When I sent you there, I expected him to cure your cockiness, not replace one form of pride with another."

"Ma'am?"

"Genuine emotion is not a problem. If Orizozabil led you to believe it is, he's wrong, and I shall have words with him."

Alara gaped, dumbstruck.

"Your problem," the prelate said, "is not an excess of emotion or a deficit of focus. It is, as ever, your pride."

"But it's not. About other things, yes," Alara said sourly, "but this is something I know I'm doing poorly."

"You are not a perfect preacher, Alara. Neither are you a poor one. You seem to believe preaching is a performance that must be flawless. But the success of your congregation will depend less upon the quality of your preaching than upon the devotion of its members to Telshi. To believe otherwise is the height of arrogance."

Alara nodded. Tears welled in her eyes.

"I have several rectors to whom I can send cocky young curates. I sent you to Orizozabil's mission because, of the cocky graduates I had last year, you were the one who had not only the generosity to serve the people there, but the fortitude to withstand the hardships." She smiled. "You are eminently suitable for the clergy, Alara. And given your association with Kaesbaro through its support of the mission, you are better suited to that curacy than anyone else in my purview."

This endorsement was more than Alara had dared pray for. She pulled out a handkerchief to dry her eyes. "Thank you, Prelate. But . . . how can I overcome the fact that every time I perform a holy rite, I wind up thinking about myself?"

"For example?"

"I did a naming in Kaesbaro, and instead of the baby I was thinking about my father and the Makutians and Dorrel and how much I wanted to be his wife. How much I want to be a mother."

"Curate Chevallon," the prelate said, as if scolding her for giving the wrong answer in class, "do you imagine I can officiate at a wedding and not remember my own? Every time I perform a naming, I remember those of my children. How could I not? That is not egotism. It is empathy."

Alara stared into the prelate's blue-gray eyes, allowing the lesson to sink in. "Rector Orizozabil never said such a thing."

"Ah. I shall have words with him, indeed."

After a few moments' silence, Prelate Dalys braced her hands to rise.

"Wait."

"Is there something else?"

Alara covered her eyes with one hand. "Oh, there's so much . . ."

She looked up, first at the ceiling, then at the portrait over the fireplace, as if that many-times-great grandfather could give her the words she needed.

Only One could do that. *Kenna, tell me what to say.*

She described, haltingly at first, her most recent visions, and the messages she'd received in Tarvag and Darshalay. The more she spoke, the more words poured out of her.

The prelate listened with her usual serene patience.

"What am I to do?" Alara asked. "Nothing in my training prepared me for this."

"Indeed." The prelate's face was as inscrutable as on the day Alara had given her dissertation. "There have been no prophets in living memory. It is not a skill to be taught. If it were, who would teach it?"

"Do you think I'm misinterpreting?"

"I cannot judge that. Only history can judge whether one is truly a prophet."

This was indisputable. When she was young, no one believed Alara was a seer, until the things she'd seen began happening. "It's daunting," she whispered.

The prelate ducked her head, her brow creased. This minuscule crack in her unflappable demeanor made Alara shiver. "I wish I knew what to tell you, Alara. All I can say is . . . let Ahbay guide you. He must be your teacher now."

They were only going to the lodge for a couple of days, but while Dorrel packed one valise, Alara packed two. He didn't concern himself too much with it. At least neither was big enough to contain one of those ridiculous crinolines.

Alara had just finished packing her journal pages and Scriptures into a saddlebag when the bugler at the front gate blew "attention."

Dorrel had been lounging by the door, waiting for her to finish packing. Now he straightened, reaching for the doorknob.

"Perhaps that's them."

"Could be." She left the saddlebags, and they headed for the stairs at a quick pace. "It might only be the Makutians."

"Seems unlikely." The newspapers had yet to report a Makutian delegation crossing the border. He and Alara practically jogged to the landing overlooking the rotunda. Below, Mehrialéna stood by the sofa in front of the open doors.

Alara shrieked with delight and scrambled down the stairs, barreling into Dad as if he were her own father.

Dorrel was close behind.

Dad held her tightly. "Oh, Alara. We were so worried about you." He eyed Dorrel. "And you." He let go of Alara so he could embrace Dorrel.

Dorrel had never been so glad to see his father. The relief was so great, he couldn't find words.

Neither, apparently, could Dad. There was a lot of back-slapping and throat-clearing, but no words.

When she was done hugging Alara, Marita eyed her warily, cupping her hand around the side of Alara's face. "Are you all right, Curate?" She stroked her thumb across the faded splotch under Alara's eye.

"Yes, Marita. Got a bit beat up, but I'm healing nicely. Nothing tragic."

"Hmm. Yes." Marita smiled slyly, as if keeping a secret. "Yes, you are all right, aren't you?" She gave her another quick hug before accepting one from Dorrel.

Shelon's father, Montus Balmon, stood quietly behind Marita. After they'd all shaken hands, and Dorrel and Alara had offered their condolences to Marita and Mr. Balmon, Mehrialéna showed the new arrivals to their rooms. Dorrel and Alara followed.

He held her hand and whispered, "I think we'll leave tomorrow, instead."

She smiled. "I think so."

While they walked down the hall, Marita said, "Alara, I packed the things from your room and brought them with me. Thought you might want them."

"Thank you. I have missed my journal."

Marita lowered her voice. "I couldn't find your sword, though."

Alara inhaled sharply, stopping in her tracks. "Oh. I . . . I was afraid of that." She turned to Dorrel, her eyes wide and beginning to tear up. "I'm so sorry."

He held her. Dad, ahead of them, stopped and came to see what was wrong.

Marita said, "It seems the Makutians took Alara's sword for a trophy."

Alara's voice was a breathy thread. "Kester, I'm so sorry."

He patted her shoulder. "Don't fret, Alara. It's only a sword."

Dorrel knew perfectly well it wasn't only a sword. But it had to be said. Because it ought to have been true.

"Is there no chapel? In a palace of this size?" Prelate Dalys asked, while she and Alara arranged chairs on a patio of the west wing.

"No. I once suggested Boh add one, but he doesn't wish to upset his father by making changes."

"I see." The prelate put the last chair in place. A servant arrived with a lectern, and she showed him where to put it, near the edge where pavers met lawn.

The sun sank behind the treetops. Inside the house, the housekeeper rang a bell to announce the meeting. Everyone soon gathered and took their seats.

The service was brief, since the prelate used only one Scripture reading and two short songs. After the second song, the prelate said, "Before we dismiss, Professor Sheeno shall come forward to conduct a piece of business."

Sheeno took the lectern. "Our commencement ceremony at Denedra was several weeks ago, but one of our students missed it."

Alara gave Dorrel's hand a squeeze.

"Now that all concerned are in attendance"—he nodded to Kester —"I am pleased, and indeed proud, to confer the degree of doctor of veterinary medicine upon Dorrel Chevallon."

Dorrel ducked his head, then stood and went to meet Sheeno at the lectern, where he accepted the roll of parchment. The two of them shook hands. Sheeno drew Dorrel closer and embraced him.

Alara had never seen Professor Sheeno hug a student.

When the professor said, "Congratulations, Dorrel," he sounded a little hoarse.

So did Dorrel. "Thank you, Professor."

Dorrel returned to his seat. Alara leaned against his shoulder to admire the diploma. "There," she whispered, "isn't that better than any rotten old letters patent?"

Dorrel grinned, nodding.

Dorrel had imagined a rustic cabin. The hunting lodge was built of great, rough-hewn timbers, but it stood three stories high with a huge kitchen and parlors larger than the public room of the West Bridge Inn. The dining room could seat twenty-eight people. He and Alara ate in the kitchen.

The top two floors contained dozens of bedrooms. They moved into a large second-floor room with a balcony overlooking the lake.

They had spent most of their adult lives rising with, or even before, the sun. So they woke each morning while it was still dark. Which isn't to say they rose.

And they retired early each night, which isn't to say they slept.

Dad had brought Willow to Shandór, so part of each day was spent training her and Bastion. But that took only a small part of each day, and the chores were slight, so they had more free time than they knew what to do with. Or, rather, more than they would've known what to do with if they hadn't each spent years thinking about what to do on such an occasion.

Although Dorrel had long wished for the freedom to indulge himself in Alara's presence in every possible way, after two weeks, he began to get restless. "You just spent whole summers like this? Every year?" He worked with a boning knife, carving the rest of the meat off the pheasant she'd roasted for their dinner. Already in her soup pot were vegetables and a generous cup of claret.

"Yes. You think us a bunch of indolent gentry, don't you?" She crushed a few cloves of garlic and added them to the pot.

"I just can't imagine stopping work for weeks at a time on purpose."

"Well, when I was at the mission, I couldn't, obviously. But when we were students, we had summers off, anyway."

"Excuse me? I worked all summer."

She ducked her head. "Sorry."

"Don't be. I enjoy my work, Lar. That's why it seems odd not to be doing it."

She stirred the pot. "Well, I hope you've enjoyed this holiday, because once we get home, there isn't likely to be another soon. I won't be able to leave the curacy for weeks at a time."

"Fine with me." He handed her the plate of pheasant meat and kissed her cheek. "A few days in Ecciston or up at the vineyard will give you enough of a break, won't it?"

She grinned. "Surely." She dumped the scraps into the pot and stirred while Dorrel washed his hands.

Someone knocked at the door.

Dorrel, wiping his hands on a linen towel, went to answer it.

From the kitchen, a long corridor led to what Alara called the front room, a great hall with a high, beamed ceiling and an enormous stone fireplace. He walked around the edges of the ornate knotted silk rug, in spite of Alara's insistence the family walked on it all the time.

Dorrel opened the door. Bóhjetien stood on the doorstep, hat in hand, dusty and sweaty. Dorrel stepped aside so he could come in. "How did it go?"

"Better than expected."

"Lar's in the kitchen." They walked that way in silence.

Once there, Bóhjetien washed his hands and face before taking a seat at the table.

"Supper is half an hour away," Alara said. "But may I get you something in the meantime?"

"No, thank you. I shall not stay long."

Dorrel winked at Alara, who, getting his meaning, took down the wine glasses while Dorrel fetched the bottle. "Claret?" he asked.

"Yes, thank you . . . Ah-ha!" Bóhjetien took the bottle to examine the label. "Arken!"

"What else? I asked Dad to bring a case with him. The rest is up at the house."

"Excellent. How much?"

"It's a gift, Boh. Don't mention it."

"Such a gift is impossible not to mention. Thank you."

"You're welcome."

Alara put out two glasses.

"Not having any?" Dorrel asked.

"No, thank you." She poured her tea over ice.

He still found that drink too strange to try.

"More for me." Bóhjetien, grinning, filled the glasses. Then he raised his. "To a successful summit."

"Ocha," Dorrel said.

Bóhjetien closed his eyes, savoring the claret. "Alara, you made a brilliant match."

"That would be true, even without the claret." Alara slid into the seat next to Dorrel.

"So they are coming, then?" Dorrel asked.

Bóhjetien nodded. "I met with Velek at the border crossing between Gadrut and Vonisayu. As I suspected, the resistance is all on King Domat's part. Velek is willing to negotiate. He shall ask Ambassador Pavud to come but shall come alone if he must."

Dorrel rolled the stem of his wineglass between his fingers. "And what did he say about the attack?"

"He denied having anything to do with it." Bóhjetien raised a finger. "And I believe him. My friend is not one to order assassins. But he did say something I have passed on to the police."

They waited for him to continue.

"The Kivatan priests in Darshalay may have ordered the attack when they heard of your wedding."

"Why would they?"

Alara sighed. "Sergeant Korig said only the priests care about a woman's purity."

Bóhjetien shrugged one shoulder. "An overstatement, perhaps. But it is possible they see your actions as an affront to their gods as well as to Velek and the king."

What business did Kivatan priests have judging a Telshan curate? Dorrel took a long drink of wine, which did nothing to settle his stomach.

"Furthermore," Bóhjetien said. "I have word from the constable. The assassins are not Makutian. They're Temhainites."

Temhain was to the east of Redíque. That country had nothing to do with the treaty.

"What?" Alara plunked her glass on the table. "Why . . .?"

"They are of the Kivatan faith, you see. But not Makutian nationality." Bóhjetien pointed at her. "So it supports Velek's theory."

Her brow furrowed.

Dorrel asked, "When will Velek and the rest get here?"

"Two weeks."

His shoulders sagged. "Another two weeks."

"I should think you would relish such a thought, yes?" Bóhjetien smiled slyly.

"Perhaps, if everything else weren't hanging over us. As it is . . ." He sighed. "I just want to go home."

Alara pulled a moue, nodded, and looked into her glass.

"I am sorry it is taking so long," Bóhjetien said.

"Not your fault . . ." Dorrel said as Alara said something similar.

Bóhjetien waved a hand. "We do what we must, yes?" He changed the subject by asking about Bastion. That kept them talking until the glasses were empty. Then he picked up his hat.

As they walked him to the door, Alara said, "Boh, do you believe this can be settled peacefully?"

"If Velek and I were left to ourselves, yes. But as long as Domat has a hand in it . . . I do not know."

Her brows pinched together.

"You must know . . ." Bóhjetien hesitated. "You have seen the papers."

"About the Makutian troop movements?"

He nodded. "They are gathering at Gadrut. In, I am sorry to say, very large numbers."

# Chapter 29

## A SPECIAL MISSION

Ever since news of the Chevallons' marriage had reached Tarvag, troops had been moving through the capital on their way to Gadrut. Sturg visited a different tavern each day to collect as much intelligence as possible. Though unable to join the campaign, he at least could stay informed.

He was preparing to go out one day when Kabed's lieutenant summoned him to the general's office. Sturg took the chair Kabed indicated.

Kabed slid a page across the desk. A written reprimand chastising Sturg for inciting armed conflict. "I haven't signed it yet." Kabed pulled the paper back. "And there's a chance I won't. The king has a special mission for you."

The iron band that had clamped Sturg's heart all those weeks loosened.

"I told you I wasn't sure what to do with you. Well, I've a commander at Lanek who must retire."

Lanek. A small town in the mountains far to the north. Nothing of note ever would happen there. Hardly the place for a king's special mission.

"You'll be sent there if the summit goes as the king wishes."

"And if it doesn't?"

Kabed folded his hands on the desktop. "What I'm about to say is never to be repeated."

Sturg nodded, his free heart leaping at the walls of his chest.

"Prince Velek is leading the summit delegation as the king's proxy. But the king suspects Velek's sympathies are with the Telshans. So he's unlikely to press for all of the king's demands. The trade agreement gives us only limited access to Glynrell's seaports. The only way to gain permanent access is to conquer Glynrell." The general smirked, and Sturg mirrored the expression. "But you heard Prince Velek. He thinks we can't do it."

"Our kill ratio against the Glynrellans in the last campaign was better than one to twelve."

"Yes, but you oughtn't brag about that statistic to anyone else, Commander. Your Glynrellan campaign isn't looked upon favorably in all quarters. And it was your man who failed to kill Chevallon. If not for that, Velek would be married to Kordelyon's daughter by now, and we'd all be getting on as usual."

"Yes, sir."

"The king knows as well as you or I the only way to recoup our nation's honor is for Chevallon and the woman to die. But his Temhainite assassins failed in their mission. Now, if Velek pursues his own agenda rather than the king's, our orders are to execute the Chevallons. If that leads Glynrell to declare war . . . so much the better."

Already on the edge of his chair, Sturg could've leapt to the task immediately. "May I ask . . . if the king doesn't trust Prince Velek, why send him as proxy? Why not send Prince Uked?"

Kabed grinned, something he didn't often do. The sight of his crooked yellow teeth unsettled Sturg's nerves. "To smoke him out. Only with proof of such disloyalty can Velek be removed from the line of succession in Uked's favor." Kabed snorted. "Then we'll all be better off."

"True."

"So I have your full cooperation."

"Of course, General."

"Good. Wait for my order. We act only if the king's demands aren't met. After Chevallon and his wife are executed, whether the Glynrellans declare war or not, we'll attack Tylan and Vonisayu. You'd be sent to the Glynrellan front."

Sturg's nerves thrilled. He longed to be sent to the front. Any front.

"That is assuming you succeed in your mission. If you fail . . ." He pushed his eyebrows together. "You go to the gallows."

"Understood, sir. But there is, of course, the possibility that though I succeed in carrying out the execution, I'm killed by Chevallon's friends on the spot."

"True."

"What happens then?"

"Does it matter?"

"Begging your pardon, General, but Ult will need looking after till he's of age."

Kabed nodded. "All right. If the execution succeeds but you're killed . . . I'll see your boy is admitted to the military academy."

Only nobility and gentry were admitted to the academy. A common boy like Ult could never get in, unless he had a high-ranking sponsor. Were it permissible in such company, Sturg would've laughed aloud. "Thank you, General."

Staying in the same building as Velek and the other Makutians kept Dorrel's nerves on edge, even though they were in the west wing, while the Glynrellans had the east wing. Besides, a company of Redíquan soldiers had been sent. Since Shandór's barracks could accommodate only one platoon, the rest were camped in the newly mowed rye field on the west side of the house. Their placement, visible from the Makutians' windows, was surely deliberate.

Since the summit wouldn't start for another day, Dorrel didn't bother with a suit. Instead, he put on a beige linen shirt Alara had ordered for him from the local tailor. Like the ones Bóhjetien wore, it was loose-fitting with short sleeves. He headed for the sitting room, buttoning the shirt as he went.

The troops had confiscated all civilian weapons, and Alara hadn't spoken of any further premonitions, so armor didn't seem necessary.

Alara sat at the desk by the window. At first, he thought she was writing in her journal. Then he saw the calendar. Her brow furrowed. She counted days, frowned, counted again.

"Something wrong?" Dorrel asked.

"It's my cycle."

"Oh." He had hoped for quick results, but how could he complain? Lots of couples had delays of months, even years.

"Is there anything I can do?" He brushed the back of his fingers across her hair.

She laughed, just a bit hysterically. "It's more a matter of what you've already done." She grinned at him. "It should've been last week."

"Ha!" Dorrel pulled her out of the chair, off her feet. He held her so her eyes were level with his and kissed her.

This left her feet dangling about a foot off the floor.

She hugged him and spoke softly into his ear. "It could be a fluke. I missed one once before. My sophomore year, I had a martial arts competition the same week as final exams. The doctor said it happens, sometimes, under duress."

"Humph. You've certainly been distressed lately." He set her down. "Ask Marita. She can always tell."

"Not yet."

"Why not?"

She kissed his cheek. "Just let's keep it to ourselves. Just until next month. Please? Our secret?"

He couldn't deny her that.

Even though the summit hadn't begun, the delegates were expected to breakfast together. On his way to the stairs, Sturg stopped at Ult's rooms. He opened the door and stepped into the empty sitting room. "Ult!"

The spaniel ran out of the bedroom, yipping at him and wagging its tail. It hopped upward, a sign it wished to be picked up.

"Sit."

The dog sat, still wagging its tail. Sturg daren't turn up at the table with dog hairs on his dress uniform.

Ult, still in his nightshirt, entered a moment later. "Sir?"

"I have a job for you." Sturg gestured the boy closer and closed the door. "You mustn't speak to anyone of this." He put his hand on Ult's shoulder. "General Kabed asked me to do something, but I can't because the Redíquans confiscated our weapons. You must go into the Redíquans' camp and get me a bow and a quiver of arrows."

"Should I wait till dark?"

"Yes, that would be prudent. As long as I have them by morning."

"Yes, sir."

"And keep wearing civilian clothes. The soldiers may think you work here."

Ult smiled. "Some of them already do."

He was a clever boy sometimes. Sturg clapped his shoulder. "Good."

After breakfast, the Glynrellans gathered in the morning room, which took up the corner of the east wing farthest from the rotunda.

Alara, unsure what to expect from the meeting, stood at one of the arched windows, looking out at the eastern garden, kneading her hands. Because the land sloped toward the lake, the morning room floor was a full story above the ground. Another rank of windows faced the lake. With all the curtains pulled back, early light filled the room.

*Ahbay, guide us. Give us wisdom.*

Father pulled an armchair with gilded feet and brown-velvet upholstery to the center of the room, where four couches formed a loose square atop a bright floral rug. He sat down and appointed Divreenan to take notes.

The others picked seats on the sofas or drew up side chairs. Alara sat on a sofa between Dorrel and Rariden.

Father made a few vacuous opening remarks. As soon as he opened the floor, Rariden spoke up. "As I hear it, they took every weapon they could get their hands on."

"That's their way," Marita said.

"Indeed. We ought to ask for the return of the trophies."

"They're unlikely to concede that, General," Father said.

"I know. But asking serves two purposes. It shows we consider the thing an affront. And it gives us something on which to make a concession."

Father grinned. "Without actually giving up anything."

"Anything that hasn't already been lost, you mean," Marita grumbled.

"Surely."

Mr. Balmon leaned over the back of the sofa and whispered something to Marita. She shook her head.

"Speak up, Mr. Balmon," Father said. "All opinions are important."

He plunked back into his seat. "My girl, Shelon. They cut off her hair. No chance of getting that back, you think?"

"I'm afraid not. Why would you want to?"

"To stop them from having it."

Father nodded, showing a concerned frown. "Of course. We'll

make a point of it, then." He turned back to Rariden. "Anything else, General?"

"Yes. After the war, we agreed on prisoners' reparations of one hundred staters per month of imprisonment. In today's currency, that's just over eleven hundred staters. They ought to pay that to Alara—"

"Surely not!" Alara gaped at him. "It's not the same."

"Yes, it is."

"Marita—"

"I agree with him," Marita said.

"But—"

"You were kidnapped and beaten," Dorrel said. "Why are you defending them?"

"I'm not defending, I'm just saying . . . I wasn't treated like . . ." She swallowed the lump in her throat.

Marita arched her eyebrows. "Like a prisoner of war?"

Alara bowed her head, her stomach in a knot. Korig had come close, but . . . "To suggest my experience even approaches that of ladies captured in the war . . ." She shook her head. "There's no comparison."

"It has less to do with how you were treated," Rariden said, "than with making them pay."

"But they only had me a week."

"Doesn't matter."

Marita folded her arms. "There was no prorating after the war."

Dorrel leaned close and whispered in Alara's ear. "Don't try to argue with them both."

The ambassadors spent the better part of the afternoon behind closed doors, working out the agenda. Late in the day, everyone gathered for apéritifs in the salon opposite the state dining room. While servers passed raspberry liqueur and vermouth, Alara scanned the room.

Sturg glowered at her over the rim of his glass. She looked away.

Velek arrived, a slender young woman on his arm and Hanik bringing up the rear. She moved toward them.

Mr. Balmon had said Shelon was found with a crossbow bolt in her back. All the Makutians had been armed with crossbows, but she gathered Korig was the expert.

"Good evening, Your Royal Highness. Lieutenant Hanik."

Hanik didn't even look at her.

"Good evening, Curate." Velek turned to the woman. "This is my niece, Navka. She's eager to meet you."

Navka ducked her head, and her pale cheeks flared pink.

"My pleasure, Navka." Alara put out her hand. "May I ask why?"

Navka, eyes still cast downward, gave a limp handshake. "Oh. Well. You had the use of a couple of my dresses."

"Oh, yes. I had forgotten." Alara released Navka's hand. "They were very pretty. Though you're very slender, and I'm . . . not. Did you get them back?"

"Yes. I meant to visit you . . . in the palace. But you were gone."

"Oh dear. You . . . saw the state we left the guard in?"

Navka nodded, her face darkening to a bright red.

"I'm very sorry."

Her voice was almost a whisper. "I understand why you did it."

"Thank you." Navka was a little shorter and much slimmer than Alara, with honey-colored hair and a delicate face. What she could see of it. "I'm pleased to meet you."

"And you, ma'am."

Alara turned to Velek. "May the lieutenant have liberty to speak with me?"

His eyebrows shot up. "Of course." Velek parted from Hanik with a nod and led Navka toward where Mehrialéna sat with Mum.

When they'd gone, Hanik gave a nod. "Good evening, Curate."

"I've something to ask, though I understand if you mayn't answer."

He waited, expressionless.

"In Kaesbaro, the first casualty was a teenage girl with long blonde hair. She was shot in the back, her throat cut, and her hair cut off. Was that done by Sergeant Korig?"

Hanik's gaze drifted away for a few moments. Then he looked her in the eye. "I suppose it'll do no harm to say yes. Although . . ." One corner of his mouth lifted. "He's Corporal Korig, now."

"Is he?"

"I told you I had connections." He winked. "Didn't you believe me?"

She chuckled. "Of course I did. Thank you, Lieutenant."

"You're welcome, Curate."

She returned to Rariden and Mr. Balmon. "General, it was Korig who killed Shelon."

"Ah-ha. Good work."

The butler called them to dinner. As they moved across the hall, Dorrel came up from behind and gripped her arm, right below her stitches. Rather firmly.

He spoke in her ear, his voice quiet but tense. "What was all that laughing and winking with the Makutians?"

"I beg your pardon?"

He tugged her to a stop. "You know what I mean."

She let the others move ahead. "I was finding out which of them killed Shelon if you don't mind." She pulled her arm from his grip and went to her seat. Her face burned.

There was no discussing the matter until they were alone, so Alara tried, unsuccessfully, not to think of it. Throughout dinner, Dorrel seemed to pretend as if nothing had happened.

As they finished dessert, Camrun started recruiting people to play cards. That seemed like a good time to take Dorrel aside, but Bóhjetien tapped her shoulder and asked her to follow him.

He took her to the same drawing room where she'd met with Prelate Dalys. "Please do not be upset with me for arranging this, Alara. It is important."

"Why would I—"

Velek appeared in the doorway. He stepped in. "I hoped it would be possible to continue our conversation from the embassy."

"Of course."

Hanik waited in the corridor.

Bóhjetien smiled and squeezed her hand. Then he left and closed the door.

She and Velek took seats across from one another.

"The vision . . ."

She waited.

"It has a great many ramifications. Certainly more than even I can guess. But I wonder"—he hesitated, swallowing hard—"if I'm not to be king . . . what am I to be?"

She drew back. "Ah. Well . . ." *Kenna, what should I tell him?*

She gave no answer.

Alara took a deep breath. "I wasn't shown that much. I can tell you Kenna said everyone is given a gift with which to serve."

"A gift?" He waved a hand at her. "Like you claim to have?"

"Not necessarily. Some gifts are supernatural, but others are not. Hanik is gifted as a healer, and there's nothing miraculous in it. Mehrialéna is gifted as an artist. I don't know what gifts Mairah has given you, or what purpose Ahbay plans for you, but I know He has a plan for everyone who wishes to follow the Way."

"And if I don't wish to follow?"

She shrugged. "Then there's nothing more I can tell you." She leaned back in her chair. "Have you read the Telshan Scriptures at all?"

"Some. Boh gave me a copy, but it's difficult, since they're in Redíquan."

She nodded. "The Scriptures have been translated into Makutian. Perhaps—"

"They have?"

"Yes. Are you unaware of the Telshan movement in your country?"

"I've heard rumors that some who live near the border go into Redíque to attend prayer meetings."

"True." She didn't mention the missionaries who operated clandestinely within Makut. She wasn't ready to trust him with that knowledge. "I'll write to Prelate Pomiren and ask him to send a copy." She stood and went to the writing table, where she jotted down a few chapters and verses. "In the meantime, here are some passages for you to study. If you need help, I can translate."

"Your Makutian is very good."

"Thank you."

"And your husband's is flawless. Did he teach you?"

"No, Dorrel's Makutian seems perfect to you because he's a speaker." She handed him the paper.

He glanced over it. "What do you mean?"

"When he speaks, people hear him in their own languages."

"Really?" Velek frowned a little.

"If you don't believe me, ask Boh." She sat back down.

The mantel clock ticked away several seconds.

Velek stared at the paper. "The curate in Nuahn once said in a sermon that Ahbay makes a path for everyone. And each person must discover that path."

"Yes. You'll find something about that in the first passage I gave you."

"But how does one find this path?"

"One prays, Your Royal Highness, for guidance."

"Oh."

During the long silence that followed, Alara did some praying of her own. *Telshi, help me to help him find you.*

As if Kenna had whispered in her ear, Alara realized Velek might not know how to pray. "Would you like me to pray with you?"

He looked up, meeting her eyes. He opened his mouth, but then closed it and nodded.

Alara was so used to holding people's hands during prayer, she extended hers without a thought. She wasn't sure what was more surprising—that she held out her hand, or that he took it.

"Telshi, we're told your way is the least dangerous. But we also know that even the least dangerous path may not be an easy one. And our human failings often keep us from seeing your path. Ahbay, guide

Velek as he attempts to discern the path you've charted for him. Give him wisdom and fortitude, for his path, whatever it may be, seems likely to be a dangerous one indeed. Ocha."

Alara let go of his hand. "I hope you don't mind my using your name alone, sir. But with Telshi, there is no peerage."

"Quite all right. I did once tell you to call me Velek."

"True."

"Thank you, Curate. You've been helpful. I think."

"You're very welcome." She spread open hands. "This is my path. It's how I serve."

"I see." Velek rose and walked toward the door. "Navka would like to talk more with you, but she's shy. If you could get her alone . . . or at least without men around . . . she has many questions similar to mine. She's spent most of her life in the gynaeceum with few chances to visit Redíque." He pursed his lips. "She's very fortunate Uked gave her permission to come. Normally, he wouldn't let his daughters go abroad without him."

Alara stood and followed him. "Oh dear. Yes, I'd be happy to chat with her." But she needed to talk to Dorrel first. "Speaking of Uked, may I ask what he said when you told him about the vision?"

He turned back to her. "Oh, he was quite satisfied. He doesn't believe your vision was truly divine, and he said he didn't need a vision to see I'm unfit to rule." He paused. "I won't tell you exactly what he said. You may value plain speaking, but I'm sure you wouldn't like Uked's sort of language."

The two princes had left, most of the Glynrellans had gone off to play games, and the diplomats, with General Kabed, had withdrawn to a corner of the salon. It was impossible for Sturg to impose himself on such company, so he tromped up to his room.

Had Kabed seen how Hanik carried on with that woman? If he hadn't, Sturg would make sure he knew of it.

Ult's door stood open. Inside, he sat cross-legged behind the coffee table. Sturg stepped in. The boy was drawing a picture of Shandór's south face. Several other sheets, already filled with pictures, lay on the table.

"Where did you get paper?"

Ult stood. "From the desk." He pointed to a writing table near the window. "The maid said I could use it."

"All right, then." Sturg turned to go.

"Sir! I have what you wanted." Ult ran into the bedroom.

"You'll not run indoors," Sturg hollered. He closed the door.

Ult returned at a walk. "Sorry, sir." He carried a drab green canvas bag in one hand and a Redíquan short bow in the other.

Sturg took the bow. "Good. What's in the bag?"

Ult unbuckled the bag's flap and opened it. "Quiver, twelve arrows, a knife, fatigues, and a few other things." He held out the bag. "I thought if I took the whole bag, the soldier might think he just misplaced it. But if I removed only the weapons, he'd know they were taken."

Sturg shouldered the bag, then tousled the boy's hair. "Well done, Ult. Good thinking." Ult grinned like an idiot. Sturg withdrew his hand and turned toward the door.

"Wait, sir. I thought you might want this, too." Ult had wiped the smile away, at least. He picked up one of the papers from the table. "This side is the Redíquan camp." Ult had drawn each tent, marking which ones likely had officers in them. He flipped over the page. "And this is the palace grounds, as far as I was able to explore today." Palace, stables, barracks, and camp were all neatly drawn and labeled. Ult had spent too much time detailing the hedges in the garden, but at least he hadn't neglected to mark the driveways and walkways. Distances even had been paced out and noted.

"Very good. A visual record of a reconnoiter always is useful."

"Thank you, sir."

Sturg went to his room to study the map.

# Chapter 30

## PUT AWAY THE SWORD

"You're making this too easy!" Dad crowed, when he and Mr. Balmon won their third game of whist against Dorrel and Camrun.

The salon, across from the state dining room, was paneled in oak and lit by wall sconces and a huge chandelier. The room contained several table-and-chair groupings.

"Another?" Dad shuffled the cards.

"No thank you," Camrun said. "I've had enough humiliation for one evening."

"Sorry about that." Their losing streak was entirely attributable to Dorrel not paying attention. "Where's Alara, do you think?"

"Who knows? Off with Lena, possibly."

"Lena's right over there." Dorrel pointed to where she sat with Shenevra and Marita and Velek's niece.

"Oh."

Alara came in a few minutes later. She passed their table and joined the ladies.

Camrun stood and picked up his beer glass. He pointed to

Dorrel's. "Can I get you a refill?"

"No thanks." Dorrel went after Alara. He didn't wish to be rude, but he couldn't think of a nice way to say it. "Where were you?"

"Just doing some counseling."

"With whom?"

"You know I can't . . ."

"Everyone is here. Except your Makutian friends."

"I beg your pardon!"

Marita put her beer glass down with a thump. "Come with me." She grabbed Dorrel's arm and pulled him toward the door.

Alara gaped. Marita waved her forward. "You too. Come along."

She dragged Dorrel by his elbow down the hall to the morning room. With the sun setting on the opposite side of the house, the dusky garden beyond the windows lay in shadow.

Marita glared at Dorrel. "Please explain why my favorite newlyweds are suddenly bickering like schoolchildren."

"Have you seen her? Laughing and flirting—"

"Flirting?" Alara squealed.

"—with one of the soldiers who kidnapped her. The same one who disabled Mr. Risdun." He threw his hands in the air. "It's crazy!"

Marita scowled at him. "You sound like my father." She put one arm around Alara. "Which fellow is he talking about?"

Alara's face turned bright red. "Lieutenant Hanik. Prince Velek's bodyguard. He protected me."

"Really? When I got there, you were black and blue."

"It could have been worse."

"Perhaps, but—"

"Dor, he put himself between me and his commanding officer. He could have died for that. And he made sure Korig was punished for attacking me."

"That doesn't make him our ally."

She clenched her fists. A sign of trouble. "It makes him *my* ally."

Marita put her arms around Alara's shoulders. "I understand, Alara."

Dorrel drew back. Oh, he was an idiot.

Marita pulled Alara onto a settee. "You know I was a prisoner of war."

Alara shook her head. "There's no comparison, Marita. Really."

"Let me be the judge of that. Mairah sometimes lets me cure people, so the camp physician had me work in the infirmary. Foul work. The soldiers used prisoners as they pleased, and when one became pregnant, they took the baby from her womb, because they knew Telshans consider that the worst atrocity."

Alara nodded, weeping.

"But he and I got along, considering."

Dorrel sagged against the wall. He should've remembered this story. His heart dropped into his stomach and made him sick.

"When I became pregnant, the doctor refused to abort my baby. The camp commander asked why, and the doctor claimed it was his own. Which was nonsense, because he was one of few who hadn't used me. He kept me safe in the infirmary until Rariden's troops liberated the camp. And when the doctor went on trial for war crimes, I testified on his behalf." She hugged Alara's shoulders, weeping. "Because he was my ally." She glared at Dorrel—rightly so. "And my father said I was crazy."

He hung his head.

Alara sniffled.

"I still can't explain why I formed such an attachment to someone who committed such horrors," Marita said, "except he protected me and my son. Dorrel will probably never understand what you feel, but —" Marita's voice caught. He was unused to seeing her display such emotion. She took a deep breath. "But I do. And it's good to know I'm not the only one who ever felt this way."

They embraced, each shedding tears on the other's shoulder.

Dorrel walked to the hall. He leaned against the wall opposite the morning room, trembling.

*Telshi, forgive me.*

Sometime later, he couldn't guess how long, they emerged.

Alara stood in the doorway for a moment, staring at him with bloodshot eyes. She let go of Marita and came to him. She put her cheek against his chest and her arms around his waist.

"I'm sorry," he whispered, as much to Marita as to his wife.

Alara would've preferred to spend the rest of the evening alone with Dorrel, but she needed to see Navka. So they walked back to the salon. "I want to do this now, because once the summit starts, I may not have time."

"It's all right, sweetest. I understand." He kissed her cheek and joined the men, while Alara returned to her seat with Navka and the other ladies.

The men started another card game.

Navka continually looked their way.

While the ladies chatted, Alara waited for Navka to pose some of the questions Velek claimed she had. But Navka remained mostly silent.

Camrun crowed over some victory.

Alara turned to Mehrialéna. "May we remove to the drawing room, where it's more quiet?"

"Certainly." Mehrialéna stood. "You go ahead. I shall order tea and apéritifs."

"Lovely." As the ladies walked down the wide corridor toward the great hall, Navka hung back. Alara slowed to draw alongside her. "Your uncle tells me you have some questions."

Navka wrung her hands. "Oh, yes ma'am. If you don't mind."

"Of course I don't mind. I'm a cleric. It's my pleasure to serve."

"Ah! Yes. Of course."

They were settled into the drawing room with tea and sherry, Mum and Mehrialéna prattling about fashion, before Navka spoke again.

She leaned close to Alara. "May I ask a question about Scripture?"

"Of course."

"Digalo says there's no noble or peasant, no male or female. But that's not true, is it? I mean, we're all nobles, and in the countryside, peasants work farms. And men and women are so obviously different . . ." Her cheeks flushed.

"Yes, but what he means by that is, as far as Kenna is concerned, everyone is the same. We may distinguish between people by their profession or appearance, but Kenna doesn't. She judges only by people's hearts and souls."

"Ah! I see."

"And in Glynrell we truly have no nobility. That was done away with centuries ago. So everyone, regardless of birth, can pursue any sort of career."

"But your father is royalty."

Alara's voice turned cold and hard despite herself. "He is not. And never will be."

Navka drew back. "Oh."

"Sorry." Alara drew and released a deep breath to banish the tension that gripped her lungs. "My father may have sought the prime minister's office because of our heritage. But he only won it because the people elected him. And he won't hold it for long. At the next election, they will replace him."

"Is that why you disobeyed him?"

"No. I disobeyed him because he asked me to do his will instead of Kenna's will. I'm a cleric. I must fulfill my calling. If that conflicts with the prime minister's plans, so be it."

Navka put down her cup and scooted forward. "So it's all right to disobey my father if it's Kenna's will?"

Alara narrowed her eyes. "Have you disobeyed your father?"

Navka looked away. "Not exactly."

"Velek told me you had your father's permission to come."

"I—I lied to Uncle Velek. Father doesn't know I'm here. If he finds out I'm missing . . ." She shook her head. "I don't want to go back."

Heavens. What had the girl gotten herself into?

"Do you follow Kenna?"

She glanced toward the door as if afraid. Her voice dropped to a whisper. "Yes. The last time I was in Darshalay, Mehrialéna and Domínarey took me to the meetinghouse. The prelate said, 'Give your heart to Kenna,' so I did. Although I'm still not sure what that means. But I took a Scripture book back with me —"

Alara gasped.

" —and I've been reading it ever since, trying to learn."

"I'm very happy for you, Navka, but do you realize how dangerous that is, taking Telshan Scriptures into Makut?" Missionaries had been executed for as much.

"Yes. I know." She looked to Alara. "That's why I want to stay here, where women are free and I can read whatever I want."

Navka surely deserved better than the gynaeceum. *Kenna, help me advise her. Can I really advocate her disobeying her father?*

Well, if she didn't, she'd be a hypocrite.

Alara and Dorrel reached the morning room before anyone else. The curtains on the wide, east-facing window were pulled back, though outside only the dimmest gray light crept through the carefully trimmed shrubs.

A silver coffee service sat on a table to the left of the door. Alara poured two cups of coffee, and they settled onto a couch from which they could look out the window to the garden. He stretched his arm across her shoulders, and she scooted closer.

Camrun came in and gave a cheery "good morning" while heading straight for the coffee. Rariden joined them shortly. Prelate Dalys and Marita were not far behind.

Alara stood, leaving her cup and saucer on the coffee table. "Do you want the furniture rearranged, ma'am?"

The prelate surveyed the room. "Let's just move this couch that has its back to the window. And I did request a lectern."

Camrun and Dorrel turned the sofa to face east. A few minutes later, after some of the others had arrived, servants brought in the lectern and some velvet-and-gilt chairs.

The prelate opened the center window and had the lectern placed in front of it. Birds outside sang up the sun. "Alara, I see you brought your Scriptures. I've selected a passage from Galardi. Would you read it?"

"Perhaps Dorrel ought to read."

"Why?"

Dorrel covered his eyes with his hand. "Lar—"

"He's a speaker."

The prelate glared at Dorrel as if he'd said something rude.

Alara continued. "If he reads, everyone will understand."

"Really? How long have you had this gift, Dr. Chevallon?"

Dorrel rolled his eyes. "I don't know. At least"—he looked at Alara —"for the love of—it's been two months now."

Two long, tiresome months they had been, made tolerable only by their marriage. She ran her fingers through his hair, just behind his ear. "Indeed."

The prelate gave him the verses, and he reviewed them silently. "Curate, you may lead the prayer of confession, then."

"Yes, ma'am."

Soon Alara's parents entered and sat on one of the sofas.

Prince Velek arrived with Navka. Hanik broke formation and spoke quietly with the prelate, then took his seat behind the prince.

The prelate glanced out the window at the increasing sunlight, then leaned close to Alara, speaking softly. "How long ought we to wait for your cousins?"

"No longer. They are not early risers."

Prelate Dalys moved to the lectern. She picked up the bell, adding its chime to the chirping of the birds.

They sang a song about how Telshi could bring peace where human hearts created strife.

Halfway through, Bóhjetien, wearing a shirt with the collar

undone and no suit coat, sneaked into a chair near Velek.

"At this point," the prelate said, "we would normally share our troubles and thanksgivings. But we are united here with one trouble. When we are finished, perhaps we shall share one thanksgiving. We have a great work before us. As we enter into it, let us remember our dead. Chairwoman Marita Graylin and Lieutenant Areld Hanik shall read the necrology."

Marita and Hanik rose from their seats.

Alara took out her handkerchief.

Marita began with Palon's name. Then Hanik named one of the students from Denedra. They alternated, taking turns reciting all of the forty-one dead, ordered by rank and age. It ended with Marita saying "Private Shelon Balmon."

Alara dabbed her eyes before her tears could fall. Someone behind her sniffled. She feared it was Mr. Balmon.

Marita turned to Hanik, extending her hand. He looked her in the eye. They shook hands.

After they resumed their seats, Prelate Dalys led the congregation in a hope-filled prayer that left Alara with more tears in her eyes. Another song was sung, this one on the theme of reconciliation.

The Scripture Dorrel read was from Galardi, who, having returned from war, wrote about the futility of human conflict and the need for people to forgive wrongs and empathize with the views of others. "For in unison we may join under the guidance of Ahbay, who will teach us to put away the sword and take up the hammer. He would have us build and not destroy."

Dorrel tried to shrug off the comments everyone made about his reading. Now he understood how Marita felt when people praised her healing gift. He hadn't done anything.

He followed the others to the meeting room at the front of the palace. Three sets of double doors opened onto the corridor. Gilded rococo carvings decorated the white door panels. Bóhjetien and Ambassador Rabicanoh entered first and took their seats at the head of a giant U-shaped table placed in front of a granite fireplace large enough to roast a side of beef. Carved into stone above the firebox was the Shardamayn family crest, painted in white and green with gilt trim. Rabicanoh's attaché sat on his left.

Prime Minister Kordelyon and the other Glynrellan delegates walked across the room to their seats, near narrow ceiling-high windows overlooking the front drive. Crisp white linen draped the table, reaching the floor. High-backed chairs upholstered in pale-blue silk ringed the table's edge.

Dorrel hesitated. What was he doing in such surroundings with such dignitaries? Opposite the fireplace, next to a convex protrusion made by the rotunda, hung a larger-than-life portrait of a king who, from the looks of his clothes, had ruled four or five centuries ago. Dorrel stared at it. *You have married a descendent of kings, young man.* Indeed he had, and if muddling through this summit was the cost, so be it.

He clutched her hand, and they turned toward the table.

Place cards marked where everyone was to sit. Prince Velek sat near the doors, across from Kordelyon. Their respective ambassadors sat next to them, the rest of the delegates arrayed down each branch of the table.

Dorrel pulled out Alara's chair.

A row of chairs for the translators and spectators ran along the wall of windows, and a few chairs had been placed against the opposite wall. Dad and Mr. Balmon took seats behind Dorrel and Alara.

The servants closed the doors. Shenevra made her way to her seat, patting Dorrel's shoulder, then Alara's, as she passed.

"Remarkable." Rariden slid into his chair on Alara's right. "After fifty years . . . the place hasn't changed."

Sturg took his seat next to Kabed. Hanik stood against the wall behind the prince's chair.

Ambassador Rabicanoh called them to order. He spoke at length about the historic precedent of the Treaty of Shandór and how pleased the Redíquans were to be agents of peace.

Sturg paid little attention, though Pavud's translator, sitting behind him and speaking in low tones, interpreted the whole thing in Makutian. Prince Bóhjetien made a similar speech, though at least it was shorter.

"And now, Prince Velek," Rabicanoh said, "you wished to say a few words?"

"Thank you, Ambassador." Velek rose.

His speech, given in Rediquan, was as boring as Rabicanoh's and was meek and conciliatory as well, going on about misunderstandings and regrets. "We have come today in good faith to restore relations with our neighbors to the west. A portion of our deliberations this week —"

Sturg could only hope the business wouldn't take all week.

"—shall concern reparations. As a token of our good faith, we wish to begin by putting one matter right." He turned, and a Redíquan captain handed him a scabbard.

The hair on the back of Sturg's neck prickled.

The Redíquan soldiers standing guard all put hands to their swords.

Velek walked between the arms of the table. He stopped in front of the woman, facing her across the tabletop. She stood.

"Curate Chevallon, I believe this is yours." He held the sword— scabbard, belt, and all—out to her in both hands as if she'd earned it in battle.

She gasped. "Your Royal Highness, you . . . you have no idea how much this means." Her voice was breathless and weak, like that of a woman for the first time in Sturg's experience. She clutched the sword to her bosom like a lost child. "Thank you."

Velek gave her a small bow. "You are welcome."

While the prince returned to his seat, the woman turned to Chevallon, beaming. He patted her shoulder, as did the big man behind them.

For that, he'd given up a well-earned trophy? For *that?* Velek couldn't have known about the sword unless Hanik told him.

Sturg clenched his interlaced fingers. He wasn't sure whom he wanted to kill more: the woman, or Chevallon, or Hanik.

Alara didn't want to let go of Nya's sword. But one of the guards leaned in from behind her. "Please place the sword on the table where we can see it, madáme."

She placed it at the far edge of the table. As she pulled her hands back, Dorrel caught the one closest to him and kissed it. She smiled.

Then her father said something about "our three great royal houses —Olmunt, Shardamayn, and Kordelyon—uniting to restore peace and prosperity."

*The Kordelyons are not royalty*, she wanted to say. *They are Telshan with no peerage, only peers.* But interrupting would only prolong matters.

After his speech, Pavud and Divreenan each had one to make, each equally pointless. Marita, who sat on the other side of Rariden, muttered something to him, and he chuckled, nodding.

He leaned toward Alara. "She says we'd have been done by now if the politicians had been quiet and let the rest of us hash it out."

# Chapter 31

## REPARATIONS

Dorrel wished he'd had an extra cup of coffee to help him stay awake through the speeches.

Once they were finished, Ambassador Rabicanoh leaned forward. "Prelate Dalys gave us an excellent beginning this morning by turning our minds to the great loss of human life. In accordance with the Treaty of Shandór, those responsible for the deaths of soldiers in combat shall be held blameless."

Marita leaned forward, looking at Kordelyon. He nodded, and she spoke. "Ambassador, may I comment upon that?"

"Certainly, Chairwoman Graylin."

"Private Shelon Balmon was not killed in combat. She was shot in the back, as were many of the students at Denedra."

Mr. Balmon hung his head.

What the Makutians were thinking was impossible to tell. But surely all the Glynrellans were thinking the same thing. It was exactly the way the Makutian spies had killed the border patrol just before the invasion of Glynrell.

Velek looked down the table at Sturg. "Is this true?"

"The fighting at Denedra began when a Glynrellan archer shot one of my men."

"But at Kaesbaro?" Velek asked.

"She obviously was going to summon additional enemy troops, Your Royal Highness. It was in the best interest of my unit to stop her."

"I object," said Kordelyon, "to the use of the term 'enemy.' In spite of the skirmishing, no state of war existed."

"We concede it was an unprovoked act of aggression," Velek said. "But she was a soldier, was she not? The risk of death is inherent in soldiering. Her death ought to be accounted as a combat loss."

Dorrel glanced at Mr. Balmon, who sat just behind Marita. Leaning forward, elbows on knees, he clenched his hands.

"We will issue a formal apology," Velek added, "if that will help."

"Your Royal Highness," Kordelyon said, "I appreciate that gesture. But we refuse to concede this point."

Rabicanoh insisted they table it. Mr. Balmon started out of his chair, but a pointed finger from Marita stopped him.

The matter of the horses was next on the agenda. Prince Velek claimed the mare Alara had taken was worth three thousand sovereigns.

Alara protested. "It was an old mare with splay feet. Her days as a saddle horse were numbered."

"Nonsense," Velek said. "It was only eight years old."

"Really?" Alara put on her mock-sweet voice. "Then why did Commander Sturg call it 'an old mare no good for eating'?"

Velek didn't answer. He produced the horse's pedigree. Bóhjetien looked it over and walked around the table, stepping between Alara's chair and Dorrel's. "It is not a first-class pedigree, but it is not a shabby one, either. Offer two thousand."

She did, and Velek accepted.

Kordelyon asked Dorrel to give Toban's value.

Dorrel left his notes flat on the table, because if he held them up, the others would notice how his hands shook. He took a gulp of water in a futile attempt to drown the knot in his belly. "Based on what the army usually pays for horses in his line, we've estimated his value at thirty thousand staters."

Sturg barked an expletive no one bothered to translate.

Alara leaned toward Dorrel. "What did he say?"

"I'm not going to repeat it."

"Impossible," Sturg said. "No animal is worth so much."

Bóhjetien asked for Dorrel's notes, so he passed them, along with Toban's pedigree, to the attaché who came for them. She took them to Bóhjetien.

Velek said, "The amount is irrelevant. The horse belonged to a member of the Glynrellan militia and therefore must be accounted as a combat loss."

Dorrel's heart clenched. They were sure to bring up that business of his being out of uniform.

"Dr. Chevallon's horse was not army property," Kordelyon said.

"But Sergeant Chevallon was called to active duty, and the horse was killed in combat. You will note," Velek said, "we have not requested compensation for the horse Commander Sturg lost in Kaesbaro."

Kordelyon and Divreenan consulted for a few moments. Then Kordelyon walked down the table to Dorrel. "I'm sorry, Dor, but we must concede this. The army will reimburse you."

The money didn't matter. He had Bastion. And Velek was right. Toban was a combat casualty. "I understand, sir."

Kordelyon clapped Dorrel's shoulder before returning to his seat.

Now Dorrel just had to think of a diplomatic way to tell the prime minister to stop calling him *Dor*.

Alara stared at the agenda. The line said only *reparations*, but she felt an uncomfortable weight on her heart, despite what Marita had said. When General Rariden elucidated, Velek leaned forward, clasping his hands on the tabletop.

"Reparations were paid, General, to prisoners of war. As Prime Minister Kordelyon has noted, no state of war existed."

"It cannot be denied Curate Chevallon was captured and held against her will, and we have the testimony of Ambassador Rabicanoh's staff doctor that she was injured."

"You cannot mean to say, General, her treatment rises to the level —perhaps I should say descends to the level—of abuse perpetrated during the war."

Alara appreciated that Velek spoke of war crimes with the same words a Glynrellan might use. She whispered to Rariden, "He's right."

He ignored her.

Velek and Ambassador Pavud bent their heads over a piece of paper. Then Velek looked up. "In light of the degree of her injuries, and the fact she was in our custody only one week, we are prepared to pay one hundred ten staters."

Before Alara could signal this was more than enough, Rariden said, "A tenth? That is an insult. There was no prorating the last time we met here."

Velek and Pavud consulted again, after which Velek said, "We shall pay a quarter. Two hundred seventy-five staters."

Rariden glowered. "No, sir."

The ambassadors argued about it for a few minutes, until Rabicanoh insisted it be tabled, along with the matter of Shelon Balmon.

If he hadn't been under orders to attend, Sturg would've walked out.

The absurd request to pay off a woman for losing a fight was followed by Rariden asking for the return of trophies. "The Kaesbaro delegation is prepared to turn over the effects of the Makutians killed there in exchange for our soldiers' belongings."

Sturg expected better from a military man.

"With all due respect, General," Kabed said, "there's no precedent for that."

Rariden smiled. "But there is, General." He gestured toward the sword, still lying on the table. "We are only asking that our other combatants receive the same courtesy as Curate Chevallon."

Kabed started to speak, but Velek raised a hand to stop him. "General Rariden, you must see the distinction. Curate Chevallon is alive. Her sword was stolen. The other items were taken from the dead."

"A theft from a dead man is a theft from his family."

Velek deferred to Ambassador Pavud, who leaned forward slightly. "That is a point on which our customs differ, General. Besides, carrying out this request would be impractical. To issue orders to ten men to return a collection of weapons—even if we did so, there is no way to return each item to the right family."

"In the case of swords and bows, that may be true," Rariden said. "But one item taken was unique. A foot-long tress of blonde hair. We demand that Corporal Korig return it."

The back of Sturg's neck turned to gooseflesh.

Velek, Pavud, and Kabed huddled briefly. Then Kabed turned to Sturg.

"How could they know this? Did Korig speak of it in her presence?"

"No, sir." Sturg glared at Hanik. "But the lieutenant may have."

Kabed got up, spoke to Hanik, then leaned over and said something to the prince.

Velek and Pavud exchanged a few words before Pavud spoke again. "We are baffled, General, by your request for such a trivial thing."

"There is nothing trivial about a memento of our fallen," Rariden said. "Corporal Korig has something that rightly belongs to Private Balmon's father."

The ambassadors argued the point until, finally, Kordelyon made a show of conceding the trophies as if it were a great sacrifice. "Peace is, of course, the most important thing we all seek."

Rabicanoh called a recess midmorning. Footmen brought platters of puny pastries while a couple of maids served coffee from a cart.

Sturg and Kabed got their coffee, then stood near the wall. "They didn't just know Korig killed the girl," Sturg said. "They knew he was demoted."

Kabed nodded. "What makes you think they got that from Hanik?"

"He was talking to Chevallon's woman yesterday before dinner. He even winked at her."

"Are you sure?"

"Yes sir. As her escort, he became . . . chummy with her."

"Huh." The general looked across the room at Chevallon and the woman. "Chummy enough to pass information to the enemy?"

It might be presumptuous for Sturg to suggest that such action deserved a demotion. Yet he was on the verge of hinting at it when Rabicanoh called them to order.

The innkeeper was given the floor.

"Fifty-two years ago," she said, "four Makutian soldiers crossed the border near Tylan in the night. They murdered the members of the border patrol by shooting each of them in the back. Once the patrol was dead, General Witek led three battalions into Glynrell and captured Tylan."

She allowed a moment of silence.

"After the war," she continued, "General Witek's advance scouts were turned over to the war crimes tribunal. They were convicted of murder, because when they killed the border patrol, no state of war existed."

Sturg didn't like where she was going with this history lesson. The hairs on the back of his neck rose like a dog's hackles.

"Eight weeks ago," she said, "a troop of Makutian soldiers approached Kaesbaro in the night. They murdered the watchwoman near the eastern bridge by shooting her in the back." She paused again. "We have already agreed no state of war existed. I therefore charge that Commander Sturg and Corporal Korig are likewise guilty of murder and should meet the same fate as their predecessors."

Sturg didn't know what had happened to those men. They weren't spoken of in Makut. But since Telshans didn't execute criminals, he supposed they spent the rest of their lives in a Glynrellan prison. He stifled a shudder. Like the innkeeper and Rariden, those men might still be alive. In prison. Being preached to by Telshan clerics.

Death would be better, even if it came at one's own hand.

Velek, Pavud, and Kabed bowed their heads together. Then Kabed spoke. "Commander Sturg was given an assignment, and he carried it out to the best of his ability."

Sturg's ruffled ego was soothed, till the general continued.

"That his best wasn't in compliance with Prince Velek's wishes is regrettable. He has been officially reprimanded. That is, we believe, sufficient. As for Corporal Korig, he was under orders and cannot be held accountable."

"General Witek's men were under orders as well," the old woman said, "and they were held accountable."

Kabed, Velek, and Pavud exchanged glances.

Pavud took the floor. "That a previous monarch thought it expedient to sacrifice a few soldiers to forge a peace agreement cannot bind the current monarch to an identical course of action. Especially since the circumstances of Commander Sturg's presence in Glynrell were so different."

"What circumstances?" the innkeeper asked.

Pavud smiled coldly at Kordelyon. "The commander was, of course, in your country already, stationed at our embassy."

"That's irrelevant," the old woman shot back. "His conduct in Kaesbaro can have no possible connection to his duties in Ayenni."

"A discussion of Commander Sturg's orders is not germane." Pavud stared across the table. "Unless Prime Minister Kordelyon wishes to go into it."

"You are correct," Kordelyon said. "It is not germane. But, as Chairwoman Graylin points out, Corporal Korig must be held accountable."

Pavud folded his arms. "One thing I must say in defense of Commander Sturg and Corporal Korig."

The old woman waited silently for him to do so.

"*They* were in uniform."

Chevallon's woman winced.

Sturg choked back a laugh.

The old woman pretended confusion. Prince Velek stated his case against Chevallon just as he had at the embassy.

While the politicians covered that ground again, Sturg watched Chevallon. To his credit, he remained expressionless.

Kordelyon tried to argue that Chevallon had acted as a private citizen, not a soldier.

Velek reiterated the fact that the militia had been called up a week prior.

The debating went in circles for almost an hour.

But all of them, Sturg, Korig, Chevallon, even the female sentry, had done what they believed needed doing, to the best of their abilities.

The matter seemed stalemated.

Pavud slapped a copy of the treaty on the table. "Whether any given soldier's action was incorrect is irrelevant. Here is the key matter: 'Prime Minister Kordelyon shall present his daughter Alara to His Royal Highness the Crown Prince Velek.' This clearly indicates that once the prime minister's daughter arrived at the palace in Tarvag, she ought to have remained there. That Sergeant Chevallon—"

Kordelyon said, "Dr. Chevallon, if you please."

Pavud spoke through Kordelyon's interruption. "—removed a member of the prince's household is an offense of the highest order. And whether one calls him doctor or sergeant does not matter. He must be extradited for espionage."

"Out of the question." Kordelyon pushed his chair away from the table and leaned back.

"Furthermore, Prime Minister, as your daughter willfully abandoned her rightful place with His Royal Highness Prince Velek to consort with a commoner —"

"I beg your pardon, Ambassador!" Kordelyon sat up straight.

"We must insist that, to comply with the intent of the treaty, you provide an unsullied bride to take her place."

A murmur ran down the Glynrellan side of the room.

"You must be joking." Kordelyon pulled back again. "What you ask is outrageous."

"These are our requirements, Prime Minister. That the Chevallons face trial in Tarvag for offenses against the crown prince, and that the Kordelyons provide a substitute to fulfill the terms of the treaty."

"Impossible," Kordelyon snapped. "How many daughters do you think I have?"

"You have nieces, do you not? Cousins?"

"That you would even make such a request shows how little you understand our beliefs." Kordelyon faced Rabicanoh. "We cannot negotiate this way. I move that we adjourn and withdraw for private meetings. We can reconvene after luncheon."

Velek seconded this motion, and Sturg added his voice to the ayes. Let the politicians take their wrangling to a back room and leave him out of it.

# Chapter 32

## A SUPERB TACTIC

As they adjourned, Alara reached for the sword, but the soldier again stepped in. "I'm sorry, Curate. I'll have to take that now."

She snatched her hands away from the rapier. "Certainly. I understand." She was grateful Barláhtiay had allowed it in the meeting room, however briefly.

While Velek and Bóhjetien went to one room and Father and Ambassador Rabicanoh to another, Mehrialéna invited the family to the second-floor sitting room.

Mum thumped into an armchair. "Unsullied bride, indeed. I would give him a few readings from the Scriptures if I thought he would listen."

"I wish they'd been so forthright at the outset." Alara sat with Dorrel on a sofa.

Camrun frowned, his arms folded. "Perhaps they were."

"What nonsense." Mum rounded on him. "Honestly, Camrun."

He shrugged.

Mehrialéna perched on the edge of her chair. Her face was tight, and her movements stiff.

"Lena, what is wrong?" Alara asked. "You do not seem yourself."

She stared at the floor, then Alara. "Perhaps I . . ." She swallowed, then jerked her chin up. "I should do it. I could be the substitute."

The calls refuting this notion were unanimous. "It is out of the question, Mehrialéna," Alara said.

Camrun put his hands on his hips. "Besides, even if it made sense and did not contradict Scripture, they want a Kordelyon. If they wanted a Shardamayn, Velek certainly would have asked you already."

Mehrialéna scooted back in her chair and folded her arms. "I doubt Velek would ask anyone. He has said he does not wish to remarry."

"This request did not come from him," Alara said. "It came from King Domat."

"Still, perhaps I should discuss it with Velek. I must marry soon, Alara. I am nearly thirty. And I know no one else who is tolerable and of my own station."

"Your station is irrelevant. And you told me he was dull."

"He is." She sighed. "But we get along, which is more than I can say about some." She glowered at Camrun, who snickered. "And what do you mean 'they want a Kordelyon?' Ambassador Pavud said cousin."

"But he said 'the Kordelyons,'" Camrun answered. "If the treaty was meant to forge an alliance between the Olmunts and the Kordelyons, bringing you into it would not serve the purpose."

"The purpose of the treaty was to lift the embargo," Mum said.

"Hrm. Yes, ostensibly." Camrun folded his arms. "And I would have agreed with you . . . until Father asked me about Reyshara Kordelyon's abdication."

"Oh, stop." Mum waved her hands. "This is ridiculous."

"What reason could he have for asking if he was not trying to undo it?"

Alara grew stiff. She hadn't considered that possibility. "You think the treaty was part of that."

"Such alliances were often formed in the monarchical period."

Mum stood and held out her hands, one toward each of them. "I will not have you talking about your father this way. It is disrespectful, and you are wrong. He was only trying to promote free trade."

After a brief silence, Mehrialéna lifted her chin, her haughty demeanor restored. "Well, I shall discuss the matter with Velek anyway."

"Do not, Lena," Alara said. "You do not love him, nor does he love you."

Mehrialéna rolled her eyes. "Have you some vision, O wise prophetess, that you speak to me thus?"

"Velek shall not be king. Uked shall succeed Domat."

Mehrialéna's expression softened. "Oh. Why?"

"I was not shown why."

"Velek sometimes comes to worship with us." Mehrialéna's voice dropped a little. "Perhaps he shall become a Telshan. The Makutians would not allow a Telshan to take the throne."

Alara shrugged. "There are many reasons why he might be removed. Or choose to step down."

"But that has nothing to do with whether I ought to marry him."

"It does if you are marrying him because of his station. Which would be the wrong reason to marry, anyway. Galardi said marriage must be founded on love, not politics. As Camrun said, if Velek loved you, he would have asked already."

"Was that you admitting I'm right about something?" Camrun smirked.

Alara ignored him.

Mehrialéna spread her hands. "What am I to do, then?"

"You are to concentrate on developing your gifts and leave the matter of a husband to Ahbay. He knows what He's doing."

Lena narrowed her eyes. "Do you know what He is doing, O wise prophetess?"

Alara sighed. "I do not know His plan for you. Only that He must have one."

The mischief disappeared from Mehrialéna's expression. "You did not become annoyed by the word 'prophetess' as you usually do."

No. It seemed her fate, whether she wanted it or not.

Sturg wasn't a pious man, but when the delegates reconvened after lunch, he begged the gods of his fathers the meeting would soon end.

Prince Bóhjetien was given the floor. "His Royal Highness Prince Velek and I have discussed the present impasse and have established a compromise. We hope, Prime Minister, you shall agree also."

Kordelyon smiled a little.

"There are two ladies involved. Alara, for whom reparations have been asked, and an as-yet-unnamed relative of hers, who is asked to fulfill the terms of the treaty. Prince Velek is prepared to yield his claim on, as Ambassador Pavud put it, an 'unsullied bride,' if you, Prime Minister, yield your claim on Alara's reparation."

"I refuse to give this 'unsullied bride' business any credence by even discussing it," Kordelyon said.

"Prime Minister," Prince Velek said, "I am, in an effort to break the impasse, asking you to forfeit your claim on the precise sum of eleven hundred staters. Yet I am yielding a claim on the freedom of one of your relatives. Since you are a Telshan, I thought you would esteem such a thing priceless."

"Indeed, Your Royal Highness. But it is a thing to which you have no just claim."

Without taking his eyes off the prime minister, Velek held his hand out to Pavud, who put a copy of the treaty in it. Velek held it up. "I daresay we disagree on that point."

"That there was a misunderstanding is regrettable," Kordelyon said, "but my relatives cannot be held accountable for an error in translation."

"Error? Ambassador Pavud." Velek put down the treaty and turned to his right. "Was there an error in translation?"

"Not that I am aware of, Your Royal Highness."

Velek looked more stern than Sturg had ever seen him. Almost kingly. He turned to Divreenan. "Ambassador, to what error does the prime minister refer?"

Divreenan said, "The Makutian phrase 'present to' was translated literally into Glynrellan. But the phrase has a different meaning in each culture. The phrase should have been rendered in Glynrellan more in accordance with its intent."

"Or struck entirely," someone muttered. Probably Chevallon.

"Yes," Velek continued, "we are all keenly aware of that difference. Perhaps, Ambassador Divreenan, if the treaty had been written in Redíquan, as was the Treaty of Shandór, the 'misunderstanding,' as the prime minister calls it, might have been avoided. Ambassador Pavud, how did you originally propose to write this clause?"

"The phrase I suggested, Your Royal Highness, was, as is often found in marriage contracts, 'shall deliver his daughter in marriage.'"

"And what did Ambassador Divreenan tell you?"

"That no Telshan father would do such a thing. So we met with Prime Minister Kordelyon."

"And what did he say?"

"That such phrasing was too blatant. That the only way he could get the treaty past parliament was to use the phrase 'present to,' which in Glynnish describes an introduction, but in Makutian describes a betrothal."

A murmur washed over the room. Kordelyon's wife leaned forward and whispered to him, but he didn't answer her.

He displayed no emotion. "I believe the ambassador and I recall that meeting differently."

"How do you remember it, Ambassador Divreenan?" the prince asked.

Divreenan stammered, red faced, looking from Kordelyon to Velek and back. "I—I—" His gaze roamed the room, taking in Rabicanoh, the Chevallons, and finally the prelate. He sighed, then faced Velek. "Ambassador Pavud's account is accurate."

Chevallon's wife clenched her fists on the table. Her cheeks flushed. He put his hand out, as if to hold hers, but she batted it away and walked out.

Kordelyon's wife stood, and Chevallon also started out of his chair. His mother-in-law's hand on his shoulder stopped him. She followed her daughter out of the room.

"Prime Minister Kordelyon." Velek opened a book. "The fourth Canon says, 'Parents must protect the dignity and purity of their children.'" He flipped to another page. "Galardi writes, 'Mere allegiance cannot sanctify a marriage.' And in the Chronicle of Wisdom"—he flipped to a section near the front—"'A woman married but unloved' is listed among those things that 'cause the ground to tremble.' Now, perhaps I misunderstand, but it seems to me that, under these precepts, a Telshan father would not subject a daughter to an arranged marriage against her will. Is my interpretation flawed, Prelate Dalys?"

"It is not, sir."

How had the prince become so familiar with the Telshan Scriptures? Not that it mattered. Using them against Kordelyon was a superb tactic.

"Prime Minister," Velek continued, "it is my understanding that you were fully aware of King Domat's intentions. He, however misguidedly, wished to get a wife for his son. And you, he thought, wished to pursue the sort of alliance that was arranged among royal families in pre-Telshan times. Am I"—he paused—"misunderstanding?"

"No one arranges marriages anymore, outside of Makut," Kordelyon said.

Just like a politician to not answer the question.

"I agree your family should not be held accountable for this clause. Which is why I am willing to concede this point. I ask in return a mere monetary concession."

After a long moment's silence, Chevallon leaned toward Rariden. The general stood, his chair scraping the floor. He walked to

Kordelyon and said something in his ear.

The prime minister nodded, then turned toward Bóhjetien. "We accept the prince's compromise."

Sturg glanced Kabed's way, eager for a sign Velek had conceded too much so they could proceed with the execution. But Kabed's leathery face showed nothing.

Alara ran, skirt hitched up, through the rotunda up the stairs all the way to her rooms. There, she collapsed onto the settee. When the knock came at the door a minute later, she didn't answer, hoping whoever it was would go away.

The door opened, and Mum came in.

"Oh, baby," she said, weeping. "I'm so sorry. I didn't know. Had I known, I'd have stopped him, I swear."

"I know, Mum."

They wasted a bunch of time in the afternoon arguing about extraditions, until Rariden asked for a recess. This, they could all agree upon.

As soon as the gavel hit the table, Dorrel jumped from his chair and went after Alara. As he ran toward their suite, he noticed Camrun close behind.

The suite was empty.

Two doors down, in the Kordelyons' suite, Shenevra and Alara were packing Shenevra's clothes.

"I've asked the housekeeper to prepare another room for me."

Camrun took a step toward her. "Mum . . ."

"You were right, Cam. I shouldn't have doubted you and Rariden."

Alara, moving things from the dresser to a trunk, froze. "What did

Rariden say?"

Shenevra looked away.

Camrun's eyes darted back and forth between Alara and Shenevra. "He said the timing couldn't be coincidental—the Makutians asking for a meeting that week."

"He told them. Didn't he? Father told Pavud when I would be in Ayenni."

Camrun shrugged. "It looks that way."

She dropped the clothes into the trunk and slammed the lid.

Briefly, Dorrel wondered why she wasn't crying. Then he saw how red her eyes were. And Shenevra's. While the others had been bickering about extradition, they'd been crying themselves out.

Shenevra put a dress into one of the trunks and went to the wardrobe for another. Her voice had a steely edge Dorrel had never heard before. "It all has to do with royalty. Druyun always had an unreasonable interest in royal lines. Sometimes I think the only reason he married me is because of my connection to the royal family. When my uncle gave him the regalia, you'd have thought it was a coronation."

The knot in Dorrel's stomach tightened. "So Velek was right when he said the prime minister was looking for some sort of old-fashioned . . ." He couldn't find the words.

"Alliance by marriage," Camrun grumbled.

Dorrel nodded. That was the phrase.

Once the packing was done, they left the trunks in the prime minister's suite and went to Dorrel and Alara's rooms. They sent for tea and waited for the housekeeper, but before either arrived, Rariden and Marita did.

Shenevra tried to apologize for ignoring his advice, but Rariden waved it off. "I have something more important to discuss with all of you before I take it to the prime minister. Sit down, please."

Marita joined Shenevra on the settee. Alara took the armchair, and Camrun turned the desk chair to face Rariden. Dorrel sat on the arm of Alara's chair.

"I've had something in mind since the beginning of the summit," Rariden said. "I've been reluctant to use it, but I think it's the only way to break the stalemate."

He stood near the coffee table, between Alara and Camrun, hands clasped behind his back. "Sturg bears primary responsibility for Shelon Balmon's killing. But the Makutians have a strong case for asking us to drop the charges against Korig."

Marita shook her head.

"I'm sorry, but they do. Yet we have little basis for asking them to drop the charges against Dorrel." His glare hit Dorrel like the lash of a whip. "What you did is against international law."

Alara clutched Dorrel's hand.

"During the war," Rariden said, "we sometimes exchanged prisoners. Six of our officers for half a dozen of theirs, that sort of thing. I believe we can similarly trade Alara and Dorrel's freedom for Sturg and Korig's."

Dorrel brushed his thumb across the back of Alara's hand. "What do you think?"

"Kenna said we are to forgive as we have been forgiven."

He nodded.

Marita folded her arms and leaned back. "That's surely true, but I don't think Montus Balmon will give in easily."

Rariden said, "Would it help if I talk to him?"

She tilted her head. "Probably." She stood. "I'll come with you."

Rariden patted Shenevra's shoulder before going.

The door clicked shut behind them. Dorrel sighed. Mr. Balmon didn't stand a chance against both of them.

Shortly after Rariden and Marita had gone, a server brought tea.

*Show us your path, Ahbay,* Alara prayed. *Keep Mum strong. Help us deal with Father. And when I see him, stop me from punching him in the face.*

Mum poured, then handed a cup to Camrun.

After a perfunctory knock, Father walked in.

Camrun brought the tea to Alara. "Thanks, Cam."

"Well, there's something I don't often see—you two being civil to one another."

"It isn't often we agree." Alara kept her eyes on her cup. "But we do agree you . . . are a pig."

"I beg your pardon, young lady."

She put her cup down and stood to face him. "You'll get no pardon from me, Prime Minister. You call yourself a Telshan. The precepts clearly state—"

"Alara." Mum rose slowly. She placed one hand on Alara's shoulder.

Hanging her head, she stepped back, grateful to find Dorrel behind her. She leaned against him. He wrapped his arms around her.

"Druyun Kordelyon," Mum began, "you make a good show of attending prayer meetings and supporting the church. But the precepts clearly state children are a gift from Telshi and must be valued as such. 'Dearer than any treasure.'" She took a shuddering breath. "She was bludgeoned, Dru. She took stitches! And it could have been worse." Mum straightened her shoulders. "You traded your daughter's dignity to a foreign prince to increase your political power." Mum seemed to be gaining strength, but her voice was strangled. She glanced at Alara. "This curate tells me neither Kenna nor the Scriptures nor the prophets give me permission to divorce you, despite your failure to uphold Telshan precepts."

"Shen, please—"

"But that doesn't mean I have to live with you. I cannot remain with a man who would endanger my child." She shook her head. "I can't trust you anymore. I'll never know when you're lying to me to get your way—"

"I have never lied to you, Shen."

Her hand lashed out, slapping his face with a sharp crack.

His head swept aside, reddening. He held it there, jaw open, eyes blinking.

"You *promised me* she would be safe!"

His brows knitted. He didn't look her in the eye.

"I have nothing more to say to you." Mum resumed her seat and filled a teacup.

Alara, trembling, didn't know what to do.

Dorrel, thanks be to Ahbay, did. "Prime Minister." He extended his arm toward the door. "I must ask you to leave."

Mum remained in her room when the delegates reconvened. As they took their seats, Alara reached out to grip Montus Balmon's hand. "Thank you, Mr. Balmon."

He shrugged. "We always knew getting those fellows into a Glynrellan prison was as unlikely as . . . well, as getting back Shelon's hair."

Once everyone was seated, Rariden made his proposal.

Ambassadors Pavud and Divreenan spent several minutes debating whether the pardons were, in fact, equivalent.

"This is not only a matter of palace security and the violation of the treaty," Pavud said. "Our national honor has been shattered."

"I daresay, Ambassador," Father said, "that if your national honor is reliant upon the conduct of foreigners, then it was rather fragile to begin with."

Pavud turned to Velek to see whether he would answer.

Velek's hands remained flat on the table. "Indeed."

Pavud paled.

"Our people have long had a notion of national honor different from that of our neighbors," Velek said. "And I cannot, through either logic or diplomacy, defend it."

Pavud started to speak, but Velek silenced him with an upraised hand. "We accept General Rariden's proposal."

Bóhjetien smiled. "May I trust, my friend, you shall withdraw your troops from our border as well as Glynrell's?"

"Certainly."

Dorrel leaned toward Alara. "There's only one more thing we need to know."

"What?"

"When can we go home?"

Sturg's muscles quivered like those of a dog straining to obey the command to sit when every instinct told him to attack. Attachés drew up three copies of the treaty. In Redíquan. Bóhjetien, Velek, and Kordelyon all signed it. They shook hands all around. Rabicanoh's gavel hit the table for, praise the gods, the last time.

The Glynrellans quickly moved away from their prime minister, talking amongst themselves, leaving him with only his ambassador for company.

While Velek and Pavud spoke with Bóhjetien and Rabicanoh, Kabed leaned toward Sturg, his voice low. His words set Sturg's nerves afire. "Commander, you may proceed."

# Chapter 33

## THE EASTERN GARDEN

Alara felt Sturg watching her while they again endured the social sham of sharing drinks before dinner. He kept uncomfortably close. And Dorrel was as tense as she'd ever seen him.

He put his half-empty glass on a table and held her hand. "I've no appetite. You?"

She squeezed his fingers, shaking her head.

"If we went for a ride, would the kitchen staff feed us supper later?"

"Surely."

"Then let's go. I need to get out of here." They went to their suite to change.

She pulled off her vest and dress and hung them up. He put his arms around her waist and kissed the back of her neck. She giggled. "Do you want to go out or stay in?"

"Hmm . . . not sure, now."

Alara turned in the circle of his embrace, looped her arms around his neck, and kissed him. "Well, think about this. We can only go for a ride while it's light. But there will be plenty of time for lovemaking after supper."

The noise he made was somewhere between a chuckle and a growl. He kissed the side of her neck. "You're very clever." He kissed her once more before letting her go.

They changed into riding clothes. He headed for the door.

She started to follow, but then hesitated. Something like a tap on the shoulder or a whisper in her ear compelled her to turn around.

Alara hadn't felt this way since the day the assassins had come for them. She opened the trunk and pulled out her gambeson.

Dorrel leaned on the doorframe, watching her fasten it. "I can't fault you for caution, Lar, especially in your condition, but—"

"We don't know for certain I am in that condition." Though she longed to be, she didn't wish to dwell on it in case she wasn't.

"I told you, ask Marita."

She huffed.

"Everyone is disarmed, and Barláhtiay's men are on their guard. What are you afraid of?"

She fastened the last buckle. "I don't know. But after what happened last time, I'm not going to ignore this kind of . . . premonition." She reached into the trunk, pulled out his gambeson, and tossed it to him. "So armor up, or we're not going anywhere."

His lips twitched into half a smile.

Alara snickered and grasped her brigandine. "Just make up your mind. There's only an hour or so until sunset."

Sturg walked double time to his rooms. He shucked his dress uniform and changed into dark-green Redíquan fatigues. He slung the soldier's bag over his shoulder and jogged down the back stairs to the nearest exit.

Within minutes, he'd perched in a leafy maple between the stables and the shore with a view across the lawn and the gravel drive to the stable courtyard. No matter which part of the house they came from, he'd have a clear shot before they reached the stable. If they had already gone, he'd get them on their return.

The quiver was on his back, the bow in his hand. He wore the knife on his belt.

The setting sun touched the treetops on the western side of the palace. The eastern garden and the drive lay in a shadow that reached toward the stables.

The dining room curtains hung open. He watched the delegates take their seats.

Finally, the Chevallons came through the kitchen door. Hand in hand, they walked through the garden, chatting and laughing.

He nocked an arrow.

The sun and garden and Alara's laughter instantly soothed Dorrel's ragged nerves.

"I need to pick a new girl's name," she said.

He chuckled. "I didn't realize you had an old girl's name."

She smirked and nudged him sideways, letting go of his hand and taking a sidestep away from him. "I used to imagine if I had a daughter, I'd name her Sarya. But I can't now, since Laneesa and Gylun beat me to it."

"Not Reyshara?"

"We can't name her Reyshara. What will people think?"

He draped his arm across her shoulders. "Since when do you worry about what people think?"

She looked skyward. "Constantly. Especially you." They stepped off the garden pavers and onto the lawn.

"What? What did I ever do—"

"Oh, admit it." She scampered a little ahead, then turned to face him, walking backward, her eyes glistening. "When we were undergraduates, you thought I was an arrogant snob."

He moved to catch her. "I never thought you were a snob."

"Ha! You admit—"

A loud *thunk*. Her eyes flew wide open. She staggered into his arms.

Dorrel glanced over her shoulder. An arrow stuck out of her back. He ripped it out. "Down!" He shoved her to the ground.

"Dor, no—" Grass bristled against her nose. He wrapped his right arm around her head and shielded her body with his own.

She could do nothing but chant "no, no," as one after another, the arrows struck him. And arrows they must be, just like the one he'd pulled out of her, still clenched in his left hand, near her shoulder. Some hit his brigandine with the same dull thud that had nearly knocked her down. Others tore into his flesh with a sickening squelch.

When half a minute had passed with no further strikes, Dorrel pushed up enough to glance over his shoulder. "Where is he?"

Alara looked at him. Blood ran down the side of his neck. One arrow stuck out of his arm. Another had gone through his calf. "Dor . . ." She stretched one hand toward the trench just under his ear.

He sat back on his right hip. His breath was short. He looked once more over his shoulder. "I don't see him." Dorrel turned to her, wincing. His voice creaked. "Get Marita."

Alara scrambled to her feet and sprinted toward the house. She wove though the twisting, hedge-trimmed garden paths.

**Go back.**

She didn't slow her pace. *Kenna, no! I can't help Dorrel. He needs Marita!*

The response was so abrupt, she stumbled.

Emptiness.

A moment ago, Telshi's spirit had flowed through her like the breath in her lungs. Now she suffocated. She stopped, gasping, drowning in silence pouring from heaven.

*Kenna, help me!*

Nothing.

Was this what Galardi meant when he spoke of those Kenna turned Her back on? And Alara deserved it. Arguing! Arguing with the Sovereign of All.

She ran back to Dorrel.

He sat on the grass by the drive, arrows poking out of his skin and armor. Only a few stuck in the lawn, having missed their mark.

As she approached from one side, Sturg approached from the other, a long knife in his hand.

Dorrel tried to stand, but his leg, penetrated in three places, buckled under him.

*Kenna, forgive me for arguing.* As she passed Dorrel, she hesitated just long enough to snatch an arrow caught in the brigandine near his shoulder.

"Lar. Don't."

But she couldn't stop. She'd been sent back just for this.

Sturg charged toward them.

Holding the arrow in her left hand like a knife, Alara ran to meet him.

Inside the house, someone screamed.

He lunged with the knife. She swept her right forearm into his, pushing the knife arm away. She plunged the arrow into his side, just below the ribs. She yanked it out. The arrowhead tore away bits of uniform and flesh.

He growled. Alara dropped the arrow. Grabbed his wrist and elbow. Pulled him around and down. Once he was on his back, she pressed her knee into his elbow.

He punched the side of her head.

She twisted his wrist until the knife came away in her hand. She tossed it to Dorrel. It landed in the grass, inches from his hand.

Sturg's arm came across her throat, pushing her away. She got to her feet and took two steps back.

Sturg leapt across the gap between them, trying to knock her down. She dodged, spun, and lashed a kick at his back.

He staggered, then wheeled on her, fists raised. He let loose a series of rapid jabs.

She bobbed, guarded, and deflected the jabs aimed at her head. But she missed the one he aimed at her ribs.

He winced, then gaped. Had he thought the brigandine just for show?

Alara threw a right cross at him, then ducked under his roundhouse punch and grabbed his arm. Hooking her ankle around his, she almost brought him down.

But, as Rariden had so often told her, almost didn't count.

Sturg kept his footing. His hand clamped around her bicep.

She pushed her other arm under his. Ducking, she butted her head into his solar plexus.

She crouched, wrapping her free arm around his leg. Rising, she lifted Sturg off his feet, throwing him back over her head.

He landed in the grass with a hearty thud.

Sturg stared at the sky.

He gasped for air. What had she done?

Her boot heel came toward his face. He rolled away and got to his feet.

She wore armor. No wonder she'd survived his shot. Chevallon was armored as well. But he couldn't stand. Sturg only had to beat the woman. Finishing Chevallon would be simple once that was done.

He charged her again, but she dodged and kicked his side.

Sturg spared his fists any more blows to her torso. He focused instead on landing an uppercut that would knock her out. But she deflected most of his punches with a sweep of her forearm. The woman landed a few kicks on his torso and got a couple of right crosses through his guard.

Finally, he got under her defense and landed an uppercut. Her head rocked back. He laughed. He swung again, a powerful right cross.

She ducked under it. He staggered a little.

Dorrel knelt on his right knee, despite the arrow that transfixed his thigh. But his left leg still wouldn't hold him up. He clutched the knife Alara had given him, watching her fight Sturg alone. And in her condition. *Telshi, help us!*

She ducked under Sturg's right cross. With nothing to meet his fist, Sturg was thrown off balance. Alara landed a kick on his back that sent him stumbling.

She glanced toward Dorrel.

"Keep your eye on him," Dorrel shouted.

"Dorrel!" someone behind him shrieked. In a moment, Shenevra knelt next to him, the billowing skirt of her copper brocade gown soaking up blood from his leg. "Hold still."

"Marita . . ."

"Right behind me." She pressed a lace-trimmed handkerchief against his neck.

"Someone needs to help Lar."

"The others are coming."

Sturg turned on Alara. She met him with a flurry of jabs. He deflected the first few, but the others all met their mark, tossing his head back and forth.

Marita knelt next to Dorrel and wrapped a dinner napkin around his left forearm, where an arrow had carved a trench.

A moment later, Camrun was behind him, a strong hand around his good arm, and a gentle one on the arm that had an arrow through it.

Dorrel felt dizzy. "Cam . . . help Lar."

"At the moment, you need our help more than she does." Camrun handed Marita his handkerchief. She added it to Shenevra's. "Besides, Lar's better at that sort of thing than I am."

With her free hand, Shenevra pulled out the arrows caught in the plates of the brigandine.

Sturg staggered backward. As he advanced again, Alara met him with a spinning roundhouse kick.

Her bootheel carved a trench in his cheek from ear to chin.

Sturg put a hand to his face and stared at the blood that came away on his fingers.

Rariden and Dad jogged past.

Sturg lunged for Alara as if to grapple her. She jabbed her boot into his stomach.

He fell on his face, gasping for air. He planted one foot on the ground, but before he could attack again, Rariden grabbed one arm and Dad the other. They pulled him away from Alara.

"Stand down, Commander," Rariden said.

Sturg only growled, tugging against them.

Alara stood there, hands on hips. Dorrel could see the scar on her armor where the arrow had hit. It hadn't gone deep, but still . . . "Lar?"

She came toward him, winded, sweaty, utterly beautiful.

"I'll take out the arrows after we get him inside," Marita said.

"Is she all right?" Dorrel asked.

Marita glanced up and grabbed Alara's wrist. She put one hand over Alara's belly. "Yes, they're all right."

Dorrel sighed, releasing the tension in his muscles. He sagged, letting Camrun hold him up.

"They?" Shenevra frowned at Marita.

"She's pregnant."

Shenevra gasped. "How do you know?"

Marita shrugged. "I just know."

"Marita's a healer, Mum."

Marita turned Alara to examine the marred armor between her shoulder blades. "That'll need a bandage, but it's not bad."

The wound on her back, which Alara could hardly feel, was the least of her concerns. Trembling, she knelt next to Dorrel and carefully put one arm around him, burying her face in his shoulder. He trembled as well.

"What in the name of all that is holy . . ." Bóhjetien jogged down the garden path toward them. Velek, Father, and the rest followed.

Alara kissed Dorrel's cheek. Then she stood. "Sturg tried to kill us."

Bóhjetien put his fists on his hips. Mehrialéna, carrying a basket of first-aid supplies, ran to Dorrel, followed by servants with a stretcher.

Marita removed the handkerchiefs and bandaged the gouge under Dorrel's ear.

Velek strode across the lawn to Sturg. "In a Redíquan uniform. A high crime indeed."

"The weapons are also Redíquan." Alara snatched one of the arrows from the ground and handed it to Velek.

Velek glared at the arrow. He held it in front of Sturg's face. "And how did you come by this, Commander?"

Sturg remained silent. His eyes focused on the sky above Velek's head.

Sturg straightened his shoulders.

Kabed approached the prince. "An affront, indeed, Your Royal Highness. Summary execution is within my rights —"

"No!" Prince Bóhjetien came toward them. "Capital punishment is not permitted in Redíque."

Velek nodded. "Indeed. General, I believe we can leave this matter to Redíquan justice."

Sturg half-expected Kabed to insist upon a Makutian court-

376

martial. But only half.

Kabed made a small bow. "I defer to Your Royal Highness."

So be it. Sturg was to take full blame. He was prepared for that. He had utterly failed. He just wished it didn't mean disgrace for Ult.

Alara's attention was torn between Sturg's villainy and Dorrel's wounds. The servants carried Dorrel's stretcher toward the kitchen door.

Bóhjetien cocked his head toward Kabed. "You mean to say, General, you believe he committed such an outrage with no orders?"

Kabed's face revealed nothing. "Much of his actions in Glynrell were without orders."

With answers like that, the general could have a future in politics. Except the general had no future at all.

*Kenna?*

She did not speak. But Her back was no longer turned. Alara wanted nothing more than to leave the others and find a quiet place to bask in Her presence. *Kenna, forgive my distrust. I'm done arguing. I'm Your servant. Tell me what to say.*

And She did. Yet Alara neither trembled nor wept. Now, Telshi's spirit didn't break her. It fortified her.

She moved alongside Velek. "The commander may be reckless, but he is not a rebel. He had his orders."

Kabed frowned. "Not from me."

"Through you."

Velek turned to her. "From the king?"

She nodded.

"Ah. Well. Now I know how far he trusts me, do I not?"

"Indeed. General Kabed can also confirm that the king hired the Temhainites who tried to assassinate us."

Velek glared at the general. "Can you?"

Kabed stiffened and squared his shoulders, but he remained silent.

Father stepped between Alara and Bóhjetien. "So you admit King Domat ordered the assassination of my daughter and her husband."

"To redeem our 'national honor,' no doubt," Velek said.

"Not only in this matter." Words she hadn't thought of poured through Alara. "During his father's reign, Makut suffered defeat in Glynrell. If he could win a war where his father failed and gain permanent control of our ports —"

Father's chuckle was as stiff as Sturg's posture. "You're speculating now, Lar."

"I am not. Kenna knows the schemes of Her enemies."

He folded his arms. "And She shares them with you?"

It had never happened before. It might never happen again.

Velek's eyebrows rose, then pushed together. "Did you foresee this? Is that why you both wore armor?"

"Not fully. If I truly had foreseen it, we would have worn swords also."

Father gave his hearty campaign laugh. "Well said, Alara."

How could he take her side now? How could he even speak to her?

"Boh," Velek asked, "have you a stockade where we can put these two?"

"Both? You are going to take her word for it?"

"She was right about the other matter, was she not?"

Bóhjetien looked from Velek to Alara and back again, then blew out a puff of air. "We have no stockade here." He turned to Barláhtiay. "Captain, take them to the jail in Nuahn and tell the magistrate what happened."

Barláhtiay saluted and moved to take Sturg from Rariden and Kester. A lieutenant moved toward Kabed.

"Your Royal Highness," Kabed said, "you can't hand me over to these foreigners on the word of a woman."

"General, I am confident that if you are innocent, the Redíquans will not convict you. Go quietly. Do not disgrace yourself with whining."

Kabed flinched, then started toward the stable with the soldiers and Sturg.

"This was an attack on Glynrellan citizens." Father put a hand out, stopping the captain. "It should be tried in —"

"Velek is right," Alara said. "Leave it to Redíquan justice. Otherwise, we risk undoing all we have accomplished here."

His eyes narrowed. "Is that from Kenna as well?"

Rariden grabbed Father's arm. His fingers dug deeply into the flesh. "Don't. Argue. With her."

He failed to stare Rariden down. "Certainly. Sorry, Lar."

Rariden let go.

Father nodded to Barláhtiay, as if his permission were needed for the man to carry out Boh's orders. But the captain and his soldiers were already moving Sturg and Kabed along. "Carry on, Captain."

Her hands clenched. She turned her back on him and closed her eyes. *Kenna, help me cope with this man . . .*

But all that came to mind was a verse about the wrath of Telshi toward servants of the Adversary.

"Perhaps," Father said, "if I had let you and Sturg fight it out at the start, we could have avoided all this trouble."

She spun around. With a right cross to the jaw, she knocked him flat on the bloodstained grass.

# Chapter 34

## ONLY ONE WAY

Alara ran to the scullery, where Dorrel lay on a trestle table.

Marita looked at Mum. "You have those pruning shears?"

"Yes." Mum took them from a nearby counter and handed them over.

Alara used her fingers to comb the hair away from Dorrel's slack-jawed face. He lay on his side, unconscious, with Marita at his back and Mum at his front.

Marita cut the head off the arrow that had gone through Dorrel's thigh. She gripped the shaft by the fletching and pulled out the arrow. She passed the pruning shears to Mehrialéna and started stitching, while Mum kept pressure on the other side.

A half-dozen shallow wounds showed where arrows had breached his brigandine. The arrow in his arm hadn't been removed yet.

"Do you need more hands?" Alara reached toward the basket of linens.

"Yes, but not yours. Mehrialéna," Marita said, "please take her upstairs and bandage that cut on her back."

Mehrialéna spoke little Glynnish, but once Mum translated, she picked up a bundle of supplies. "Certainly."

Alara kissed Dorrel's temple, then followed Mehrialéna.

"See if you can find Kester," Marita said. "I could use his oversize hands."

In the hallway, Kester leaned against the wall, looking glum. He gave Alara a quick hug before going in to help with Dorrel.

The Redíquan captain commandeered a carriage to take Sturg and Kabed into the town of Nuahn. To the jail. They had the rear-facing seats. Two Redíquan privates sat opposite them.

How did the woman know the king had hired the assassins? Kabed wouldn't have given that information to Hanik.

After a long time, Kabed broke the silence. "No death penalty in Redíque."

Sturg kept his gaze fixed on the piece of sky he could see through the small rear window of the coach. "Yes, sir."

"Life in prison."

"Yes, sir." Of course, the king would get Kabed out. But since Sturg was meant to take the blame for the whole operation, he'd do so. Without whining.

"They have twelve."

"Yes, sir." Two officers and ten soldiers. And two of them.

"Erkan was right, you know."

Sturg swiveled to face the general. Erkan, that legendary warrior of Makut's distant past, had said many things. Of course, the first thing that came to mind in the present circumstance was, *It is better to die in battle than in bed.*

"Yes, sir."

Kabed nodded.

Their hands were tied behind them, but a well-placed kick put Sturg's boot into the face of his opposing private. The blow knocked him unconscious. Kabed's opponent didn't go down so easily.

Sturg threw himself into the other private, pinning him against the side of the carriage. Kabed pummeled the boy till he collapsed.

Sturg folded his torso, pulling his bound hands around his hips and legs to the front. The burly general couldn't do the same. Sturg took the first private's knife and cut Kabed's ropes. Then Kabed took the knife and freed Sturg.

They slit the privates' throats and took their swords.

One at each door, they paused, eyes meeting. Kabed said, "Now," and they leapt out.

A horseman shouted to alert those ahead. Sturg cut the back of the horse's leg. It went down, shrieking. The soldier, a lieutenant, his sword already drawn, scrambled to his feet and advanced.

Sturg met him, sword raised. The lieutenant struck first, a clumsy chop aimed at Sturg's sword arm.

He dashed it aside with a sweep of the rapier. Sturg stepped in with the knife, jabbing it between the lieutenant's ribs.

Kabed beat off the blows of a sergeant still mounted. The other soldiers left their horses. Their boots pounded packed dirt as they came at them, some from the head of the formation and some from the rear.

The lieutenant staggered away. Sturg pulled back the knife. The lieutenant pointed his sword at Sturg's chest. "Stand down."

Several men took Kabed down, looking more like a rugby squad than soldiers. Several more came toward Sturg.

The lieutenant didn't press his attack.

The Redíquans didn't mean to kill them. They'd capture and imprison. Here, it seemed, there was only one way to die in battle.

*How often have I told Kenna 'but' or 'no'? The height of arrogance.* Alara hadn't finished writing in her journal everything that needed to be written. But the sun was setting.

She peeked in on Dorrel, still motionless. Marita had said the anesthetic was unlikely to wear off before morning.

So Alara left him and the unfinished journal entry and walked down to the western patio. Prelate Dalys placed her Scriptures on the lectern. "Alara, I didn't expect to see you here."

"I'm of more use here than watching Dorrel sleep."

The prelate nodded. "Then you may read the Scriptures."

Most of the household turned out, though her father did not. Velek and Navka took seats at the front with Bóhjetien and Mehrialéna. Kester sat next to Alara and squeezed her hand. "Marita's a miracle worker. He'll be fine."

Alara smiled. "I know."

"You sound confident. Have you seen something?"

"Not seen, exactly." The feeling was more like a premonition. A good one, for once.

Halfway through the final song, a Redíquan sergeant rode in at a gallop. He pulled next to the patio, jumped down, ran to Bóhjetien, and whispered in his ear. Bóhjetien waved to the prelate, who signaled a stop to the singing.

Bóhjetien nodded to the soldier, who addressed the prelate. "On the way to the jailhouse, General Kabed and Commander Sturg attempted to escape. They killed two men in the attempt. The general was recaptured, but the commander turned his knife on himself. He died before we could reach the doctor in Nuahn."

A murmur ran through the congregation. The prelate bowed her head.

Hanik, sitting behind Velek, leaned forward. "Sir? We must tell Ult."

They left their seats and hurried inside.

Alara watched them go, feeling an odd tugging, as if she should follow.

It wasn't odd. It was a direction. She ran after them.

In the corridor leading to the stairs, she caught up to them.

Hanik said, "He can't go back. There's no life for him there now."

They started up the stairs. Velek asked, "What about his mother?"

"She died in the epidemic."

"Where's his father?" Alara asked.

The men stopped so abruptly, she nearly bumped into Velek. He paused, one foot on the step above, and stared down at her. "With all you know, you don't know that?"

Alara shook her head.

Hanik's eyes, heavy as thunderclouds, caught hers. "Commander Sturg was his father."

"Oh, no. No. I never once saw him behave in any way fatherly. Not once." She jerked her chin in Hanik's direction. "You were more fatherly to him."

Hanik snorted a half-laugh and continued up the stairs.

On the second floor, Hanik paused at a door near the stairs before rapping sharply several times.

Ult, in dungarees and an untucked white shirt, opened the door. He said nothing, but his eyes widened when he saw the prince and grew wider still when he looked at Alara.

Then he burst into tears.

He couldn't have heard already. She wanted to embrace him but refrained until he said, "I'm so sorry, ma'am. I didn't know he was going to—" He turned away.

Alara pushed past Velek and Hanik. She put her arm around his shoulders and ushered him to the settee. He leaned on her shoulder and sobbed for a minute. Hanik crouched in front of them. Velek stood nearby.

Ult's spaniel trotted out from the bedroom and sat by his feet, whining. Alara patted her lap. The dog jumped up, then walked from her lap into Ult's.

He scratched its ears absentmindedly.

"He didn't tell me why he wanted them. He just told me to get them. So I did."

"Get what?"

"The weapons. And the uniform. I took them from a soldier's tent."

His voice rose to a childlike wail. "I didn't know he was going to hurt you!"

"Oh, bless your heart." She hugged him again. His face went bright red. "But that's not why we're here." She looked at Hanik and braced for another cloudburst of tears.

Hanik, his voice low and calm, explained what had happened.

Ult frowned. Then his head bowed a little. He put both hands on his dog's head, scratching one ear with each hand. "He told me not to let the dog on the furniture."

Alara patted his shoulder "Boh won't mind."

They sat silently for another minute. Velek sat in the armchair.

Ult's face twisted into a fretful grimace. "What's going to happen to me? Will I be reassigned?"

Hanik shook his head. "You're not enlisted. You don't have to stay with the army unless you want to."

"I don't have anywhere else to go."

Velek inched forward in his chair, leaning on his knees. "Ult, I'm going to tell you something that only a couple of other people know, but you must swear to keep it completely confidential."

"Yes, Your Royal Highness."

"I've arranged to buy the property on the north shore of the lake from Prince Bóhjetien."

Alara caught her breath.

"Are you shocked, Curate?"

"Well, there's been talk in the family for decades of selling it. But I never expected it to be sold to a foreigner. Begging your pardon."

Velek waved his hand as if to show no pardon was necessary. "After the summit, I'll return to Makut just long enough to pack my things and . . ." He met Alara's eyes. "And retrieve my mother." He smirked. "Then I'll come back here." To Ult he said, "You're welcome to stay with us if you like."

"Oh! Oh." Ult said nothing more for several moments. Then he looked at Hanik. "Begging your pardon, sir, but . . . could I go with you?"

Hanik stiffened. "I am in the employ of the prince. If he relocates to Redíque, so will I."

"Oh." Ult frowned.

Alara said, "You don't have to make a decision today, Ult."

"Of course not." Velek leaned back in his chair. "I'll need a few days to settle matters with Prince Bóhjetien. And even after I leave for Makut, Navka will stay here with Princess Mehrialéna. I believe if we ask, the Shardamáyns will let you remain till I get back."

Alara stared at him. "Navka's staying?"

"Yes. She refuses to go back. Ever. Not even to get her things. You and your family have truly encouraged her with your talk of Telshan equality."

"Are you displeased?"

"Not at all."

Ult turned to Alara. "Will you be here?"

"Yes, for a few days, at least. I don't know when Dorrel will be able to travel."

Ult winced. "I'm so sorry."

"None of that, now. It wasn't your fault."

"Thank you, ma'am." He paused for several moments. "I heard a maid downstairs say you hit your father."

"I did. Shameful behavior for a Telshan, but I can't say I regret it."

Ult hugged his spaniel to his chest. "I know what you mean."

# Chapter 35

## WHEN THE TIME COMES

Dorrel slept in eerie stillness. Alara kept one hand on his chest so she could feel his heart beating. Her own sleep was intermittent. Each time she woke, she gave thanks he was alive, made intercession for Ult, and confessed her anger at her father.

After several cycles of sleep and prayer, she was unable to sleep again.

In the sitting room, she curled up on the settee with her Scriptures. Velek's question plagued her. *Kenna, if he's not to be king, what is he to be?*

She didn't get an answer.

Arrogance! Velek wasn't a Telshan, so why should Kenna reveal his purpose? Even if Velek did join the church, as Mehrialéna suspected he might, there was a curate in Nuahn to advise him. Just because Kenna had spoken to her about a couple of things didn't mean Alara had to handle everything.

Perhaps that was true of Navka as well. *Kenna, protect her from her father. She's chosen a dangerous road, and —*

Dorrel groaned.

"Dor? I'm here." She jogged into the bedroom.

He rubbed his forehead. "How long have I been out?"

"All night. It's nearly morning." She sat next to him.

He growled—a furious sound—and tried to sit up.

She pushed at his shoulder. "Don't."

"There's a splint on my leg."

"Yes. Marita doesn't want you to stand on it until she looks at it."

Moaning, he dropped his head back onto the pillow. "Useless. I was utterly useless to you."

"Nonsense! You saved my life."

"You had to fight him alone."

"Which I was able to do because you protected me."

He reached up and stroked her cheek. She lay down, her head on his chest. He brushed his hand over her hair.

A few minutes later, Marita arrived. She removed the splint and examined Dorrel's knee, making him push it against her hand side to side, up and down. "See if it'll hold your weight."

Marita held his hands while he got up. Alara held her breath. *Mairah, you've worked miracles through Marita before. Please . . .*

The knee held. Dorrel took a few steps.

Alara released a sigh. *Thank you.*

After the sunrise prayer meeting, Alara stood by, ready to catch Dorrel's arm as he eased himself out of his chair. But though he moved slowly, he stood without help.

Camrun stood behind her. "Dor, I didn't expect to see you on your feet."

"Marita's a miracle worker," Kester said from Dorrel's other side.

"It's Mairah's doing, not mine," Marita said as she passed.

Smirking, Dorrel met Alara's eye and offered his arm.

She looped her hand through. As they turned toward the door, Navka intercepted them. "I'm sorry. May I speak with the curate?"

"Surely." Dorrel kissed Alara's cheeks and walked with the others to the dining room for breakfast.

"I hear you're staying," Alara said.

Navka grinned widely. "Yes! Mehrialéna said I could stay with her family until Uncle's house on the north shore is built." She gripped Alara's hand. "Thank you for your advice. I think you're the only one who understands."

Alara patted her hand. "I'm afraid I understand too well. I pray you'll be happy in Redíque."

"I'm sure —" Navka shook her head and switched from her native language to Redíquan. "I am certain I shall."

Velek approached. "Navka, let's go in to breakfast."

Alara released Navka's hand. "Your Royal Highness. When you told Boh I was right about 'the other matter,' were you talking about the north shore?"

"Yes. He and I have discussed it for years. I had imagined it as a winter retreat, not a permanent residence. But after you told me about your vision . . . hearing I wouldn't be king was . . . liberating. A king must have wives, and I don't want to remarry. A king must worship at the temple, and I . . ."

He looked at Navka, then toward the hallway. By then, the others had all left, except Hanik. Velek excused him. Hanik stepped outside and closed the door.

"No one knows of this but Navka and Boh. And you mustn't tell anyone. Not until my mother and I are safe back here. If word reaches Makut before then, I might never make it out again."

Mehrialéna had been right.

"The day before the summit, after you gave me those verses to study, I talked to Boh —as I often have—about this 'freedom' he always speaks of Telshi offering. Because it seemed to me Telshan precepts are limiting —"

"I know it seems that way, but —"

"But they're to protect the soul, I know. Boh explained that. Perhaps he should explain it to the prime minister."

Alara snorted.

Velek gave a little smile. "Boh told me all that was needed was to pray to Kenna. Is that true?"

"Yes. Well, if you wish to join the congregation in Nuahn, the curate will ask you to make a profession of faith in worship. And proper discipleship is a lifetime's work. But the prayer is all that's needed to begin. I take it Boh led you in that prayer?"

Velek nodded.

*Thank you, Telshi.* Alara wondered what effect the prince's new faith might have on his loyal but agnostic bodyguard. *Kenna, if I could not change Hanik's mind, perhaps Velek can.*

After breakfast, Kabed's lieutenant was dispatched to Gadrut with orders to withdraw the troops. Ambassador Pavud and his entourage departed soon after. Bóhjetien and Alara withdrew to the sitting room, where Velek put the pardon into Alara's hand.

"Thank you, sir."

"Thank you, Curate. Your advice has been very helpful. I had never considered abdicating. But Uked is better suited to be king."

"That is debatable, given what we saw this week. But it was not my advice. That message came from Kenna." She stole a glance at Bóhjetien. He looked away. She turned back to Velek. "May I ask a question?"

"Certainly."

"You realized joining the family of faith is so important, it is even worth giving up your title."

"Yes."

"Would you please explain that to Boh? He does not listen to me."

Bóhjetien spluttered indignantly, while Velek just looked confused. Bóhjetien started for the door but stopped and faced Alara. "I tried to dismiss what you said as one of your usual antimonarchy diatribes. But your words have haunted me."

He leaned against the door and rubbed his forehead.

"I read the precepts, and prayed about it, and spoke with Domínarey." He came to stand in front of her. "She wondered why I would cling to the crown when I have always said I hate court life."

"It does seem contradictory."

"Yes, but I never thought of it as a choice I could make. Because it would not only affect my family and me. All the nobility would lose their titles, also."

"Are you afraid that in the future, it shall be deposed nobles who throw eggs at you?"

Bóhjetien screwed up his face as if trying to get angry. Then he dragged his hand down his cheek and blew all the air out of his lungs. "Perhaps."

"What are you talking about?" Velek asked.

Bóhjetien sighed. "About whether I ought to follow the example set by Alara's illustrious ancestor Reyshara." He put his arm around Alara's shoulders. "I can only say I shall consider it. But I cannot say what shall happen when the time comes." He frowned. "Do you know when that time is?"

She shook her head.

"But if you are shown, you shall tell me?"

"Certainly." Alara hugged him. "Thank you for at least thinking about it."

"How could I not? Only do not tell Mehrialéna. If she hears of it, there shall be no end to her complaining."

Although Alara was eager to return to her new home and ministry, Marita forbid Dorrel to travel for two more days, so Alara sided with her. They kept him occupied by helping him exercise as much as Marita would allow.

On the morning of their departure, Mum stopped by their suite. She wore tan riding trousers and a teal shirt with billowy sleeves. "Are you sure you're well enough to ride?"

"Marita said so." He tucked the last few things into his haversack.

Alara was packing her bag as well. She turned her back and stifled a snicker.

"Perhaps you should take a carriage. Bóhjetien will lend you one."

"A carriage is more likely to tip over on mountain trails than a horse is to lose its footing." Dorrel tied his haversack shut.

"Oh!" Mum spun around and stalked out of the dressing room.

Alara picked up her bag and stopped to kiss him on her way to the sitting room. Her eyes flicked in the direction Mum had gone. "I'm sorry she keeps mothering you."

"It's all right. I don't mind."

She smiled and went to the outer room.

Mum was there, pacing. "What am I to do with you?"

"Mum, stop fussing." Alara gathered her books and papers from the desk.

> On the rostrum of Kaesbaro's meetinghouse, Alara leads the congregation in prayer. After their "ocha," she draws a songbook from the lectern.
>
> She looks up. Dorrel sits near the front, holding a toddler in his lap: a little girl with brown eyes and a long mop of jet-black hair.
>
> Alara opened the book. "Please turn to canticle number—"
>
> The door bangs open. A breathless soldier enters. He wears the forest-green field fatigues of the Redíquan army.
>
> On his left arm is a black band of mourning.
>
> The whole congregation gapes at him. Alara cannot pretend there is no urgency in his demeanor.

As if from far away, she heard her mother say, "She didn't hear you. It seems she's having a vision."

Alara blinked, her sight returning, unsure whether to rejoice or grieve. "Is it that obvious?"

"I recognize that look."

Alara scooped up the papers she'd dropped and left them on the desk. "I must talk to Boh." She walked toward the door.

"Can you tell us what you saw?" Mum said.

"Yes, but come with me so I don't have to do it twice." She darted downstairs, Dorrel and Mum close behind.

The sound of arpeggios played on the pianoforte rang down the hall that led to the morning room. Under the music ran a babble of conversation.

In the doorway of the morning room, Alara stopped. Camrun, who had remained behind with Mum after Rariden and the others had returned to Ayenni, pulled a volume of music from a shelf and took it to Navka, who sat at the piano, her delicate fingers flashing across the keyboard. She flinched when Camrun leaned in to place the music before her. He backed away but leaned on the piano, speaking in a voice too low to carry.

Bóhjetien and Mehrialéna occupied a seating group in the middle of the room with Velek and Ult nearby. Ult's dog lay on the floor beneath his chair. Hanik stood on duty against the wall near the door. He glanced at her, then looked away again.

Dorrel's hand pressed against the small of her back. "Are you all right?"

"Yes. Yes," she whispered. "Just trying to decide if it should be shared with . . . everyone."

He waited, bless him.

She moved into the room. Navka played as if she were familiar with the old Redíquan folk tune Camrun had chosen.

Alara moved to the center of the room, uncertain whether she should interrupt the pleasant scene with unpleasant news. The linen of Boh's shirt was cool and crisp under her hand when she gripped his shoulder. She crouched next to his chair and dropped her voice. "You asked me to tell you when I knew more."

His smile faded. His cheeks paled. "Yes. Tell me."

An account of the vision bubbled out of her.

The blank look on his face degenerated to a frown when Alara mentioned the black armband. "Mourning."

"Yes." Alara stood and slid onto the settee next to Bóhjetien's chair.

"Because Jentiérri will have died."

Mehrialéna gasped.

Mum folded her arms. "But how do you know that, baby?"

"I cannot explain, Mum. I just know." She rubbed her forehead. "Bóhjetien, you have only a few years to prepare."

Mehrialéna lifted her chin. "I am sure Bóhjetien is prepared to take the throne at any moment."

What Alara and Bóhjetien had discussed could not be shared. Not with Mehrialéna.

Bóhjetien grabbed Alara's hand. "How do you know it will be within a few years?"

Alara smirked and looked over her shoulder at Dorrel. "Because by then our daughter will be about two."

## THE END

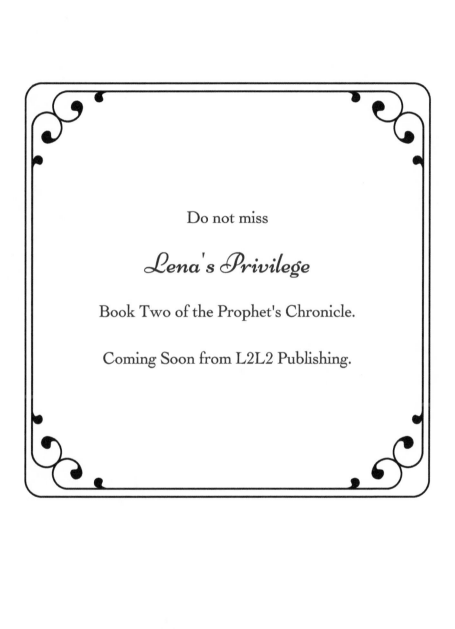

Do not miss

*Lena's Privilege*

Book Two of the Prophet's Chronicle.

Coming Soon from L2L2 Publishing.

# AUTHOR'S NOTE

One of the more challenging aspects of writing a secondary-world fantasy like this one is creating a believable set of cultural mores and belief systems. Discerning readers will already have figured out that Telshanism is closely modeled on Christianity. Kivatanism, on the other hand, is loosely based on polytheistic faiths like that of the Greeks.

While inventing Telshan Scripture, I brought in additional elements so it's not a strict duplicate of the Bible. These elements support the egalitarian premise of the Prophet's Chronicle series. I even slipped in a verse referring to the consent of the governed.

In Chapter 30, Navka asks Alara about the Scriptures, alluding to a verse you'll see in full in Book Two of this series: "Among those who live in the light of Kenna, there is no noble or peasant, master or slave, male or female, for all are one in our anointed Redeemer."

The Telshan Scriptures are largely, but not entirely, drawn from the Christian Bible. I sometimes paraphrase our own Scriptures. For example, the verse above is modeled on Galatians 3:28, which says, "There is no longer Jew or Greek, there is no longer slave or free, there is no longer male and female; for all of you are one in Christ Jesus" (NRSV). This wisdom is almost two thousand years old, yet we still struggle to achieve racial and gender equality. One of the things I wanted to explore in this storyworld is what life would look like if people lived as if they really believed this verse is true.

One fact the church has historically used to rationalize the sidelining of women is that Jesus, the Twelve, and the apostle Paul were all men. Meanwhile the first evangelist, Mary Magdalene, is unjustly slandered as a prostitute, and Junia, whom Paul called "prominent among the apostles" (Romans 16:7), is all but forgotten. Many have even tried to recast her as a man.

What would my storyworld need to prevent the marginalization of women if a verse that says "there is no longer male and female; for all of you are one in Christ Jesus" wasn't enough?

How about a feminine Redeemer? If your Savior were a woman, you'd find it difficult to justify oppressing women. But I didn't want to marginalize men, either. The point was to show equality. A matriarchy would violate the "all of you are one" principle just as much as a patriarchy. If the Trinity were entirely feminine, that would tend to create a matriarchy. Given that some of us assign feminine qualities to the Holy Spirit to balance the masculine qualities of Father and Son in the Christian Trinity, I chose to flip this and make the Counselor masculine.

Collectively, the godhead is called Telshi.

Mairah is the mother, the Creator. Her purview is birth, healing, and death. She makes you what you are.

Ahbay is the father, the Counselor. His purview is guidance and governing. He shows you what to do.

Kenna is the child, the Redeemer. Her purview is forgiveness and prophecy. She restores you to right relationship with Telshi.

I fully realize, given the reaction of conservatives to *The Shack*, that a feminine Redeemer will offend some Christians. My decision to use a feminine Redeemer anyway was not made merely to provoke. It's an attempt to inspire introspection. If people are bothered by the idea of a feminine Creator or Redeemer, they should consider *why* they're bothered.

My faith tradition teaches that God is beyond gender, because God is not human. God is Other, but since both male and female are made in God's image, we can conclude that God's nature encompasses masculine and feminine — and far more.

I've been told that my feminine persons of the Telshan Trinity push my story out of the realm of Christian fiction. Maybe that's true. But I am a Christian, and my hope is that these stories will appeal to Christian readers because in Kenna they will see a reflection of Jesus.

— Kristen Stieffel

# ACKNOWLEDGMENTS

If I try to list by name all the people who contributed to this book, we'd have a whole other book on our hands. So I'll hit the high points, and from those omitted, I beg forgiveness.

My very first readers, Susan Lundine, Rachel Pereira, and Beverly and Tip Tipton, reassured me this book was good enough to see publication. Your encouragement and critiques were invaluable.

Jeff Gerke, my book doctor, called the early draft of this story "brilliant" and "bloated." He told me which parts were boring and needed to come out and which parts were skimpy and needed beefing up. Jeff, I could not have done this without you. You're the best.

Eva Marie Everson and my critique partners in her fiction workshop, in Word Weavers, at Jeff's Anomaly forum, and in American Christian Fiction Writers' Scribes all helped me smooth out the rough cut. I owe especially huge debts of gratitude to beta readers Rebecca P. Minor, Robynn Tolbert, Will Ramirez, Luke Scott, Shae Hamrick, and Gretchen E.K. Engel. The whole crew at New Authors' Fellowship provided both emotional support and shining examples to follow.

Thanks be to God, I grew up in a house full of books, where I was welcome to read all of them. I have been reading for as long as I can remember. Mom tells a story about when I was around three years old, and she told Dad I could read. He figured I was just reciting the stories she read aloud to me. Until I climbed in his lap and read the newspaper to him. After that I took off, and my parents always encouraged my creative and scholarly endeavors.

So thank you, Lee Kirkpatrick, for imbuing me with a love of learning, encompassing science, history, geography—more topics than I can think of. And thank you, Helen Kirkpatrick, for teaching me the most important thing anyone can learn—how to read.

—Kristen Stieffel

# ABOUT THE AUTHOR

Kristen Stieffel is a writer and freelance editor specializing in speculative fiction and is associate editor of *Havok*, a flash fiction magazine focused on the science fiction and fantasy genres. She has edited a variety of projects, including business nonfiction and Bible studies, but she is a novelist at heart and has edited novels in many genres for both the general market and the Christian submarket. Kristen sees teaching as her primary gift and approaches editing as an opportunity to educate. She often teaches at writing and editing conferences.

Kristen is a member of the Editorial Freelancers Association,

Christian Editor Connection, and American Christian Fiction Writers. As co-chair of the Florida Writers Association youth program, Kristen helps organize its annual conference and leads an online critique group for middle and high school students. She is also a mentor with Word Weavers International and serves on the planning committee for Realm Makers, the only conference for Christians who write speculative fiction.

Prior to becoming a freelancer, Kristen spent twenty years at Orlando Business Journal, a weekly newspaper, where she filled a variety of roles including page design, copyediting, and writing and recording a daily stock market report for a local radio station.

An elder in the Presbyterian Church USA, Kristen serves as clerk of session at her church and teaches adult Bible studies. Despite living in Florida, Kristen is an avid knitter. In the state that pioneered air conditioning, most sweaters are worn indoors.

You can learn more about this intriguing author, editor, and instructor at www.KristenStieffel.com.

# LIST OF NAMES

This list describes the principal people and places in *Alara's Call* with pronunciations. Note that accents in Redíquan names do not change vowel sounds; they show which syllable the emphasis falls on.

Telshi: (TELL-shee) the one triune deity
Mairah: (MAY-rah) one person of the Telshan trinity; the Creator
Kenna: (KEN-ah) one person of the Telshan trinity; the Redeemer
Ahbay: (AH-bay) one person of the Telshan trinity; the Counselor
Ocha: (OH-cha) the Telshan term of affirmation
Telshan: (TELL-shən) a worshipper of Telshi

Alara: (ah-LAR-ah) a curate in the Telshan church
Apanumon: (ah-PAH-noo-mon) Glynrell's neighbor to the north
Ayenni: (ay-EN-ee) capital of Glynrell
Barláhtiay: (bar-LAH-tee-ay) Redíquan captain
Bóhjetien: (BO-zhət-yen) crown prince of Redíque
Camrun: (CAM-run) Alara's younger brother
Chevallon: (CHEV-ah-lon) Dorrel's family name
Dalys: (DAL-iss) prelate of the Telshan church in Glynrell
Darshalay: (dar-shah-lay) capital of Redíque
Denedra: (den-ED-rah) mountain range north of Ayenni
Domínarey: (doh-MEE-nah-ray) Bóhjetien's wife
Dorrel: (DOR-el) a veterinarian; Alara's suitor
Dorváir: (dor-VAIR) home of the Redíquan royal family in Darshalay

Druyun: (DREW-yun) prime minister of Glynrell

Gadrut: (gah-DRUT) a Makutian town

Glynrell: (GLIN-rell) Alara's homeland

Hanik: (HAN-ick) a Makutian lieutenant

Ivepafras: (ee-vep-ah-frahss) chaplain at the Redíquan embassy

Jentiérri: (zhen-tee-AIR-ee) king of Redíque

Kaesbaro: (CASE-bah-row) Dorrel's hometown

Kaesrynne: (CASE-rin) river in Glynrell

Kordelyon: (core-DELL-yon) Alara's family name

Korig: (CORE-ig) a sergeant in Sturg's company

Makut: (may-KÜT) country to the east of Glynrell

Marita Graylin: (mah-REE-ta GRAY-lin) innkeeper, chair of Kaesbaro's town council

Mehrialéna: (mare-ee-ah-LAY-nah) Bóhjetien's sister

Navka: (NAHV-kah) Velek's niece

Orizozabil: (or-ee-ZO-zah-bill) rector of Alara's mission in Apanumon

Palon Madrew: (PAL-ən mah-DREW) Glynrellan army captain

Pavud: (PAY-vùd) Makutian ambassador to Glynrell

Rabicanoh: (rah-bee-cah-no) Redíquan ambassador to Makut

Rariden: (RARE-ih-den) Glynrellan elder statesman; retired army General

Redíque: (reh-DEE-kway) a country to the southeast of Glynrell

Reyshara: (ray-SHAR-ah) the last Glynrellan monarch

Shandór: (shan-DOR) Rediquan palace belonging to the royal family

Shardamayn: (shar-dah-main) surname of the Redíquan royal family

Shenevra Wyndur: (shen-ev-rah win-DÜR) Alara's mother

Sturg: (stərg) Makutian commander

Tarvag: (TAR-vag) capital of Makut

Toban: (tow-bən) a bay (i.e., chestnut with black mane) stallion charger

Tylan: (TIE-lən) Glynrellan town near the borders of Makut and Redíque

Velek Olmunt: (VEL-ek OL-munt) crown prince of Makut

# REVIEWS

Did you know reviews can skyrocket a book's career? Instead of fizzling into nothing, a book will be suggested by Amazon, shared by Goodreads, or showcased by Barnes & Noble. Plus, authors treasure reviews! (And read them over and over and over . . .)

If you enjoyed this book, would you consider leaving a review on:

- Amazon
- Barnes & Noble
- Goodreads

. . . or perhaps even your personal blog? Thank you so much!
—The L2L2 Publishing Team

# More from L2L2 Publishing

## If you enjoyed this book, you may also enjoy:

Bound by Heaven. Hunted by Hell.
Liz Brantley is desperate for a normal life.
Able to see and fight demonic forces, she has spent her life
alone, battling the minions of hell bent on her destruction,
running from the God who gave her this curse. Drawn to her
abilities, the demon Markus unleashes havoc on her
hometown and pulls Liz further into the throes of battle. She
wants nothing to do with any of it. When she meets a
mysterious man who seems unaware of the mystical realm
that haunts her, the life she's always wanted moves within
reach. But her slice of normal slips from her grasp when an
old flame, Ryland Vaughn, reappears with secrets of his own.
Secrets that will alter her destiny. Torn between two worlds,
Liz is caught in an ancient war between good and evil.
And she isn't sure which side to choose.

# More from L2L2 Publishing

If you enjoyed this book, you may also enjoy:

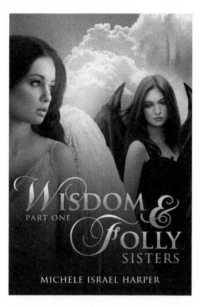

Wisdom. She may have crafted the worlds by the Maker's design, she may have been by His side since the beginning, but her heart aches. Her sister is gone. Defected, to a group of rebels who loathe their Creator with every fiber in their beings, who plot His downfall. Her new assignment? Fight them. Defeat them. But how can she fight her sister, when all she wants to do is bring her home? Folly. Fury seethes within her. Jealous of the attention the Maker lavished on her sister, she turned to a new master and became his favorite. Or so she thought. Determined to prove herself, to become invaluable, she realizes destroying her sister just may be the key to Lucifer's heart. Her plan? Engage Wisdom. Distract her, defeat her. If only there wasn't the minor detail she wasn't counting on.
Missing her sister.

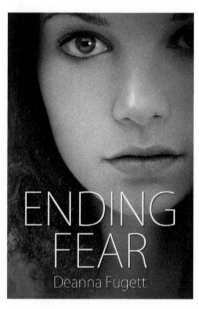

CPSIA information can be obtained
at www.ICGtesting.com
Printed in the USA
FFHW02n1009230818
47929612-51632FF